Mobility

Also by Lydia Kiesling

The Golden State: A Novel

Mobility

A NOVEL

Lydia
Kiesling

Crooked Media Reads

A zando IMPRINT

NEW YORK

**Crooked
Media
Reads**

Excerpt from "On Form and Subject-Matter" from BRECHT ON THEATRE edited and translated by John Willett. Translation copyright © 1964, renewed 1992 by John Willett. Reprinted by permission of Hill and Wang, a division of Farrar, Straus and Giroux, and Bloomsbury Academic, an imprint of Bloomsbury Publishing Plc. All Rights Reserved.

Excerpt(s) from CANTO GENERAL by Pablo Neruda. CANTO GENERAL © Fundacion Pablo Neruda. Translated by Jack Schmitt. Copyright © 1991 by The Regents of the University of California. Published by University of California Press. Used with permission.

Crooked Media Reads is an imprint of Zando.
zandoprojects.com

First Edition: August 2023

Text design by Aubrey Khan, Neuwirth & Associates, Inc.
Cover design by Evan Gaffney
Cover art: Flame Towers © cescassawin | Getty Images; Oil spill © Timothy Malone / EyeEm | Getty Images

The publisher does not have control over and is not responsible for author or other third-party websites (or their content).

Library of Congress Control Number: 2022946745

978-1-63893-056-3 (Hardcover)
978-1-63893-057-0 (ebook)

10 9 8 7 6 5 4 3 2 1
Manufactured in the United States of America

For Tim

Petroleum resists the five-act form . . .

—Bertolt Brecht

Upstream

1998

$13.45/$8.03

THE PICNIC

The grass of the picnic field was strewn with broken watermelons, their flesh warming like human tissue in the punishing sun. A dozen men stepped away from the gobbets of fruit in the grass, picked fresh melons from a wheelbarrow, and formed two lines, facing each other at a remove of three yards. From within a great fog of boredom, fifteen-year-old Bunny Glenn watched these men—in baggy cargo shorts, in unsuitable suit pants, in jeans from which bellies strained crisp polo shirts. Pale heads grew pink without hats. When a whistle sounded, each man hurled his watermelon at the man across the way. It seemed terrifying to Bunny to have a melon lobbed at you, and she noted how some of the men flinched, while some seemed to run toward the impact. Bunny's own father was among this group, a reedy white man wearing a look of stoicism beneath which Bunny detected a wholly deserved note of misery. Country music crooned raggedly from a speaker.

Bunny sat at a table under a large tent and watched this scene, with sticky inertia, with a sort of swollen, bursting stillness with which she had been afflicted for days and weeks. Before her on the table, two flies feasted on the remains of rice and eggplant. A British *Cosmopolitan* lay open, its pages already read and digested, dog-eared to denote the women Bunny one day hoped to resemble and the products she one day hoped to buy.

Her father had stepped away from the watermelon toss and now drank a beer with two chubby middle-aged men, American, maybe British. Bunny watched him wearily, knowing from years of Fourth of July celebrations on foreign soil that they would not go home until a recording of the national anthem in a lilting female voice had been played and they had admired some meager display of fireworks. A woman waved at Bunny from a neighboring table—a pert, brown-haired woman with round rosy cheeks, thin lips, and a kindly expression—and the effort of producing a sullen hello felt Herculean to Bunny, like sending a watermelon hurtling through space. Bunny was so bored she could die.

The picnic tent was situated on a yellow field on the edge of the city, edged with clumps of artemisia and tall grasses that gave way to an arid plateau in various stages of development. There was a chain-link fence surrounding the field, upon which were threaded the banners of the oil companies that were pumping oil from beneath the Caspian Sea. Even out of sight the Caspian was ever-present in Baku, a faint salinity announcing vast waters that were neither ocean nor lake. Vicious winds blew onshore in the afternoons, the strongest Bunny had ever felt. She thought the plane might break apart as it banked over Baku, the day they arrived at the beginning of the summer.

A noise broke through the thunk of watermelons, the clink of warm beers, the buzz of adults speaking, the cries of the few young children playing on the grass—a sound of male activity that was somehow louder and more male than the other sounds. Bunny looked up to see a cluster of boys, of young men. One of them she recognized with a surge of joy. Upstairs Eddie, as the Glenns called him, lodged with the Qadirov family in the apartment above the Glenns' embassy-assigned dwelling. He was British, and young, somewhere in his late twenties. He was short but not too short. He was thin but wiry and he had a close-cropped, bullet-like head that was saved from brutality by the sensitive line of his jaw. Upstairs Eddie was in Baku to make a documentary about oil wells and the Nagorno-Karabkh war. He had occupied Bunny's nearly every waking thought from the moment they met, him dragging his duffel up the marble stairs of their building until today, the picnic, when the local population of young men of interest to Bunny suddenly exploded.

The men with Upstairs Eddie were making a lot of noise. They looked, Bunny noted with amazement, like seniors just graduated from Stanhope, the boarding school where she and her older brother, John, would return in the fall: gorgeous in the aggregate if not individually, white boys with gently shaggy hair, bronzed, golden-furred legs in khaki shorts and dirty running shoes. They were drinking Heinekens fished from a cooler full of lukewarm water, from where Bunny had earlier fished her own tepid Coke.

Where did they come from, these young men? Bunny yearned to know. She cataloged them slyly as they moved in a group to the buffet line. One had reddish-gold hair, slight but with broad shoulders across which stretched an ancient Harvard crew tee. He had a long nose and a rugged beard of a slightly different color than his hair. As he ladled mutton onto his rice he spoke to the boy next to him, who had tousled dark brown hair and brown eyes that crinkled as he laughed at something the redhead said. He was lithe and tall; Bunny and her female peers often lamented that boys got, without effort, the willowy bodies that the girls had to achieve through other measures. Finally there was the largest man of the group, with brown hair somewhat unevenly cut. There was a slight bulk to this man, which he carried with surprising grace. He was wearing a tank top upon which a counterfeit Minnie Mouse spoke the words "Love from Baku" in a neon-pink bubble. There were small patches of black hair growing on his shoulders, but the shoulders were broad and powerful to the extent that the better-looking boys seemed frail beside him.

This last had blue eyes that fell on Bunny where she sat, as he and the other young men walked in her direction. Now Bunny understood what an athlete felt when they had lined everything up perfectly and the ball fell miraculously into the appointed spot. She dropped her eyes to her magazine and raised them when she heard a voice saying, "Is this seat taken," in the voice of Forrest Gump, a joke that instantly confirmed the bearer as American, although Bunny had already known, the way one just knew. You could tell by hair, by mien, by decibel, and barring that you could always tell by shoes. In their travels the Glenn family had discussed this at length, how shoes conveyed nationality more than any other article of clothing—at least until their last posting, where men wore black leather coats like bathrobes, the likes of which the Glenns had never before seen.

Bunny gave a horse laugh and shook her head, furious at the blood that rushed almost audibly to her face. She saw the man in the tank top sway lightly as he sat down, steadying himself with a hand on the back of the folding chair but keeping his plate level and his Heineken tucked between his arm and his body. He leaned into Bunny's airspace and peered at her magazine. "What are we reading?" he asked as Eddie arrived with the other two men.

"Hello, Bunny," said Eddie fondly. "This is my downstairs neighbor, Bunny," he said.

It made Bunny squirm with pleasure to hear Eddie speak her name. "My real name is Elizabeth," she explained to the newcomers. "But people call me Bunny."

"Ho ho," said the big man. "Bunny from Baku." He leaned close and began to read aloud from her magazine in a deep voice, "Drive him wild with the latest in hair removal," just as Eddie said, "This is my friend Charlie," putting his hand on the man's hairy shoulder. "The most hated American in the former Soviet Union." Bunny closed her magazine, mortified, and put it under her plate.

"Bunny's parents are with the embassy," Eddie told Charlie, who made a face.

"Diplomat brat," he said mockingly, but with a directness of gaze that pleased and disconcerted Bunny.

"That's me," she said primly, thrumming with adrenaline. She had already adopted a kind of haughty insouciance about this, used to telling people her father was in the Foreign Service, a diplomat, as if it were the most boring, vaguely embarrassing, but also very important, thing in the world.

"How is life in Baku for young Bunnies?" the man named Charlie asked.

"It's okay," said Bunny, shrugging.

"Where were you before?" he asked.

"Yerevan. DC before that. Athens before that," said Bunny.

"Woof," said Charlie. "Yerevan. Worse than Baku. Better than Kishinev." He said this with authority.

"I was only there for, like, four weeks," said Bunny. "I go to boarding school because there was no school in Yerevan or something." There was a school, but it was very small. Her younger brother, Ted Junior—Small Ted, Teddy Bear—had gone to it for the year, while Bunny and John were sent away.

"It's certainly no Athens," said Eddie. "Athens," said one of the gorgeous boys derisively. Bunny bridled at this. She loved Athens, and missed her room in the apartment they had lived in for four years, as she missed her favorite taverna, the cats on her street, the Cokes that tasted better than Cokes anywhere else.

It had shocked Bunny, how much Yerevan was not Athens. On their first day in Armenia they had driven past a flaming trolley cable that was snaking and sparking in the street like something alive, small box-like cars darting around it like the cars in cartoons. In their apartment the lights went in and out and there was a chemical smell of gas from the sewer. Conservators placed buckets of water under the paintings in the national museum. This decrepitude was distasteful to Bunny, who aspired to a house like her Uncle Warren's in Nederland, Texas, where there was a separate room for every function, a lawn, a car, a smoothly paved street for Rollerblades.

Baku represented an improvement, Bunny felt. They had flown to Yerevan on Armenian Airlines, the air smoky, the tray tables creaky, the leather of the seat pockets worn and creased. But to Baku, they had flown British Airways, a new plane, newly nonsmoking. Bunny could be brought to panicked tears if even a little bit of mayonnaise touched her food, and yet she liked the plane sandwich, with its soft squares of cheese and its limp cucumbers, almost gently pickled, its smear of something creamy on the white bread. It had raised her hopes. And Baku did feel different from Yerevan, with a blue sea and select small signs of immense wealth, a certain frenetic quality, restaurants like Sunset Café where you could get a hamburger that almost passed for American.

"How do you all know each other?" she asked the young men, hardly knowing which face to look at, overwhelmed with sudden abundance. "Charlie and I know each other from Moscow," said Eddie. "We were in the same Russian course. I assume Charlie knows them because he knows everybody."

"Prep-school jerkoffs," said Charlie, gesturing toward the other men. "I found them in the Lord Nelson, where I was celebrating our independence."

"They're adventurers," Eddie interjected, introducing the other boys. "They rode horses and trains from Kamchatka to the Caspian Sea."

"Not exactly," said one in an amused drawl.

"We met this dude from the CIA who said that we'd get killed if we went that way," said the other, not to Bunny, but to Charlie and Eddie, and he and his companion laughed together, sharing a private joke of bravery and disaster.

"Maybe we'll get a job at Charlie's newspaper," one of them said languidly.

"Strictly a one-man show," said Charlie, and he burped voluptuously. "No CIA moles allowed." He put his arms over his head and Bunny could hear cracks down the length of his spine. She could smell a mix of off-gassing from his shirt's Minnie Mouse appliqué and a faint funk from underneath. He was the center of gravity at the table, all attention on him.

"What newspaper is it?" Bunny asked, and all the men smiled.

"Well, Bunny," Charlie said, "It's called *The Intercock*." Bunny couldn't tell if he was joking and looked around at the men's faces. "*The Inter-Caucasian Times*," Charlie said. "I cover foreign activity in the former Soviet Union. I like to think my influence stretches beyond, though." Charlie put an enormous spoonful of rice, laden with pieces of lamb and apricot, into his mouth and chewed cursorily before speaking again.

"And what does your father do at the embassy?" He smiled somewhat meanly. "Or maybe it's your mother who's the career gal." Bunny noted the phrasing, "career gal." This is what her mother called the women who worked at the embassies. Some of them even had trailing *husbands*, an arrangement that seemed inconceivable to Bunny.

"My dad. My mom's back in the States right now. He's in Public Information," said Bunny, thinking of her mother and her younger brother in Texas. It was good for Bunny, today, that Maryellen Glenn was not here. If her mother had been here, Bunny would not have been allowed to wear the shorts that she was wearing, which were a flat-front khaki with a two-inch inseam. She would have been less liberal with her shimmering plumeria body lotion. Her mother would have frog-marched Bunny around the tent to shake hands and answer questions politely.

Charlie made his fingers into a steeple. "Jeff Brathwaite. No. Ted Glenn." Bunny was startled. "How do you know that?"

"Charlie knows every foreigner from here to Norilsk," said Eddie. Bunny heard the rifle shot of her father's laughter and looked over to see him with watermelon down the front of his polo shirt.

Charlie drank most of the rest of his beer in one gulp. He looked intently past Bunny, and Bunny followed his gaze. She saw a man who had been doing the watermelon toss talking to Aybeniz, one of the FSNs from the embassy. Aybeniz was short and curved, with black hair and eyebrows so beautiful they made Bunny regret the excessive plucking she had done along the top of her own, now turned into pencil-thin remnants in spite of Maryellen's remonstrances. Charlie spoke, looking at the man. "That guy is named, I am not shitting you, Kermit. He probably flew here from Sani Abacha's funeral." Bunny did not know who this was. He put his hand over his eyes and squinted. "Her, I don't know who she is, but I hope to be intimately acquainted with her soon."

"That's Aybeniz," said Bunny. "She's married to one of the marines," she added with barely suppressed resentment. Bunny felt frumpy and young, and hated the woman, found her tacky yet threatening. Bunny was not encouraged to fraternize with marine detachments—had specifically been told not to parade up and down past them—but since she was a small child in Athens she had fully and automatically fallen in love with every marine she saw, the men anyway, beautiful in their uniforms, polite, upstanding, friendly to kids and young women, representing honor and commitment.

Charlie continued to scan the tent. "And there's the tiny little cunt," he said, and everyone at the table looked too. He stuck his arm and his finger out in front of him, his huge arm reaching to the middle of the table, and Bunny saw that it was the woman who had waved at her earlier, the petite and friendly looking brunette. He put his index finger and thumb together and squinted as though to squish her head.

Eddie groaned sepulchrally. "What?" said Charlie. "That little pip-squeak is the Station Chief!" He pointed now with his middle finger. Bunny looked down at her plate. The explorers were convulsed with laughter. "Come on, dude," one of them said. Eddie slapped the back of Charlie's head. "One day someone's going to shoot you in the head, mate," he said.

"Good," said Charlie. "I will be fucking ecstatic. I hope they cut my dick off first."

Bunny kept herself in willful ignorance of the workings of the embassy. Political, economic, USIS, USAID—they were to her an amorphous mass, the world of grown-ups, the world of work. But she knew that a Station Chief was CIA, and that it was not a secret, exactly, but not a talked-about thing. She was surprised that this post was held by a woman, and such a small and friendly looking one at that. The position conveyed secrecy and authority; it was held, she thought, by tall and confident men.

The sun was going down and the men went back to the buffet. As she watched them join the line for the food, Bunny saw them gesticulate among themselves. Charlie put his hands in front of him as though he were clutching something, then put them by his head and mouthed *Oh my god* to Eddie, who shook his head, laughing. There were probably a hundred people at the party now, and a softball game had begun in the open field beyond the boundary of the tent. The US ambassador ran to make it to a base and lost his Marlins cap. Earlier in the party, Bunny had been trapped between her brother and father in the sun while this ambassador had speechified about the new and flourishing relationship between the United States and independent Azerbaijan, one of the most dynamic and abundant countries in the world. Bunny now saw her father and John, physically two peas in a pod, her brother bringing a candid and friendly face—a golden face for a golden child— to the tall, angular frame they shared.

John was on the Stanhope cross-country team, where he held the eighth-fastest time for a 5K course on the eastern seaboard. He was single-mindedly focused on getting it below fifteen minutes and fifty-eight seconds for their hilly and unpleasant course. His roommate, a white South African named Paul de Waal who was covered in freckles, had the third-fastest time on the eastern seaboard. Now, every morning John invoked Paul de Waal and stepped out into the heat of the city, snaking through back streets and darting around Ladas and Nivas in their clouds of poisonous exhaust. Every day he ran himself ragged on the streets of Baku, sometimes getting lost, gathering whole groups of people to him, goodwill radiating from and to him as he gamely tried a few words in Russian. Twice he had been brought back to the house in someone's old car, the driver not believing that John would ever be able to find his way home. He had joined the ubiquitous expat overseas running club called the Hash House Harriers. The participants, almost without exception foreigners, would meet and follow a mad course, predrawn with chalk scrawls earlier that day by some appointed person. At the end of the race the adults would drink buckets of beer and participate in arcane rituals. John and Ted had run the Hash in Yerevan, in Athens, and now in Baku. In Athens Bunny had gone to the family-friendly walking version with Maryellen, but she had not gone in Baku; the prospect of running in front of a group of strangers was simply too mortifying.

Looking around the tent Bunny saw Charlie in animated conversation with a stout older woman from the catering line. The woman laughed and pinched his cheek and then pulled from a box a bottle, which she gave to him along with a sleeve of plastic cups. They embraced. Charlie returned to the table with these, and the other men. "Krepkaya," he said, brandishing the bottle. "Collector's item."

Charlie set out the cups and poured several fingers from the bottle. He set one in front of Bunny. "No," Eddie protested, putting his head into his hands. "Charlie, she's not allowed to have that."

"Bunny, how old are you?" Charlie asked. Bunny desperately wanted to say sixteen, but she wasn't, and she knew that nothing sounded more babyish than saying you were almost the age that you almost were. "I'm fifteen," she said. And then she said it anyway. "Almost sixteen."

Charlie patted Eddie on the back. "Lighten up, Edward! I give teenagers vodka all the time." Bunny looked around her. She knew her father would not have forbidden her a swig of vodka, in the right context, but she knew already this was not it. She swiftly drank and put her cup back down. Charlie took it, and Eddie took the bottle from his hand. "No," he said. "For god's sake." Bunny was struck by the crystalline pepperiness of the vodka, so cold and spicy it was almost sweet, like a candy cane. She tried to look blasé. Those elements of her nervous system that were constantly humming at Stanhope, fear and arousal, had given way in Baku to inertia and boredom, to hours spent in silence on an embassy-provided couch, the wind blowing hot off the inland sea. They were activated now, to an almost-unbearable degree. These young men were wilder, nearer versions of the boys at Stanhope. She had an encyclopedic awareness of those Stanhope boys: what girls they had dated or hooked up with, their sports, their academic standing, their hometowns. It was destabilizing to see this group, adult, overgrown, but somehow the same. Her heart thumped in her chest.

"Where are we going after this?" the beautiful explorer asked the other men. "Someone told me there's half-price drinks with an American passport at the Ragin Cajun."

Charlie groaned. "Jesus, not the fucking Ragin Cajun. *No* Ragin Cajun. *No* Margaritaville. And *no* fucking Fisherman's Wharf. Fucking oil choads. I consent to Universal and that's it." The explorer ignored him. Eddie shook his head. "I'm sorry, Bunny."

"Don't worry about Bunny," said Charlie. "Bunny's heard it all, haven't you, Bunny? You can't faze Bunny."

"Have you been to the beach yet?" Eddie asked her, rerouting.

"We went to one. It smelled like oil," said Bunny. It was not an unfamiliar smell. Bunny had smelled a version of the smell in Athens when they drove out of the city on the way to the Isthmus of Corinth. When they visited her Uncle Warren in Nederland and the wind was right she smelled the smell too. "That's the smell of money," Uncle Warren had told her when she wrinkled her nose.

Bunny felt a hand on her shoulder and froze, feeling caught out in some impropriety. She looked up and saw her father standing behind her.

"Hello, Bunny," he said. "You found friends. Eddie, nice to see you." Eddie stood up and shook hands with Ted Glenn, who looked at the other men at the table. Charlie stood up too. "Charlie Kovak," he said, sticking out his hand and pumping at Bunny's father's hand enthusiastically. Bunny was surprised to see her father smile in recognition. "I know you by reputation," said her father. "I'm genuinely sorry to hear that," said Charlie in a way that suggested he had said it before. The violence that arrayed itself around him dissipated as he assumed a relaxed adult posture. Bunny could see him clearly now, a good-looking, intense, slightly bulky white man in dirty Adidas Gazelles and a silly shirt.

"I get your newspaper in my press packet," said her father with a smile.

"Again, I'm sorry to hear that," said Charlie.

"I learn something new every issue," said Ted. "Although I hope you aren't regaling Bunny with your more salacious stories."

"Sir, never," said Charlie. Her father shook hands with the other men and asked Eddie how his documentary was going.

"Going well, thanks very much," he said. "And really, thanks again for introducing me to Mehmedov," he said. "I wouldn't have gotten onto Oily Rocks without him."

"I'm glad to hear it," said her father. "He can be evasive, but I think ultimately he's not just looking out for number one."

"Yes, I think you're right," said Eddie. "He was quite forthcoming."

Eddie's project, he had told the Glenns when they had him over for drinks their first week in country, would highlight the disparity between the vast wealth that was currently flowing in from the Caspian oil consortium and the continued debilitating infrastructure problems and environmental degradation of Azerbaijan. He spent a lot of time recording long establishing shots of Sumqayit, which was famously full of rusted-out pumpjacks and tin huts and mud. He also took footage of Azeri refugees who had been displaced from the disputed territory between Armenia and Azerbaijan. There had been a war between Armenia and Azerbaijan, Bunny knew; lots of people had died, Armenians had been killed and driven out of Baku, and many Azeris had been driven from their villages and were now living in awful conditions mostly outside of Baku. No one had satisfactorily explained the war to her. It was sort of ongoing, she thought, and she tended not to listen when it was spoken of. Ted's colleagues at the embassy spent a lot of time talking and thinking about the war but had not yet solved it.

Eddie introduced the prep-school jerkoffs, and briefly mentioned their travels. Bunny watched them. The brunette was so handsome that Bunny almost felt her loyalties pulling away from Eddie. But no, the brunette was like Paul Walker, slightly alienating in his perfection, and Eddie was like Pacey from *Dawson's Creek*, except British, and thus exotic within the boundaries of Bunny's habitus. Not so symmetrical, but warm and giving and with eyes that really saw who you were. Upstairs Eddie was still ahead. She could not quite place how Charlie fit into her taxonomy of beautiful boys.

"You can do a talk for us at Public Affairs," said Ted to one of the boys. "We have a lecture series, if you've got photos."

"What'd you bring out there?" Eddie asked one of the explorers. "Digital SLR?"

"Canon PowerShot," said the explorer. "It's a good little camera." The men nodded solemnly, Bunny's father, even Charlie, respectful of equipment and gear.

Ted waved to another man, who stopped at their table to say hello. This new man was also handsome, Bunny decided, but older, more decidedly an adult. Ted introduced him to the younger men, and they all shook hands. "We can thank him for the first Azeri-English dictionary ever printed, at least that *I* know of," Ted said. The man looked pleased. "Well, you can thank Exxon," he said, and Charlie made a "chuh" sound. Bunny noticed that the man pointedly avoided looking at him. "We did the Cyrillic one a few years ago," said the man.

Bunny knew the dictionary, which sat in the middle of the Glenns' embassy-assigned coffee table, mostly unconsulted by her, along with a photo book called *Azerbaijan: Land of Fire*, which carried the logos of Statoil and BP. Oil was the big thing about where they lived now, Bunny knew. "The government works hard, but the oil companies work harder," her father sometimes said at home, inscrutably.

"To public-private partnership," Charlie sneered at the man who was responsible for the dictionary, holding up his glass. The man ignored him.

At that moment the PA made a ringing sound and then a man's recorded voice blared forth to say, "Please rise for the national anthem." Bunny surreptitiously plucked her shorts out of her butt. She didn't want to have her back to the men, to show the red marks of her legs from the hard folding chairs. The big American voice of an unknown woman belted the anthem from the PA, and Bunny's eyes smarted involuntarily when the voice quavered at the high notes.

Bunny was moved to imagine the other Americans overseas at that very moment, eating hot dogs made of strange local meats, the flag waving above foliage unseen on American soil. She teared up with a wellspring of national sentiment, feeling both stirred by the profundity of the American enterprise—the one that Ted and Maryellen reminded them they were a part of every Thanksgiving and Fourth of July and new posting and new move—and sorry for herself. She thought about the cul-de-sac in Nederland where her Uncle Warren and Aunt Christine and her two cousins lived. Her little brother—Ted Junior, Small Ted, Teddy Bear—would probably be riding bikes with them or playing video games or watching *The Simpsons*. When the PA buzzed off after the wavering final notes, fireworks erupted weakly over the field.

In the car Ted Senior sat next to Murad, the Glenns' driver, and they spoke in Russian, Bunny noting with disdain that her father's Russian was clumsier than that of Eddie, who sounded so elegant and fluid when he spoke. Ted Senior was at a slight disadvantage in Baku, where he didn't speak Azerbaijani and Russian was less dominant than he'd anticipated. Murad, though, spoke Russian. He and his wife, Lale, who left food for the Glenns every week in Maryellen's absence, between them provided every one of the Glenns' material comforts. When the television broke, Murad had driven John through the entire city, picking up people along the way; the new passengers guided him down a narrow street where a part was replaced by someone who had recently been in Moscow. Bunny thought Murad looked like Tony Shalhoub.

In the back seat, John and Bunny were silent. John had been ignoring Bunny since the end of the school year. He had not spoken to her for the entirety of their flight to Baku—except to steer her to the right shuttle line, except to remind her to check and make sure she had her diplomatic passport, the black one, not the blue one—and he did not speak to her now.

Before they had flown to Baku, Bunny and John had left Stanhope for the summer and gone home with Stanton Cartwright, a boy who ran cross-country with John. The weekend had begun with movies and furtive beers shared in a hayfield on the property and ended in the living room on a Laura Ashley couch across from Stanton's mother, who had found Bunny emerging from Stanton's room in the middle of the night. Stanton's mother had flawless skin, rich chestnut hair shaped into a helmet, and she wore a purple twinset, a pair of khakis, and loafers that Bunny's magazines had taught her to recognize as expensive. Stanton stood by a window on the other side of the room, somehow outside the conversation. Mrs. Cartwright looked very directly into Bunny's brown eyes with her steely blue ones. "You shouldn't sell yourself so cheaply," she told Bunny, to which Bunny could find no response except, "I'm sorry." Stanton had said nothing until his mother stood in silence and left the room, when he shrugged and offered his own one-word apology. When Bunny slunk out to the Cartwrights' pool, febrile with shame, her brother and the other Stanhope boy somehow already knew. Since then John hadn't spoken to her. But he also hadn't told their parents why, and that was all that mattered. Now in the back of the car, as she did every few hours, Bunny remembered the mortification of Stanton Cartwright's mother's eyes upon her, and felt thoroughly disgusted with herself.

Moving through space without expending any effort at all was Bunny's favorite sensation and so she shook Mrs. Cartwright's face out of her mind, put her window down, and leaned out. It was very dark for the first part of their drive, the unlit, bumpy roads that would take them to their building, a *Stalinski* affair in pinkish-beige Baku limestone—similar but distinct from the checkered darker pink tuff of the buildings in Yerevan. It was, the Glenns had been told by the facilities person, smaller than some of the gorgeous vault-ceiling apartments of the late-nineteenth century, the Nobel era, the Taghiyev era, the oil-millionaire era—even those that had been subdivided under the Soviets—but it was still much more spacious than a Khrushchev building. "It could be a lot worse," was how Ted put it to Maryellen when they first arrived. Murad left them in front of the building and they climbed the cracked marble tile stairs, lit with a single dim bulb, up to the second floor, the sound of their footsteps echoing all the way up the dark stairwell.

Bunny left her brother and father in the living room watching CNN and went to her room with its unforgiving bright light. Their apartment was furnished, like most embassy housing, joylessly, with an assortment of heavy furniture, and the walls were a cream that had aged into yellow. There was little Bunny could do to make the room hers, except leave her habitual nests of clothes all over the floor, but she had plastered over one wall with her collection of Absolut ads, carefully transferred from her dorm at Stanhope. There was a ponderous varnished armoire with fogged glass inside of which more clothes lay in a mound. The curtains were chintz with pink peonies. Bunny pulled them back and opened her window, looking out onto a courtyard that was pitch-black at night. Car horns and other city noises came in and she leaned out, wondering where Upstairs Eddie and the explorers and Charlie had decided to go. She pictured them moving in a group down the Bulvar by the lapping Caspian, smiling at the women they passed, sitting down to have a tea in one of the all-male cafés before ending up at Ragin Cajun or Margaritaville or one of the other new restaurants filled with foreign oil workers and young women. She wondered whether she would hear Eddie come home, his athletic, almost martial footfalls taking the cracked steps two at a time, or the creaking of the heavy door of the Qadirovs' flat, the original door, beautifully carved wood. Zeynab Xanim would probably leave him a plate of food, and she pictured him taking it to their balcony and eating it looking out over the city, his mind's eye on the hundred miles of platform cities floating far from shore on the dark waters of the Caspian.

Bunny lay on her hard bed with her magazine and finished an article about sugar waxing, resolving to try it if she could find the means. The boys at Stanhope spoke of gross vaginas, although how exactly they could be gross Bunny didn't know. She was desperate that her own vagina not be gross. She moved on from the sugar waxing to "8 Ways to Heat Up the Summer" and then imagined sliding ice cubes down

Eddie's chest and that of one explorer, then the other. Her mind balked at Charlie's chest. And yet it slotted him into the scene, watching approvingly from the side. She squirmed against her hand. When she was finished she crept to the bathroom to begin the complex ministrations to her face and teeth that would increase her odds of driving a man, any man, a particular man, wild.

THE EPISODE

Maryellen and Small Ted had left Baku after only two weeks at their new post because Maryellen's mother, Bunny's grandmother, had started to behave erratically, covering the walls and floors of her fine house in Beaumont, Texas, with newspaper, old towels, and masking tape. She had always been a fastidious woman, a fretful woman constantly in motion, constantly tidying and wiping up, but Uncle Warren had impressed upon Maryellen that her cleanliness of late had become a kind of mania, and Maryellen despairingly agreed, mere days after setting up her fifth overseas home in fifteen years, to return home to Texas and help out.

Before she left, Maryellen and Ted Senior had argued about what to do with the children, specifically with Bunny, and Bunny had listened to them from her position on the couch in the half dark, the fan aiming at her, the living room window shuttered against a howling wind that pelted the glass with minute scraps of rock. Ted believed that Bunny needed to learn how to be independent, and Maryellen believed that idle hands were the devil's playground. "There's not really that much trouble she can get into," said Ted, "and she needs to learn how to navigate in new places." Maryellen had cast her eyes dubiously at Bunny lying limply on the couch. "Ted, it's simply different with girls," she told him, "and you know it."

"People stare at me," Bunny had added plaintively, not wanting to go with Maryellen, necessarily, but wanting to be pitied and heard. John, reading *The Economist* on the other side of the room, rolled his eyes. "That's right, everybody is obsessed with Bunny, everyone's trying to trade Bunny for five camels," speaking of Bunny but not to Bunny, in keeping with his embargo. The staring and attention from people on the street in Baku was ubiquitous. Bunny could not tell if the staring was of greater magnitude because Baku was different than Yerevan or because she was now, as Maryellen put it primly, more of a young lady than she had been before. Some stares were simply from interested people who could tell immediately that Bunny was not from Azerbaijan. Some were pointed but mostly playful: "Hello, beautiful girl!" Some scared her, boys who followed her until she could walk fast and resolutely to a safe and crowded distance. "Monica Lewinsky! Monica Lewinsky!" one of them had yelled, cracking up. Bunny cursed the slutty intern as she broke into a humiliating jog.

Ted Senior had finally convinced his wife that he could handle Bunny, and so Maryellen had left, bringing her youngest child and reluctantly leaving the older ones behind. And then Ted threatened Bunny with tutors, telling her at dinner that she must learn Russian, or Azerbaijani, or trigonometry. He implored her to study the history of Baku, which was thousands of years old, a stop on the Silk Road, a crossroads of many empires and cultures, Persian, Russian, Turkic, Indian, Chinese. It was the first independent Muslim republic, briefly, he told Bunny, and had the first secular school for Muslim girls. (Ted and Maryellen reminded Bunny, often, that education for girls was hard-won and never guaranteed.) He reminded her of the brilliance of everyone who had come through the Soviet system, which he admired in spite of being a Cold Warrior himself. "Just about everyone you see in this city can recite a poem *and* fix a car engine," he would say with feeling. "These places have literacy rates that would put any other country to shame!" He reminded her that she was also an ambassador of her nation, in a way, and should be improving herself and representing the United States. But without the iron will and attention of Maryellen in the house, Bunny's father was unable to follow through on his threats.

What happened to Bunny? her parents had been asking each other, and Bunny, for the last two years. She had been a bright, outgoing child with prodigious interests and an uncanny memory. When she was six years old, she could recite all of the world capitals. But then she became the kind of student who would receive a worksheet for homework and lose it, crying the morning it was due as she pulled sheet after grubby, crumpled sheet from her bag. She nearly failed freshman biology her first year at Stanhope, which was, as Ted pointed out, all about memorization. Her grade in Spanish was a C, her grade in precalculus a C+. John made the honor roll. Bunny could not focus; Bunny could not do anything except read magazines, compare perfume samples to one another, look in the mirror, and think about boys and which boy liked which girls. Bunny on her own merits would never have been accepted to Stanhope, which had an application process more rigorous, it seemed to the Glenns, than most colleges. But John and Bunny were a package deal, and the federal government would pay full freight for them to attend while their parents were abroad, and they had a letter of recommendation from the US ambassador to Indonesia, whose own children had attended Stanhope and then gone on to Kenyon and Yale.

"Y'all have spoiled that girl," Bunny's grandmother told Maryellen when they were on home leave at her house in Beaumont, before her brain eroded and she began covering the house with newspaper and towels. Bunny listened at the door. "Spare the rod, Maryellen." But

Maryellen, raised with the rod herself, had for the most part spared the rod, wondering often and aloud whether that had been a mistake.

After Maryellen and Ted left Baku, Bunny stayed inside for a few days until she couldn't stand it anymore. The Glenns' selection of television channels was very small, all in Russian or Azerbaijani, and their selection of worn VHS tapes miscellaneous. She had read the book that Stanhope assigned for the summer, *Look Homeward, Angel*, which she found boring. She read *Bridget Jones's Diary*, purchased in the airport and now her favorite book of all time, three times through. So Bunny did what her father asked and explored, taking the city map he had bought and annotated for her, sometimes listening to her Dave Matthews Band CDs on her anti-shock Discman, one half of her mind taking in her surroundings—watching for intruders and malfeasants—and the other cataloging the triumphs and humiliations of her sophomore year.

Bunny liked the glamor of the old oil-millionaire palaces down by the shore, the stone buildings done in a Gothic style, French style, Venetian style, European style, others with embellishments she could only vaguely conceive of as "Eastern." There was so much to look at. Giant bas-relief bronze faces emerged from apartment walls bearing names and dates she could not read or understand, strong faces rendered in bronze, Cyrillic and Latin letters commingling on plaques that her father had told her were to commemorate the poets and folk artists of the Soviet years. She could not fix on the style of the city, the look of the city, which felt like Yerevan but not, like Athens but not, like Paris but not.

Then there was the ancient novelty of the old inner city with its warren of stone streets, the grand houses with old wooden enclosed balconies, curtains drawn across the glass. Sometimes she would navigate the old winding streets to the Palace of the Shirvanshahs or the sturdy Maiden Tower, a stone building of disputed purpose comprising an ancient and peculiar shape. She would wind through and down and then along the stretch of waterfront, the Bulvar, the paving stones loose on their sandy dredged seabed, little patches of water pooling up from beneath the cracks. She envied both the lovers canoodling in gondolas in the miniature canals of "Little Venice," and the young children on the rickety carnival rides of the Bulvar. She longed for companionship.

Bunny was in awe and vaguely afraid of the Baku metro, which was nothing like the cement tunnels of Washington, DC, but otherworldly in its grandeur, glittering with mosaics and marble, lighting schemes that ranged from a burnished gold to surgical white, embellished with the heroes of the revolution, the poetic heroes of the Persianate past clasped in romantic embrace. She was alarmed by the precipitous escalator, of the rush of dank, cool air that swept up from the depths of the station and the speed and angle of descent. She was too scared to find a space in the crush of people who occupied the car up to the very door, the smell of rayon and hot bodies and perfume making her wrinkle her nose. Sometimes she would let one car go by, then another, then another, watching the people crushed up against the door, too embarrassed to wedge herself in.

Sometimes she found herself in homier neighborhoods, places that might once have been villages, drawn into the tissue of the city as the city sprawled out, the aboveground oil pipes that snaked through the dirt roads and knobby paved streets and in between houses forming its sinews and veins. Here the dwellings were not the huge block apartments but were one or at most two stories, run-down but clean, garlanded with explosions of bright green pomegranate leaves and their brilliant orange flowers, riots of grape vines growing up to shade walls from one central ancient stump, generous fig leaves spilling over limestone brick, mudbrick, painted plaster, mulberry tendrils creeping over corrugated tin, fences cobbled together from old doors metal and wood, ramshackle gates pushed open to reveal a cat and kittens in a patch of sun, laundry on the line, potted geraniums lovingly tended, familiar sites, homey sites. She felt a kinship with these places, perhaps more accurately a surface familiarity, a visual recognition. They reminded her of the Glenns' years in Greece, the whitewashed trunks of plane trees and ash trees sending their shadeful canopies over the narrow street, fending off the winds, the heartrending summer scent of fig leaves growing in the sun, their gentle roughness against her fingers like a cat's tongue when she reached out to touch.

Sometimes people in these neighborhoods assumed Bunny was lost and tried to question her about where she was going. "*Sağ olun, sağ olun*," she would say, *thank you, hello*, trying to smile while continuing to walk briskly. Her great fear, besides being kidnapped or *molested*, as she thought of it, was that she would need to go to the bathroom. She carried a package of Kleenex in the Herve Chapelier bag she had begged Maryellen to buy her after seeing the other girls at school with them, because toilet paper was not always present. People used sprayers and buckets of water after going to the bathroom, a combination that mystified Bunny. If there was not also some kind of toilet paper, and a strong, substantial kind, how would you avoid just getting all wet and then putting your clothes on with wet spots? It was mysterious to all the Glenns, and not the kind of thing you could ask your new neighbors.

Bunny's favorite walk was up Azadliq Street, the way to the American embassy. There was a lot of activity on the narrow pavements that abutted the wide street with its speeding traffic, a level of bustle against which she could almost disappear. There were small dark shops in the basements of old buildings where you could get a paper typed up on a typewriter or a computer. There were internet cafés where Bunny would stop and email her hallmates, scanning her Hotmail futilely for an email from Stanton Cartwright. There were shops for handbags and underwear and tucked-in lunch counters for grilled meat wrapped in bread, their delectable scent filling the air. Bunny would walk up the street, a gentle slope, and feel an involuntary relief when she saw the impenetrable gray walls of the embassy, the police booth in front, the inevitable line of people waiting to come in, a scene that replicated itself across the entire world. She might go in herself, showing her passport and waiting for her father to collect her, selecting a book from the listless library of English-language paperbacks inside, or she might simply take in the feeling of comfort and carry on with her walk, maybe roaming as far as the leafy green area of the medical school, before finally turning home and walking on sore feet to the apartment, where she would devour the food that Lale had left.

In the evenings, Bunny would go upstairs to the Qadirovs' apartment where Upstairs Eddie lived, to watch *Santa Barbara* with Zeynab Xanim. Bunny had never heard of *Santa Barbara*—in Athens there had been *The Young and the Restless* and *The Bold and the Beautiful* with Greek subtitles, which Bunny had watched with her babysitter Edna, who came from the Philippines and was married to a Brit in the merchant navy. But in Baku it seemed people loved *Santa Barbara*. Zeynab Xanim also watched *Guadalupe*, which as far as Bunny could tell was not even a proper American soap, but a Mexican one, and sometimes Bunny watched that with her too.

Dr. Qadirov, or Zeynab Xanim, as the Glenns had instructed Bunny to call her, meaning something like Mrs. Zeynab, was a recently retired epidemiologist from Azerbaijan Medical University, and her husband worked at the Ministry of Health. Their cramped but majestic apartment had not been updated as the Glenns' had but was furnished similarly, crowded with dark and ornate wood. A small study was lined with medical books belonging to both Qadirovs, and a likeness of I. Akhundov, the father of epidemiology, hung in a gilt frame on the wall. The other Dr. Qadirov, Zeynab's husband, Fuad Bey, Mr. Fuad, was seldom home when Bunny was there. He kept a parakeet named Khosrow in a cage that moved between the kitchen and a small balcony, and he was at war with a man in the apartment building across the street, who kept a hutch of pigeons on his roof, one of which had attacked Khosrow when he was taking the breeze on a ledge outside the kitchen window. Fuad Bey was in his seventies and very fit thanks to a complex regime of calisthenics he undertook to fight the effects of his wife's cooking.

Zeynab Xanim had made herself responsible for the Glenns' happiness from the moment they dragged their suitcases up the dingy stairway. The Qadirovs had two daughters, one of whom was studying economics in Hungary and one of whom lived with her husband in Moscow, and so Zeynab Xanim, an empty nester, had in particular taken Bunny under her wing. In retirement she had replaced the activities of her professional life, which had been characterized by campaigns against first malaria, then HIV, with cooking elaborate meals for her female friends and colleagues, some assortment of which came over several nights a week. In the evenings Zeynab Xanim took a break from her titanic meal preparations to sit down and watch *Santa Barbara*. Sometimes she was joined by a former colleague from the university, an irascible Russian woman named Alla, sometimes by her cousin Farida.

Bunny found Zeynab Xanim's attentions stifling and *Santa Barbara* cheesy. Zeynab Xanim seriously disapproved of Bunny's sojourns alone around the city, fussed at her, fussed at Ted Senior, and, if she heard Bunny's door open when she was at home, would stick her head out and interrogate Bunny about her destinations. But Bunny accepted her ministrations because Zeynab Xanim was funny, she spoke good English, and she was a wonderful cook. Moreover, in Zeynab Xanim's kingdom lived Upstairs Eddie, and Bunny lived for the glimpses of his room she got when she used the Qadirovs' bathroom—the sight of his bed neatly made, either by himself or by Zeynab Xanim. Every once in a while she was rewarded for her attention to the tortured narratives of *Santa Barbara*, dubbed in Russian and completely baffling to Bunny, by a glimpse of Eddie himself, and the sound of his footsteps in the hallway spurred the beating of her heart. When he swept in after a day visiting some monument to the depredations of the oil business, Zeynab Xanim would insist that he sit with them and tell them what he had seen.

Eddie spoke Russian beautifully, but he tried to make Zeynab Xanim speak Azerbaijani with him too. Zeynab Xanim spoke Azerbaijani of course, and Russian of course, and English, and French too. Fuad Bey spoke the first two, to which he added Persian, although it was unclear to Bunny whether he spoke it or had just memorized long stretches of poetry in it, which he would recite to Zeynab Xanim when she shouted at him about the parakeet cage. Bunny spoke no language but English. A singular dialect of pleasantries and restaurant phrases from four countries and her half-apprehended Stanhope Spanish ran pointlessly through her head, while her mouth formed only the crude self-taught American vernacular of her age and cohort. But Bunny had learned to tell the difference between Russian and Azerbaijani. Azerbaijani was rapid, rhyming, poetic, the mouth making vaulted sounds even at high speed, whereas Russian had a pinched quality, the tongue pressed high up in the mouth, something happening in the nose. Occasionally a new word would catch like a burr on the springy, obliging matter of her brain, and she would whisper it to herself while walking through the streets.

The night after the Fourth of July picnic, Bunny knocked on the Qadirovs' door at the customary time. Zeynab Xanim brought Bunny a glass of tea, and there were biscuity things on a silver tray leftover from a party she had for her friends the night before. She turned on the television and said, "Now, Mr. Mason." Zeynab Xanim loved Mason Capwell, the ne'er-do-well son of the wealthy Capwell family around which the events of *Santa Barbara* circled. Because it was dubbed in Russian, Bunny was frustratingly in the dark about what actually happened in the show beyond what Zeynab Xanim would explain.

Footsteps boomed in the stairwell, and Bunny entered on high alert. She never came to see Zeynab Xanim without immersing herself in a cloud of body spray on the off chance that Upstairs Eddie would be in, but she still felt sensations of panic. She didn't like the shirt she was wearing, which created back fat if she didn't sit up straight. She heard the sounds of men in the hall and then the door opened and Eddie and Charlie, the man from the Fourth of July, appeared at the entrance to the sitting room.

"Oh, wow," said Charlie, as if involuntarily. He looked at Zeynab Xanim, who creakingly stood, an eye still on the television screen. Eddie spoke to her in Russian and then Charlie spoke to her in Russian and she gestured him to the armchair adjacent to Bunny's side of the couch. "Hello, Bunny," Eddie said. "We've interrupted story hour." Bunny smiled and Eddie started down the hallway into his room with his hand up as though to say "I'll be right back," and Zeynab Xanim went into the kitchen to get things for them to eat, Eddie stopping to say something protesting to her in Russian, at which she laughed and swatted at him in the air. There was the clattering of one of two refrigerators where Zeynab Xanim stored the materiel of her hospitality. Bunny still had not spoken.

Charlie leaned closer to her, his body looming in Zeynab Xanim's French empire chair. He rested his forearms on his knees and looked at the screen and then around at the books and pictures on the wall. Then he leaned forward and looked intently at Bunny, who reflexively scooted back into the sofa. "Bunny," he said. "How are we today?" He followed her eyes to the screen again, where Sonny Sprocket, Mason's evil double, was kissing Cruz Castillo's ex-wife. "And what the fuck are we watching?" "It's *Santa Barbara*," said Bunny. Charlie nodded. "Our great cultural export," he said. "Is this what you do all day?" he asked Bunny, using his head to gesture around the Qadirovs' living room. "Watch soaps with *xala*?" *Xala* meant "auntie" in Azerbaijani,

Bunny knew. "I go out and walk around," she said almost apologetically. "I mean, I don't exactly know a lot of people." Zeynab Xanim and Eddie came into the room at the same time, Zeynab Xanim with a tray. She gave Charlie a dish of spoon sweets that he accepted with Russian expressions of gratitude, and then he put his knees together in an almost maidenly posture to make a surface for the dish. Eddie sat in a chair next to the television.

Night had fallen in Santa Barbara, and blonde Eden Capwell was home alone in the dark. Some gloved hand had cut the lights and the phone. It was silent in the Qadirovs' living room but for the whir of the fan and the clink of spoons on Zeynab Xanim's china. Bunny moved closer to Zeynab Xanim. Someone prowled in the dark. Blonde Eden, gentle and defenseless, cried out. She was struck in the face by the man in black and shoved to the ground. She moaned, and the dubbed Russian voice cried "Nyet!" in a hysterical register which made Bunny want to laugh. Zeynab Xanim put her arm around Bunny and her hand in front of her eyes, partially in jest. The man lay on top of Eden. The man traced the tip of a knife down her breast, slicing through the fabric of her blouse. Charlie guffawed and Zeynab Xanim spoke to him sharply. He replied, his hands raised in a mock defensive posture. Eden was now on the beach with the prowler, who forced a pill into her mouth. Charlie covered his mouth to suppress his mirth.

When the final credits rolled the Qadirovs' phone rang and Zeynab Xanim went to a side table to answer it, responding to the caller animatedly in Azerbaijani. Eddie had his head to the side, listening. "She's talking about the show," he said, laughing. "Someone's called her up to talk about it."

Zeynab Xanim put the phone down. "Farida," she said to Bunny. "She can't believe this." She pressed pastries on the men. Eddie looked at Charlie, who put his dish on the table and smiled broadly at Zeynab Xanim. "Shall we?" said Eddie to the other man.

"Where are you going?" asked Zeynab Xanim in English.

"I'm having dinner with someone from SOCAR, and Charlie invited himself," said Eddie. Bunny knew vaguely that SOCAR was an oil company of some kind. It was often referenced at the adult dinners and drinks that were a constant of embassy life.

"Next time we'll bring you, Bunny," said Charlie, putting his hand on Bunny's shoulder as he stood. She smiled wanly. "My Bunny stays with me," said Zeynab Xanim. She patted Bunny on the knee and kissed her cheek. Bunny did not like her own parents to touch her, but she could tolerate this much from Zeynab Xanim, and she let herself be cuddled briefly against her shoulder.

After several moments Bunny extricated herself, bringing her dishes to the kitchen as her mother would have wanted and extending a finger tentatively toward Khosrow, whose sharp beak made her nervous. Eddie followed her and jostled chummily against her while they each put a dish in the sink, Zeynab Xanim protesting from the doorway that they should leave them. Blood roared throughout Bunny's body at his nearness, the softness of his shirt, the hair on his arms. She could weep.

"Still digesting the drama of *Santa Barbara*?" he asked. She couldn't think of anything to say in response to this, and in fact had had very few long conversations with Eddie at all, so she just elbowed him back.

"I don't know," she said. "I don't have anything to say I guess." The touch of his skin on her arm made her feel physically weak, as though her knees might buckle and lay her out on the linoleum of the Qadirovs' kitchen floor. She dreaded the moments it would take for her to get from the spidered enamel of the Qadirovs' sink to her own ugly room with a key that could be turned in a lock. She turned away, and Charlie was behind her close enough that the ruffle at the bottom of her skirt brushed his jeans as she turned. "Whoa," he said, his hands up. "Sorry." She fled, beet red, and got herself out of the apartment and down the clattering stairs.

The Glenns' apartment was empty. Ted was at a function and John had gone with him. Alone, Bunny went to her shoebox of treasures at the back of her bureau, removed the package of Congress Lights she had secreted there, and went to the window. She opened it and leaned far out over the sill, surveying the courtyard to make sure it was empty and dark. For the fourth time ever and the first time at her own home, she smoked a cigarette.

Bunny had bought the cigarettes during a windless and stultifying afternoon two days after Maryellen left. She had set out in search of a place to buy pads or tampons, which she had forgotten to bring from the States. She had been wadding up and bleeding through their stash of American toilet paper, and she would have to be brave and find where to buy them in Baku. She longed for stores—big stores, huge stores, the kinds of stores her Stanhope hallmates' parents brought them to when they visited the dorms. With these Stanhope hallmates Bunny had been taken to Target, to Bed Bath & Beyond, to Walmart, none of which Maryellen or Ted would ever have shopped at even back home. They abhorred chain commerce for what it had done to the American landscape, to bustling main streets, and to the professionalism of employees. But Bunny longed for the brightly lit aisles of the superstores, bearing thing after thing after thing. Her hallmates had stacks of fluffy towels. They had giant containers of Paul Mitchell shampoo and conditioner. They had multipacks of razors and endless clean socks and underwear and sports bras. What Bunny would give for this abundance!

In Baku, after finding the pads in a cramped store on a corner several blocks from their house, too embarrassed to make eye contact with the proprietor as she paid, Bunny had walked and walked until she came to a small open-air market, where an assemblage of goods was piled on low shelves and tables, shielded from the sun by strung-up tarps. A middle-aged woman oversaw a cart with small piles of loose cigarettes and mysterious boxes bearing unfamiliar names, no Marlboro or Camels that Bunny could recognize. After waffling between Ambassador and Congress brand, Bunny had pointed wordlessly at a box and handed over her manat. When she had received her change and the cigarettes, she mustered, "*Sağ olun*," and the woman smiled at her, revealing teeth shining beautifully with silver.

Now Bunny pulled tentatively at the smoke and only coughed once. She held the cigarette between two fingers by her face, her forearm straight and her elbow tucked at her side in a chic manner. When it was done, she threw the butt out into the dark and put her clothes in a ball at the bottom of her dresser. Maryellen had forbade Lale from tidying up after Bunny, wanting Bunny to take responsibility for her things, so her room remained mostly undisturbed.

Bunny returned to the Qadirovs' for *Santa Barbara* eight out of the following ten days and did not see Upstairs Eddie even once. She went on three walks along the Bulvar with her brother and purchased a single pink lipstick from a table selling cosmetics in a crowded underground passage, downstairs from the park with the giant statue of the poet Fuzuli and near the old Grand Hotel with its cracked and empty tiled fountain. She had lunch thrice with her father near the embassy and each time replaced a Michael Crichton paperback and took another from the community library. The only people she spoke with were her father, her brother, the Drs. Qadirov, and Khosrow the parakeet, who finally hopped onto her index finger and bit her thumb so hard it bled, just as she had feared he might.

She shuffled between her CDs until they skipped and juddered hopelessly. She lay on the couch and riffled through the pile of *The Economist*s that came in the diplomatic pouch for her dad, and then she lay there with her eyes closed, building a dreamworld for herself that

involved marrying each of the individual boys who orbited Upstairs
Eddie, and Upstairs Eddie himself.

One night Ted arranged for her to babysit for an embassy family who
had a two-year-old. Normally they had a nanny, a woman they had
brought with them to Baku from their last posting, but she was away.
Murad drove Bunny to their apartment where, the child already dis-
patched to the crib, Bunny gorged herself on a bag of Kit Kats she
found in their cupboard while she watched their videotape of *Friends*.
The couple was a tandem couple, *both* the husband and the wife posted
to the embassy, the first that Bunny had ever encountered. Bunny's
mother became a Foreign Service spouse at the end of an era but firmly
within its temporal boundary, when wives were meant to be employed
with the work of the home, and to assist the ambassador's wife in her
social duties. They would be called over to the residence before a function to fold napkins and devil eggs and lubricate the proceedings in a
way that would reflect well on their husband. But Maryellen had been
a career gal too, before she married Ted; she had been a flight attendant
with TWA when she and Ted met, in a bar in Athens when he was out
of the Peace Corps and on his way to the Foreign Service. Ted's career
was not capacious enough to accommodate the continuance of hers.

Ted made occasional laughing references to "TWA boot camp," but
he would follow it with an earnest litany: "Your mother had to sit
through three interviews and a written and oral test and language
training, just like I did for the Foreign Service." He repeated this with
such regularity that it had become a kind of mantra to the children, the
meaning of which they had forgotten. But they would listen spellbound
to Maryellen's stories of inebriated passengers, operatic barfing, an
emergency landing in a field in North Dakota, the flight attendants
who were fired for gaining two or four pounds. When they wanted to

be deliciously scared, they asked their mother to describe the flights filled only with flight attendants, where pilots did a series of terrifying maneuvers in the sky. This was literally the worst thing Bunny could imagine, but it gave her an odd sense of security to know that her mother had done it and could fly entirely without fear. The Glenn children listened to Maryellen's stories until they were as worn and beloved as an old baby blanket.

"It was the best job in the world," Maryellen would say. "It's a different world now."

Bunny looked at the photos arranged around the apartment of the tandem couple. She didn't think the woman was beautiful, maybe she could be called *handsome* or *striking*, but the man was handsome. Their wedding photo was on a table in their foyer and she inspected the bride's dress, which was modest and tea-length, not really a wedding dress at all. She wondered how the woman had lured the man.

She looked through her closet, which was a lot of Ann Taylor and low heels. She had birth control pills on her dresser, Ortho Tri-Cyclen, which Bunny had heard from her friends was the best one to go on. She used her father's credit card number, which she had memorized, to call the ATT 1-800 number and place a long-distance call to her hallmate Arden, nine hours in the past in Shaker Heights, Ohio, but no one picked up the phone. The parents came back after eleven. Before they drove her home the woman gave her a bag with some books and magazines and the *Friends* tape, along with a twenty-dollar bill and a handful of manat.

"You probably don't have much to do," she said with sympathy.

THE PARTY

Bunny was lying on the couch, her bony shoulders against one end, her ankles propped up on the other. She watched the TV and from time to time looked down at her legs, vigilant for stray hairs, for patches of dry skin, for veins, for cellulite. The TV was showing a large building with its front blown off, each room exposed like a monstrous dollhouse, like the building in Oklahoma City, which had blown up when Bunny was in the eighth grade. A smoldering pile was next to the building on the screen, which had been the US embassy in either Nairobi or Dar es Salaam. The bombs had gone off at the same time and the coverage was undifferentiated and ubiquitous and had dominated the TV for more than a week. Bunny peered at the screen for evidence of bodies, of blood and injury, both wanting and not wanting to see, but the visible carnage for these events was always architectural. Papers fluttered in the breeze, an image that was beautiful in its incongruity.

The targets were the embassies, the primary victims Kenyans and Tanzanians, hundreds of people. A dozen Americans had died, but the world was so small that Ted knew one of the dead, a guy from his first posting. Ted put his head in his hands when he sat on the couch in the evening and watched the footage. Bunny had never seen him cry and he did not cry now, but he looked gray and regretful and very tired. Maryellen back in Texas entered a transatlantic panic that traveled through the phone line and rippled even the still air around Bunny, a specific draft of fear that whispered in and out of their lives depending on where they were. In Athens, in childhood, someone from the embassy had gotten blown up in his car by a Marxist-Leninist bomb. "His head came off," one of the other embassy children had whispered while they played at a dinner party, and Bunny ran to her parents and cried.

The normally comforting stiff hair and firm voice of Bobbie Battista was not enough to quiet Bunny's needles of fear as the screen showed the demolished buildings from every angle. She turned the TV off and read *Ali and Nino*, a book the tandem couple had given her and which appeared on every list of recommended reading provided to new families in Azerbaijan by the State Department and auxiliary expat-serving entities. It was a love story, which intrigued her, but it felt alien to her, foreign and stuffy in its prose. She wished she had *The Clan of the Cave Bear*, which she had read with secret, electric amazement at her grandmother's house, her hand finding itself in her pants once she put down the compact and velvety paperback.

Bunny shuffled through the magazines on the coffee table. She flipped through the glossy magazine about Azerbaijan put out by an American woman with no obvious connection to the country or any governmental or nongovernmental institution—a woman about whom the adult Glenns endlessly speculated. She read something about textile production in rural areas and then put it aside. Underneath an *Economist* was a magazine with a startling cover, the rubble of something she recognized as one of the embassies. "Whoops," it said across the space between the two remaining buildings, the words *The Intercock* emblazoned above. Bunny thought of Charlie, unencountered since she saw him in the Qadirovs' apartment. She paged through the rest of the magazine, references upon references, crude cut-and-paste jobs and collage, nothing she could understand. On one full-page spread titled "Caucasian Graft Report" were photos of smiling white men, grown-ups, with a block of text each. "Viktor Kozeny: Dooney & Jerkoff"; "Gary Best: Retard Rambo"; "Roger Tamraz: Pipeline Putz"; "Graftin' James Giffen"; "John Deuss: Putting the Party in Apartheid."

At the end of the feature was a small row of photos of women, all unrecognizable to Bunny. "Ladies' Room," went the headline, followed by more text: "We at *The Intercock* want to recognize the brave women who have broken the glass ceiling and joined the pantheon of Caspian Graft. These women have taken the physical defects nature dealt them and let them curdle into the fermented mare's milk of ambition, joining the hall-of-famer grafters despite the limitations imposed by their sex." One of the women, with a name Bunny didn't recognize, was a Black woman with light skin. "The Hoover Institution is the Big House and Chevron carried her over the threshold," a caption below her photo read. Bunny could tell that these were jokes, and she wished that she understood them better. They seemed to be in line with what she and her friends at Stanhope liked to look at on the internet—like The Spark, or a website called Fat Chicks in Party Hats, narrated in broken English by someone who called himself Miguel, that Bunny thought was the funniest thing she had ever seen. But this, Charlie's newspaper, was written with a level of knowingness that evaded her. Another page, "War Porn," had a photo of a funeral procession, a line of coffins carried by brown men, a procession so long that the coffins couldn't be counted.

Bunny wondered how Charlie had gathered all this information. She wondered how old he was, where he had gone to college, if he had gone to college. Bunny knew very few people who had not gone to college. Even her Uncle Warren had gone, although he had not finished, to a small Christian college in Texas, not a school that anyone from Stanhope would attend, or want to attend, or have heard of. Maryellen had gone to Baylor. Bunny's father had gone to Harvard; there was no chance of Bunny following him there, although John, she imagined, had a shot. There was nothing more important than where you went to college, Bunny knew.

Bunny was considering that next year she would need to go on college tours and wondering who of her parents would return to the States to take her when she heard the heavy footsteps in the stairwell that she somehow could identify as her father's, the particular sound of his glossy office shoes on the steps.

"Hello, Bunny," Ted said, when he had come into the apartment and set down his briefcase, a gift from Maryellen with his initials on the front flap. "You're exactly where I left you this morning."

"I moved," she said sullenly.

"Where's your brother?" he asked, seating himself on one of the overstuffed armchairs that surrounded the coffee table.

"I dunno," she said. "Running."

He peered at the magazine propped against her knees and frowned. "I'm not sure that's an edifying thing for you to be reading," he said.

"I don't understand a single thing in it," she said. "What is it even about?"

"It's inside baseball. About oil mostly."

"Why is he so . . . mad?"

Her father considered for a moment. "His view is that since the collapse of the Soviet Union, there's been a gold rush for resources, and that a lot of unscrupulous people are making money in very corrupt ways. Which is true." When the Glenn parents were together, she sometimes heard her father lament the quality of men with whom he was now expected to engage, and the variety of work he was expected to do. Bunny, despite her sense of alienation from her father, knew he was a very smart man. His bookshelf was filled with forbidding books by Aleksandr Solzhenitsyn that Bunny sometimes tried and failed to read.

"Hmm," said Bunny. "I thought it was good to have, like, business. After communism." Bunny also knew from her father that the problems of Armenia and Azerbaijan had to do with communism, which was something that seemed like a good idea at the time but which had been perverted by the naturally corrupt nature of people and groups.

"Yes," her father said, leaning forward, tenting his fingers, pleased to have engaged Bunny in any kind of dialogue, a suffusing happiness that Bunny could instantly and warily perceive and which shamed her with its simplicity. "But there are so many corrupt practices built into these places that it's very unlikely that regular people will see a lot of benefit. Many of the same people who clawed themselves to the top during the Soviet era are now going to be in charge. Regular people may have more ways to *spend* money. But if they're not making any more money, there's no point." Her father had long talks with the Qadirovs upstairs about pay cuts at the Ministry of Health and the medical school. "And in Azerbaijan, because it has natural resources that, for example, Armenia doesn't have, the gold rush is at a fever pitch."

"Huh," said Bunny, and she moved on. "When's Mom coming back?" she asked.

"Soon, I think," said her dad. "I hope. You miss her, huh?"

"No," said Bunny rudely. "I was just curious." This was not precisely true. She longed to be away from her mother when she was near her mother, because her mother issued litanies of tedious rules, but she felt bereft without her. It was odd not to smell her mother's Lubriderm or hear the sound of her hair drier in the hall, hear the swish of her skirts, her Keds and her espadrilles, or find traces of her everyday lipstick, a gentle coral, on a mug.

Her father sighed. "Would you like to go to a party tomorrow?" he said. Bunny rolled her eyes. "An embassy function, great."

"This one will be interesting. Lots of crooks like in the magazine there," he said, gesturing at *The Intercock* with a look of fatigue. "One of the prospectors renovated an old oil-baron mansion for his company and they are having a big reception tomorrow. I have to go, and I thought you and John could come too." Bunny sighed. "It should be interesting," he said again, helplessly. "You could wear the thing your mother spent so much money on for your spring dance."

Her father flipped open the top of the briefcase and dug inside until he found an embossed card that he handed over to her. There was the outline of a ruined medieval building and details about the party.

"Fine," said Bunny. Her heart beat a little faster in spite of herself. Already she felt the evening accrue to it a significance she had hitherto only felt at the sound of footsteps, hoping she might glimpse Eddie from her spot on Zeynab Xanim's couch. She would wear her beautiful dress.

Bunny's dress was beaded pink tulle from BCBG. This, in Bunny's estimation, placed it very high on the hierarchies of fashion. There was Jessica McClintock, which had been the source of her dress for the freshman-year spring formal dance, and then there was BCBG, which was more expensive and for which she had lobbied her parents over the course of several phone calls on the dorm pay phone before they relented and transferred the requisite funds to Bunny's account. Maryellen was the stricter parent, but on certain matters of fashion, if Bunny's and her tastes aligned, she could be a light touch. They were from Texas, after all, she sometimes reminded Ted Senior. Frocks were important. Maryellen was less of an asset for things like outwear, which were also important, but there Ted could be persuaded for reasons of practicality. This is how Bunny had gotten her North Face shell in black and red, which was the correct jacket to have at Stanhope.

The dress was an asymmetrical sheath that fell at its longest point to mid-shin and at its shortest point a few inches above the knee. Its base layer was a clingy synthetic material above which the tulle floated, tucked in with a stitch here and there, so that the lines of the body could be seen below. It was the most beautiful dress Bunny had ever seen. She would do her eyebrows tonight, she decided, her mind already racing. She would paint her nails. She had twenty-four whole hours to make herself beautiful.

Bunny began her ablutions at noon after eating the small, gemlike dolma that Lale had left in the fridge. She washed her hair and then blow-dried it with a paddle brush until her arms ached. When John left for his run, she painted her nails and sat on her windowsill to dry them, smoking a cigarette, looking around first to see that no eyes were upon her. She raided her parents' bathroom cupboard for any spare beauty products that had not traveled back to Texas with Maryellen. She smoothed a forgotten silicone serum onto her hair for frizz. She curled the ends of her hair under. She searched her plucked eyebrows for signs of redness. At five thirty, she started on her makeup. John was home now, watching soccer in his shorts. At six she slithered into her dress. Her father came home as she was going upstairs to the Qadirovs'. "Don't you look nice," he said. "I told Zeynab Xanim I would show her my dress," said Bunny, embarrassed to be caught in the act of caring. Everything was a source of mortification; her body was aflame with it every moment of the day. Her father made her stop while he went to go get the camera. "John," he called to her brother in his own room. "Come take a picture with your sister."

John came down the dark corridor in his shorts and T-shirt, saw Bunny, and laughed. "I'm not even dressed yet."

"That's okay," her dad said, ushering him toward Bunny. "We'll take another one when you are." John and Bunny stood next to each other, their arms barely touching. "Come on," said her dad. "Get together. Mom will want to see some pictures." They reluctantly scooted in. "Cheese," said their father, and they smiled wanly.

Zeynab Xanim, too, took a photo when Bunny knocked timidly on the door. "*Vyy*," she exclaimed, and she called to Fuad Bey. Upstairs Eddie came down the hall too, a tie untied around his neck. "Bunny, fabulous in her frock!" he said. Zeynab Xanim got her camera and took a picture of Bunny, and then a picture of Bunny and Eddie and Fuad Bey, and then had Fuad Bey take a picture of her with Bunny. She made Bunny and Eddie sit down on the sofa and went into the kitchen. Fuad Bey sat down in the imposing armchair. He offered them candy from the saucer on the table.

"Why are you going to the party?" Bunny asked Eddie. "Isn't it, like, an oil guy's party?"

"It is," said Eddie. "Part of my film talks about these people like our host, who made millions of dollars by being at the right place at the right time." He interpreted this for Fuad Bey, who said in accented English, "Mr. Five Percent."

"What does that mean?" asked Bunny.

"There was a man, Calouste Gulbenkian, an Armenian from the Ottoman Empire who became a British citizen. He was an oil engineer and larger-than-life character. His big achievement was brokering the merger of the Royal Dutch oil company and Shell and getting them the rights for Mesopotamian oil. Iraq. And he kept 5 percent of the shares, which at that scale was just absurd money." He issued a rapid stream of Russian to Fuad Bey, who spoke animatedly back.

"Anyway, our host tonight was like that. He got in on the Contract of the Century—the oil consortium with the new government of Azerbaijan. . . ." He looked at Bunny to make sure she understood, and she nodded weakly. "He showed up in Baku just as the Soviet Union was collapsing. No real expertise, just an instinct about what might happen with the oil and gas here. And it turned out he was right, and by the time the majors got involved he had met all the right people in the new government, which is not hard to do in a small country, and cut himself in to the new deals. His percentage was smaller, but the amounts in question are so huge that he became tremendously wealthy overnight."

Bunny had heard again and again of the Contract of the Century, without knowing exactly what it was. Something about oil, different companies working together, revitalizing decrepit wells, blah blah blah. It was as impenetrable to Bunny as the warren of pipes and factories that ran through the Black City, the industrial east of Baku where she had been told not to go. Eddie translated again for Fuad Bey, who made a derisive gesture, almost as though he were spitting. She noted his pronunciation of Azerbaijan, with the *j* that danced between the hard j of *jam jar* and a softer *ʒh*, his barely voiced *"ai"* and the broad *a* that stressed "jan." Bunny involuntarily repeated it to herself, the same way she repeated his pronunciation of Baku, which actually had no "oo" at all, but something more like the *i* in "kill." Eddie thought for a moment about how to translate.

"He said between British Petroleum and the Americans and the Russians and SOCAR and these Mr. One, Two, Five Percents, what's left for Azerbaijan?" Bunny looked at Fuad Bey and shrugged her shoulders sympathetically. He reached across the table and pinched her cheek. He was an affectionate and handsome man, in a craggy and bristle-eyebrowed way that Bunny had not yet learned to appreciate.

"That really is a lovely dress, Bunny," said Eddie. Bunny let herself imagine briefly that Eddie and Bunny were a couple, say a royal couple, going off to a state dinner, being wished goodbye by one of their fathers, she wasn't sure whose. Eddie had recently come from the shower, Bunny knew from his damp hair, the visible smoothness of his cheek, some faintly herbal smell. Zeynab Xanim came with the tea, and when Bunny finished it she went back downstairs.

Murad drove them to the party, which was not far away, in the ancient inner city, but it took a long time for the car to navigate the other line of cars through the narrow, curving streets within the stone city walls. The mansion, a beautiful limestone building that had mellowed from white to biscuity gold, was lit up from within, and cars were disgorging their passengers, who trooped up the stairs to the ornate door. They were met by a willowy brunette who asked for their invitations and showed them to an area to leave light summer coats and wraps and then toward the inner room with bar and food. The walls were hung with suzanis and rugs, delectable rugs, the rugs that drove the foreigners wild. Ted Senior was immediately accosted by colleagues to whom he briefly introduced his children. Bunny heard herself tell several people her name, where she was in school, and how she was liking Baku, and she said thank you for compliments about her dress or her looks. John had received familiar greetings from a few adults, which puzzled Bunny until she remembered with resentment that he had been spending his Sundays running with the Hash, making friends. In a moment between introductions Bunny slipped away to a table laden with food, caviar and cream and nuts and candied fruit and savory pastries. The room was full of smoke. Bunny teetered in strappy heels she had ordered from a website called Bluefly that promised real designer brands at reduced prices. They were four inches high and had maimed her feet within moments.

It was early in the evening, but there was an air of license at the party, in the opulent interior, in the presence of a number of unidentified attractive women. Bunny felt it was the kind of party where she and a friend could really get away with things. John was encircled by his group of runners. A male server passed by with champagne and Bunny looked around before smiling and taking one from his tray. She put her arm across her body, loosely tucking the flute into the opposite armpit. Her prized Kate Spade purse, another Bluefly purchase, dangled from her shoulder. The hall of the mansion was packed now, and she followed the flow of people to the back of the building, through a library and out a French door into a courtyard where some ruined

ancient structure, something like a tiny mosque with a squat minaret—
different from the skinny minarets of the Turkish mosque on Martyrs'
Lane—was silhouetted against the dark sky. Groups of people were
gathered in the courtyard smoking or lined up at another bar. Grass
tickled her ankles and her wretched toes and there was a gentle smell
of cat underneath the smoke.

For an hour Bunny roamed the jewel-box mansion, her shoes rubbing her feet raw. Twice she took champagne flutes from unattended
trays. She saw her brother standing over the hors d'oeuvre table, pil-
laging the caviar. She overheard groups of red-faced men, a cacophony
of phrases. *Karabakh. Azeri-Chirag-Gunashli. Shahdeniz. SOCAR.
OPEC. Clinton. Berger. Morningstar. Lewinsky.* She lost her sense of
which words were English and which were not. The building was a
welter of noise and laughter. Her head spun pleasantly. Her father came
round the corner from the receiving room to the hallway where she
was about to climb the stairs to the second floor, the banister adorned
with a ram's head carved from wood.

"Are you all right, Bunny?" he said.

"Yes," she said. "I was going to look upstairs."

"Don't get into trouble," he said. "We'll stay a little longer." And
then two men were upon him, and hands were clasped all around.

Bunny imagined she made a dramatic spectacle as she ascended the
circular stairway, swaying on her heels. At the top of the stairs there
was a hallway with a beautiful kilim down its length. The corridor was
lined with closed doors bearing plaques. At the end of it a door was
open and smoke and voices drifted out. She walked down the hall and
into the room, an octagonal room laid out like a cozy den, low benches
lining the walls.

In this room she saw Charlie Kovak poured into an armchair, his
legs dangling over one of its arms. He wore shiny polyester slacks and
a short-sleeved button-up shirt. He held a cigar in one hand, in the
other a saucer filled with ash. Across the hearth from him was a

gray-haired white man, very tall and lean, his elbows on his knees. A cluster of other men, Eddie among them, was by the heavy drapes of the open windows, some blowing cigarette smoke into the night air. Bunny realized with force that Charlie and Eddie were men, to be incorporated seamlessly into the circles of other men. She felt her age, irrelevant in the loving sitting room of Zeynab Xanim and Fuad Bey, and now noticeable, unwelcome, pathetic. The gray-haired man saw her before Charlie did and buttoned his lips into a flat non-smile, and Charlie turned and laughed riotously and gestured to the ottoman by his chair.

The ottoman was low and Bunny played out in her mind the awkwardness of seating herself on it gracefully in the tight dress. She stood for a while until she saw a high-backed dining room chair and pulled it up an intermediate distance from the men. Charlie said, "Joe, this is Bunny. Bunny is Ted Glenn's daughter, from USIA or whatever they call Useless now." This was a joke about Public Affairs, which Bunny had heard before. USIS was called Useless, and she knew it was currently in the process of being reorganized in Washington in a way that caused anguish. The man named Joe glanced at Bunny and gave her a queasy, preoccupied smile before his eyes returned to Charlie, who continued speaking to him. She was conscious that she had nothing to occupy herself with. No book, no magazine. She looked across the room to the cluster of men where Eddie stood, and he smiled and waved.

Charlie spoke again to the man. "So tell me. I have lots of sources who say Clinton's guys are pushing BTC, but I don't know what the consortium wants." The other man looked pained, and drunk. He glanced at Bunny, visibly willing her to go away. She looked down and busied herself with her purse, beloved purse. She took a tube of lip gloss from her bag and applied it delicately with a small wand. Charlie reached beneath his chair and produced a bottle of vodka, which he poured into a water glass in front of the man.

The man named Joe drank from the water glass. His face soured. Charlie tapped his cigar in the saucer. The room was fetid. "Did I write one single word about your weekend in Batumi?" Joe's face twisted into a kind of resigned rage. He stood abruptly, threw his cigar into the empty fireplace, and stalked out of the door. The jettisoned cigar let off a solitary plume of smoke. Bunny tried to look blasé. "Pull up a chair," said Charlie, waving to the vacant seat. "Finish Joe's drink."

"Gross," Bunny said, but after a pause she bent forward for the man's glass and sipped its astringent contents with a grimace.

"What was his deal?" she asked. Eddie had abandoned the group of men by the window and joined them, and he seated himself in the armchair and looked intently at Charlie, who assumed a didactic, almost vacant expression.

"That guy is a functionary at Amoco, which is the largest American partner in the consortium to pump Azeri oil out from under the Caspian. British Petroleum is *just* about ready to buy them, so he is now about to become a functionary at BP Amoco. Right now the oil they are pumping is going through at least one pipeline that travels through Russia. The Clinton administration is hoping that they will pump this oil via a completely new pipeline, which someone will have to build, and which will bypass Russia, and Iran, because the Clinton administration does not want to rely on Russia or Iran. They want to bring the oil through Georgia to Turkey, where it can then go on tankers to Europe. They have been back-channeling for years to make this work."

"Why was he so mad?" said Bunny.

"Because I happened to be present when Joe spent two nights of a working weekend on the Black Sea with a lady of the evening named Yuliya." This made Bunny feel sick. Her parents had spoken in a veiled way of "Natashas," some of the young and beautiful women who hung around the clubs, but it was new to imagine that a man who looked like her father might visit one of these women. "Ew," she said, shocked.

"So what did he say," said Eddie, looking at Charlie.

"He said it's close," said Charlie. "Who knows what that means."

"Does . . . ," said Bunny. "Sorry, this is, like, so stupid." She looked at Eddie, whom she trusted not to make fun of her. "Does the oil, like, literally go under the ground?" This was not what she learned about in school. At Stanhope they read *The Turn of the Screw* and parsed its hidden meanings.

"Yes," said Eddie. "And it's an astronomical project. It's digging a trench through three sovereign nations, getting all the politicians to agree, ploughing up people's fields, allegedly compensating them. It's staggering to imagine the logistics, let alone the costs."

"What's the point?" she asked.

Charlie spoke. "Because the United States does not want to be in a position where Russia or Iran can say, 'Fuck it, we're shutting down this pipe today,' and suddenly the oil stops flowing, or it costs much more to flow. The want oil to flow west more than they want it to flow east, in every sense. And they want Azerbaijan to feel friendly and rich. They don't want 'instability' in this part of the world." He made quotes with his cigar and his fingers. "Chechnya's bad enough."

"But isn't it the oil company's oil?" said Bunny. "Ah," said Charlie, brandishing his cigar, and Bunny felt included, conspiratorial. "The US Government would like to dictate how the oil gets to market. Where it has to travel from in order to get where it's going. What it will cost when it gets there." He drank freely from the bottle. "They think the oil is gonna run out. They have to go shopping to find more. So the State Department flunkies are very interested in this place, and it's probably the main point of their jobs right now, to make sure that US companies get a piece, and guide the pipeline where they want it to go. It's about who *gets* to get rich. Oil companies a hundred years ago spent half their time trying to make sure no one developed Iraqi oil before they were ready to do it themselves. A lot of people need to get rich from the end of the Soviet Union. The US wants to make sure the right ones do."

Bunny thought with a flare of interest of her mild-mannered father, his boss, his boss's boss, and all the way up the rungs to the president of the United States. She thought of all the jowly men at the Fourth of July picnic, the people she had slipped in between like a ghost, and marveled that these frumpy grown-up men might be of some central importance, some giant machine that made the world move. It was both overwhelming and very boring to think about.

Charlie gazed languidly at the room, which was now empty but for two men speaking some northern European language near a window. He seemed to settle farther into his chair, content with Bunny and Eddie as his audience. Bunny had a feeling of illicit coziness, that this was her family now, enswathed in smoke and the imbricated luxury of the antique mansion.

"Do you want to hear the story of oil in the former Soviet Union, Bunny?" said Charlie.

"I guess," she said, taking care to sound as though it were a minor imposition, to have something explained.

"Every single person at this party, except you and me and Eddie and probably the girls, has been roiled up in some sleazy deal for more than ten years, since the moment it seemed like the Soviet Union was going to come apart and Moscow was going to lose its hold on thousands of miles of territory." Eddie was looking at Charlie with affection, and Charlie had his arms stretched out wide, the glass clutched in one hand. "The Soviets had lots of brilliant engineers and had been doing oil extraction for years, but they weren't raping the earth to its fullest potential; they didn't have the technology to find all the reservoirs. And then all the local rulers, the guys who saw independence coming, the Azeris, the Kazakhs, the Turkmen, the colonized guys, whoever had something that might be of value, they're looking for how they can maximize that value once Moscow is more or less out of the picture." He looked at Bunny, a film of sweat over his face. "You're aware that the Soviet Union no longer exists, Bunny?"

She rolled her eyes. "Yes, I'm aware."

"So Kazakhstan was the real prize at first, just ungodly amounts of oil underground. The field they knew about ten years ago, that's Tengiz. That's under the Caspian too, but on the other end, the Kazakh end. So in the late 1980s and '90s, everyone is trying to get a piece of that, but especially BP on the British side, and Chevron on the American side. So guys from both of these companies are flying out to Kazakhstan every month and pulling all-nighters with the just-about-to-be-autonomous leaders, the oil ministers, the fixers. BP's flying them to Disneyland, BP's buying them new American dentures and sending them on fucking cruises, meanwhile Chevron's back-channeling with Gorbachev, who still has a few moves left in him—he's promising he'll give Kazakhstan to Chevron while Kazakhstan's new leaders are making other plans with BP." Bunny's head spun pleasantly.

"Meanwhile," Eddie interrupts, "you have the people we were talking about with Fuad earlier tonight, the Five Percenters. Two Percenters. They get themselves worked into these deals too. Like our host."

"Yes," said Charlie. "There's basically never been a better opportunity for graft in the history of the world than right here, right now. Or the last decade, anyway." Bunny was losing the thread, but she didn't care. Charlie drank the rest of his vodka. "And also, Bunny, you have to realize that all this shit, all these sweaty fucks staying up all night eating horse and drinking vodka and smelling each other's farts, they're only bargaining for the right to *negotiate*. For years they do this. And if they finally get it, it's only good for one year." Bunny poured some more vodka into a discarded glass on the floor. "There's so much fucking money that it's worth it to suffer like that," Charlie said. "One of the oil guys told me, 'With oil and gas you don't pay to fuck. You pay to talk about the *possibility* of fucking.' But really, you pay to get fucked. You just hope you manage to nut too."

"Ew," said Bunny.

"So anyway, with Tengiz field, it ended up being Chevron. Despite everything that BP threw at it, trying to get the negotiating rights, Chevron had Gorbachev on his last legs, it had Condoleezza fucking Rice flying over to personally negotiate for them. So Chevron finally got it. Then Gorbachev told BP that as a consolation prize, they could have negotiating rights in Azerbaijan, different country completely but no problem, they could have everything under the northwest Caspian, that's here." He belched quietly. "So then BP had to start fucking off to Baku instead. But here they were already behind, already at a disadvantage, because people like our host were already here, the unaffiliated guys, all the pissant treasure hunters who showed up before the big boys arrived." Eddie had taken out a small notebook from his pocket and was jotting something down. "You're a fucking dork, man, Eddie," said Charlie, and he drank again.

"Anyway, Bunny, they finally got the deal done here, BP did, but in the end they had to share it with Turkey, with the Saudis, with Amoco, with Exxon, with Norway. The fucking US government was the one who made sure Exxon got their 5 percent. They personally intervened. Aliyev's government gets a $300 million bonus for 'infrastructure,' plus a one-off $5 million to build a new hospital. This is on top of the off-book millions they had to throw in to sweeten the deal when they were negotiating." He paused. "Not that the US is any fucking different, you pay to play there too. But it smells different here." He threw his own cigar into the fireplace. Bunny wrinkled her nose against the dense smoke.

"Most of the foreigners here are either stone-cold mercenary freaks *or* the guy that sweetens the deal for them." At this point Charlie was swimming in his own mind. "They show up somewhere, they say, 'You can't do this without us. You need us.' And then they fuck you, and a small percentage gets rich, and everyone else stays poor." He drank again. "And there is always some local asshole, some Sani Abacha willing to fuck everyone else to stay on top." Bunny was not sure who this was.

"Everyone has some lie they tell about it." He looked angry. "Here they say, 'What a shame about these *Soviets*. All these wonderful educated people left in the dust. Now they're going to live so much better.'" Charlie sloshed his drink in his glass. Bunny was puzzled, because that's what she thought too.

"They hear about the 'opportunity,' and then they're suddenly flying out every three weeks staying in the Old Intourist hotel bitching about the rusty bedsprings and the roaches, eating mayonnaise salad and complaining like they're here as a favor. A guy who owns a fucking handbag company flies in from Aspen trying to buy the state oil company." Charlie swung his legs off the chair. "The Caspian is a banquet, and they're the vultures come to feast." He looked at her and then at Eddie, each with great intensity. Bunny felt his look smolder in her very soul, too young to know he could be looking at anyone like that, that it didn't matter who was in front of him, that this was a story he had told again and again. And then he broke the moment, stretched, and laughed.

"And then Eddie and me are the flies," Charlie said. "Like a third of the foreigners here right now are probably journalists. They fucking love it. It's got everything. Oil, hookers, Chechen warlords, shitty suits, names they can't pronounce. You go to Club 1033 and it's like the guy from the *Times* dancing with the guy from the *Journal*, with Eddie filming them." Now Eddie laughed and stuck up his middle finger. "Wanker," he said. "Of course only Charlie is pure."

"There she is," Bunny heard from the door, and she looked behind her to find her brother, flushed with the heat of the party. "Hi," she said. Her father was shortly in the room too. "Gentlemen," he said to Charlie and Eddie.

"We're explaining the BTC pipeline to Bunny here," said Eddie.

"Ah," said her father. He looked at Bunny. "Will you be ready for a quiz on US energy policy?"

He put his hand on her shoulder. "Time to head home, kiddo." She shrugged the hand off her shoulder, horrified to be called *kiddo*. She stood with as much dignity as she could muster, said goodbye to Charlie and Eddie, physically pained to leave this conspiratorial moment. She walked out of the party with her brother and her father, her blood buzzing with secret alcohol.

THE POOL

On Friday evening Ted Glenn came home early and sat at the dark varnished dining room table with John and Bunny, eating the meal that Lale had prepared. "We have activities for the weekend," he said. "We can go to the Hyatt pool," he said. "And on Sunday there's an excursion to Gobustan. The CLO organized it. It's a national park with petroglyphs."

"Great," said Bunny lugubriously.

"It's a World Heritage Site," said her father. "You'll like it."

"What about the Hash?" said John.

"Oh," said her father.

"I'm supposed to get my name soon," said John with as much of a plaintive waiver in his voice as he was capable. A major conceit of the Hash was the bestowing of sobriquets. Someone from World Bank was called World Wanker. A woman who worked for the IMF, one of the few women in the Hash, was called Ima Motherfucker. Ted had worn his Stanhope Cross-Country sweatshirt to the first Hash he ran and had been made to drink beer out of a shoe for promoting "racist" behavior. Racist, according to Hash conventions, was behavior that indicated any sense of competitive spirit. A joke.

Ted looked perplexed. It was not usually his older child who was trying to get out of family activities. "I suppose you can stay here," he said, and he sighed. "I'm assuming you aren't interested in going to the Hash," he asked Bunny.

"No," she said. "I'll go on the field trip, I guess."

"And tomorrow, the Hyatt pool," said Ted with a desperate cheeriness. They had been told again and again about the Hyatt Regency, which had opened a few years ago and was the first major modern hotel chain to come to Azerbaijan. Ted had been there for drinks. The oilmen joshed Ted Senior that he was lucky to have missed the days of the Old Intourist hotel, where all the foreign companies, and the American embassy itself, had previously set up shop.

After they had finished Lale's food, they watched several of the *Friends* episodes from the tape Bunny had been given. Bunny loved Rachel's and Monica's outfits—so sleek and put-together. Afterward they called their grandmother's house in Beaumont and spoke with Maryellen and Ted Junior, as they did every sixth or seventh night. Bunny was not accustomed to thinking about her father as a person, and she noticed with surprise that his voice filled with some new sound when Small Ted came on the phone. "Teddy Bear," he said. "How's my boy?" Bunny herself felt a squeeze in her chest when she heard his voice. "Ashley and Tyler have *Super Mario Kart*!" he squeaked over the line. She had hardly seen her younger brother since she and John had gone to Stanhope. When Small Ted had been born in Athens, Bunny had been seven, and he had been her baby. She put him in her toy wagon, surrounded with stuffed animals, and pulled him around their apartment while her mother sat watchfully. "I miss you, Teddy Bear," she told him. "Come back soon." But she didn't want him to come back, exactly. She did not want to spend all day with him and her mother in the Baku apartment, dreaming of Upstairs Eddie.

They opened the windows and a faintly damp night breeze came through, blowing out the fug of the day. The night air made every one of Bunny's sinews scream with the urge for flight, for action. At least tonight she had a project. When Ted and John had gone into their rooms, Bunny shut her own door and took from a corner of her suitcase the small bag of CVS products she had carried with her across the ocean. The swimming pool meant a bathing suit, meant addressing her bikini line, which meant the deployment of a system that was not perfect but was as close as she had come, in many months of experimentation. The timing was not ideal—ideal would have been a day or two for her tender skin to recuperate, but she had to work within the conditions presented to her.

She filled a bowl with water and wet a washcloth in the bathroom and returned to her room, locking the door. She changed from her second-best underpants, black satiny ones from Victoria's Secret, to her worst underpants, which had little flowers and holes where the cotton was pulling from the elastic band. She put a white towel on her bed and perched on it, her legs butterflied with her heels pressed together. She took from her toiletries bag the little pot of what was advertised as crème bleach and used the small plastic spatula to spread the cream onto the black hair that spread out from her crotch onto her thighs. She used a hand mirror to survey her face and made small dabs to the fuzz that grew toward her jawline, below the point where she felt her sideburns ought to stop. She put twenty minutes on her alarm clock and waited, reading *Ali and Nino*. When the timer went off, she took the wet washcloth and carefully wiped all of the bleach from her legs and crotch, seeing with satisfaction that the hairs were now blonde and rust colored.

She wrapped the towel around herself and took herself and her toiletries bag and her alarm clock and her book to the bathroom, where she mixed a poisonous powder with a little water in the bowl. Sitting on the edge of the bathtub, she applied this new paste to her skin and continued reading while the timer counted down. At the appointed time, she took a different plastic spatula and, holding her skin taut, scraped it across the flesh, watching the defenseless bleached hair come away with the paste, contorting herself to reach the inner recesses where she had applied it. Everything burned, but it was the purifying burn of improvement. When she was finished, she flipped the switch on the water heater, waited the accustomed time for the water to heat up, and ran the water while she inspected herself. She knew her breasts were too small, her hips too wide, her thighs too big; unless she stood with her legs slightly apart they rubbed together at their tops; she longed for a gap between them. She sighed and pushed the excess flesh from her hips toward her back, giving herself a slightly different silhouette, the one that would be ideal. She felt the water, which was warm, and stepped into the shower to wash away the residue of an hour's work.

Murad left them at the entrance of the Hyatt in the heat of midday. It was a large pool surrounded by chaise longues and a small area of tables and umbrellas where a few people were eating and drinking. The family members went to their respective dressing rooms and emerged by the pool, a thrilling moment. Bunny had heard so much about the Hyatt: the Hyatt, so much better than the Old Intourist; the Hyatt, finally an American chain; the Hyatt, they didn't hire anyone over twenty-five; the Hyatt, they were training a brand-new workforce in American-hospitality-industry standards.

Bunny had been dying to go to the Hyatt, and indeed, it was a very nice pool. Bunny surveyed the people present. There were a lot of men, a few women, of middle age, few of them actually in bathing suits. One table of men were in suits, although a couple had removed their jackets and rolled up their sleeves. A group of what she perceived to be Azeri teen boys were wrestling by the deep end and alternately pushing one another into the pool, and she wondered what it would be like to know them. Her father waved to a few people she didn't recognize around a table and led his children over to be introduced. She resigned herself to the company of adults, the skin of her bikini line smarting under her shorts. Azeri pop music played, a woman's voice sobbing over a minor key.

Ted cursorily presented Bunny and John to someone from the embassy, someone from USAID, and a middle-aged woman he introduced as a scholar of the Caucasus, a professor or academic of some kind. John and Bunny smiled politely and set their belongings on an adjacent pod of chaises. It was irrelevant to them. They were "embassy people," which could mean anything. It could mean the political or economic section, their chain of command the ambassador, then the deputy chief of mission, then the political counselor. It could mean public affairs officers like Ted. It could mean consular, which was where newbies fresh out of the Foreign Service Institute spent eight hours a day hearing the petitions for US visas from people who brought their families, brought sheafs of documents demonstrating their financial and physical health, brought cookies and cakes, brought wads of hard-won cash they held out in pointless supplication. There were the spies, who disguised themselves among the regular diplomats with vague titles and pledged fealty to their Station Chief, who Bunny knew now was the small brown-haired woman. There were the Foreign Service Nationals, the locals. Then there was everyone else who might get invited to the Fourth of July. AmCham types. Oil types. UN types. Members of obscure do-gooding organizations. Furiously intent and offputting Jehovah's Witnesses, adrift in Babylon.

John pulled off his shirt and dove into the water, where he began doing laps. Bunny tentatively removed her shirt and shorts and surreptitiously inspected her crotch for chemical burns or errant hair. The skin was red and painful but mostly covered by the bottom of her bathing suit. She took a number of mincing steps to the steps of the pool, careful not to let her body jiggle more than was necessary. At the steps she submerged herself in the safety of the water and looked around. Scanning the cluster of tables she saw someone looking at her, and she did a double take. Under a terrible hat and stupid sunglasses like the Johnny Depp poster of Hunter S. Thompson that the Stanhope boys put in their dorm rooms sat Charlie, hunched over a notebook and gripping a bottle of Xirdalan beer but unmistakably looking her way.

Bunny hesitated, then put up a hand, and he did the same, the shyness of the gesture incongruous. There was no world in which Bunny would leave the pool and walk over to say hello. Wordlessly they arrived at a kind of compromise. Bunny swam herself to the edge of the pool close to the tables, and Charlie stood casually, stretched so that his T-shirt showed the furred band of olive skin beneath, and walked almost absentmindedly to where Bunny was treading water.

"Fancy meeting you here," he said to Bunny.

"Hi," said Bunny. He sat down and put his feet in the water. "What are you doing?"

"I'm undercover," he said.

"What do you mean?" she asked.

"This is how I write my newspaper," he said. "I go to venues where oil executives and government collaborators give each other hand jobs and watch them arrange to sell off the country piece by piece."

"Oh," said Bunny. "They do that in the pool?" she tried to be arch.

"Ha," said Charlie humorlessly. "No, they do it sitting in the chaise longues while placid fucks from USAID," he gestured in the direction of the people Bunny had just met, "who are supposed to be helping women and bringing benighted places into the modern era so they can enjoy the fruits of capitalism, sit next to them and pretend they can't hear it."

"Oh," Bunny said.

"I should interview your dad," he said absentmindedly.

"I don't even know what he does," said Bunny. This is what she said at school when people asked, which conveyed an air of mystery that Bunny knew, in her heart, was not really justified.

"He's a propagandist," said Charlie. "He organizes cultural-exchange shit. He makes newsletters with meaningless phrases about 'US-Azerbaijan' partnership. He organizes training programs for Azeri teachers in America so that Azeri school teachers who speak three languages can become as full of bullshit jargon as American ones. He reads memos from the Azeri-American Chamber of Commerce about how to make things easier for the oil companies." Bunny was agog at Charlie's ability to summarize the faults of his enemies without any *like*s, *ah*s, or *um*s. Bunny was always being halted mid-sentence by her parents, who could not stand for her to say *like* or *um*.

Bunny was surprised and offended to hear someone denigrate her father's work, and she felt incensed on his behalf. Before he had joined the Foreign Service, Ted Senior had been in the Peace Corps in a village in Thailand. The 1970s. Old-school. He had washed himself in a bucket and helped people.

"Or," Charlie laughed, "here's a new one. That woman," he pointed at the scholar in Ted's group. "She's angling to get a million dollars from the Chamber of Commerce to start a program at Harvard to lobby for Azerbaijan." He put air quotes around *program*. "She's probably working for SOCAR. Or the CIA. Or Mossad. Or all of them at the same time. And your dad is going to help her."

"What a boring reason to drag us all the way here," said Bunny, trying to sound cavalier.

"It's not fun for you here, I gather," said Charlie, as though to himself. "No, why would it be? You don't really get to capitalize on the fun parts." They watched John make a balletic dive off the diving board.

"We're going on a tour tomorrow, some cave-paintings place," said Bunny.

"Oh yeah," he said. "Gobustan. Eddie is going on that." Bunny's heart sang at the news.

"Are you going to come?" Bunny asked.

"I wasn't planning on it," said Charlie. "I've been there before. But maybe I should. Maybe there's someone I can make fun of for the newspaper."

"Probably," said Bunny. "It's an embassy trip, I think." She felt she should say something bold. "These things are usually pretty gay," she ventured. This was the insult of choice they used at Stanhope.

Charlie laughed. "Indeed." He scratched himself and went on. "I don't know why Eddie's going. Surely he has been to the premier site of touristic interest within one hundred miles of Baku in his six weeks of shooting video of busted oil derricks." He paused and smirked. "Maybe because you're going." He looked at Bunny suggestively, an eyebrow arched.

Bunny felt blood rush into her face above the surface of the cool water. "Yeah right," she said, the only other thing she could think of to say. She sank under the surface and came up again, the motion she used to make when she pretended to be Ariel from *The Little Mermaid*.

Now Charlie looked sneeringly at her. "No, Eddie is a little bit too scrupulous for you, I regret to report," he said. "Fifteen is a little bit beyond the pale for old Edward, who is a gentleman." Bunny was stung; she bobbed under the water and came up again. "Looks like I hit a nerve," said Charlie unkindly. "Don't worry, Bunny; if you're looking for an older man to rape you, you're in the right place," he said, spreading his arms wide to enclose the whole of the club.

"Ew," said Bunny. "You're gross." She looked around to make sure her father or another grown-up couldn't hear any of this.

"You got it," said Charlie. "I am gross. I take drugs; I'm a disgusting person." He grinned and saluted her. She dunked herself under the water again and swam away. When she emerged on the side of the pool closest to her chaise, she turned and saw Charlie settling himself back in his chair at the table. He raised his beer to her and swigged it. She stayed in the water, splashing aimlessly in the shallow end until he got up and walked into the clubhouse, unable to bear the thought of walking away from him in her bikini.

THE OUTING

The next day dawned cool and clear, the sky a peerless blue enamel. Bunny awoke at seven thirty and got ready. She wore a khaki skirt that hit slightly above the knee and a white camisole with a short-sleeved pink polo shirt over it. She wore the gray New Balance 990s that she had bought after seeing everyone at Stanhope wear them. Her feet weren't finished growing and they pressed painfully against the tip of her big toe. She carried her Herve Chapelier tote, in which she put her UK *Cosmo*, *Ali and Nino*, and, in a secret pocket, her Congress Lights. She had an image of herself alone standing above the petroglyphs, which she had not seen but could picture scrawled upon some glorious promontory, and everyone away from her while she smoked a cigarette until Eddie walked up beside her and took it out of her hand to kiss her against the setting sun. Eddie, who was too scrupulous to touch her.

They were early when they were disgorged from Murad's car at the gate to the old city, where small tour buses and dilapidated vans congregated. There were only a few scattered people, none of whom Bunny recognized apart from the CLO, who had organized the event. Her father went up to speak to her, a white woman with brown-streaked gray hair, resolutely sporty in jeans, a boxy polo, short white socks, and pristine tennis shoes. She was a spouse, like Maryellen; Community Liaison Officer was a position designed for spouses, a friendly job with a modest salary.

The CLO ushered them into the idling minibus. Bunny went in first and crawled to the very back right corner. Her father sat next to her, and six other people filed in after. The CLO perched in the seat next to the driver, a man named Turgut from the embassy motor pool.

"We'll give it another five minutes to see if we get any stragglers," she said. Bunny looked out the window and saw the stragglers—Eddie and Charlie, emerging from a battered Lada driven by a man who took their money with a cigarette in his hand. They got onto the minibus, Charlie stooping in the doorway. "Hi, hi, sorry, sorry," he said.

Before they settled themselves, Charlie turned to their row, gigantic in the small minibus. "Ted," he said. "Hot off the presses." He reached into his bag and pulled out a newspaper, which he handed to Bunny's father. Ted looked at the cover and then turned it over in his lap. "Oh no," he said. Bunny made to take it out of his hand and he gripped it tighter. "You can have one too, Bunny. You will recognize the art." Charlie handed her one. It took her a moment to understand what she was seeing on the cover, which was Eden Capwell's beautiful maimed face. "You have no idea what lengths I went to get this image," said Charlie with satisfaction. Superimposed over the raspberry the rapist left above Eden's mouth were the words "LAYING PIPE," with smaller writing below: "BTC in the Bag." "THE INTERCOCK" blazed across the top of the paper. The letters of *cock* grazed Eden's forehead.

"Oh my god," said Bunny. "It's Eden." She looked at Charlie, feeling both obscurely betrayed but also pleased to be in on the joke.

"Who is Eden?" asked Ted.

"From *Santa Barbara*. The show I watch with Zeynab Xanim. She got, um, molested in one of the episodes." She and Ted had never had a conversation about sex, and they never would.

Charlie and Eddie whispered to each other, and Charlie put his arm around Eddie's neck and crushed Eddie's head into his chest. They were like puppies, their play incongruous in this vehicle full of professional people. Bunny felt embarrassed, somehow, as though it reflected on her. She leaned her forehead against the window.

The bus began to move. The CLO went over the schedule: They would have a tour, and then they would be allowed to wander around the site for twenty minutes. They would reconvene at the bus, be driven onward to the famous mud volcanoes, and then turn around and have lunch at a seaside resort on the way back to town. She introduced their guide, Hasan, a man in his forties or fifties with a salt-and-pepper mustache and tanned skin, who sat in a seat behind the driver and gesticulated at the passengers while the minibus rattled through the winding interior streets of the city.

Bunny stared out the window as they turned onto the main road that would take them out of Baku, lined with fine ornate buildings, buildings embellished with wrought iron balconies and scrolled eaves, buildings where the leaders of the world had sat, Hasan told them: Stalin, Charles de Gaulle. Hasan pointed as they passed a streamlined blue-gray building formed of stacked rectangles, almost like an oil tanker or an ocean liner. "There is your first embassy," he said to the group, pointing to the building. "The Intourist Hotel. Also British embassy and British Petroleum offices. Every embassy was located there in the first years of independent Azerbaijan." Bunny was sick of hearing about the Intourist. But the building was sprucer than she had imagined. There was a café-bar in one corner. "This is where all business in Baku was done," said Hasan.

The countryside surrounding Baku began to reveal itself, a beige hardpan surrounded by short striated cliffs, brown with scrubby foliage, lined with a few very large houses around the top. They passed a field full of oil pumpjacks working, moving up and down, some blue and orange, some the color of dull rust, spindly towers of steel between them and a few small, embattled trees. "This is Bibi-Heybat field," said Hasan. "Since 1844, the oldest drilled oil field in the world. Older than Pennsylvania and Texas," he said, with pride. "The longest continuously operating field, anywhere." He peered out the window and then looked back at them. "Azerbaijan oil is the oil that defeated Hitler," he said, and Bunny felt for a moment the solemnity of this, although she was confused. The Americans defeated Hitler, she thought. The only good war, she was given to understand. Hasan continued. "In Azerbaijan, oil production is 2 percent onshore, 98 percent offshore." As they moved south he pointed out the window of the rocking minibus toward the Caspian, endlessly blue beside them, littered with the complex, gargantuan metal snarls of machinery and offshore rigs, the hulking metal whales that were the tankers. "I worked offshore eighteen years," he said. "Four days on, twelve days off." He smiled at them and held up a hand showing three fingers and one thumb. "Then I go to war with Armenia," he said, pointing at the missing space in his hand. Charlie said something in Russian, and Hasan laughed. He pointed at Charlie. "Watch out for him," he said. "A bad boy." Bunny couldn't tell whether they already knew one another or if they simply fell into the camaraderie that seemed immediately and infinitely available to a specific kind of boy or man, something easy, comic, kindred.

The bus dodged potholes and careened around stalled cars, coming to a promontory on which was a grand sand-colored mosque, gleaming new, with the same rotund, almost squat minarets as the ones in the old city. "This is Bibi-Heybat Mosque," narrated Hasan. "It was destroyed by Bolsheviks and now this last year it is rebuilt." He pointed. "Azerbaijan is a Shiite country, like Iran, but not like Iran. You don't hear Adhan here because it was banned by the Bolsheviks." Bunny had heard the Adhan in Istanbul when the Glenns visited during their Athens posting. Azerbaijan did not feel Muslim the way Turkey had felt Muslim to Bunny. Occasionally she saw a woman in hijab. As though reading her mind, Hasan continued. "If you see a woman in burka in Baku, she is coming from the Gulf so her husband can drink our vodka." He winked.

The landscape continued to rush by, the Caspian on her left, its turquoise waters, its monumental pieces of floating infrastructure. She had expected it to look murky, but it was a postcard sea, a turquoise that deepened to aquamarine and then a deep, oceanic blue on the horizon. On the right she saw occasional dilapidated blocks of apartments, some newer buildings in construction, some large single-family homes, very grand with mansard roofs. It was an architectural hodgepodge, the kind Ted and Maryellen would lament, no planning, they would say no harmony, mansions with no context, landscaping that popped fully formed and incongruous out of the hard yellow earth. She saw, too, large warehouse buildings bearing American names.

Soon they came to a large complex under construction, a warren of steel rising from the pale earth. Before it stood a tall billboard with a photo of President Heydar Aliyev, a man whose face Bunny had seen everywhere. It was a distinguished face, Bunny thought; he looked like a movie star from the 1950s in the sunset of his life. But Bunny knew he had been in the KGB, the three letters about which she knew only to respect and fear. An effective, if harsh and corrupt man, Ted sometimes opined. Hasan pointed. "This is new Sangachal Terminal, which now is taking oil and gas from Caspian to Supsa and Novorossiysk on Black Sea." He continued as if reciting. "This project is owned by British Petroleum, Amoco, and SOCAR State Oil Company, with a few other companies. It was built after the Contract of the Century was signed in 1994." He cast a look around the van. "America has just a small part," he said mirthfully, putting his extant fingers and thumb together.

Ted turned to his daughter didactically. "Looks kind of like Motiva, doesn't it?" Uncle Warren, Maryellen's brother, worked at the refinery in Port Arthur, near Nederland where they lived. Maryellen's father had been a landman, and had been grimly resigned when his only son clawed his way back down to a line job at Motiva, although Warren had now been at a desk for years and earned a seemingly huge amount of money.

Soon they had reached the turnoff to Gobustan, passing through a small village, mudbrick houses with fruit trees and plants growing in oil cans, a beautiful fruit stand, the fruit like gems nestled in jeweler's boxes, and then onto a road lined with huge rocks, a plateau that rose up from the flat plain.

The bus parked below a mountain-sized pile of colossal boulders, heaped against one another as though by god's hands in the middle of the arid plain. The parking lot, such as it was, was empty apart from one other bus. They filed out and stretched and gathered while Hasan lit and took a few deep drags from a cigarette and someone vanished behind a rock to pee, avoiding whatever hole in the ground would comprise the bathroom. When everyone was convened, they followed Hasan up a wild, winding footpath into the boulders, stopping halfway up the plateau around a flat stone into which had been carved, or eroded, a perfectly round basin that was now filled with water with no perceptible source. Bunny's mind wandered as Hasan explained the significance of the site and the water hole. They were high up now; she walked to the edge of the massive flat stones and looked below at the flat apron of land that led out to the Caspian, the Absheron Peninsula spread before her. The water sparkled; she counted nine tankers, tiny against the variegated blues. It was like a painting, the rigs and tankers peaceful and immobile, nothing in motion at this distance, the monumental platform city of Oily Rocks far out of view where Bunny imagined it as some strange, broken-down floating island, a creaking vestige of Soviet production. There was a light breeze and the sun warmed her head and shoulders. She could smell the leaves of the fig tree that sprang from the rock along with thorny shrubs, yarrow, and thyme. The boulders were smooth, giving the impression of cleanliness, of divine order. The group moved along and stopped before her, where Hasan gestured out onto the same plain where Bunny gazed. His finger paused at a complex of buildings, small in the distance. "Azerbaijani Alcatraz," he said. "Our most famous prison. My neighbor is there after he killed his wife, a very stupid man." He delivered this so calmly that it created only a ripple in the group. Bunny laughed nervously and he looked at her, noticing her for the first time, and pinched her cheek.

The group moved on and Hasan steered them past a small school group, hustling along lagging children so his own group could convene at each boulder to see its petroglyphs—cows, horses, fecund female figures without heads, a row of dancing men, their movement unmistakable across the chasm of millennia. Some of the petroglyphs were forty thousand years old, Hasan told them, and some only five thousand. They came from a time when the valley had been wetter, the life easier. Even the Roman Legionaries had left a mark when they came through after the birth of Christ: someone's name and a rank, the name of the emperor.

Bunny wandered away from the group and scrambled up higher and higher onto boulders beyond the path. She worked her way back to a small cave reached by a narrow gangway that seemed to disappear into rock. She heard footsteps behind her and, before she could turn, a voice said her name without inflection. She turned and saw Charlie and turned back again to the rock, aware that she must make a nice tableau, a *meaningful* tableau. She was moved by the vision of herself contemplating the marks of the past, the ineffable mysteries of life. She could feel him standing behind her, close, and then she could feel his hands on her shoulders, large and hot, but gentle on her, not heavy. She felt like she had been struck in the pit of her stomach, at the top of her underwear, that something inside was folding in on itself. First the hands rested and then they squeezed, gently and then harder. Involuntarily she brought her shoulders to her ears and as quickly as the hands had arrived they were removed, so that her shoulders, now untouched, strained toward the potent warmth they had briefly felt. "Hi," she said, turning to face the figure behind her, but he had already walked away. She thought to follow him toward the next patch of boulders but felt suddenly embarrassed. She turned again to the dancing people and forced herself to stand there for several more minutes. Her face was full of blood.

She counted to twenty and looked around. Charlie was now out of sight and her heart had stilled in her chest, leaving her only with the new information of hands on shoulders. She felt like a codebreaker with this information, prepared to turn it over in her mind and parse it endlessly. Hands on the shoulders meant something. Bunny knew. She walked away from the painting and looked for Charlie ahead of her on the horizon, but he had vanished among the uncomprehending boulders.

Midstream

2009

$71.99/$34.14

BEAUMONT

The sky was filled with huge, rolling clouds as Bunny navigated her grandmother's Oldsmobile down the highway that led from Houston to Port Arthur, springtime in Texas, the road lined with pink and purple smudges of evening primrose, bluebonnets and coneflower, yellow riots of coreopsis and sneezeweed, the warm breeze a humid caress through the windows, which were down even while she ran the AC, its cool jet through the heavy air keeping her alert on the endless road. She had learned to drive later than her peers, but she had, in her month in Beaumont, perfected the art of driving in Texas—a fountain Coke in the cupholder, the radio on whatever pop station had a song she could stand, her soul broadening on the open stretches of green, secret wet parts glinting through tall grasses, the tree-lined expanses of oak and pine.

Bunny had a job interview that afternoon, at a temp agency called ManPower, and she had taken a very long drive to pass the time until the appointed hour. Driving was how she spent these aimless weeks, in between filling out job applications and writing unsolicited emails, dutifully attaching her résumé, writing, "I have taken the liberty of attaching my résumé"; writing, "To whom it may concern"; writing, "Self-starter." In the Oldsmobile she had learned to drive around the Golden Triangle—Beaumont, Port Arthur, Orange—and soon ventured farther and farther down the long straight road to Houston, where she was at first too nervous to manage the perilous interchanges, the terrifying drivers, before she eventually mastered her fear. Eventually she had even driven down to Galveston, marveling at the insane steel structures of Texas City over her shoulder with their sudden evocation of Baku, but not Baku in the chop of the dark waves, the dilapidated gentlemen's clubs, the stilted houses of the Gulf, and then, eventually, the murky windswept waters of the beach.

Bunny had never before spent more than a week in Texas. Now she was in a humid limbo, and her long drives were opportunities both for puzzling through and zoning out, for thinking and looking and forgetting. She drove and drove and hoped that the phone would ring, and finally it had, and now she was easing her nerves, careful not to spill her Coke on her interview blouse, keeping her elbows up so she wouldn't sweat, willing the time to pass until she would navigate the Oldsmobile to the low-lying beige strip mall where the temp agency was located.

Bunny was living, temporarily, with Maryellen in her deceased grandmother's mock-Tudor house in the oldest part of Beaumont, Texas. She was twenty-six years old and praying to get hired by an agency called ManPower. She could not quite believe that things had come to this. The economy had collapsed, she knew, although she could not feel it in her daily life beyond the steady drumbeat of the TV news that Maryellen turned on in the evening. Bunny was dealing with something more consequential—her boyfriend of three and a half years had broken up with her, her father had left her mother—for which these world events served only as a confirmatory background hum that things had gone awry.

The world had been awry, in any case. During Bunny's first week at Connecticut College, a hail mary acceptance off the waitlist, she had awoken with a hangover to learn that two planes had flown into the buildings three hours down the road. And then a war had started, and George Bush had become the president again, and the world had just seemed an unrelieved parade of horrors. So Bunny had kept her attentions local—to parties, and her sporadic attendance of classes, and to boys. College offered so many boys, although in the end they were mostly the same boys as at high school—sometimes literally. She woke up more than once in Stanton Cartwright's bed before he finally graduated and exited her life.

She had started hooking up with Evan, the eventual boyfriend, in the last months, until they had graduated and she had gone to Greece, where Ted and Maryellen were on a second posting. She ate ice cream from the periptero boxes and looked half-heartedly for jobs while her parents prodded her, all the while sending escalating emails back and forth with Evan. They had a series of murmured phone calls during which he told her unambiguously, unabashedly, unapologetically, that he loved her, and she decided to move in with him in Pittsburgh, where he was starting law school.

Ted and Maryellen had been befuddled. John was in his second year of the Peace Corps in Ukraine. But Bunny, although troubled with a vague sense of prematurely thwarted ambition as she watched her peers prepare for MCATs and LSATs, had no explicit ambitions except to make enough money that she could buy things without having to ask her parents, and to have sex with Evan in an apartment that, miraculously, they would share.

In Pittsburgh Bunny found a Craigslist job as an assistant for a man who had the world's largest collection of ephemera about the Ohio River Valley. On Mondays, Wednesdays, and Saturdays she sat in his attic taking things out of boxes and entering them into a spreadsheet. On interim days and afternoons she worked at an upscale baby store. Bunny disliked both jobs, but she had been content to earn money and wait until Evan finished school to figure out what she wanted to do. So Evan went to class and she went to her jobs, and in the evenings she shopped for groceries at the Giant Eagle and attended Zumba class and felt pleasingly adult. She could pay her half of the rent and her gym membership and her $120 student loan payment. Barack Obama won the election, a great victory for American goodness. Evan was awash in loan money, and it felt like they lived well enough, even flying to Greece once to visit her parents. At night Bunny would drink wine and make meatloaf and a salad and tell Evan about her day while he sat with his law notebooks spread across their kitchen table and his sock feet propped up, his arms behind his head. Until one day he told Bunny that his feelings had changed, and that he was no longer content. Part of the reason why, Bunny heard more than he actually said, is that Bunny's very contentment with their arrangement had turned Evan off. Bunny and her wasted potential, her vague drifting.

And so suddenly Bunny was washed-up. She spent evenings looking for roommates while Evan tactfully stayed at the library. And, while she was responding to Craigslist ads and cursing herself for not reading the signs, her father, after thirty years of marriage, told Maryellen he was leaving.

"I have some news that may be difficult," is how he had put it to Bunny on the phone. It gave Bunny the feeling she had hitherto only associated with being in trouble, with doing something very wrong at school. The movie of her mind played her whole childhood, John and Small Ted and Bunny and their mother and father rattling over foreign roads in the station wagon that followed them to every post in a shipping container, the whole world contained in the car's interior. It was inconceivable that this could be gone. It had been real, and now it wasn't.

Ted left Maryellen, but of course, being on an overseas posting, Maryellen was the one who had to leave. And so Maryellen had gone back to Beaumont, to a strange folly of a house built in the 1920s, Maryellen's mother's pride and joy, the culmination of a life of scrapping. Maryellen had not grown up there but in a small kit house a few miles down the road (Bunny's father, on the other hand, had grown up in Houston, with, as her mother put it, "a silver spoon in his mouth").

For as long as Bunny could remember, Maryellen had disliked the Beaumont house—which had for years been filled with her own mother's inveterate, unceasing fretting—as she disliked Beaumont, disliked the Golden Triangle, disliked Texas itself, even while she couldn't bear for it to be slighted by the patrician types she encountered at embassy functions overseas.

Now Maryellen was back in this house she had always hated, a mismatched marriage of fussy Britishism with anarchic Mediterranean wrought iron embellishments, and she and Bunny floated around the crumbling building like ghosts, drinking gin and tonics and eating plates of spaghetti with cheese and butter. Ted had taken a TDY assignment in Dushanbe to put himself as far away as possible from the trouble he had caused. He had always yearned for posts that were remote from the imperial core. He had floated Dushanbe to the family periodically, when it was time to bid, and Maryellen had always batted it down. "Nothing east of Ankara," she told him after Baku.

Bunny felt both obliged to be in the house in Beaumont and unable to think of anywhere else to go. But she could not stand to be in the house all day with Maryellen, who was crushed and defeated, and who had only Bunny to talk to, and so Bunny drove and drove, burning gas and spending down the $352 she had in the bank. Today, the day of her job interview, Bunny had driven nearly all the way to Houston on I-10 and then turned around and come right back, skipping the patch of I-10 that would take her straight to Beaumont and instead speeding the car down SH 73 past the cows and armadillos—endlessly startling and delightful creatures to Bunny—the road elevated over wetlands and marshy spots.

If there was anything in Texas Bunny loved it was this big sky and soft green and the shimmering waters, dark pockets of bayou tucked in between trees, the salt tongue of the air, the sudden relief after the strip malls and stacks of giant pipe, the mounds of gravel and sand that she now left behind as she navigated the Oldsmobile east from Houston. She drove and drove, and after the healing green of the wetlands, she was in Port Arthur and the giant metal nest of Motiva.

Out of her open window Bunny took in the flat green lawns, small houses built directly on the grass, the sheer incongruity of the scene of these well-loved, slightly shabby homes set against the behemoth refinery, a shadow city made all of steel, belching clouds that cast a pall over the sky. She drove down past the main access road and saw a playground, a frail, bright, and beautiful thing, directly across the road from the main refinery gate. She turned onto the old main-street-style road toward the Gulf, lined with fine old buildings that seemed deserted, empty lots by the Hotel Sabine. Even with her fundamental ignorance of Texas, Bunny had the information in her mind that Port Arthur was a Black town, confirmed by the sight of the occasional resident tending their yard. This information was in her mind the way it was in her mind that Maryellen's parents had moved from Port Arthur to Beaumont in the 1960s for unspecified reasons.

Bunny turned inland onto the road that would lead to Nederland— where Warren and Christine and their children had recently moved into a newly built and piteously ugly house on a cul-de-sac, four bedrooms, three bathrooms, a gigantic swooping A-frame faced with stone and brick, with an oddly narrow yet soaring foyer and the first walk-in closet Bunny had seen—then onward, passing taquerias and unprosperous-looking local businesses that became Family Dollars and chain stores, finally reaching the strip mall where the temp agency was nestled among a medical clinic, a Lowe's, a Hobby Lobby, and a nail salon.

The unrelieved ugliness of these strip malls caused Bunny physical pain. She knew strip malls, of course; she had happily availed herself of their wares during Target runs and nail appointments in college. But now they assaulted her with their ugliness, with the unpleasantness of trying to get anywhere, save within the tree-lined old quadrant of Beaumont or the splendid but curiously vacant downtown, where the stately buildings bespoke an era that seemed now to be over. Out on the highways the only people on foot looked fragile amid the cars, young men wheeling broken-down bikes, young women pushing strollers on cracked sidewalks while trucks sped by.

Bunny knew that somewhere people had to be together doing things in pleasant surroundings, but she could not tell where. Houston, she imagined, a place that had soon come to seem like her best option for a better time. Bunny had begun to revise, haltingly, her taxonomy of nations. America had the good appliances, the toilets that could suck down any filth. But its aesthetics were impoverished, and she wilted as she drove along these strips or sat in her idling car in a drive-through line, waiting for her Coke.

The temp agency was freezing cold after the warm wind of Bunny's long drive, and it was staffed by a middle-aged white woman named Annabelle. First she had Bunny sit at the computer and complete her Microsoft Office tests. Bunny's scores in each were exemplary. She could type 120 words per minute, she could format, she could add things up in Excel.

"Can you tell me about your work experience, honey?" Annabelle asked. Bunny thought of her jobs in Pittsburgh, both of which had been deeply unsatisfactory.

"Well, I worked for a private collector as his personal archivist and administrator." She had prepared this line in advance. "It required a lot of organizational skills, research skills, cataloging skills, and computer skills, mostly with Microsoft Excel." She thought of the quiet in the collector's attic, its particular heft, the nearly imperceptible buzz of the lights, the thick carpet that muffled the footsteps of the collector, who startled her when she had been farting with the false assurance of solitude, or picking her nose, or briefly looking at Perez Hilton or Jezebel on the laptop where she cataloged his ephemera.

"Interesting," said Annabelle. Bunny crossed her legs in her black interview pants.

"Well, I'm an English major, so you kind of have to be ready to do anything." Annabelle laughed and Bunny laughed too. Bunny had started to see the humor, in a beleaguered way, of the disconnect between her present circumstances and the way she had spent her time in college. It was funny, the chasm between the way she had been encouraged to spend her time, reading books and writing papers, and the methods by which she was now expected to earn money. She felt, much of the time, like an unbelievable, irredeemable loser.

"And then I also worked part-time at a high-end baby store," she said. Noise to the collector's silence, eight dollars an hour to his twenty. She hated the smell of the shop, sticky toddlers and desperation and diapers—both the powdered smell of the clean ones or the heavy biological funk that floated from the Diaper Genie in the back hall. Bunny had been fascinated and repelled by the pyramid display of breast pumps.

She went on. "So for that I used the point-of-sale service, did inventory, assisted customers, things like that."

"Your Word scores are the highest I've seen," said Annabelle. "So we should be able to get you into something, even with the economy how it is. Oil prices are starting to creepy-crawl back up a teensy bit," she made a pinching gesture with her fingers. Bunny felt surprised for a moment to think that might have something to do with her. "So hopefully some places will start staffing up; we'll see."

"Well, I'd love to be considered for anything," Bunny said, and she would. She had, after all, $352 left in the bank, although the beauty of coming to Beaumont was that she now lived rent-free.

In the parking lot Bunny sat back in the Oldsmobile, removed her interview cardigan, and sipped from her watery Coke. Before she turned the car on, her phone rang, a long sequence of numbers, an international number that signified her father. They had spoken only briefly since the schism. There was the problem of *where* she would even talk with him, since she and Maryellen shared a house and it felt awkward to have his disembodied voice enter that house, not to mention the outrageous time difference. She picked up.

"Hi, Dad," she said.

"Hi there, kiddo," said her father's voice, crackling over the line in a city Bunny could not picture.

"What are you up to?" he asked. She told him about her job interview, and he made vague sounds of encouragement. "How's your mother?" he said, and she felt a flare of anger that returned her to age fifteen. "Why do you care?" she said. "Bad."

"I'm sorry to hear that," her dad said. There was a silence.

"What are you doing with yourself apart from looking for a job?"

She sensed that he wanted to give her advice, but she could also hear in his voice that he was trying not to cause offense. "Driving around," she said sullenly.

"You could go and look at the Taco Bell field," he offered. Bunny had forgotten about this. Ted had grown up in Houston, somewhere fancy, something Oaks, his father a lawyer, his grandfather a lawyer. Ted had gone to a private school that had been in a movie. His parents had died young, so Bunny had few memories of them, but she knew that Ted's inheritance had been what bought the Glenns' nest egg, a baggy craftsman home in Washington, DC, that they rented out throughout all their postings and which Maryellen yearned to one day renovate and occupy.

The Taco Bell field was a joke, something Ted's grandfather had gone in on with a few other men, a place to camp before Houston sprawled like it did today and which Ted's father had then inherited with a couple of dozen other people—and of which now Ted Senior held something like a 1/78th share. It was a patch of grassland halfway between Houston and Galveston that had once produced oil and provided a small amount of income to the various parties involved, and which now housed a Taco Bell and a rusty garden of derelict machinery, the well fallow and cashless beneath. The senior members of the family who held larger stakes were in a continual state of warfare over this field, whether to sell off the surface immediately for further development or keep it in case a better deal came along. Selling the surface did not mean that they sold what was underneath it, but what got built on the surface affected the underneath; this was the most Bunny understood of it.

"No, thank you," Bunny said. She was between warring instincts: she both never wanted to have a conversation about feelings with her father, and yet couldn't believe he thought there was anything else to talk about. The feelings generated by his actions had, at this moment, a totalizing effect on her and Maryellen's life. How could he make small talk?

"I hope you're taking care of yourself." Ted's voice sounded helpless. "Do you need money?" She hated the way this sounded, hated that money was of course a constant hum in her brain. Twenty-six, a college graduate, unemployed! She prayed that Annabelle and ManPower would come through.

"Not if I get a job soon," she said. "But if I don't then yes, I guess."

"Okay, well," he said.

"Well," she said, "I better go."

"Take care," her father said. "I love you."

"Okay," she said. She got off the phone before she started crying.

She could not believe her father had done this, and there was no one to discuss it with apart from Maryellen, with whom she did not want to discuss it. She felt remote from her brothers. While John had eventually reversed his silent treatment of his slutty sister, he was now in Ukraine, his Peace Corps term winding up but feeling no compunction to go home as he partied in Kyiv and cast around for his next thing. Small Ted had just started college at George Washington. Bunny envied her little brother, that he was now busy with classes and new friends. They exchanged text messages occasionally, but somehow the unusual parameters of their upbringing had not led to closeness. In any case neither of her brothers had shown an inclination to discuss their parents' divorce at length. More than once Bunny had almost called Evan to talk about it—he knew her parents, had been to their apartment in Athens—but she held on to her dignity, beyond the private mortification of stalking him on Facebook late at night to see if he had another girlfriend, just as she stalked Stanton Cartwright to see him in Patrick McMullan–watermarked photos from parties in New York City, with beautiful thin girls Bunny felt she knew without knowing.

She finished her Coke, flapped her armpits, and angled the Oldsmobile toward home.

THE WEDDING

Bunny stood on the worn pavers of her alma mater, her stomach full of froth. It was summer, the grounds empty, but she could almost hear the sounds of the Stanhope students as they streamed through the old wooden doors of Dow Hall and then the women's buildings, Cuttner and Grosvenor and Alice James Halls, across green lawns and flagstones and hidden courtyards that linked the daisy chain of stone buildings around a central bell tower. It had been eight years since Bunny left Stanhope, but she could almost see the bad boys coming from the woods, the spot they called the Office since it was filled with castoff desk chairs and filing cabinets, where they took hits from a glass piece called the Falcon that a flaxen-haired boy had smuggled to school with him in his bag. Bunny had lost her virginity in the Office, to the very same Paul de Waal whose 5K time tormented her brother, so freckled he was "practically disabled," Bunny had opined before the same freckled body hovered over her in the dark.

She could almost see her brother and Paul de Waal now, galloping down with the other boys from the upper floors of Dow Hall, floors where new freshmen boys quailed at the bathroom, five showerheads and a central drain, where there was piss in the shampoo, the water turned from freezing to scalding, everyone whapping each other's balls with stinging wet towels.

Bunny looked across the fields to the girls' dorms, dorms made of cheap stucco that had once reverberated with the sounds of hair dryers and high-pitched exclamations, corridors that were a decade ago scented with Bath & Body Works Pearberry, with Davidoff Cool Water, with CK One, with CK Be, with Ralph Lauren Romance, drains that foamed with suds, Nelly blasting on the stereo of a girl whose father was high up at Bank of America. "If you wanna go and take a ride with me," the girls had sung together, knowing and singing every word, the N-word included, most but not all of the girls white, their skin damp, their hair sizzling in flat irons. They looked at themselves in the mirror and at each other; they said "I'm so fat," "You're so tan." They said "That's so gay"; they said "That's so ghetto"; they said "That's so funny." They pulled on their light dresses, their illegal Rocket Dog platform flip-flops, their J.Crew sandals, and they skipped out the doors in clouds of scent, arm in arm and hand in hand, soft paws fixing stray hairs, buttons at the nape of the neck, voices sounding across the fields they crossed to sign in for breakfast.

Bunny was back at Stanhope for a wedding, one that she and Evan had been invited to together, months before they broke up. Allison, the bride, had been Bunny's sophomore roommate at Stanhope. Bunny had not been a very good roommate, to Allison or anyone else, but Allison was a loyal kind of person and Bunny had made her laugh with her constant, catastrophic lateness, her vicious impressions of the teachers.

The cocktail hour after the brief ceremony took place on a promontory overlooking the lake where the crew practiced. It was a small wedding; Allison was very rich but in the kind of sturdy, sensible way that did not entertain frippery. When Allison spotted Bunny with a drink sweating in her hand, she gave her a radiant smile and Bunny, who had been filled with an incredible sense of self-loathing since she set foot on the campus, felt glad that she had come. She looked at Allison's beautifully broad face, cheekbones that fanned out from her nose like the wings of a moth. Bunny caught a glimpse of the ring as Allison pushed a hair out of her own eyes and reflexively reached for her friend's hand.

"*Oh. My. God. Allison,*" Bunny cried. "This is so stunning." *Stunning* was a word that Bunny was starting to hear and read places, and she liked the sound, emphatic and somehow more adult than *amazing.* Rings were stunning. Brides were stunning. Allison was stunning in her strapless A-line satin Vera Wang—classic—her chapel-length veil surreptitiously removed after the ceremony. Weddings were stunning. Bunny learned this the way she had learned to say "I'm down for whatever" or "I'm good."

Bunny had had few opportunities to see an engagement ring up close. Her own mother didn't have one; Ted was parsimonious and found the practice distasteful, and Maryellen wouldn't have wanted anything that drew further attention to her as she went about her errands overseas. Allison's ring was glorious. It was an emerald-cut— Bunny knew from the furtive googling she had done when she imagined that Evan might one day propose—perched coolly between two smaller rectangular diamonds. It was an architectural ring, almost streamline moderne.

"Wow, Allison," Bunny said, forcing herself to look away from the ring. How she yearned to try it on! A grasping, unexpected form of envy rose in her. But she hadn't seen Allison in five years or more, and she could feel herself being creepy. "I'm so happy for you," she volunteered. "Thank you so much for inviting me."

"I had to have my Rowdy Roomie!" said Allison. "I'm sorry your man couldn't make it."

"We actually broke up," said Bunny, but then she rushed to say, "But it's okay!"

Bunny had only told her small group of friends from college about the breakup, fielding a few sympathetic texts and calls. She asked them to look out for jobs where they worked, but they were all doing AmeriCorps or studying for the LSAT while their parents supported them.

Allison saw someone see her out of the corner of her eye, but, always a well-mannered girl, she held the conversation with Bunny for another beat before looking apologetic.

"Get out there," said Bunny, making a shooing motion. "We'll talk later!"

After Allison bounded off to greet her other guests, Bunny wandered across the promontory and scrambled down an embankment to one of the places where the Stanhope students used to smoke, although, judging from the absence of errant butts, they did no longer. She would have killed for a cigarette. She had quit smoking for Evan, and even in the prolonged period of sadness and nihilism that attended the breakup, even in the gloom of the Beaumont house, she had stayed strong. Bunny did not want to be Rowdy Roomie, with everything that went along with it.

The day had been too hot, but now the sun slid below the edge of the fields that abutted the forested acreage of Stanhope, suffusing the air with custard light. Bugs moved languidly across the surface of the water. Here in this place where she had so often hidden it was not the memories of school that flooded in but the interstitial times, the day-long flights to and from. She and her brother had ridden planes where gray skeins of cigarette smoke hung in the thin air of the cabin, defying overworked filtration systems. They had ridden planes with chickens clucking and peeping in boxes. They had ridden planes where terrified new fliers prayed aloud during the unholy moment of ascent. They flew with their parents; they flew alone with their unaccompanied-minor placards around their necks. They spent one night in a hotel with a British Air "nanny," probably an off-duty gate agent, when they missed a connecting flight. Bunny remembered coming back to Stanhope after that first and only Baku summer, the frantic freshening in the bathroom to erase the damage of eighteen hours in transit, the clench of her stomach as the shuttle entered the school gates.

And then she looked around and found herself back, age twenty-six, on the grass by the pond, where a cute but slightly slovenly white man, just rounding into what Bunny considered middle age, was slipping inelegantly down the slope in soft brown loafers. He had the full, flopping hair that should have gone on the head of a man five or ten years his junior, and he wore pink pants—Nantucket reds, their proper name—and a pale blue shirt that had parted just above his belt, revealing the white of his undershirt.

"Ahoy," he said, and Bunny laughed. As if conjured by some louche minor deity the man produced a pack of American Spirits from his pocket and offered it to Bunny.

"This is the only reason anyone comes down here, right?" he said. Bunny took one without hesitation and then accepted the flame from his lighter.

"Thanks," she said.

"I'm assuming you're here for the wedding," he said.

"Yep. You?"

"Allie's my cousin. I went here like six years before her." Bunny tried to do the math. Was he thirty? Thirty-one? Thirty-two?

"We were fourth-form roommates," Bunny said.

"Ah," he said. He stuck out his hand. "I'm Rob. Rob Phillips." Bunny felt her mind begin to scan the genealogies that were still indexed in her consciousness.

She looked at him and saw that he had the straight, low brows of Allison, of other faces she could recall. How peculiar to recognize the features of a given family when its individual members were strangers, like, she imagined, marble busts of famous Romans. She pulled on her cigarette, which was glorious. She instantly began to worry about where she would find enough cigarettes to last her for the rest of the evening.

"Where did you come from?" he asked.

"I just moved from Pittsburgh. I'm in Texas now. Houston, kind of," she said ruefully. What about you?"

"I'm in the City," he said, meaning New York City, the only city.

"Ah," she said. His eyes were blue and there was a little bit of gray in his hair. She imagined him in high school. He might have picked her off of the herd with two of his friends and asked her slightly mocking questions about what it was like to live in . . . what was it called again . . . Azervagina? Or he might have found her in some secluded place where she waited to be found and spoken to her softly until they were out past the tennis court and lying in the damp grass. She was grown-up now, she reminded herself. It didn't matter what he thought about her. He was looking at her with a friendly, apprais-ing expression—she was wearing a magenta Nanette Lepore dress she had bought on sale at Nordstrom, and his face more or less confirmed that it looked great on her—when the gong rang.

"Oh my god," Bunny said. "Allison." The bride had employed the school's gong, the one that called the students across the fields to din-ner every afternoon. Only the senior prefect assigned to the task had the key to the cabinet where the gong was kept, although one year the senior prank had been to replace the gong with a turkey leg.

Bunny tossed her cigarette butt and gingerly stepped on it with the toe of her shoe.

"What's your name?" he said, stopping her before she reached the slope.

"Oh, I'm Elizabeth . . . Bunny."

"Bunny," he said. "Okay."

"Shall we," she said, and they scrambled up the slope, his hand hov-ering at her elbow as her heels sank into the soft dirt.

Together they drifted toward the board with table assignments and then separated toward their seats. Bunny dreaded learning at which table of cast-off friends and relatives she had been placed.

Allison had been a cornerstone member of the Stanhope Choir and a champion diver, and her choir friends and diving friends were sitting together at their own boisterous tables, half of them with plus-ones. Bunny was at a sort of odds-and-ends table with one face she recognized, Celeste Gaudette, looking just exactly the same to Bunny as she ever had. The same pale blonde hair, the same intent eyes and beautiful brows swooping up into slight points. Bunny and Celeste had not been friends, but Stanhope was so small that she was as familiar a sight to Bunny as though they came from the same family. The young women leaned into one another for a weak and loveless hug. "Nice to see you," said Celeste just as Bunny said, "Great to see you."

Looking around the room Bunny could almost see it populated with other members of this imagined family, some of them present in the flesh, most of them not. Bunny slipped into memory like a once-beloved dress. She remembered goading the boys into telling her what they thought of all the girls, as though by obsessively parsing the physical traits of others she would learn the things they wouldn't tell her about herself. There was one young woman who had the most perfect ass the school had ever seen, it was said. It had gotten an award, at some talent show, in veiled terms. There was another who was gorgeous, stunning, like literally perfect, like could be in movies, but she wouldn't have sex because she was saving herself for someone very lucky. There was a girl whose crooked teeth made you want to slap her, one boy had said. Sitting at the choir table was Mr. Li, the choir teacher. He was Asian, and strict, and lived in Dow Hall, so some of them had called him Chairman Dow. Bunny had, certainly.

Bunny felt a hand and looked up to see Rob, red-faced and standing behind her chair. His gaze passed from Bunny to Celeste, then back to Bunny.

"Hello again," he said.

"Hi, Rob," Bunny said. "This is Celeste, from my class."

"Hi," he said. "Mind if I pull up a chair? My table sucks. What are you guys talking about?"

"Just catching up," said Celeste, eyeing Rob with suspicion. Bunny remembered that she had always been a very principled girl. Bunny said, "Have a seat."

He settled himself between the women.

"What do you do?" Bunny asked him.

"I'm a trader."

Bunny looked at him blankly. "I literally don't know what that is," she said, and he shrugged.

She had had about four drinks and was feeling free and magnetic, like she had pulled this rumpled, slightly red-faced apparition to herself, one who probably dated women who did complex kinds of exercise routines. She was both mildly repelled by him and anxious to capture his approval. He was peeling the dissolving label off of his beer.

"Like, when you go into your office, what do you do?" she asked, with unexpected vehemence.

"I go in, I get coffee from the machine, I turn on my computer," he said, and then he laughed at his own joke. "I mean, what do you want to know? I buy low and sell high." This was facetious, Bunny assumed. "What do *you* do?"

Bunny felt so free that she barely tried to disguise the nature of her situation. "Well on Tuesday I'm starting a job at an engineering firm," she said, thinking "firm" sounded more important than "company." A few days before she had come to Stanhope for the wedding, still wondering how she would pay the credit card on which she had put the plane ticket, she was clicking around on her laptop and drinking white wine on the screen porch, her mother supine in the hammock a few feet away, when she received an email from Annabelle at ManPower with her first assignment as an administrative assistant at Miles Engineering

Consultants, with a pleasing salary of fifteen dollars an hour. In her message, Annabelle wrote that this was a family company where a little bit of ingenuity and loyalty could go a long way.

"But up until now I was working *two* jobs," she added comic emphasis, "one as an . . . archivist for an insane man and one at an upscale baby-and-child consignment store." She shimmied her shoulders at this last, seeing Celeste watching her.

Rob laughed. "What's an upscale baby-and-child consignment store?" he asked.

"A place where you can get expensive strollers gently used," she said. "And baby clothes and shit. I made eight dollars an hour." She chugged the rest of her drink.

Rob whistled.

"Ooh, fancy, what do you make?" Bunny said, which came out sexually provocative to an extent she hadn't intended.

"More than that," he said putting up his hand to stall further inquiry.

"Can I have a cigarette?" Bunny asked. She had masticated the entirety of her too-small beef medallion, and waiters were beginning to collect plates from the tables in the gentle roar of the dining hall, the noise of cutlery against a hundred gold-rimmed plates that had fed hundreds of people a thousand times.

Outside it was very dark and there was the knife edge of cool in the air. Bunny remembered the heartbreaking moment when autumn stole in—the chill mornings, the darkening afternoons, the sun sinking below the earth as she gasped, sandpaper-throated, through the last half mile of the cross-country course. And then the quicksilver moment when spring exploded in the morning light, spring at Stanhope a parody of itself, baby ducks on the pond and a riot in the blood of every student, young limbs stretching out to feel the sun after a season in the dark. She shivered in the night air.

"I'd offer you my jacket, but I don't have one," said Rob, which Bunny thought was considerate. The bar is so low, she reminded herself. Evan had been considerate, truly considerate. He just didn't love her. She didn't hold his interest. She could barely hold her own interest. So she smoked with Rob and they exchanged a selection of memories, an endless number of alumni names and college classmates to ask about and pass the time. Rob asked if she knew his buddy Tom, another sexy, malignant presence at the school, roving around with a group of other boys causing ripples of anxiety and desire.

"I remember he and his friends played a game," Bunny said. "One of them would lie down and someone else would hit him in the crotch with a Wiffle Ball bat as hard as they could."

Rob laughed. "Classic."

Rob had his phone out and was tapping at it. Before Bunny could apprehend this as rudeness, he put his hand out, one index finger up, and said, "I'm not being rude. I am checking something." Bunny put out her cigarette and reached over his arm into his breast pocket where the pack of American Spirits was visible. As she did it, she could feel heat flood through her, not specific to Rob himself but from the feeling of touching a man. As she did it she could see Rob's eyebrows rise up in the glow of the lights from Dow Hall, which cast its warmth almost to the part of the quad where they stood. It became clear to her, clear as frost on the fields in October, that she could have sex with Rob Phillips. Rowdy Roomie resurrected.

They wandered back into the school, down the empty corridors, past the gun cabinet, wherein were displayed the armaments of various wars foreign and domestic. They walked past the rows of photos, arrayed against green felt in glass cabinets, of the school's founding patriarchs and board members. The Gothic embellishments to the central halls gave the illusion that Stanhope had been standing for six hundred years instead of ninety. It was eerie now, empty, its dark classrooms reverberating with the memory of sound. Bunny remembered her younger self, moving through the same corridors with one boy or another, prowling for a secluded nook. Bunny had not slept with anyone since Evan, and now she was intent that it would happen. But first they would go back to Founders Courtyard and drink more with the group assembled there. They would watch Allison and her new husband dance, and they would listen to toasts, and they would dance more, Allison yelling, *"Rowdy Roomieeeeeee,"* as she danced by, and they would sing "Don't Stop Believing," an all-white party dancing before an all-Black wedding band, their voices drifting up, up, up into the dark sky over the mid-Atlantic.

Morning found Bunny in the Holiday Inn in town, in a room that was not her own, one strappy shoe still on her foot. The shower was running, and she recognized that she was in the miraculous purgatory, just exiting drunkenness but not yet across the Acheron to the crushing hangover and pervasive feeling of dread that was her final destination. She knew that if she could make the proper interventions and make them quickly, there was a slim but important possibility that she might avoid the next part of the journey and return to happier shores. She didn't deserve it, but she wanted it. She was braless and her dress was a circle of fabric around her waist. Her underpants were on, although what she remembered of the wee hours had them most definitely off. She spied the condom wrapper on the nightstand. She remembered thrusting. Orgasm was an impossibility in these conditions. She couldn't remember whether she had faked one to end the evening's festivities or tried drunkenly to overturn the laws of the universe.

She decided that under no circumstances would she attend the post-wedding brunch back on the Stanhope campus. She would take a cab to get a fountain Coke and cigarettes, and then she would get the shuttle to the airport and hope that she saw no one on the way. She found her bra and pulled up her dress. She gripped the nightstand and bent over dangerously to see if her other shoe was present. The sound of the shower stopped and the door opened, exuding steam and a clean, Irish Spring–like smell.

"Rise and shine," said Rob Phillips, a towel wrapped around his waist, hair dappling his soft and unassuming body. Bunny smiled sheepishly at him.

"Oh my god," she said. "Big night." He dug in a duffel bag and then put on boxer briefs in a swift movement that barely disturbed his towel. He put on a T-shirt and a pair of khaki pants.

"That was fun," he said, which she thought was kind of him. Her vagina felt sore.

She remembered a thought she had shortly before they boarded the shuttle to the hotel. He seemed too old to be unmarried, in the circles she imagined he ran in. She herself wanted to be married by age twenty-eight, a number inscribed on her consciousness, perhaps by one of her magazines, as being the ideal age for marriage. And here she was, twenty-six and being drunkenly poked by a frat boy too long on the shelf. She remembered demanding he tell her his exact workday routine, pulling his coat around her against the chill.

"You're *so weird*," he had said, his voice rasping with the cigarettes they had smoked one after another. "I get an egg-and-cheese with ketchup and salt from my bodega guy," he said. "I get a small coffee. Then I take the subway or sometimes the crosstown bus or *sometimes* a cab. And by then my small coffee is done, so I get a *large* latte with a shot of caramel." She had made fun of him for this, but she almost felt she loved him when he said it—there was something vulnerable about his small, touching preferences.

"I go to the elevator and say hi to Diane, who does admin for my group. I check my charts."

"Do you have a girlfriend?" she had blurted out then, and he said, "I was engaged, but my fiancée and I recently ended things." It was a euphemistic way to put it, Bunny noticed. She didn't ask what had happened.

Later he had said, "You should get a job in the City," and later, "I'll hook you up with Diane. She makes a fuckload more than eight bucks an hour, I guarantee you. She probably makes more than me."

Bunny found her clutch and her room key. She wanted badly to ask Rob for a cigarette for the road, but it jarred too much with the scent of soap and the sight of his clean hair combed away from his forehead.

"Well," she said.

"Are you going to go to the breakfast thing?" he asked.

"I'm not sure yet," Bunny said. "I don't think I'll be ready in time. I can't go like this, obviously."

"You should come," he said, and suddenly she worried that she loved him. The bar was so low. She wondered again what had happened with the fiancée.

"Can I have a cigarette?" she decided to ask.

"Wow, dirtbag," he said. "We smoked them all. *You* smoked them all, mostly. Also you lost your shoe on the shuttle."

"Womp womp," she said weakly.

"Okay, I'm going to go take a shower," she said. She wondered whether she should hug him or shake his hand. He gave her a half hug, around the shoulders, and opened the door.

"See ya," he said. She slipped her remaining shoe off, revealing a raw place across the top of her foot, and limped down the hall like an old woman.

Two hours later she was at the airport, four hours too early and nursing a gin and tonic in a malodorous bar outside security, making periodic trips outside to smoke the cigarettes she had crossed the interstate from the Holiday Inn to buy. The sporadic memories of her night with Rob jostled for primacy with the other memories that the smell of the airport ushered in. Herself, fifteen on the way back to Baku for winter break, in a glassed-in cabana in the bowels of some European airport with the other smokers, John spying her on the way back from the bathroom, standing outside the glass and glaring at her before moving his face slowly closer and closer until his nose was squished against the glass and she laughed with relief, the only moment of levity in the sixteen-hour trip.

John was always effortlessly good, in the manner of the other upright Stanhope children. This is why he now had an interesting and exciting and valuable and fulfilling life in Ukraine, Bunny thought, and why she was in an airport bar nursing her blister and her hangover and sense of worthlessness. It was hard to believe she and John had ever been physically close. And yet they had. In Buenos Aires, two years old and thrashing with ear infection, horizontal between their parents' bodies and forming the shape of an *H* in the sweaty sheets. In Washington, DC, in a furnished apartment, John crawling in where Bunny already lay, together a semicolon between the parentheses of their parents. In Athens, during that once-in-a decade Athenian snow-storm, an asterisk on Ted and Maryellen's bed with their new baby brother. She could barely picture him now, away in Ukraine. It hurt to remember those times, before times, times that were now inaccessible not only through time and space but by the way recent events seemed to reorder everything that came before.

At the other end of the airport bar was a small group of bros watching a baseball game, her age or slightly older. They had started as a pair and accumulated further members although it was unclear, from Bunny's vantage, whether they knew one another or were simply so certain of shared affinity that they could join ranks with only a glance. She recalled making Rob give a lengthy and meandering explanation of what was involved in buying low and selling high. Where had he acquired this specialized knowledge, she demanded of him. She considered the bros of her acquaintance at college, who had participated in the same disappointing bacchanals as she and yet, to a man, seemed to have ended up in this kind of job. What was the class you took that qualified you to effortlessly earn money? What was the class where you learned what the stock market was and how it operated? "I was an econ major," Rob had offered, shrugging. "I got an internship in the City junior year."

Bunny squeezed in one last cigarette and a Bud Light before she went through the ordeal of security, removing her shoes and her liquids, thinking briefly while she did so about bombs in airplanes, but also of the face of the shoe bomber, whose mug shot she had found hilarious even though she sometimes lay awake worrying that someone would explode her in the sky. She raised her arms and spread her legs for the body scanner, exposing a moon of flesh at her midriff. When Maryellen had started her job, everyone could just walk onto a plane. Bunny found herself wanting to discuss this with someone and realized she was drunk.

She walked with purpose to her gate and then onto the plane, where she had another drink to remain drunk. She felt good. She effusively let her seatmates go to and fro to retrieve things from their bags; she admired every single flight attendant, male and female, for their beauty. "My mother was a flight attendant in the golden age of travel!" she wanted to tell them all. She loved everyone now, half in the bag and enormously tired. She recognized she had been suffering from a disease of the mind, a disease of negativity, and vowed to eradicate it. She had been dreading the trip back, the yawning void of Texas and Maryellen's sadness before her, but now she was glad to leave the past behind, she thought. She would now flip it and reverse it. She was going back where no one knew her. No one knew Rowdy Roomie; no one knew that her strappy sandal was lost for good and her vagina ached and her blood was coursing with alcohol. She would shower, and she would help her mother, and she would be positive and do well at her new job, and she would start getting her life into shape and her body too. She wanted only good things and blessings for all of the people around her, she was thinking when she fell asleep, sending the smells of Marlboro 27s and Bud Light into the cabin in an act of unwitting discourtesy to her neighbors.

2010
$83.98/$70.77

THE BEAR

I n a windowless interior room of the only Class A office tower in southeast Texas, an assortment of women sat around a table. They were all white and ranged from just north of Bunny's age to somewhere in the late sixties. Some were slender and some were padded and some were corpulent, some dressed at the lower end of business casual and some in smart dresses and dressy tops. Together they exuded an air of prickly camaraderie. A handsome woman with chunky blonde highlights and a gentle network of very fine, soft-looking wrinkles under her eyes stood at the head of an oval table and greeted Bunny as she came in.

On a felt wall of the conference room there was a travel poster for the United Arab Emirates that always created a flicker of possibility in Bunny when she saw it. She sat down next to a beautiful, plump woman named Melody with caramel-colored hair and perfect eye makeup.

"Welcome to hell," Melody said cheerily to Bunny. "Saved you a seat."

"Thanks, babe," said Bunny. "No one I'd rather be in hell with."

On Bunny's other side was Rose, her oldest colleague in the pool, and Rose said, "Did y'all see the bear?" At this, a taut and sinewy woman with dark-blonde hair and rough-textured but unlined golden skin who was passing by the room poked her head in the door. She wore orangey lipstick and black patent leather platform pumps. "That bear," she said. "That damn bear is taking up three freezers in my garage right now." The women in the room laughed dutifully and she left the doorway in a cloud of scent.

They all swiveled back to Tara, their leader, who stood at the front of the room.

"You have no idea the shit I had to go through for this," she said, sotto voce into full strength, "but as of this week, you ladies will finally be *free* of the engineers' bullshit." She smoothed her bangs into their accustomed sweep across her forehead. The girls looked around at each other. Melody put her chin on her fist and angled her face toward Tara. "You have my attention," she said, and they all laughed.

"We now have a new program called Document Locator that is *specifically* for engineering projects and *specifically* to get control of the doc revisions," she continued. "The way it works is that everyone has to be in Document Locator. When you work on a document, you check it out. While you have it checked out, no one else can work on it. When you're done, you check it back in, and then you let your engineer know that they can get in there. And then they can do whatever they need to do, and the program automatically tracks all the versions, and if we need to we can go back to an old version. It's going to make our lives so much easier, I am telling you."

For all their romance with exactitude, the engineers at Miles Engineering, the older guys especially, were cavalier about document hygiene; they would ignore the draft that had been returned to them and would make their own changes to some primordial draft parked haphazardly on their desktop computer. When an engineer did this, it meant that the girl assigned to him would have to repeat the same work she had already done, and extraneous time accrued to projects that had already exceeded their billable hours.

Melody furrowed the beautiful porcelain skin of her brow. "Okay," she said. "But what if they just keep only working on documents on their local drives or their desktop or whatever?"

"Yeah," said Rose. "Are they gonna have a training too?"

"That's a good question," said Tara. "The first answer is that if they do that, I'll find them and I'll fucking slap them." She lowered her voice again for the last part, and all the women laughed. "But the second part is that they won't be able to do that, or at least they won't be able to do that without us noticing. Because if they email you some random document or call you and say, 'Okay, my doc is in the P Drive,' you're just gonna say, 'Oh, Fred, sorry, I can't work on a document unless it's in Document Locator. Tara and Ainsley won't let me.'"

Melody again looked skeptical. "Okay, but what if they then put their fucked-up version into this new document thing and then are like, 'Okay, you can check it out,' but now there's *two documents* in there."

Tara pointed at her. "They won't do that because they *can't* do that. Because part of this new program is that I am now a 'Document Control Administrator'"—at this all the women oohed supportively and clapped as she did a little dance—"which means that anyone who wants to start a new project document has to go through me. *I'm* the one who will load a template in and give it a name and number and set the permissions for who can access it. Does that answer your question, Ms. Melody?" She looked affectionately at Melody, for while Melody was a squeaky wheel and a pain in the ass, Tara knew that their lives were easier thanks to Melody's unmatched skill with Microsoft Word.

Tara told them there would be a training in a week and that for now they were dismissed. "I want to tell you that the company has spent *a lot* of money on this program, and they want to see us succeed." The women exchanged looks.

"All this because a bunch of scientists couldn't follow instructions," said Rose as she unwrapped a stick of gum. "And they think we're the dumb ones." The women laughed.

Bunny walked back to her cubicle, a molded kidney of a desk bracketed by felt-lined partitions, and opened her email to see that she, like all the staff at Miles Engineering Consultants, had gotten the email. "Thought you might like to see the bear we bagged on Kodiak," said the text, above a photo of an immense brown creature, shaggy and prone next to a body of water, peaceful as in sleep. Beside the bear a hefty man was almost miniature. The bear's paw lay by its face, floppy and gentle, a broad soft pad with claws extending harmlessly from the fur. Bunny brought her face close to the photo and then clicked it closed with disgust.

Miles Engineering Consultants provided client satisfaction in the diverse fields of geophysics and seismology, hydrology, hydrogeology, and construction support. In the admin pool their job was to format and standardize the documents that seemed to Bunny to be the entirety of the work of engineering—not the building itself, but the paper edifice constructed beforehand out of spiral-bound reports produced in-house on a hulking printer, a machine that was as long as her grandmother's Oldsmobile and cost just as much. The documents had to be crystal clear in their meanings, free of spelling and grammatical errors, and formatted in Microsoft Word according to the standards of the Miles Engineering Consultants stylebook. A nuclear power plant (NPP) project ("the Project") would suck in the tepid water of what they were required to call the Arabian Gulf, changing every instance where an engineer called it the Persian Gulf—or Prsian, or Presian, or Person. Regardless of what the gulf was called, the report promised its readers that the water sucked in, heated up, and spit back out by the Project would not perturb its coral and its fish. The women ensured that the specifications of the documents were as stringent as those of the projects themselves. Bunny soon learned to spot the difference between a bulleted list that was 1.25 space with eight points after and one that was simply 1.5.

Bunny read hundreds of pages she did not understand about environments she could not picture—under seas, under mountains, stratigraphies and topographies that carried with them a temporal exoticism. Abyssal plains. Megaturbidites. Landslides and tsunamis and volcanic eruptions taking place twenty thousand years in the past and now having resonance in the present as cited in Subsection 2.5.1.1.1.1.4.3 or attached Appendix B.

The correspondence of headings and subheadings was one of the crucial places where the engineers' tinkering could mangle a revision, and the women combed through their pages to make sure each heading corresponded with every such reference in the text. It was remarkable, what could happen to a document passed between ten different people of various temperaments and work styles, in two different countries on fifteen different computers with software and hardware of wildly disparate age and quality. A paragraph lifted from a colleague's report written on Word 1995 or Word XP and then stuck into a template provided by the admin pool in Word 2008 was a wrench dropped down a deep well, ricocheting off steel until the entire mechanism was mangled with error. From the women at Miles Engineering Consultants, Bunny learned to fish, to delicately lower the cable down into the depths until the offending part could be located and removed. Why had the cursor stopped blinking? She could make it start again.

Sometimes the women gathered in the Repro Room to carry out collective feats of construction: printing, collating, folding, and assembling documents produced by the majestic printer. They might be tasked with putting together thirty-five copies each of four different documents, each two hundred pages long. Each one had to have the correct divider papers, the correct tabs for each section and appendix, image sections, folding maps, front and rear covers, and spiral binding. These would be sent to the United Arab Emirates or Peru via FedEx, consigned to the Pavilion Mall FedEx that stayed open until eleven. Tara would race them to the mall in her car, boxes full of documents that thirty-five unknown people on the other side of the world would come together around a conference table to read. One of these shipments could cost thousands of dollars, they were told, and a single mistake would ruin the whole batch. In the fluorescent light of that windowless room, the printer generating immense heat and noise, the women of the admin pool achieved something like flow. They exited the Repro Room and wheeled dollies loaded with FedEx boxes into the parking lot only to find that it was night, and they would glance briefly at the stars.

Apart from Melody, who had a quick and fiendish mind and was the pool's acknowledged master of Microsoft Word, Bunny found most of her colleagues careless in their work. The majority of the girls considered it enough to do the required formatting of bullets and headings, scan for key terms, and run spell-check, and this was simply not enough to reduce the infelicities that found their way into every document. Bunny read every single line, once and then again. She printed each document, marked it up, and highlighted each pen mark once she had input the change to the original document in Word. She corrected grammar and eventually noted inconsistencies in the text itself, even as the realities that the text conveyed remained completely opaque. She imagined how it might feel to understand what these documents communicated. Bunny by this point knew the engineer bios as intimately as she knew her own life story—knew where on the P Drive she could find "Carl_Phillips_Hydro_Resume" and how and when it should be deployed instead of "Carl_Phillips_Nuclear_Resume." The senior engineers sat on innumerable boards and had ingratiated themselves into myriad professional associations, causing Bunny to ponder the mysteries of expertise and how it was gleaned—or if indeed it was the claiming of the mantle, at some point around age forty, that became its own proof of knowledge.

She complained to Tara about the other admins' sloppiness because it reflected poorly on all of them. As a consequence, shortly after her six-month mark, when she came on board full-time at seventeen dollars per hour *plus* benefits, her paychecks coming from Miles Engineering Consultants instead of ManPower, she was made the proofreader, and thenceforth no report left the pool without her appraisal.

Bunny went through the rest of her emails, sending an obsequious reply to one of the engineers she liked who thanked her for a timely formatting of his report. "Appreciate the edits," he said, which made her squirm with pleasure. Most of the engineers called what the admin girls did "formatting," and Bunny was defensive and resentful about this, knowing that ultimately she had no idea what they were talking about, but also knowing that she was doing her best to make it better.

Bunny, after a moment, reopened the bear email and forwarded it to her Gmail, and then to her brother in Ukraine. This was how they kept up correspondence rather than through phone calls or any real exchanges of information. "Yeehaw," she wrote. She put on her screen saver and walked down the halls to the break room where the bear hunter, Ainsley's husband, was telling an engineer about the bear while some of the admins listened. Miles Engineering Consultants was the legacy of the recently deceased William "Bill" Miles, and it now belonged to his children, Phil and Ainsley, the COO, who was married to Jeff, the CFO and bear hunter. Phil, the CEO, lived in Houston and was rarely in the office in Beaumont, instead spending much of his time on the road for what was called "BizDev." Since the activities of the Miles Engineering Consultants scions by blood or marriage were of general interest, it was widely known that Jeff was a sharpshooter and gun enthusiast, and people always listened to him when he held forth in the break room.

"It's all about the Ruger, baby," he was saying. The three admins craned their necks to listen to him from their seated positions. Jeff was not handsome, but he took up a lot of space in the room and gave the impression at all times of wearing a bulletproof vest under his clothes.

A crane-like admin named Rayelle tilted her head. "Aren't you, like, scared the bear is going to charge you?" She had white-blonde hair that required, Bunny knew from their conversations in the admin pool, a lot of maintenance. She was the most put-together of the admins; she drove a car that looked like the armored jeeps they used to carry cash away from ATMs, and stepped gracefully out of its warlike doors every morning in three-inch heels.

"You know I had my Glock too. The ranger out there said if one surprises you, the Glock is going to be your best friend—says he never walks alone in Alaska without one. But this ol' guy was chilling by the water, taking a drink."

Bunny thought of the bear's surprise, its head down between its big paws to lap at the lake, the pain blooming under its fur. She finished her lunch and returned to her cube to read about Abyssal plains and look for errant headings. She resolved she would drive to Houston that weekend and walk around some place with restaurants and shops and different people. She was not satisfied with her life.

THE HOLIDAY CARDS

Bunny and Maryellen were sitting in the living room, drinking eggnog and watching a *Poirot* rerun while Bunny worked on her eBay listings. She had devoted herself to the disposition of some of her grandmother's household effects, upon the sale of which she received a 25 percent commission as agreed on by her mother and Uncle Warren. Every day the house lost some Victorian furniture or decorative porcelain item ferreted out by Bunny's grandmother from an antique barn. "Stunning antique cranberry glass vase, circa 1880s," Bunny typed, hunched over her computer, a knee up by her chin. "Collector's item." When she had sold enough of her grandmother's possessions, she was going to buy herself something expensive; what, she had not yet decided. Perfume, maybe. Or get her hair done. The admin girls gave her shit about her wet bun, which she wore every day because she could never wake up in time and did not care enough to do something different. She was not Rayelle, with her $200 recurring highlights.

When she had finished her listings, Bunny sifted through the avalanche of holiday cards that had found Maryellen in Beaumont, forwarded from whatever APO address had last been carefully recorded in wifely notebooks. These cards, with their long printed inserts, were the method by which Foreign Service families kept one another abreast, even as Facebook was beginning to supplant the need for regular updates—news of postings, promotions, children in college, retirement or the annual upkeep of property stateside.

Bunny skimmed, looking for glimpses of children she had once known. They were at Smith, they were at Michigan, they were at Washington University, they were at Rice and Denison or at an internship. It was hard to imagine them as adults out in the world. In her mind they were in the dim hallways of embassy housing, making forts from an empty box. They were in a courtyard thwapping each other with a length of rubber pipe left by the workmen. Their parents were having drinks on the veranda and the ice clinked in glasses while the children frolicked in gardens or piles of rubble. It was peculiar to picture them now, somewhere in America, wheeling a cart through Target, these blossoms cultivated in other soils.

One card showed a middle-aged woman on a lush mountainside on what a caption identified as the island of Papeete.

"Who is this again?" Maryellen looked over, and Bunny saw her unnerving visage of the last year, wan face, hair in a braid—not even a French braid—her highlights grown out, her body in a neat sweatsuit, her small feet tucked up beneath her. Maryellen squinted as Bunny held the letter up, creased from where it had been folded into a card showing the Madonna and child wearing tropical flower crowns.

"Oh," she said, looking back at the TV. "That's Sue Whitehead."

"Who's Sue Whitehead?" said Bunny, reading over Sue's list of achievements for the year.

"We were at Breech together," Maryellen said, nodding her head toward the wall, where for decades among the family photos a group photo had hung, Maryellen with her Breech cohort, boot camp for flight attendants, 1978: beautiful young people, mostly white women, one Black woman, a handful of white men, one Black man. They were off duty, wearing college sweatshirts, track pants and sweats, their legs pressed together, their arms thrown around each other's necks, used to close quarters in the trainee galley, used to going out dancing after they practiced sliding two stories into rafts floating in the swimming pool. Bunny had always been fascinated by the photo. Her mother had the short hair of the period and reminded Bunny of the photos of young Princess Diana. This was Maryellen's life before. Sometimes she asked Maryellen if she missed it. "I miss people listening to me," she once said with amusement. "It was like putting on a show, stepping into the plane. Suddenly people paid attention." Bunny found this surprising, since Maryellen had put the fear of God into her as a child.

Maryellen spoke again after a few minutes. "Sue found out she had some kind of inner ear thing, vertigo. She had to quit." She turned down *Poirot*. "I felt so bad for her; she was devastated. But then she did this travel-booking certificate program they had instead, and she ended up managing a high-end guest house in Bora Bora for years," said Maryellen. "She married an Australian guy out there. Now she's retired. Never had any children," she said, the matter finished. Bunny admired the way that Maryellen and Ted knew so many people with very interesting lives.

Bunny looked furtively at her mother, whose eyes were back on *Poirot*. The question of what Maryellen should do now was an open one. She could hardly return to her flight attendant career of thirty years' prior, although Bunny suggested this periodically. Therapy was out of the question for anyone in the Glenn family, although Bunny had suggested that too, even though it sounded horrible to her, something for people who could not handle their problems, who could not pick themselves up and apply to jobs and just find something to do and get over themselves. But it seemed to Bunny that Maryellen, who had previously been, in her way, the doing-est person Bunny had ever known, had a problem.

Bunny knew money was one worry. Maryellen had gotten a lawyer, and it was assumed that she would end up with some kind of alimony, not to mention some money from the sale of the house they owned in Washington, DC. For now, though, she had no income and was paying for expenses and house maintenance on a home equity loan. Although the house Bunny and Maryellen currently inhabited had a farcical grandeur to it, Maryellen's parents had not been truly rich; the house was the extent of what Warren and Maryellen had jointly inherited. When Bunny and Maryellen sat together at the dinner table at night, Maryellen spoke bitterly of nearly three decades of her own lost income. "Your father always told his stupid joke that it was harder to get a TWA stewardess job than get into Harvard," she would say. "But it was. It was harder than getting into the goddamned State Department back then. They didn't fire you from State for having a fat ass."

Bunny, who had absorbed several narratives about divorce from the culture at large, namely the phrase "for the sake of the children," wondered if her father believed he was doing Maryellen a favor by making his break when their last child was out of the house. But it seemed to her a cruelty, to wait until Maryellen had no more activities to arrange, 85 percent fewer logistics to deal with, and, of course, no job. As the holiday cards demonstrated, now was supposed to be the time for the wives to shine—the women with whom Maryellen had labored in the bad old days, or the very end of those days when FSOs were given promotions based on their wives' appearance and demeanor, when they were still expected to call upon and help out the ambassadors' wives, their husbands' bosses' wives, fold napkins and be on hand for events, swiftly remove squalling babies from garden parties they were obligated to give, babies they had fearfully delivered in foreign hospitals after a few weeks of language training. These were women who moved every one or two or four years, their things in storage units around the world, the children always changing schools, their furniture lost or broken every time it crossed the sea. Now was the time that they were meant to retire on generous federal pensions, start their own businesses, display their textiles, renovate homes they had waited decades to inhabit. Or if their husbands had truly ascended, it was time to shine in another way, at last with the amount of help that entertaining on a dignitary's scale required. Not only had Maryellen lost her partner, she had lost the future that had been part of the bargain. She was fifty-three years old, and her whole adult life had been spent on the road. Unlike her brothers, Bunny understood this implicitly, not that she wanted to be the one to fix it. "There's no reason Mom can't find something to do," John had said on GChat. But Bunny, lamenting her own loss of anticipated future outcomes, could at least feel a faint reverberation of what Maryellen must feel.

The most unsettling thing for Bunny was seeing some elemental, hidden self of Maryellen. Bunny had always sought to escape Maryellen's many rules, her rigidity, her martial cheeriness, her never-ending corrections, not only of Bunny—John and Small Ted were also corrected—but especially of Bunny. She knew the searching, scanning look of Maryellen, on the hunt for an errant hair or chipped nail polish, as well as she knew her own face. And now Maryellen was adrift, weeping, laid low. Only just out of the years of constant fighting over Bunny's grades, Bunny's clothes, what Bunny could and could not do, Bunny had no idea how to comfort her mother, felt both repelled by her and unspeakably sad. She did not want to hear her mother's laments and in response to them could only muster the kind of language she would use for her girlfriends in college—"He doesn't deserve you! He sucks!"—stretching her *Sex and the City* education to fit the completely alien frame of her parents. Often she just ended up yelling at her, and then they would both cry.

"What should we eat for dinner?" Bunny said, putting all the cards aside. Maryellen had cooked all the meals in Bunny's childhood apart from the ones Lale had made in Baku—varied, nutritious meals—and Bunny now occasionally tried to do her part by at least getting stuff at the grocery store.

"I wish we could go to Strofi," her mom said, a legendary taverna in Athens with a view of the Parthenon. Bunny worried that this would lead to painful reminiscences, but her mom had a thin smile on her face and she allowed herself to travel with her. "I'll learn how to make moussaka," Bunny said. There was a silence.

"I can get us a pizza," she tried again, and Maryellen nodded with resignation.

AINSLEY

One day Ainsley Miles Sullivan, wife of Jeff the bear hunter, spotted Bunny walking down the hall and called her into her office. Bunny found Ainsley horrible and scary—everyone in the admin pool knew she had a program that let her read their emails to make sure they weren't online shopping or talking bad about the company—but nonetheless held her in something akin to awe. Her heels were so high, her acrylics so long, her clouds of scent so commanding, her laugh so brassy, her tone so sharp as she berated her husband in front of their colleagues, that there was a majesty in her presence. She had a grim jocularity about her as she drifted through the admin pool distributing gift cards or Oilers tickets acquired through a charity raffle. Her title was COO, but she did whatever needed doing and took a fantastical salary. She had four sons in middle and high school and drove a red Porsche Cayenne with a license plate that said "BoyMom."

Today Ainsley was wearing a pencil skirt and a camisole, her arms tanned under its straps and her suit jacket draped over the back of her chair. She had her glasses on, with their red frames. Bunny marveled at how unselfconsciously Ainsley inhabited her own reality, the reality of a female scion of a small but prosperous engineering business in East Texas. Ainsley gestured toward a chair.

"Tara tells me you've been doing a great job for us," she said, and she looked intently at Bunny, who felt girlish in her Gap cardigan, her Rockport loafers. "She says you're very detail-oriented and catch a lot of issues with our docs. She says you're good at writing."

Bunny warmed at the compliment. This made Bunny feel indispensable, and perhaps nothing satisfied her more than that feeling. "Thank you so much," said Bunny.

Ainsley let down the hair from her tortoiseshell banana clip and retwisted and clipped it in a swift and utilitarian motion. "You haven't lived here long; am I right about that?"

"That's right," said Bunny. "I moved here after my grandma died to, uh, help my mom. I was in Pittsburgh before."

"What were you doing there?" asked Ainsley. "Tara said you had some kind of international background."

"My dad is with the State Department," Bunny explained. "But in Pittsburgh I was kind of an archivist, like an assistant for a collector who had a bunch of papers to organize. I was an English major."

"That's interesting," said Ainsley, not sounding interested. "So, like, military? You know Jeff was in the Coast Guard before he came on here."

Bunny gave her customary spiel. "Yep, we lived in Greece twice, Argentina, Armenia, Azerbaijan, and Washington. And now my dad's in Tajikistan."

Ainsley raised her eyebrows. "Wow," she said. "How interesting for you."

Bunny nodded. "Yeah, it was definitely a really great experience."

"You like working here?" said Ainsley, looking at Bunny with something like suspicion.

Bunny did not enjoy working at Miles Engineering Consultants, exactly. She thought of the all-staff emails from the office manager she sometimes forwarded to John, about dishes in the sink or Chick-fil-A fundraisers to support the troops, festooned with grammatical impossibilities and signed with a sparkling GIF of a young boy carrying an American Flag. She thought of the 374-page Environmental Impact Assessment on her desk. And yet at work Bunny felt pleasurably severed from the rest of life, free from the gloom that hovered over the house in Beaumont. When she got into the car at 7:45 for her very reasonable commute, her fragrant hair bundled into a neat-enough bun, the air was still cool and she listened to NPR. When she sat down at her cubicle, when she took out her highlighter and her pen and her small Post-it Tabs, she felt a pleasing sense of order. The supply closet was vast and held piles of fresh notebooks, boxes of pens, felt-tip and ballpoint, card stock in every weight, binding coils and binder clips. There was a sterile plenitude to the break rooms, with new coffee makers that used something called K-Cups that came in many flavors. There was an excoriating cleanness in the routine. She liked the electric snap of her hand on the doorknob after whispering across the stiff new carpets in her mini-wedge shoes.

Bunny had even come to love the long Repro nights and their time-and-a-half pay, the way she imagined an athlete would love an away game at a distant stadium. When she looked at her bank account every two weeks and saw that $1,072 was deposited there, she felt a miserly happiness. She spent money on nothing but gas, Zumba, Starbucks, and her share of groceries. She packed spartan and sensible lunches, sating afternoon hunger with salted almonds and La Vache Qui Rit. She was always slightly hungry, the hunger forming a slender iron rebar that held up the habitual laxity of her character and flesh. She ate her peanut butter sandwiches with smug slowness while her colleagues went to Buffalo Wild Wings. Her bank account fattened as her body attenuated.

"Oh, absolutely," said Bunny. "Everyone at Miles has been so great. I'm really thankful for the opportunity."

"That's great," Ainsley said. "I'm glad to hear it. I'm going to think of other things we can use you for." She stood, forestalling excess small talk. "I'll walk out with you. Keep up the good work."

Bunny said, "Thanks so much," and she matched her steps to Ainsley's until Ainsley peeled off at her husband's office suite.

The same day Bunny finally agreed to go to lunch with the girls from the admin pool at Olive Garden. "I can't believe you've never been to the fucking Olive Garden," Melody said, when Bunny revealed that this was her first time. "She's weird and foreign," said Tara, waving her hand as the girls all tittered and sipped their Diet Cokes. Bunny thought her soup was bad, but there was something very compelling about the unlimited breadsticks and the salty, well-lubricated salad, and she ate them until she felt sick. She drank two Cokes. Restaurants were always dangerous for Bunny, her control over her appetites so tenuous.

Around the table the women of the admin pool talked about the engineers, their primary antagonists as well as the main source of frisson in the office. They were mostly men, and there were forty or so of them—half of them white men in their sixties, the others younger, only three of them women. The younger ones came from all around the world. HR spent its days processing H1-B visas for this pool of talent, from China, Turkey, India, Brazil, Nigeria, Iraq, Mexico, each engineer working together in the international languages of English and math, each courteous when their name was mangled by their colleagues, some going so far as to adopt names more accommodating to foreign tongues. New engineers were added every week, as quickly as they could be hired. The recession did not seem to touch Miles Engineering Consultants, probably due to the late Bill Miles's good planning, the admin pool speculated. There was a reverence throughout the company for the late Bill Miles.

Some Miles engineers were friendly, some were exacting, some were cooperative, and a very few were all three. Some of them were incredible pricks, the women agreed. Everyone had been shouted at more than once. There was a thrill in getting one of the good-looking ones. Bunny's favorite was Eduardo from Argentina. She had told him, shyly, apologetically, that she had been born in Buenos Aires but that she couldn't remember anything, and he was politely unimpressed. He had a photo of a pretty girl on his bulletin board. There was no engineer that Bunny had not imagined, briefly or at length, having sex with, although she would never say this at the Olive Garden, where they might discuss attitude, general hotness, or fashion sense but always stopped short of being lewd.

The girls talked about *The Bachelor* and Bunny half listened, thinking about the Environmental Impact Assessment sitting on her desk. "So, what did you think?" Melody asked mirthfully as they walked across the parking lot to get back in cars for the five-minute drive back to the office along unwalkable roads, the sun out from behind heavy gray clouds and flashing off the glass, the air heavy with moisture. Melody gestured up at the Olive Garden sign, two stories high on stilts to signal to the drivers on the highway that they should pull off.

"Wonderful," said Bunny, eager for the fluorescent peace of her cube.

THE CHRISTMAS PARTY

t was a Wednesday—hump day—when Phil Miles, Ainsley's brother, arrived at Bunny's desk and asked her if she would look at a proposal for him. Phil was fit and attractive with a pointed, fox-like face and incongruously wide eyes that narrowed pleasingly when he smiled. He had a dimple and an air of such ease in his conversations with employees that it was clear to Bunny why he was in charge of winning new business. Melody, who knew everything, told Bunny that he was actually Ainsley's half-brother, a former playboy, and recently married to his second wife.

Bunny was unused to dealing with Phil but liked his pleasant manners. Unlike the other Miles Engineering Consultants executives, who wore boxy shoes and bad suits, Phil had a Waspy style of dress that still stirred something in Bunny. For Texas, there was something sleek and slightly fey about him, what she and her college roommates might have called *metrosexual* in years past. Today he wore tennis shorts, clearly on his way to somewhere else, and unwittingly she noted the golden hair on his calves, the cleavage between the taut muscle of his thigh and the bones below. He had only the faintest hint of a Texas accent. She estimated he was in his late forties or early fifties, but Bunny was still young enough that she had no idea how old anyone else was.

"Ainsley tells me you're the person I need to talk to if I want to make sure something sounds good," he said.

"Well, that's very nice of her to say," Bunny said, crossing her ankles and looking up at him from her ersatz ergonomic chair.

"I'm going to email you a letter for a potential client. It's not a report or proposal, so it doesn't need to go through Tara and whatever that new system is; it's just something I'm doing on my own steam."

"Of course," said Bunny. "I'd be happy to." She was elated by the recognition, the sense that her status was growing. Thus far Ainsley's efforts to find more for Bunny to do had resulted merely in assigning her to run training sessions for some of the other admins, some of whom had been there many years longer than Bunny and plainly resented her tutelage.

After Bunny had marked up the inoffensive BizDev letter and sent it back, Phil began sending her things to check several times a week. One day she passed him as he walked with Ainsley down the hallway and he stopped and put a hand on her shoulder.

"Ains," he said, "Bunny is my go-to gal." He gave Bunny a friendly squeeze. "She catches all my mistakes." Ainsley lifted her eyebrows.

"You're not stealing her from admin, are you?" she said, hitting him lightly in the stomach. They were very different, Bunny noted. The peculiarity of siblings. She thought of John in Ukraine, doing god knows what, and Small Ted napping in his dorm room or sitting in a classroom. It was so strange to think of Small Ted as a young man. She wondered what Small Ted would end up doing, whether he would find himself in a cube in an office park one day.

"She's wasted there!" said Phil. "She needs to help me with marketing."

"Okay," said Ainsley. "We'll sit down soon." Bunny felt elated. She liked the idea of working on the proposals, which usually fell to marketing, a department of two women who couldn't spell. The proposals they did eventually see in admin, usually after they were a fait accompli, were awful—nineties graphics, bad formatting, stilted language, a hundred pages of CVs with grainy headshots. Even Bunny, with zero investment in the Miles Engineering Consultants empire and still no clear understanding of what hydrogeology was, sensed they could be doing much better at presenting their business.

"I'd love to work on marketing," she said. "Or whatever would be helpful." Phil patted her back and ushered Ainsley down the hall.

"Keep it up, kiddo," he said over his shoulder.

In November Bunny received an email invitation to Phil's home for his holiday reception. "This is *not* the MEC holiday party," he wrote. "This is something special my wife and I have done the last couple of years since we renovated our new place. Her family business, some key folks from Miles, and then some of our friends from around Houston. You'll have a good time." The invitation itself read cocktail attire and gave an address that Bunny saw on MapQuest was a Houston condo building west of downtown.

Maryellen came and stood in the doorway while Bunny was getting ready for the party. Bunny had bought a green silk number from Banana Republic with attractive lines, not tight, festive but still sort of office-y. She had blow-dried, then flat ironed, her hair, and was now using a curling iron to try and reinstate loose waves in a hair routine for special occasions that had not deviated since college.

"Why won't you wear your hair up?" Maryellen asked. Bunny ignored her. Maryellen was going to Warren and Christine's for dinner that night, something she did about once a month whether she wanted to or not. She had never liked her sister-in-law. "I wish I were going to a nice cocktail party," she said teasingly, and Bunny had briefly imagined bringing her. Phil Miles had gotten remarried. Why might Maryellen not meet someone, maybe someone like Phil Miles? Her mother was beautiful, Bunny thought. She was petite, had always been smaller than Bunny, the same height but somehow more slender. She complained she was going to seed, but to Bunny she always appeared the same, immaculate. No one could make a white shirt stay bright, gleaming white longer than Maryellen. She had wide dark-blue eyes that could look friendly, stern, or incredulous with the slightest movement of eyebrow. When she looked a certain fearsome way Bunny still found herself saying, "Yes, ma'am," only partly joking.

Maryellen was not back to her old self, whatever that would look like from now on. She was in a protracted legal struggle with Ted that kept her going through documents and tracking down other documents, and she had gone to Washington, DC, to facilitate the transport of their personal effects from a storage locker in Arlington, Virginia, to another storage locker in Beaumont. Some of the time, though, she seemed better. She had, surprisingly, looked into resuming work as a flight attendant but was quickly bogged down by the amount of retraining involved and the obvious and profound ways the job had changed. She had long phone calls with women she had known over the years, other flight attendants, other foreign service spouses, and Bunny was heartened, intrigued, even, to hear occasional peals of laughter from the study where the ancient landline still lived. Maryellen went on walks around the neighborhood and spoke idly of going to visit John in Ukraine. She began looking for volunteer positions, assuming she would not qualify for any jobs. "I'll just spend down that home loan till it's gone," she said to Bunny brightly when she was in a joking mood. At Bunny's suggestion they went to get their hair done together, Bunny researching the salon with the best reviews in the Golden Triangle. Bunny had decided to get an ombré. In a place in West Beaumont she and Maryellen sat together under their foils, sharing wordless looks, askance at the appearance and conversation of their fellow patrons. Bunny hated the ombré but had felt warmth, a tentative ease with Maryellen for the course of the afternoon, until they had gotten drinks after and Maryellen took up the topic of Ted like a dog worrying a mangled bone.

Ready for her party, her disastrous ombré flowing in sculpted waves around her shoulders, Bunny raced down I-10 until she reached the industrial zone east of Houston, after which the tall towers rose up like Oz. The afternoon sun gleamed off the black mirrored windows of the soaring structures, sleek buildings radiating grandeur, permanence, stability, the solidity of guaranteed infrastructure, piercing the sky and dwarfing the faded beauties behind her in downtown Beaumont. Houston. The City. After more than a year at Miles Engineering Consultants, she thrilled to it, had gotten herself a cheap motel room near the site of the party, planned to treat herself to a nice brunch before driving home the next day.

She nervously navigated the roads to the address provided and then circled for a few blocks, missing turns until she finally found the parking garage indicated in the invitation. She blasted herself with the air conditioner before exiting the car and smelled her own breath, her armpits, reapplied a touch of Michael Kors perfume from a primordial bottle she'd had for years. In the dark of the parking lot she pulled her underwear out of her ass, straightened her tights, did squats and arm waves to get her dress away from her body, and walked the block to the palatial glass foyer of the towering building where Phil and his wife lived.

Bunny was greeted by a doorman, his voice rising over the gentle burble of a sleek fountain that stood in front of a giant pebbled wall. Huge plants sat serenely in the corner. Bunny had suddenly a vision of the new Hyatt in Baku, at that time the newest-seeming building she had ever been inside, despite the smell of swamp gas in the bathrooms. "Wow," she said, looking around, and the doorman laughed. He was Black, heavyset, older than she. He pressed the button of the correct elevator, for apparently each traveled somewhere different. "Enjoy the party," he said.

"Thank you," said Bunny, and the elevator soared upward.

When the door opened it was clear that it was opening onto a private foyer that was for Phil and his wife's apartment alone. Bunny experienced a reorientation. The anodyne modesty of the term "small family business," the aggressive bland ordinariness of the office building in Beaumont, were profoundly at odds with what she saw before her—a foyer with glass on both sides where you could see out over the city, a white marble entryway into an apartment that seemed to stretch out for miles into glass and more glass. Ainsley Miles Sullivan, she knew from photos of a Fourth of July picnic she had not attended, lived in a seven-bedroom house in Beaumont's West End, and the other executives lived in pastoral McMansions in a town north of Beaumont called Lumberton. This felt more in keeping with what Bunny had always assumed Miles Engineering Consultants could offer at its peak—the inelegant comfort of Costco millionaires. This, too, was different from the wealth she knew at Stanhope, the Cartwright's horse-country spread, for example, or stately homes built in 1975 to look Antebellum, in white suburbs circling Black towns.

As she boggled at the view, a nicely dressed woman, Latina, Bunny thought, greeted her and took her name and her coat. She gave Bunny a ticket, tucked a corresponding ticket into the coat's pocket, and gestured her into the apartment, where mercifully she did not stand for long before Phil appeared before her, flushed and smiling, holding a tray of champagne flutes. "Bunny," he said. "I'm so happy you could come." He handed her a glass and then smoothly handed the tray to a passing server. He put his hand on her back, the faintest touch, and steered her down the hallway to an open-concept room that looked out over the city. "Let's go meet my wife, Estelle," he said, gliding like a ship through the understated luxury of his apartment. "We absolutely lucked out with this weather."

"This is an incredible apartment," said Bunny with open awe as she looked around.

"It's wild, isn't it?" said Phil, his hand on her back again as he maneuvered her around a corner to a freestanding staircase that appeared to rise through the ceiling into open sky. He spoke over her shoulder as she walked carefully up the stairs, making room for a server bearing a tray in the opposite direction.

"I had the house thing with my first marriage," he said. "Piney Point, big lawn. That was marriage number one. Too much *stuff*. When Estelle and I got together, we said we weren't going to do *stuff*. We bought this place, told the architect to go crazy, and we're just thrilled with the result." Apartment life seemed right for Phil, Bunny thought. It aligned with her previous ideas of him as a sporty, slightly foppish divorcé. But she had pictured some cookie-cutter condo, some extended-stay hotel with a black leather couch. Not this palace in the sky.

As they emerged through the opening at the top of the stairs, she could see that the party was actually taking place on a rooftop. There were standing heaters, an awning, two small bars where barmen were strenuously shaking drinks. There must have been fifty people on the roof. Everyone seemed white and older than Bunny with the exception of two Black women, one statuesque and light-skinned, wearing a silver sheath, the other in a slightly boxy mauve suit. Phil led her to a group whose focal point was a jolly-looking man, elderly, with white hair in a sort of fluffed tonsure around a bald pate. Beside him was a petite white woman wearing a strapless dress in red shantung with a jaunty asymmetrical bow and an emerald choker, a Texas outfit that strode purposefully to the line between bold and gaudy and stopped a hair's breadth away. She had honey-blonde hair swept up into a conch shape above toned shoulders.

"My lovely wife, Estelle," Phil said. "Honey, this is Bunny, who has been acting as my assistant at Miles." She put her arms out to Bunny, as though she were going to embrace her, but clasped her arms above the elbows instead. "Aren't you darling," she said.

"This apartment is stunning," said Bunny. She estimated that Estelle was forty-five? Fifty? But she was stunning too. "You're stunning," she blurted, her glass of champagne doing its work and her cheeks turning red. Now Estelle put an arm around her shoulders and squeezed. "That's the best Christmas present there is."

Phil turned to the jolly man beside her. "And this is my father-in-law, Frank Turnbridge." He had smooth, rosy cheeks and white eyebrows that made little rainbows of perpetual surprise over small, shrewd eyes of pale blue. "How do you do," he said to Bunny in a comically deep drawl.

Phil demonstrated a hospitable awareness of Bunny's presence as more people joined their circle, but Bunny had stood in enough circles with strange adults to know that sometimes you could do your interlocutors and yourself a courtesy by drifting away. And so she drifted, to the edge of the roof where the sun was making its watery descent to the horizon, a thin layer of haze floating above the city in the winter sky, Memorial Park green before her and the buildings of downtown arrayed dreamily beyond. She drank up her champagne and found a waiter bearing another one. She faced the skyline in a corner of the roof to discreetly eat a tuna canapé, her mouth open wide to encircle it. After a while in her orbit around the roof, from canapé to canapé, from tray to tray, from vista to vista, she passed in the orbit of one of Phil's circles. They made eye contact, and he beckoned her over. He was standing with his father-in-law, Frank, and a reasonably well-preserved woman who Bunny surmised was Frank's wife. She was looking fixedly and smilingly at Frank, who was speaking to Phil and two men.

"You want to talk about *technology*. You know how they used to get oil?" Frank was explaining to them animatedly. "The Burmese dug a big ol' hole. And then they climbed down there and dug some more till they hit sands. They couldn't stay down there more'n a minute at a time, and then they had to recover for twenty once they got back up top. They had the women stay up top and hoist up the cuttings they dug up. They were catching oil centuries before any Rockefeller ever thought to do it. They had to do it naked, with rags around their mouths, these little brown guys, but by god they did it." He laughed. "Took two years to dig one hole." Bunny held her face in her fixed expression of listening.

"And now my guys at Spraberry complain if they don't have a god-damned cable box in the trailer. HR is telling me I could offer 'baby-bonding leave.' I'm supposed to pay these guys to go and hold a baby for two weeks? Eileen'll tell you when our kids were born, I held 'em, gave 'em a kiss, and then I was back in the pickup."

Phil was laughing uproariously and a touch ruefully, shaking his head. He patted his father-in-law on the back. "Well now, Frank, big guy, times have changed just a little bit since then."

"Don't I just know it," said Frank with visible disgust.

Phil turned to Bunny. "Frank owns one of the last family oil companies in America," he explained. "And this is my mother-in-law, Eileen." The woman next to Frank put her hand out, a gold bracelet with two bejeweled tiger heads encircling her wrist. "Hello, dear," she said sweetly.

"Bunny came on board as our UAE project started heating up," Phil told them. This was the project that kept the girls in the Repro Room so many nights.

Frank grunted. "Emirates. Did I ever tell you I was over there?" he said. "Went over when Estelle was just born. I had seen the seismic they had on the seafloor off Dubai. Everyone was showing there was diddly-squat under there. Flat surface. But when I got a look at it, I could tell it was too uniform. Not like a seafloor at all." He pronounced this like "a-tall." He looked intently at everyone in the circle, who had fallen silent in a way that Bunny could tell was customary. "So I got my boss to get me the money to do a six-fold stacking shot, get a real view. You think you know Dubai, boy. It was a shantytown. Nothing there. I stayed in the worst hotel you've ever seen. But when we reshot that seismic, well, they found out what was underneath."

Bunny smiled and nodded. "Amazing," she said. "I had no idea."

"Something interesting about Bunny," Phil said, as his wife joined him and put her arm through his. "Her father was a diplomat. So she grew up a little bit like Estelle did. You moved around a lot, Bunny, isn't that right?"

Bunny smiled warmly. "We sure did," she said, unconsciously adopting some flavor of Frank's speech. "My brothers and I. Every two to four years or so." Eileen put her hand up.

"Oh, honey," she said. "I would have killed for four years." Estelle laughed.

"I think we figured out that we moved something like twenty-eight times before I finished high school. We were doing four to six *months* half the time."

"That was the job," said Frank solemnly. "I worked damned hard. And I put your mother through hell twenty-eight times and she never complained once, just set up house, organized everything." Eileen put her arms around Frank and kissed him on the cheek, wiping the lipstick she left with a practiced thumb.

Bunny felt a kind of fascinated revulsion as she watched them. She thought sorrowfully of Maryellen back at home. The way it was supposed to happen was some better, less-Texas version of this, she thought, her parents together looking happy, on their way from some educational riverboat tour to the next, Maryellen finally fixing up the

Washington house the way she wanted, no more moves, no more language training, no more putting everything in storage and sending their car across the ocean, no more temporary guest quarters, no more orientation, just presiding over her domain. Bunny realized that she would never see her parents standing side by side like this again, and it surprised her, the way it took the wind out of her sails.

One of the unnamed men in the circle found his opportunity to ask the Turnbridges something, "Are you going out to Governor's this year," and before long Bunny was drifting again, orbiting again. As she loitered by a table bearing mini quiche and other delicacies, she spotted with perpetual, unconscious radar an appropriate man, meaning a man of her approximate age, trim and nicely dressed, something a bit round and surprised in the face, but clean-cut, good-looking enough. He came toward the table and as he reached for a quiche, he looked at Bunny, acknowledging her with a frankness that she accepted like water on parched earth.

"I haven't met you before," he said. "I'm Francis." He put down his tongs and held out his hand, which she took.

"I'm Bunny," she said. "Nice to meet you." They moved in synchrony away from the table to the edge of the roof, where they admired the last sliver of sun in the sky and nibbled at their quiches.

"How do you know Phil and Estelle?" asked Francis.

"Phil's my boss," said Bunny. "What about you?"

"I'm a rando," said Francis. "I met Phil at an event last week with my boss, and he invited both of us."

This charmed Bunny. "He's good at collecting people," she said.

"It seems like it," said Francis.

"Where do you work?" she asked Francis.

"I'm a consultant," he said.

"Cool," said Bunny. "I don't really know what that means." She had some idea that they were an elite class, like marines or people who worked at Google, and had to be able to answer questions at job interviews like how many golf balls could fit in an airplane. Evan had talked about possibly applying for one of those jobs, when he got out of law school. "Did you have to figure out how many golf balls would fit in a plane?" she asked this new man, purely to make conversation. He laughed.

"Nope, they didn't ask me that," he said. "I think that's a myth." He held his gaze with Bunny in a way she liked, an intent and direct gaze.

"Are you in oil and gas?" he asked her.

"Oh, no," said Bunny. "Phil's business is hydrogeology, like dams and nuclear plants stuff." She drank the rest of her champagne. "Not oil." She made a look of mock horror, although it did suddenly horrify her a little. Francis laughed.

"Watch out," he said, and he mimed elbowing her. "You're in the Oil Patch." He spread his arms to encompass the roof.

"I know," said Bunny, looking around again. She felt if nothing else this man would give her a conversation, and was not someone she had to work with. "But, like . . . I saw *An Inconvenient Truth*." In fact she hadn't seen *An Inconvenient Truth* because it had seemed too depressing to watch, but she knew the gist of it. Francis rolled his eyes.

"Okay," he said.

"But the earth is getting warmer," said Bunny. "It's, like, a fact. Species are going extinct every minute?"

"True," said Francis. "But look at all the other stuff human beings have achieved. We can figure something out."

Bunny felt destabilized. It did not seem lately like human beings were achieving very much. "I don't know," she said.

He raised his eyebrows. "When it's 105 in the shade, do you want to be able to turn on the air conditioning?"

"Obviously, yes," said Bunny.

"Okay, so someone in Bangladesh should be able to do that too, right?" he said, looking accusatory. It felt impossible to argue with this. Everyone in Bangladesh should of course be able to have air conditioning. Bunny thought of Ted Senior in the Peace Corps, and John now following in his footsteps. Francis swigged his drink and his face softened. "You want to have kids?" he said, with a note of genuine curiosity in his face that Bunny found sort of creepy but compelling.

"I don't know," said Bunny. "No. Maybe?"

"You should," he said, flirtatiously.

"Okay," she said, blushing in spite of herself. "Noted." She rolled her eyes. It felt so rare, this attention.

"Where would you want to have them? In a hospital? With machines in case anything goes wrong? Or, like, outside in a shed?" His certainty now irritated her. She felt she was in a debate she had not enrolled in, with the captain of the opposing team. She got enough Republican bullshit at Miles Engineering Consultants, where Rose in the admin pool sent all-admin forwards with Tea Party themes until Bunny told her she didn't think political forwards were appropriate in the workplace and now they didn't speak.

"The shed," she said in a deadpan, and he laughed. "Right," he said.

"Well what about what just happened in the Gulf?" Bunny rejoined. She and Maryellen had watched the sickening red and rainbow sheen billowing out and out and out across the surface of the waters, the seabirds covered in filth, the fireball, the fire that had burned for days, the crying families, the eleven dead men, the ruined shore.

"Deepwater?" he said. "That was human error. Process error. It should never have happened."

"Well BP and . . . Schlumberger or whatever are supposed to be the peak of the industry," she said, proud that she had reached for and found the correct names from watching Judy Woodruff with Maryellen on *NewsHour* every evening.

He laughed at her. "Baby girl, it's pronounced *Schlumber-jhay.* Not *hamburger.*"

The "baby girl," felt incongruous, a phrase he was trying on, a southern-gent phrase that didn't match this young man's accent or serious mien. Bunny was surprised by the frank condescension of it, but also its frank testament to his interest. Bunny realized that it had been more than a year since she had spoken to an available sort of man, and she reeled a bit. She had been badgering Maryellen to try one of the dating apps, OkCupid or Match.com, but she couldn't bring herself to get beyond a cursory look at an array of what she felt sure were meatheads, illiterates, or people who didn't believe in abortion.

"You got me," she said. "I just proofread documents. I don't know about any of this shit."

An older man, presumably Francis's boss, came over and began talking with him, and instead of waiting to learn whether he would be polite and introduce her, she drifted away, still mortified and now wanting the bathroom. "Schlumber-jhay," she whispered out loud, like she had once whispered *Sağ olun*, like *Efxaristo*, like *Shnorhakalutyun*, intent on cementing it into her lexicon. She spotted the blond mass of Jeff the bear-killer and wheeled away in the other direction.

After she had descended the staircase back into the apartment and been directed by a caterer to a hallway powder room, she wandered through the apartment, feeling furtive. Soon she was outside a snug office with a view, and she peered inside, taking in the bookless shelves, the antique globe, the magnificent view. She peered at family photos, Phil with a nice-looking teenage boy and girl she imagined must be his kids. She felt a presence and found Phil beside her, his loafers quiet on the carpet.

"Ah, sorry!" she said. "I'm not sneaking around. I was just admiring the office." He waved this away. "Please," he said. "Make yourself at home."

She thought for a minute about how they were alone in this tucked-away room with a faint, almost undetectable alarm. It didn't *feel* sexual or predatory. Phil was a grown man, married, and seemed very above-board. It's true he gave her a lot of compliments about her work. No, there was an odd purity to Phil, she felt. Of course she knew that every man had something of the Schrödinger's lech about him. But they were manageable in the workplace, if you gave them a chance to instruct you and then wowed them by anticipating things they would later forget hadn't been their idea to begin with.

As if sensing her line of thought, Phil spoke, looking at her affectionately. "I'm just so glad you came to work for us, Bunny," he said.

"Oh," said Bunny. "I'm so grateful for the opportunity."

"What's your vision of staying on with us?" Phil asked her.

She thought for a few seconds. "I don't know," she said. "I'd love a chance to travel for work," she hazarded, boldly. "Understand the business more." Nothing about reading a 374-page Environmental Impact Assessment required her to board an airplane. "I have a lot of experience overseas," she said, thinking of her college-admission essay, which had leaned both heavily on her overseas experiences, her earliest memories—the sights and smells and how they had enriched her in some vague but meaningful and virtue-imbuing way.

"Maybe I could be more valuable to the company if I could see how things worked on the different projects," she said. Phil patted her on the shoulder.

"Stick with me," he said.

2011

$108.88/$85.66

THE VISIT

The DC metro smelled exactly the same way it had smelled when Bunny was in middle school, between the first Athens posting and the year in Yerevan, before Baku. It was cool and dank, reminiscent of the elephant house in the National Zoo, a smell Bunny could likewise conjure effortlessly. Perhaps it was the smell that prompted Bunny to step, almost without thinking, out of the Red Line doors at Cleveland Park and text her little brother to meet her at the zoo instead of at his dorm in Foggy Bottom.

The house that had been Ted Senior and Maryellen's nest egg had just been sold for twice what they paid for it, home prices finally rebounding, at least in the desirable neighborhood where they had bought long ago. The sale had been the source of great financial relief to Maryellen. She was upset with Bunny for going to see Ted, but as Bunny pointed out with futility when Maryellen said something shitty about it, Ted was her father. And he had bought her plane ticket. "What am I supposed to do?" Maryellen would have been happy, Bunny thought, if none of the children had ever spoken to him again.

Bunny had tried to appease Maryellen by pointing out that she would be able to check on her little brother, something that only made Maryellen feel worse. Apart from dropping him off for the first day of his freshman year, and the horrible visit when she had sorted out her share of items from the storage unit, Maryellen had not been able to make any of the traditional parental college visits she might otherwise have made, bringing trays of homemade food and bags of supplies from Target to her baby boy. Maryellen was sullen as Bunny left the house for the airport.

Bunny climbed the escalator to Connecticut Avenue and understood the subterranean urge that had drawn her out of the metro at this stop. There was the library to which she had ridden her first big-girl bike, where she had borrowed *Zlata's Diary* or *Then Again, Maybe I Won't*, imagining herself the central figure of each as she turned the pages in one of its worn orange seats. There was the movie theater where she had seen *Outbreak* and lain awake for a week, picturing all her family bleeding into nothingness. There was the gift store where she had begged Maryellen, *begged* her, to buy her more stickers for her album—some iridescent, some furry, some oily with mysterious shimmering fluid underneath a thin skin of plastic, Mrs. Grossman's and Sandylion brands. Her parents, she remembered, had hated the sticker-collection craze. "It's just an excuse to buy things," Ted said, exasperated, when she came home with new sheets of small, fuzzy animals. "At least with stamps you're learning something." She could almost see the sticker book now, its waxed oblong pages. It had been her pride and joy in the sixth grade.

Bunny carried her precious things around like a hermit crab for years, every year something else falling away, until now it seemed she had nothing from her childhood left at all. Bunny thought of other precious artifacts long abandoned to some dustheap. Her pink Hello Kitty pencil case, bought from the Greek stationery store. It was rectangular, plastic, compartments on either side, but with the top lid puffy, faintly soft, depicting the heroes of the Sanrio pantheon. It was a technological object, full of built-in and secret places, buttons that revealed hidden drawers and a pencil sharpener. She had treasured this object, cradled during car rides and on the ferry boat. She had loved those Greek stationery stores, their stacks of perfect soft composition notebooks with blue plastic covers, the smell of rubber erasers. She thought of other stores that had come and gone: Eleftheroudakis, the Virgin music store. Now, here in Washington, she passed the Italian deli, the smell of dough coming through the cold fall air, and she could almost taste the focaccia and the thin slices of pizza.

Bunny had not expected to feel so much of anything here. They had moved away in 1996; she had never been back. And yet she felt she could remember every old tree, that she knew the number of worn bricks in the apartment buildings that lined the street, and that somehow these memories led her to memories of every other place and street and tree, moments that had hitherto seemed to belong to separate worlds, separate lives. She traversed the bridge that spanned Rock Creek and went through the pillars of the National Zoo, the boxy, dated font of its stone sign. She felt, for a moment, pride that such a world-class place was free, that every museum in Washington was free. She passed the cheetahs, took the path that curled around the American bison.

Bunny waited for her little brother at the panda enclosure, sitting on a bench and watching the two pandas, not the Ling-Ling and Hsing-Hsing of memory, those beloved gifts of the Chinese government now long-dead, but some other, different pandas. Bunny wondered where her mates from her public school had gone. She knew some of them had ended up on the gifted track within the public high school, ultimately attending the same tier of colleges as her Stanhope peers. She assumed many of them were on their second or third or fourth postgraduate moves. It was strange, she thought, how her peers from elite institutions had lately seemed to enter the peripatetic existence that characterized her younger years. They operated in program spans: law school three years, business school three years, med school five, six, seven years. They moved constantly for school, for internships, for jobs, for opportunities, either their own or a partner's. It seemed Bunny was once again out of step, wandering in childhood and yet now, as her peers wandered, coming back to the place her grandparents had called home.

When Small Ted arrived at the enclosure, he shuffled, bearing with him his own miasma. He was tall like John, but running to plump where John ran thin. He wore track pants and a ratty T-shirt and Adidas slides. When he leaned in weakly for Bunny's deep, almost violent squeeze, he had the pronounced odor of someone who was very hungover. "Dang, Teddy Bear," Bunny said, elbowing him. "Are you still drunk? Do we need to cross the street and go to 7-Eleven?" she asked. "Do you need a Froco?" He groaned and waved his hand away. Her nervous system vibrated with sympathy.

"How you doing, buddy?" she asked him, looking him over, touching his shoulders and tweaking his ears. His skin was awful, and his hair was a mop. It occurred to Bunny that there may be a person in their family worse off than Maryellen, more pathetic than Bunny.

"I'm fine," he said. "Fucking hungover." She could smell the alcohol and sorrow seeping out of his pores.

"Sit," she said. "We can wait for Dad. I told him we were here." Her brother put his head in his hands on his knees and Bunny rubbed his back, her eyes stinging with the closeness she still felt to him, her baby brother, although his daily life was utterly foreign to her now and had been for years.

When Ted Senior walked down the zoo path in a coat and tie, he looked like he should be coming in the door at 8:00 p.m., just in time to sit down for the dinner Maryellen had made. He carried the same battered briefcase Maryellen had bought him decades ago. He was exactly the same, Bunny thought, tall and thin, with reddish blond hair, fading slowly to gray, very slightly Redford-esque. He looked tired and worn-out. She had not seen him in two years, since before the divorce, and she could barely bring herself to hug him. She avoided pleasantries by pleading on her brother's behalf. "Teddy Bear's dying," she said. "We have to get him sustenance. He tied one on last night."

"Teddy Bear," he said, looking with disappointment at his child. Ted Senior was not much of a drinker, had never been drunk, he alleged, even when foreign people had forced him to take shot after shot of strong national brews. It went with the job. Small Ted groaned. "Poker night."

"I see. Well, toughen up," Ted Senior said. "Where should we eat?" The Glenns were accustomed to moving through emotional moments by formulating plans.

"What about Hamburger Hamlet?" asked Bunny. She looked at her little brother. "Remember that? Or were you too young?" He was almost two presidential administrations younger than she. She could remember the heft and juice of the burger. "That doesn't exist anymore," said Ted Senior.

Bunny frowned. She liked going to places she had been before. Small Ted groaned. "It has to be close to here." Bunny looked at her father and they conferred for a few more moments before deciding to walk back to the Cleveland Park strip mall. They watched the pandas for another moment in silence before walking back out of the zoo, Small Ted making a visible and Herculean effort to pull himself together as they traversed the walkway. Bunny felt a rush of pity and love for this, her little man.

"How is your mother?" Ted asked Bunny as they walked back over the bridge, Small Ted looking over the edge as though he might jump.

Bunny looked at him in disbelief. "What do you think?" she snapped.

"Fair enough," said her father. He tried again. "How is the job going?" he asked. "You said it was an engineering company?"

Bunny had been feeling proud of herself for things she had recently accomplished at work—she had streamlined a few of the proofing processes and reorganized all the computer drives, in addition to delighting Phil Miles with her improvements to his docs—but when she considered how to put it into words it suddenly felt stupid, absurd to care. "It's stupid," she said wretchedly. "I was a temp. I proofread engineering reports. Now I'm a full-time administrative assistant, whoop-de-do." Bunny felt a curling bitterness inside her body. She felt like her heart was actually getting smaller inside her chest. Perhaps this is what Maryellen felt like all the time.

As they reached the business district, they decided to go to an Irish pub, which none of them had ever been to but was a sure bet, something that had stood there for many years as a comforting and cozy-looking presence. Inside, Bunny cheered at the sight of booths and the smell of decades of beer. She ordered a pitcher and tried to revive Small Ted.

"You need to drink this," she said. "It's the only way." She saw her father looking back and forth and wondered if he was disappointed, his drunk and dirty-looking son, his grumpy and undistinguished daughter pouring him a drink.

"Do you see each other since you're both here now?" She directed this both to her brother and her father, deciding to try and get the conversation going. She drank her beer quickly. They ordered fish and chips. Small Ted began to perk up the smallest bit. Bunny would feel disgusted with herself later, she knew, but for now she would lather her fried fish in tartar sauce and wash it down with as much beer as it took. "Sometimes," said Small Ted. "Not really." Bunny felt festive with the reliable warmth of alcohol and fat. She could tell her father was trying to encourage festivity—it was transparent as he ordered chicken wings, more beers. She thought of Maryellen, who was probably alone crying at that very moment, and then she thought to hell with her, what's so wrong about having fish and chips with your own father?

Ted Senior told them about his TDY assignment in Dushanbe. He had nice colleagues in the embassy. He stayed at a small apartment near the opera house. He was learning to play the surnay, a kind of Tajik horn. He had done a trek in the Tian Shan mountains. On the second day he had gotten sick and asked the guesthouse proprietor for help, and an old Tajik man had come with an old leather bag and a bunch of glass hypodermic needles and injected him with nameless cures.

"I was just grateful he put out his cigarette before he opened up his doctor's bag," Ted said bemusedly. He had endless stories of this kind, overseas stories of characters met, hazards surmounted, adventures had.

Small Ted was by now lively enough to offer his own contributions to the conversation. "What are you going to do next?" he asked. Back stateside, Ted Senior was currently on the Bureau of International Information Programs desk.

"I might be going back, it looks like. I bid on Dushanbe," he said. He looked sheepish.

Bunny shook her head. "Wow," she said, unexpectedly stunned. She didn't know why this should matter. She was an adult. "You must really like it there," she said. It was so far away. The brief effervescence of beer soured, but the false courage remained. "Do you have a girlfriend or something?" Her father looked unsettled. Her brother said, "Welp," and got up, shuffling toward the bathroom.

"I have a friend," he said, looking at her resolutely and then looking away. "But it doesn't"—he grasped for a word—"predate." Bunny let her disgust show on her face. "How could you do that to Mom?" she said.

"Your mother and I . . . ," her father started, unable to find the words to continue. He started over, "Everyone is entitled to happiness," he said with pain on his face. He seemed like he was ready to say more, but Bunny couldn't stand to hear it. "Never mind," she said, suddenly livid. "I don't want to know."

Small Ted returned and they moved on, Ted Senior prodding about his classes and professors and Bunny prodding him about girls—"or boys!" she added—as they waited to pay the bill.

They went to see *Tinker Tailor Soldier Spy* at the same theater where Bunny had once watched *Outbreak*. Ted Senior, who loved John le Carré, suggested it. In the warm dark of the theater, Small Ted, finally overcome by his hangover, fell asleep and gently snored. Bunny was amazed at how boring the movie was. "I'm so confused," she whispered to her father, who was rapt. When it was over they took the metro back to Ted's sublet in Ballston, Small Ted getting off halfway and promising to see them tomorrow.

Ted lived in a nondescript high-rise building, one of innumerable such buildings in the near DC suburbs. They rode the elevator and traversed the long corridor to his apartment in relative silence. Bunny took in the bare-bones furnishings with faint alarm. It looked like a sanatorium. There was a calendar showing the wonders of Central Asia on the wall that was Ted's, as well as a framed reproduction of a poster from the 1959 US Trade and Cultural Fair in Moscow. This would have been one of the few items Ted took from the storage unit during the distribution of effects. Bunny was touched to see framed photos of herself and her brothers on his IKEA dresser, a random assortment of ages. There was a small ugly loveseat pullout for Bunny in the tiny living room.

It astonished Bunny, that this Spartan mode of living had seemed preferable to Ted than the life he and Maryellen had led. *He defected from his own life*, she thought to herself, contemplating the movie they had just seen, Tom Hardy's criminal blond wig. Perhaps her father had lived undercover for years.

To get ready for bed she and Ted had to awkwardly cede each other the bathroom, which was in Ted's bedroom. Bunny dreaded having to pee in the night. She slept in yoga pants and a sweatshirt, not wanting to be in pajamas in front of her father, for no reason she could name.

Bunny woke up early, bruised from the wire skeleton of the pullout, and folded it up neatly. Her father emerged from his bedroom and began removing things from the fridge for breakfast with a kind of humility, unused to hospitable domestic gestures. "I don't know what you eat for breakfast," he said. "I got some yogurt and some eggs. Granola." He started the coffee maker, while Bunny bundled all her clothes together and her toiletries and went into the bathroom, peeing with tremendous relief. She pulled on her jeans and put on her moisturizer and sunscreen, as Maryellen had impressed upon her to do every single day no matter what.

They sat at the small table, pale light streaming through the large window, which looked out onto the identical high-rises, the Potomac somewhere out of sight. Today they would return to the city, go to the Smithsonian, find a hamburger at Chadwicks, reunite with Small Ted. Bunny took small bites of the granola, which was stale.

"So tell me more about this job," her father said. "What kind of prospects do you have there?"

Bunny felt shamed by the question. "I don't know," she said. "Not very many, probably."

"Are you enjoying the work?" he asked. She considered. "No, but I don't know what work I would enjoy more." Everything else seemed out of reach. What was work, anyway?

"You could take the Foreign Service exam," her father said earnestly. Bunny rolled her eyes. She had heard her father's theory, that anyone could pass the Foreign Service exam if they read *The Economist* for six months. "I don't want to live in Dushanbe," she said.

"Well, do you want to live in Beaumont?" her father said, looking genuinely curious. Her Houston-born father had never showed any interest in living back in Texas; it was one of the things, Bunny assumed, that had united Ted and Maryellen when they first met, in the Galaxy bar on top of the Athens Hilton. Bunny admitted that she did not.

"Well," he said. "It's probably good that you are there to help your mother with the . . . transition." She hated him when he spoke of her mother. She could not accommodate this new reality where her father and mother spoke so stiffly of one another, could not sit in a room without a paid third party. She spooned out the sweet milk at the bottom of her bowl, unwilling to look her father in the face.

"Just don't forget to make a life for yourself too, Bunny," he said. "You're a very smart young woman, with a wonderful education," he said. "That's an incalculably valuable thing." He sounded imploring.

"Whatever," Bunny said.

THE ARRANGEMENT

The other girls had gone to lunch and Bunny was hunched over a *Vanity Fair*, her sandwich still in its Saran wrap, when Phil leaned over her cubicle. He was wearing a pink button-down and his graying hair was silvery-blond in the fluorescent light. He had on his glasses, which added depth to his wide eyes. "Can I take you to lunch?" he said. "I want to talk to you about something." Bunny looked around, thankful her podmates were away and wouldn't witness this. "Sure," she said, uncertainly. "That would be great." She got her bag out of the bottom drawer, stood up, and smoothed her skirt.

They drove separately to the nearby golf club, a dumpy mid-century building, a modular wedding cake, long and flat, with unconvincing columns. They were seated at the mixed grill, about which Phil made apologetic murmurings. His criticism of the venue made sense to Bunny, now that she had seen the style to which he was accustomed. The sky outside the slightly dirty window that looked out onto the golf course was pale with heat and refinery haze on a windless day. Bunny ordered a chicken Caesar salad and a Diet Coke, and Phil ordered Dover sole.

"So," said Phil, rubbing his hands together. "I have to ask you, Bunny, to keep everything that we discuss today confidential." He leaned in.

She nodded. "Absolutely."

"Everyone will know these things in due time, but for now it's between us, okay?" Bunny nodded, curious. He began.

"So, Miles Engineering Consultants is coming up on an opportunity as a firm. You know from reading our proposals that we're one of the top-rated midsized consultancies who can support hydrogeologic and seismic work." Bunny nodded again, and he went on as their food was placed before them.

"Now, you know this, but Texas is an energy state," he put his hands out to indicate the world around them. "And in this state, we're in an extreme minority of firms that basically don't touch oil and gas. Which always has worked for us. We've got great engineers and we compete all over the world on big projects, and we have competence to do things in the region too—flood analysis, groundwater stuff. But a lot of the companies that were already bigger than us before are getting just huge. They're buying companies right and left and kind of offering full-service suites, engineering, IT, oil and gas." He took a respectful bite of Dover sole and wiped his mouth with his napkin. "So we're having this problem where we're starting to lose out on projects that normally would be right in our wheelhouse, because we just don't have the manpower to expend on the proposal and bidding process, or the certifications depending on where the project is." Bunny tried to think ahead to where this was going. "We offer a really great service, and we're not technically a little guy, size-wise, but we're kind of falling between the projects that are better suited for little guys on the one hand and the projects that just eat up a lot of time and manpower on the other. So that's us."

He paused darkly and drank some of his Pellegrino and ate some more of his fish. Bunny sawed at the giant chicken breast flattening the limp lettuce below.

"Now, a lot of the jobs we bid on, or are subs for, end up having a federal component. And a certain percentage of federal contracts are supposed to go to women-, or minority-owned businesses." He had the kind of wedding ring she approved of for men, a plain gold band, not tungsten or whatever other chunky metals the married engineers at Miles Engineering Consultants seemed to favor. He clasped his hands with his elbows on the table on each side of his plate.

"Now Ainsley has always been more invested in Miles Engineering than I am. She's in the office every day, Jeff's there too. So, as we have been thinking about how to grow the company, we've come up with a plan where we restructure our ownership stakes so that she owns more than I do, and then we go through the certification process to make Miles a woman-owned business." Bunny could not imagine why she was being told all this. Phil sat back now, opened his hands. "It's not just a pretense; she'll also truly be in place to take the reins. She was running the company for Dad for a while anyway." He paused and sipped his drink. "That sounds great," said Bunny.

Phil smiled.

"I've always come and gone. I went away to business school after college, I worked in finance for a bit in my twenties, and you notice I like to be on the road or in Houston more than I like to be here in Beaumont," he said.

"Well, I saw your apartment," said Bunny. "I don't blame you." She put a friendly smile on her face to make the joke clear, and Phil gratified her by laughing.

"So, yes, that brings me to the other news. You met my father-in-law, Frank, at the party." Bunny nodded. Phil looked at her intently.

"Frank Turnbridge is responsible for one of the oldest family-owned oil companies in existence," said Phil. "All in family hands, incredible staying power. He is simply one of the best businessmen I've ever met in my life." Bunny pictured Frank at the Christmas party, his blue eyes and white hair as he described the men climbing into holes in Burma.

"Frank doesn't say this out loud, not in so many words, but even with all the benefits and insulation of being private, some of the smaller guys—and they are still technically the little guys—are starting to feel nervous about diversification. The industry has always been boom-and-bust, volatile, but now there's more uncertainty. Political headwinds. Environmental stuff." He leaned forward. "So there's an advantage to them to add some new kinds of capabilities."

Bunny said, "Hmm." She felt her mind begin to wander, her eyes ranging over Phil, stretching behind him to the other patrons in the club, out the window. This was taking a long time.

"Now I won't say that my father-in-law is always the easiest man to deal with. He's been successful because he has hung on tight to that business and kept it strictly within the family. But he's also a very shrewd man, and he's watching his competitors—and they are truly only a few, because it's so rare to find a family-owned oil business of any longevity. Anyway, he knows he's got to think ahead." Phil began his descent to the point, and Bunny, sensing the change, put up her seat and tray table. "Frank has given me the go-ahead to think about a kind of separate arm of Turnbridge Oil that would look at technology. At first most of it would probably be oil and gas tech, drilling improvements, stuff he could apply to his actual exploration and production, operating his own wells. But over time, it would invest in other kinds of technology, renewables, batteries, clean energy." Bunny cocked her head. "That sounds great."

"I'm telling you all this," said Phil, "because I'll need some help." He leaned his chair back again and framed the air before him with his hands.

"This was my thought. In the beginning you would come on half-time with Turnbridge Energy Solutions—that's what I'm calling the new arm right now—and stay half-time with Miles Engineering doing admin and the stuff you've already been doing. Over time you'll train someone at Miles and then switch over 100 percent to Turnbridge. In order for me to sell this new arm totally to Frank, I'm going to be involved with his core business too, a bit, and you'll have things come up here and there, do projects for him too." He looked at her intently. "Eventually for this to work, you'd need to move to Houston." The opportunity was as vivid as a door opening from a dark hallway into a bright room. Bunny lit up inside.

"Wow," she said.

Phil leaned forward. "With the economy like this, jobs like this, where someone is giving you a chance to shape something new? I've been in business a long time; it's a rare and wonderful thing when something like this comes along."

"Absolutely, yes," said Bunny. "Thank you so much. Is that . . . going to work with Ainsley?" She also wanted to ask, "Why me?" but managed to keep it in.

"I already handled it with Ainsley," he said. "She's annoyed but she says as long as you prioritize redoing the Miles stylebook and training a new girl, she's okay with you going to half-time." He seemed to intuit her unasked question. "I like working with you, and I don't want to deal with someone I don't know as I make this big transition. You're very methodical and meticulous, smart, very easy to get along with," he smiled and gestured for the bill. "You just bring something pleasant to the table."

Bunny set her fork and knife side by side on her plate and superfluously wiped her mouth with her napkin. "Well," she said. "I'm honored. Of course, I'd love to help however I can. Thank you so much, again." She was a blossom under the sun of his approval.

"Great," said Phil. "I'll talk to Tara. You'll keep track of your hours and meet with me every week. First it's mostly going to be coming up with a prospectus for Frank, maybe a marketing plan, doing some of that proofreading, and then just kind of assisting me with other things as they come up. Sitting in on meetings, taking notes." Bunny drank the last of her Diet Coke. "It sounds really interesting," she said. "Thank you for thinking of me."

Two months later, Bunny met Phil in the parking lot of the Turnbridge Oil Company office in Houston to inaugurate his new venture with Frank Turnbridge. Bunny had woken up at six to deal with her hair. Phil had chided her once for her wet hair at the Miles office. "My mother always said we'd catch cold like that," he had said. When it was dry, she got an iced coffee at the drive-through and drove like a maniac into Houston, to a place called the Energy Corridor, where Turnbridge occupied a short but substantial tower among buildings bearing the logos of companies she recognized.

Bunny wore black slacks, a cream blouse from Ann Taylor, and camel Stuart Weitzman heels she had gotten on sale when she bought the dress for Allison's wedding. She wore a plummy lip gloss from Sephora. She had a fresh notebook and set of pens tucked into an aging Longchamp tote, which she had bought in college and spot-cleaned with a toothbrush the night before. She arrived thirty minutes early out of nerves and sat on a bench near the entrance, waiting for Phil. When he stepped out of his car, a Mercedes E-Class, he looked her over.

"Well, this is a transformation," he said, which made her feel embarrassed but proud of the efforts she had made. She smelled the faint humidity of herself, the scent wafting from the pomade she had dabbed in her hair to keep it from frizzing.

Frank Turnbridge's office was less grand than she had imagined, but it had a view of the other towers of the corridor and was large enough to contain two leather couches on either side of an oblong coffee table. They were brought in by a casually dressed white woman of middle age with what Bunny thought of as a mom cut who introduced herself as Jody. Frank greeted Phil warmly, his hands outstretched, one to clasp Phil's hand and the other to clasp his forearm. "The man of the hour," he said. He was wearing suspenders and a gold class ring. "Frank," said Phil. Bunny marveled at the performance of it all, the way it approximated some old movie about businessmen. Three other men were shown in, white, not noteworthy to Bunny in any way. These were, she gathered through their introductions to one another, Frank's vice president of something or other, the business broker for Turnbridge, and a lawyer. They all sat down and Frank began to speak.

"I don't have to tell you, Phil, what it means to be part of a family company, but I'm going to go ahead and do it because it matters that much to me that everyone knows the gravity of it." Bunny's eyes wandered from his nicely shined shoes, his socks patterned with what appeared to be little bells, his knobby, incongruously thin knees prominent in their neat gray suiting.

"I want you to look outside that window," Frank said, bending forward to look at Phil, the business broker, the lawyer, even Bunny, each in turn, extending one hand to the glass to compel them to truly look. They all looked. "You will not find another family oil company, privately owned, on the Energy Corridor." He kept his hand outstretched and completely still, the ridges of veins on the leathery back of his hand radiating strength. His hands looked rough, as though he himself had wrested the oil from the ground, which Bunny supposed he had. "You will find only a couple in the state of Texas, only a handful in the entire United States of America." His delivery was weighted and his timing flawless.

Everyone in the room was still. Frank snapped his hand closed like a dancer and broke his posture, leaning back. He looked at Phil. "You're my son-in-law." He put a hand on the knee of the man beside him. "My son is my CFO," he said. "My daughter is my COO. My grandson is finishing school right now, and he's coming in after. I have another grandchild on deck. I have raised this family in the business, and every decision I make is about legacy, about planning, about keeping them invested in making sure this company lasts another hundred years or more." Phil reached out a hand, facing down, and awkwardly grasped Frank's hand, an almost-feminine gesture. Frank looked intently at him.

"We don't think in economic cycles, we don't think in election cycles, we don't think in presidential administrations. In this industry, we think in *earth* time. Geological time. There's no short-term problem we can't wait out, can't think our way through. *If*." He put his fingers together and jabbed them forward through the air. "*If* you keep your business organized right." Bunny felt goosebumps on the back of her neck.

"When I started this company, we were a trailer outside of Midland and Eileen did the books. She did everything. She ordered the machinery, she fended off our creditors, she drove with me all over hell to find prospects." He took a sip of his coffee. "I watched other private businesses, so-called family businesses, go down in flames because owners make moron decisions or put moron kids in charge before they are ready. They say 30 percent of family businesses make it into the second generation, and maybe 10 percent into the third." He looked intently at Phil. Bunny wondered what masculine rituals, what displays of loyalty Phil had participated in to be shepherded into this sanctum after only five years. He seemed patently of a different breed than Frank, although which breed was better at doing business Bunny hadn't the faintest idea.

"Now I've got five hundred people on my payroll across the state. I am taking care of these people whether oil is one hundred dollars a barrel, or whether it's twenty-five dollars a barrel." Frank began to look wrathful. "And not a single one of these," again he pointed out the window, "not BP, not Chevron, not Shell, can say the same thing." He coughed and pounded his chest. They all waited in silence for him to recover himself.

"When the going gets tough and they have to stand in front of their shareholders and tell them where their money is, not a single one of them can get through that without slashing their payroll to the bone." He scanned the room to look at everyone's face. "But *I* don't have shareholders," he said, the anger in his voice faintly at odds with the mirthful curve of his eyebrows. "I have *family*." He smiled. Bunny felt like clapping. In spite of herself, for a moment she believed whatever this man said. She wrote down, "Family. No shareholders. No stocks. Geologic time."

2012

$105.42/$83.59

THE HOLIDAY

Bunny landed in Frankfurt groggy and agitated from uneasy Ambien sleep, the sound of *Mission: Impossible—Ghost Protocol* blaring through the headphone that jammed into her ear pressed against the window of the plane. She was an anxious flier the older she got, attuned to every bounce of turbulence, but there was also something soothing and atavistic about a long-haul flight, something she hadn't experienced since she and the late-lamented Evan had flown to Athens in 2007. The friendly welcoming video, the ecstatic piano of "Rhapsody in Blue," put her in mind of a thousand flights of yesteryear. She could remember the airline's old playlist that had buzzed in the little marshmallow headphones, "Return of the Mack" playing while she unwrapped the scalding foil-wrapped meal or paged through the Hammacher Schlemmer catalog, now gone along with the old headphones, "Return of the Mack" replaced with a new song. The seats were smaller now, the service shabbier, but she remembered the sense of being safe in the womb of service and motion, a time capsule from the end of history. As Bunny watched the flight attendants, she pictured Maryellen before Bunny and her brothers were born, before Ted, moving deftly through the aisles, her uniform designed by Ralph Lauren, lighting cigarettes, smiling, serving. Bunny was disgusted when she saw the amount of trash people left on the plane, how people simply refused to follow instructions.

When the bell dinged on the tarmac in Frankfurt, Bunny chewed a piece of gum and made her way off the plane unsteadily, following the crowd and the signage through long corridors noisy with the warbling of many tongues. As she moved her leaden body through the terminal, she was overwhelmed with the sensation of return. While she waited in line at customs to submit her passport, she thrilled to the chirp of airport employees calling one another *Kollege* in its spunky German inflection. At a café near her gate, she bought a cappuccino and a baguette with a limp slice of ham. Surveying the row of European breads in the brightly lit window, hearing the hiss of the steam, smelling the mingled perfume and cologne of the travelers behind her, she felt elation and some deep, nearly erotic pain. She was twenty-eight years old and overcome by the airport.

John had suggested Greece. He was teaching English in Kyiv, or consulting at a school, or doing something, Bunny didn't quite know what. He had met a Swedish woman named Sofie, a journalist, and they lived together. Bunny had never met Sofie, although she sometimes looked at her photos on Facebook. Sofie didn't appear to use Facebook in the way that Bunny's cohort did—as a celebratory, perhaps competitive, repository for hundreds of photos of weddings and bachelorette parties. Sofie, who appeared to be a few years older than John, posted articles and was occasionally tagged in blurry photos of groups of people smoking in bars in places like Bogotá or N'Djamena, scenes that made Bunny think fleetingly of Charlie, of the boys at the Fourth of July picnic, whom she felt sure must no longer exist, had ceased to move in 1998, like mosquitoes in amber. In 2010 Sofie and John had gone to Greece and John posted a photo of her laughing on a boat, holding a beer and shielding her pale face from the sun. Bunny had felt unbridled envy at this photo—more so, even, than at the shot of Evan's new fiancée on a wine weekend in Napa Valley.

During one of their sporadic GChat exchanges when their time zones aligned, John told Bunny that they were planning to go to Greece again. "Oh, I'm so jealous," Bunny had typed.

"You should meet us there," he suggested, perhaps only to be kind. She thought about it for only a few hours before eagerly messaging him about dates. She had the money for her ticket. Things were going well. "You going to bring anyone?" Her brother had typed into the window, and she had written the words "No. Single and ready to mingle (sorry)."

"Okay, gross," John had written. "But seriously, come. Sofie wants to meet you."

On the plane from Frankfurt to Athens she opened her laptop and tried to sort through the notes that Frank Turnbridge had given her before she left. After ten months of split time that incurred the ire of her admin poolmates and Ainsley, who was deep in the certification process for her woman-owned business, after ten months of sporadic three-hour round-trip commutes to the office in Houston, Bunny had finally been made full-time at Turnbridge. She retained the title of administrative assistant and reported to Phil as a general Girl Friday whose utility would be applied both to the fledgling Turnbridge Energy Solutions and to Turnbridge Oil Company itself. It was clear that Phil had finagled her full-time employment by pitching Bunny primarily as a competent extra pair of hands, and she spent a lot of her time reading through Turnbridge Oil Company documents, some of which were similar in appearance to the engineering documents of Miles Engineering Consultants—seismic or surveying reports, for example—others, like limited partnership proposals for drilling, less so. Bunny didn't care. She had just gotten her very own apartment, the first of her life, in a corner of Memorial five minutes from Hershey Park and the Buffalo Bayou and a thirty-minute walk to work if she wasn't too lazy.

Bunny, with Phil's help, was realizing her potential. Her intellectual life was withered, and she decided to rise to the challenge of navigating an enterprise that she found entirely opaque. Miles Engineering Consultants was a company hired to build things, or to consult and assess the possibilities of things that would eventually be built by someone else, or to diagnose the problems of something that had already been built. Turnbridge Oil Company, on the other hand— Phil's plans notwithstanding—was fundamentally an oil company, and as such its role was to find prospects, which once acquired became their own to drill and operate. Bunny felt unease about this part, but she held on to what Phil had told her. He was taking the company in a new direction. He was looking for new technology solutions to the energy challenges of the future.

He had, moreover, given Bunny an assignment that had genuinely excited her—a research-y sort of job, a documentarian's job, a job for someone who was an English major and had spent her work-study hours in the library. It was conceived of by Phil and the small marketing team as a long, glossy pamphlet to be published on the fiftieth anniversary of Turnbridge Oil Company's founding. Since the family angle was ultimately what set them apart, even with their new suite of services, they would turn Frank's mass of industry recollections and wisdom into a bio for marketing purposes, which could be excerpted when they eventually did a website redesign. Frank, on the other hand, simply wanted to set down his memoirs before they got away from him.

Bunny was now at an age that she knew put her squarely, alarmingly, into the realm of adulthood. She had noticed that among the friends from high school and college with whom she haphazardly kept in contact, many of them seemed to have become things, or were in the process of doing so, and she wanted to be some kind of thing too. After reading an article online about how to advocate for yourself at work, she had asked Phil if Turnbridge Energy Solutions would pay for her to take some extension business courses. She began availing herself of the Turnbridge Petroleum Library, a wood-paneled room at a local college that Frank had donated and which he arranged, through Phil's intercession, for her to be able to use. On Saturdays after she went to Zumba and got bagels with Sarah, a girl from Stanhope who also lived in Houston and was, to date, Bunny's primary nonwork acquaintance, Bunny checked out books. She read some of them in the plush chairs of the reading room, others at night before bed.

She did all of this in and around the process of extricating herself from the house in Beaumont, searching for her own place to live, taking Saturdays to drive through Houston looking at neighborhoods, touring studios, testing commutes, balancing the unsettling awareness that Maryellen would be left alone with her own eagerness to leave. This small sense of motion, of momentum in Bunny's life, had been intoxicating.

She read elementary textbooks on oil, which were useful but boring, and narrative histories, which she infinitely preferred. Especially after reading the rambling, stream-of-consciousness recollections Frank had thus far scribbled out for the purposes of the memoir—his working title was "Just Where I Want to Be"—Bunny could appreciate the value and the difficulty of an orderly, well-structured oil narrative. She remained bewildered by the financing, the business structures, the rights, the downstream, the derivative products, the financialization. She couldn't take in the full enormity of the thing, however hard she tried. The history, too, was labyrinthine: Burmah Oil Company begat Anglo-Persian Oil Company begat Anglo-Iranian Oil Company begat National Iranian Oil Company and British Petroleum Company.

Standard Oil Company of New Jersey begat Jersey Standard begat Esso and Enco begat Exxon. It went on and on and on like this. But she could now more or less grasp the engineering, which was pleasingly literal, rooted in the earth itself.

The frankness of the metaphors made her laugh. "Making hole," they called it when they dug for oil, these men desperate to plumb the vast geologic structures underground. There were dry holes and wet ones; there was lubricating mud, and rocks too tight to bring forth the oil secreted within. In her mind's eye she drew up a vast and stylized map covered in translucent, overlapping jewel-toned circles, the major oil and gas fields of the world. She heard the music of their names: Carabobo, Hibernia, Kashagan, Cantarell, Ghawar—that supergiant among supergiants—and felt something like desire prick the base of her stomach. The names were an evocation of unknown places, places that were more interesting than the fluorescent lights of the Turnbridge office. She read names that echoed from the Baku days: Azeri-Chirag-Gunashli, Bahar. *Bahar* meant "spring," she remembered. She thought of the wind off the Caspian, the soporific heat of their old apartment.

When geopolitics appeared in these narratives, sometimes Bunny thought nostalgically of her father and of the Glenns' old life together. She enjoyed the books about famous discoveries—the personalities, the Herculean struggles for dominance. She could sense, reading some of the accounts so lovingly, cinematically described, how much their authors had wanted to convey the grand enormity of the stage on which all these oil stories played. And she could feel how much the men in these stories had wanted the oil, their frustration over hours of negotiations, long nights filled with double-crossings, interminable moments idling on desolate tarmacs. She imagined their pain over ruinous dry holes—"Mukluk," she said the word aloud to remember it—billions of dollars of expense, the desiccated disappointment of earth with no liquid beneath. She pictured soft Permian salt domes, honeycombs of porous rock, hydrochloric acid injections that widened each fissure. She pictured metal drills, hard enough to crack geologic time, hard enough to bore a mile, two miles, below the seafloor, their passage eased by gentle mud, mud mixed with oil, oil begetting oil— light, highly pressurized oil of surpassing quality. It was hard to imagine the relief, oil coming through rock after four hundred million years of slow grinding. She read that when the papers were signed and the oil spurted out the men would daub it on their cheeks.

There were of course dead people and filth strewn all over the pages of these books. She read about blown wells that burned for months, that incinerated the very air, columns of fire that could be seen from space, celebrity firemen who shut down oil infernos and were played in the movies by John Wayne. The flares, the sour gas, the oceans slicked with crude. Seagulls cleaned off with toothbrushes and Dawn dishwashing soap. Bunny was surprised at how quickly some of these incidents, so consequential at the time, had been disappeared from the pool of generalized knowledge in which she swam. Exxon Valdez, of course she knew that—it was the prototype for malfeasance, the villain of her childhood. Deepwater Horizon, it seemed, would take a similar place in the collective mind. But Texas City? She had driven past it and never known. Piper Alpha? Bohai? Ocean Ranger? Kielland? The tragedy and waste and environmental degradation sobered her. And yet in the accounts found in the Turnbridge reading room these tragedies were made small against the inexorability of a steel tube drilling down thousands of feet, drilling sideways a thousand feet more, seeming to subvert the laws of geology or physics. Literal pipelines laid under the ground and spanning two continents, traveling under the ocean itself, to bring them their standard of living. There was no arguing with it, Bunny felt. Astronauts died going to space, she told herself.

Bunny's own flight was bumpy now, but not enough to terrify her. The plane banked and the Aegean came into view, dotted with the lace archipelagos of islands and the serene brown bulk of the mainland. She closed her laptop and pressed her nose against the window, her finger on the blue. Among many not-quite homes, the closest thing. The plane bumped on the drafts of air that swept across Attica and touched down. Dutifully Bunny waited for the seatbelt sign and then shuffled into the corridor of the plane, littered with blankets and the plastic wrapping of headphones. She gathered up what she could carry of other peoples' detritus, thinking again of Maryellen as she deposited them in the trash inside the terminal. It was the new airport, had not been Hellenikon in years, no more clouds of indoor cigarette smoke, only the suggestion of smoke drifting through the hallways, hallways that had once been spanking new and now had the light patina of wear, hallways that were just slightly too airless and warm, gently smelly with the fug of travel. When she stepped out of the airport into the baking July heat, her heart sang.

John and Sofie had already checked into their hotel in Plaka. Bunny had suggested an Airbnb, a newish thing which she had not yet used, but she had seen her friends speak of it enthusiastically on Facebook. She had been amazed to see that with this program you could rent your very own luxurious and furnished apartment with a view of the Parthenon. John had balked.

"Look at what happened in London," he GChatted back when she had sent him the link. "The rents went up so bad with short-term rentals that people got evicted." He sent her an article about the London Olympics that she didn't read, and, feeling her own suspicion at the niceness of the advertised apartment, she acceded to his selection, a dingy but clean hotel on the south side of the Acropolis where the avocado tiles of the bathroom were poetic in their age and ugliness.

In this dark green bathroom Bunny took a shower and brushed her teeth. She put on a linen dress she had bought for the trip, stopping to see herself in the distorted mirror of the bedroom. She had preemptively lost five pounds, knowing she would gain it back with the food she planned to eat, the daily ice creams from the Delta and Algida boxes. She had developed a sixth sense about her weight, finely honed her practices, observed the changes borne of her slightly more advanced age. She counted her calories religiously, restricting herself so that she could binge when she wanted to, always on a seesaw with her desire and her resolve. The results were undeniable as she saw the drape of her dress, which fell pleasingly in a straight line to her calves. She opened the door to the tiny marble balcony and looked up at the Acropolis, the Parthenon itself out of sight. The apartment where she and John had lived as children was two neighborhoods over, the top floor of a solid old building, a small but beautifully proportioned space with a wide veranda and a direct view of the Acropolis and Hymettus. She looked down now at the narrow Plaka streets and watched a group of begrimed kittens eating dry food out of the bottom of a sawed-off water bottle. Her new smartphone, for which she had gotten an international data plan, pinged. She left her room and took the narrow elevator to the lobby, where her brother and his girlfriend were waiting.

When Bunny saw her brother she perceived with shock that he was an adult. A tall, rangy, slightly beaky man like their father, in a faded blue T-shirt and canvas slip-ons. She felt a florescence of love that surprised her. They embraced with awkward warmth, and she turned to meet Sofie.

Bunny's first impression of the other woman was that she was untidy. She had caramel-colored hair that was obviously straight and thick but that had been pulled into a ponytail from which looping cowlicks protruded. She had wide-set eyes of light brown and a wide mouth. She was wearing a very lightweight blue baggy sweater with a boatneck that didn't quite look intentional. She wore beige linen pants that were still too heavy for Athens in August. On her feet were a pair of grievously stained Saucony Tigers from a previous era. She had a canvas shoulder bag with Thai writing on it and the logo of what looked like a grocery store. She laughed and extended a hand to Bunny, who disregarded it in favor of a spontaneous embrace.

"Everyone is very jealous of me," said Bunny, meaning Maryellen, "that I get to meet you."

Sofie said, "And now I finally meet the famous Bunny," in English that was unaccented but un-American in some only faintly perceptible way. The three stood awkwardly in the lobby, surrounded by faux antique panels depicting the gods of Olympus.

They had agreed beforehand that their first destination would be the taverna that in their memory had the best pork chops in Athens. They threaded their way through the narrow crowded streets of Plaka, past the noisy courtyard with the rooftop cinema, the brightly lit shops selling lewd T-shirts, classical replicas, products made from olives, until they were on the thoroughfare of Vasilissis Sofias. They passed the Megaro Mousikis concert hall, which was not there during their first posting, newly built during their second. They passed the American embassy, which had mushroomed in size, buildings exploding out from its central tidy and extraterrestrial Bauhaus design. Bunny remarked on this.

"Oh my god! It's huge!"

"They have to hold more intelligence guys now, I bet," said John derisively. "So Obama can launch his drones."

Bunny was surprised at this. Obama was heroic to her, a symbol of the victory of good over evil. And he had gotten Osama bin Laden, whatever that was worth—although after the disasters of Iraq and Afghanistan, it did seem a little beside the point. Frank Turnbridge had said, "Finally, something good out of Obama-nation," and Bunny bristled within.

The restaurant was in a quiet neighborhood off the busy main street. As they walked, Bunny looked up at the grimy facade of apartment buildings to see the awnings and balconies overflowing with plants, sagging air conditioners hanging over graffitied stucco, drips and drops falling from above and accreting slime on the pavement. Every building called out to her. Her whole life she had heard the denigrations of Athens. The Paris of the Balkans, they said, just as Buenos Aires, her birthplace, had been the Paris of Latin America, Baku the Paris of the Caucasus. Maryellen used to joke that she was on track to be posted to every Paris except the real one. But Athens was beautiful and stately and energetically itself, even in its shabbier quarters—not, of course, that Bunny had had much exposure to those. But she had wandered through Exarcheia, wandered through Omonia, gotten off the train and found herself lost in Piraeus. It was, to her, a perfect place, where sometimes its narrowest sidewalks, covered with cat shit and nameless excretions from the pipes, were old marble out of which grew olives and figs. She thought of the smallness of her existence in Beaumont, its expansion now that she had moved to her apartment on an unremarkable but tree-lined street in Houston. Life had been feeling bigger, but now it was small against the vivacity of Athens, with its narrow streets, its dense life.

They reached the restaurant after nearly thirty minutes of walking, climbing the city stairs and stepping off onto the cement platform dotted with tables under a cozy lattice of honeysuckle and grape leaves. Bunny heard herself say the words for a table for three. "*Eimaste tria atoma*," she said, *We are three*, atoma like atoms, like three separate entities gathered together in the golden light of the lamps. Sofie gave her a look of surprise to which Bunny thrilled.

"You speak Greek," she said.

"No," said Bunny. "Vestigial memory."

"Well John doesn't have it," said Sofie. "He was hopeless on the bus."

"Bunny was always better at languages than me," said John. Sofie pulled a pack of Winstons and a lighter from her bag and placed them on the table next to her cell phone like a Greek. "Interesting," Bunny said to her brother. "I see smoking is allowed now." John, the runner, had always been disgusted by smoking.

Sofie laughed. "He doesn't like it, so we compromise. I smoke only one a day unless I'm on a deadline or vacation." The waiter returned to the table, and Bunny asked him in Greek for a half-kilo of house wine and water from the tap, the words warming her like a flame, like the coppery wine when it arrived in its vessel.

John put his arm around Sofie and looked briefly, lovingly, admiringly at her face and Bunny saw now that Sofie was beautiful, a revelation that made her reevaluate what she thought she had apprehended of her until now. There was some faint challenge to the symmetry of her face that kept it from placidity and added to its charm. It was the kind of face you wanted to keep looking at, a listening and seeing face that emanated friendliness but kept its own counsel. Bunny could see what a striking couple Sofie and John made and felt the sudden force of her own loneliness. She also felt a whisper of uncanny déjà vu, thought of all five of them sitting around the table, Ted, Maryellen, Small Ted, John, and Bunny. It brought pain in a phantom limb, the same way at Maryellen's house she instinctively took five forks from the drawer to set the table. But it was impossible to feel lonely under the warm lights and vines of the cement slab in downtown Athens. Bunny felt the privilege of being in this great city, in this handsome couple's orbit. She took one of Sofie's cigarettes and lit it.

"How's Mom?" John asked her.

Bunny thought for a moment about how to answer, thought about Maryellen, who she saw every Sunday. She was doing things. She volunteered twice a week at the children's museum in Beaumont, bringing expansive warmth to the role that surprised Bunny. She had expressed an interest in becoming a Texas Master Gardener through a course offered by the A&M AgriLife Extension program but had missed the application cycle for that year.

"I don't know," said Bunny. "Better. But she's still sad. What the fuck is wrong with Dad?" she asked, even though she was not sure she wanted to talk about it, was not sure that John was the correct interlocutor. "What was it like when you visited him?" John and Small Ted had gone to see Ted in Dushanbe. Bunny had looked at the photos on Facebook, the three of them by horses against snowy mountains, by a government building that reminded her of Baku, by a statue, by a mosque. She had felt an ache of regret that she hadn't gone, and renewed fury at her father.

"I don't know, fine," said John. "He seemed good."

"Well, Mom still cries, like, every week," said Bunny. It had been three years and Bunny doubted that Maryellen could ever fully exit the shock of the change. She ashed her cigarette. "She's fucking . . . destitute. I don't think she'll ever get over it. I'm not over it." Now she felt naked at the table with these strangers. John shrugged in a way that Bunny found irritating, putting her back into the role of unserious little sister.

"Well, not exactly destitute," John said pedantically. This was true, monetarily speaking. The judge or arbitrator had taken the attorney's tallying up of what Maryellen would have earned in twenty-six years of TWA salaries had she not moved every one to four years in support of Ted's career, while also raising his children. Incredibly, Ted's attorney's returned fire with charts showing that due to airline deregulation and Carl Icahn's restructuring of TWA, which led to furloughs and bankruptcy following the explosion of Flight 800, Maryellen would have earned much less, had she retained her job at all. "I'm surprised the sonofabitch didn't try to argue that I would have been *on* Flight 800," Maryellen had told Bunny bitterly. The judge had taken the numbers and performed his own calculations and named a monthly sum that Ted was obliged to pay. This was Maryellen's income, with which she could live and make payments on the home equity loan that had gotten her through the first years.

"I mean, like, spiritually destitute. We were, I don't know, a team," Bunny said haltingly. Inside the station wagon, around the dinner table, life had been warm and complete.

"Yeah. But not once we went to Stanhope, honestly," said John. "When we weren't there, they had to just deal with each other for once. Dad always wanted to do shit like go to Afghanistan and monitor elections, and she didn't want to do that. You know, 'nothing east of Ankara,' all that shit." He waved the smoke away from his face and looked at Sofie with annoyance.

"What's she going to do with the house?" he asked. Maryellen had always planned to go elsewhere, but lately her peerless ability to make a house nicer fought with her goal of impermanence. Thus, she had focused her attentions on their late grandmother's dismal grass yard, its fussy plantings. She had covered everything with plastic and was starting the garden over.

"I really don't know," Bunny said. Some days Maryellen said, "I want to move to a big city," and other days she could barely bring herself to drive into Houston to meet Bunny. Sometimes they met in Big Thicket and hiked around, talking over current events and fighting about whether or not Maryellen should look at Facebook for hints from their old life, which Bunny said she should not, even though Bunny did exactly the same thing.

"How does your other brother take it?" Sofie asked.

Small Ted was a cipher; Bunny talked to him even less than she did her older brother. He was barely hanging on in school in his last year and had become something of a competitive poker player. He spent most of the last summer in Las Vegas, growing pallid under fluorescent light. Bunny and John had invited him to come on this trip too. He would actually have had people to see in Athens, places that knew him. But on GChat he said, "Maybe next time."

"Maybe he's the one that's the most fucked-up by this," Bunny said. She turned to John. "He was with them alone the most. What did he say when you went to Dushanbe?"

John laughed at her. "You think we had a big feelings talk? We went on a twelve-hour hike and he bitched the whole time. He kept saying Osama Bin Laden was going to jump up and snatch him. Well, he was dead, one of the other guys, what's-his-name. Zawahiri. Then he got diarrhea."

"Are your parents divorced?" Bunny asked Sofie.

"Yeah," said Sofie. "But they divorced when I was small, and they both remarried. My father consolidated wealth by marrying a terrible rich woman, and my mother found a new rich prick to replace him."

"Ah," said Bunny. "Good for them, I guess." Bunny wished Maryellen would "put herself out there." Then again, Bunny herself felt little inclination to put herself out there, and she hadn't been married for thirty years like Maryellen.

John was tearing bits off the edge of the paper tablecloth until Sofie stilled his hand with one of her own. Bunny looked at her. "What kind of journalism do you do?" Sofie blew a long stream of smoke up at the greenery.

"I mostly cover environmental stuff, mostly in Europe," she said. "Sometimes economy stuff. Last year I took a little time to go to the States and cover Occupy. And I came here to cover the austerity protests. But generally my beat has been the polluters, the bad boys." Bunny thought back to Sofie's Facebook photos, fixing in her mind an image of dirty and riotous tents in New York City, a movement that had registered only the slightest disapproving flickers in Bunny's consciousness. "Maybe they would be happier if they got jobs," she had probably said to Maryellen while they watched the occupation on *NewsHour*, a point upon which she and Maryellen could vigorously agree.

"Interesting," said Bunny. "Do you work for a newspaper or what?"

"I was working for a paper when I met John, but now I follow my own stories and freelance."

"Cool," said Bunny. She looked at her brother. "And what do you do, anyway? Mom is worried you're a USAID gangster." Maryellen had always wanted John to take the Foreign Service exam like his father.

Sofie laughed and John rolled his eyes.

"I sometimes pick up contract consulting with NGOs," he said, "But mostly I teach English. I work at a private school that has a lot of money. They pay me well and the hours are good. I coach track." He shrugged. Bunny noted the way that he seemed satisfied with this, her over-achieving brother.

"He makes dinner," said Sofie, rubbing his back. She looked at Bunny. "And what do you do? John tried to explain to me but I don't think he really knows."

Sausage arrived, and three brown pork chops, the fat on the bone crisped, perfect yellow fried potatoes sprinkled with shreds of white cheese.

"Oh my god," said Bunny. "I dream about these." She put out her cigarette.

She cut into the pork. "I was working at an engineering firm. First I was a temp and did administration and proofing, reports and stuff, and then there was a management change"—she paused and considered how to continue—"and I went with my old boss to help him start a new venture, and now I still do admin but also work on proposals and special projects." She felt her decision not to elaborate like a bad odor in the breeze and was sorry, because she realized as she summarized that she was proud of herself, in some small way, for working her way a few rungs up the ladder in the manner she had seen extolled by others. She had not worked particularly hard, she thought, but she had been exacting and methodical. She couldn't help but to make her work as good as she could. You had to work.

"It's not the most interesting work, but my boss gives me a lot of flexibility and I finally have my own apartment. No more living with Mom, thank god." She chewed the salty fat. "I still see her every weekend for dinner though." She felt relieved to be thousands of miles away.

"So what does the new company do?" Sofie asked. Bunny already liked Sofie because she asked questions and then appeared to actually listen to the answers. In her heart of hearts Bunny wanted to talk about things from work more than she had the opportunity to do. How else could she process the frustrations of engineers, of warring Microsoft Word versions, of working for a while at two companies in two cities doing two jobs?

"Well the first one was an engineering company that did, like, dams and nuclear power plants and seismic stuff, but then the company my boss left for is a small family-owned energy company." She could hear her avoidance of the word *oil* and decided to plow ahead. "Well, it's an oil company, but my boss is starting a new part of it that will work on renewables and green tech."

Sofie's eyes widened, narrowed, twinkled while she chewed a very large bite. "Fascinating," said Sofie when she had finished. "Tell me everything. What's the company?"

"It's just small," said Bunny. "I mean, not small, but not like a multinational. It's called Turnbridge Oil Company, named after the guy. So now we're Turnbridge Energy Solutions. TES. My boss at the engineering company is married to his daughter, and I think the two of them kind of convinced him to let my boss come over and try to diversify the business." Bunny searched Sofie's face, which was neutral, friendly.

"I can't believe you went into the oil business," said John. "Do you talk shop with Warren?" Bunny felt this was a low blow. The last time John had come to Texas, for Maryellen's mother's funeral, shortly before Ted's desertion, he and Warren had shouted over the funeral meats regarding Warren's views on Barack Hussein Obama, and Christine said that Maryellen was being prejudiced because Maryellen said Sarah Palin was white trash.

"It's literally trying to move out of the oil business," said Bunny. "And, like, find new technologies." She felt a familiar disdain from her brother, an implication that she did not, and would not ever, have all the facts.

She looked at Sofie, feeling the urge to impress and appease. "You can probably tell me a lot more about what we do than I already know," she said. "I've been taking classes, but they are a lot." The classes had not been going well. They were evening classes at the Houston Community College Global Energy Center, and they bewildered her. After the first session of one class, "Managing the Firm in the Global Economy," she had spent eight hours on the homework assignment, which was a case study of a global business. She had chosen H&M and immediately felt overwhelmed by its scale.

"There's so much to take in about how everything works," continued Bunny. "It's completely overwhelming."

"Subterranean estates," said Sofie.

"What does that mean?" said Bunny.

"It's from a poem about Standard Oil," Sofie said. "Pablo Neruda." She lifted her glass and looked up with faux pomposity. "'Fire shot up through the tubes, transformed into cold liquid . . . it encountered a pale engineer and a title deed.'"

"Wow," said Bunny, impressed always by people who knew things, and she clinked her glass against Sofie's. They finished their meal as the spell cast by faithful quotation dissipated with the smoke from their Winstons.

Bunny woke up to the sound of the rooster and lay blinking at the ceiling of her whitewashed island room, noticing the shaft of light that came through the rattan blinds and beatified her toiletries. Across a small gulf from her own twin bed was an empty one, which brought to mind a thousand sun-soaked Greek mornings in rooms like this she shared with her brothers, waking up dazzled by the light, spoiled with beauty, spoiled for beauty going forward. She could hear tender murmurs through the wall that adjoined John and Sofie's room. Last night she had heard them laugh drunkenly as they struggled to move the bed away from the wall and then there was a period of suspicious, loaded silence that she tried not to dwell on. She rose from the bed and brushed her teeth and looked at her skin, the creases of sleep on her neck, which she feared would become permanent lines. She rubbed sunscreen carefully around her face and on her neck and put on her dress and found her bag where she had dropped it stumbling into her room after too much retsina.

Bunny walked down the three concrete stairs to the dirt path that fronted their block of rooms. An empty lot spread with stones and thistles sloped down first to several rows of low white buildings, then to the aquamarine waters of the small port. She saw Sofie standing on the other side of the plastic partition that divided their concrete veranda. Sofie stretched her arms up to the sky and then out beside her and then behind her back, rolling her shoulders and looking out at the sea. She was wearing a faded blue wrap around her body, knotted at the back of her neck. Her hair was loose and she looked disarmed, her face soft and open. Bunny could see the outline of her breasts, which were large and slightly pendulous, and felt a surge of surprised envy. "Hi," she said, her voice rusty from sleep.

"Hi," said Sofie, yawning. "Where are you off to?"

"I'm going to get a coffee and something to eat. Want me to wait?"

Sofie stretched again. "I'll go with you. He wants to sleep more," she said. "He can't hold his liquor. One sec." She went inside and emerged wearing a boxy white shift and a straw hat under which her face bloomed with health. "Let's go," she said.

They walked down the dirt road to the rough asphalt and in a few minutes reached the port road and the row of cafés with small groups of foreign holidaymakers. After a brief conference they sat down on the dingy white cushions of wicker armchairs and inspected a laminated menu card. Familiar curlicues of prices were handwritten next to printed descriptions in syntactically creative English, half the prices blank or regretfully crossed out with marker. They ordered freddo cappuccinos of medium sweetness and bacon and eggs.

When their coffees arrived, they both lit cigarettes, Bunny having acquired her own pack. "I hope John isn't wiped out," she said dryly. "I want to go to an actual bar tonight. I want euro music, I want G&Ts, I want a Gordon's Space, I want to see men who are not engineers from Texas." John and Sofie had spent the previous night at a taverna regaling Bunny with their tales of hitchhiking around eastern Europe.

Sofie laughed. "I don't think they even make Gordon's Space anymore, my dear. But all the other things can be arranged," she said. "He'll rally around. And if he doesn't, I'll still come with you."

Their breakfast came, the yolks an electric orange fresh from the coop, the bacon soft and fatty, the village bread toasted crisp and dusted with oregano.

"Look at this," said Sofie, stubbing out her cigarette. "Beautiful."

It was a change from the refrain of most women Bunny knew in Texas, her mother and the admin girls, who would always say, "Lord, this is so much food." For as long as Bunny could remember, Maryellen would take half the portion of an American restaurant meal and conspicuously separate it onto another plate to be taken home or left behind. The admin girls, with the exception of Rayelle and her salads, would eat everything and then suffer and seethe throughout the afternoon. Here Bunny had promised herself free reign. She would resume her spartan habits and meet the deep, sensual bite of hunger upon her return. One half cup of nonfat Greek yogurt, 76 calories. One tablespoon of honey, 40 calories. One-fourth of a cup of walnut quarters, a shocking but healthful 180 calories. "Nothing tastes as good as being thin feels," she and her friends used to joke while they gorged on pizza. Their mothers had the line on the fridge, even before Kate Moss made it famous. Bunny went back and forth on whether it was true.

On the way back to the room they stopped to get John a *bougatsa* from the bakery, greasy flaking pastry bursting with warm cream and so tempting that they bought a second one and shared it as they walked back to the rooms.

"I'm glad you like to eat," said Sofie. "*My* sister doesn't eat anything. No butter, no oil, no wheat."

"Well, normally I don't" said Bunny, "But here it would be wrong not to. I think about this food every day."

Sofie went to rouse John, and Bunny changed into her bathing suit and came back out into the midmorning heat. She trod the dirt path to the beach along tilled fields, where sheep sheltered in the shade of low stone walls. The air buzzed with cicadas and smelled of wild thyme and goat droppings, and her shoulders crisped in the sun. The land sloped gently up from the path, the hillsides rippling, here and there arranging themselves around lines of hand-hewn terraces. On one ridge there were the skeletons of six cement cubes lined up like vertebrae on the backbone of the island. Undoubtedly these were aborted rental villas, casualties of the economic collapse. A finished house next to an old threshing floor, laundry on a line stretched across the veranda, had a roof bristling with concrete rebar, a hopeful gesture toward a future in which a second story was possible. On the ground Bunny spotted the red plastic and rust of an old shotgun cartridge and remembered that when she and John and Small Ted were young, their parents had made them fill a garbage bag on family treks, coming upon fields strewn with refuse, empty plastic water bottles and toilet paper and the ubiquitous shotgun shells mixed in with potsherds, some bearing a bit of ancient paint. During their posting the Glenns kept these pieces of antiquity in a bowl on a table in the foyer. When they left they scattered the sherds over the side of a mountain, nominally satisfying the Archaeological Authority's prohibition on removing Greek patrimony and confounding the archaeologists of the future.

Eventually the trail brought Bunny out of the fields and onto a small cliff that followed the edge of the sea, from which intrepid beach-goers had forged small treacherous paths down to the tiny rocky beaches and caves below. She continued on until she had passed a small taverna, hours yet from the lunch rush of midafternoon, and a small grove of sheltering scrub pines. Finally she reached the canonical stretch of white sandy beach that was not yet crowded, the fleshy bottoms of pale people, Brits, she thought, growing red in the weak shade of a beach tent at one end of the beach, and a group of young Italians in Brazilian bikinis doing group exercise at the other. The Greeks would come later.

Bunny laid out her towel and took off her dress, taking a moment to rejoice that she had finally been able to get six sessions of laser hair removal using a Groupon. It didn't solve all the problems of hair, but it had helped a lot. She waded in, walking out and out in the slowly deepening sea as though she could walk all the way to Naxos, laid out beguilingly in the distance. Tears came into her eyes as she lay back and floated on the infinitely gentle, infinitely kind water of the Aegean.

She was treading water a fair way out from the sand when she saw Sofie in her straw hat standing on the embankment surveying the beach. Bunny waved both her arms as high as she could and in a moment Sofie saw her. She began paddling herself toward the beach, and when she was able to stand, she gestured to the place where she had left her towel. Back on the beach she watched surreptitiously while Sofie took off her white bag dress and revealed a faded bikini in a dusty purple color, high-waisted boy-short bottoms, slightly stretched out, exposing the very slightest glimpse of her butt cheeks, and a triangle top with a sturdy band. Her body to Bunny looked both beautiful and useful, productive. Blonde hairs glistened on her legs. She had no cellulite, the perpetual bane of Bunny's life, but rather a kind of hard-won slack to her long thighs. The flesh expressed itself as something strong and flexible rather than dimpled and diseased, which was how Bunny saw her own flesh in the harsh light of the dressing room where she had tried on her one-piece. There was the most gentle curve to Sofie's belly, negligible beneath the swell of her breasts. It was a body that had denied itself nothing but that also had no need to deny. Her hair was down, cut blunt across and reaching the back band of her swimsuit, and she looked absurdly alive. Bunny was surprised to receive the sight of this body with something other than envy. Perhaps it was the fact that Sofie was the girlfriend of her brother, de facto removed from the sphere of competition inside of which Bunny had typically assessed the appearance of women. There was no fear of male adjudication when the male was her brother, the odd beaky man who was laid out in his rent-rooms by a few carafes of wine.

"I like that bathing suit," she said to Sofie as she scooped handfuls of water onto her shoulders and neck at ankle depth.

"Aw, thanks," she said. "I got it on Tenerife. The only one that wasn't a thong. Did you do sunscreen?" She looked appraisingly at Bunny. "You Glenns are quite pasty."

"I sprayed my back," said Bunny, and she remembered that the spray was supposed to be bad for the environment, she had heard somewhere. "It's the only kind I can do by myself," she offered as though to apologize. Sofie ran and dove and began to swim with a confident crawl toward the horizon.

Later they lay on their towels side by side. "I brought two Aflas," said Sofie, and she produced the beers from her bag. She used her lighter to pop the tops off and they sat drinking them, looking out at the boats in the water, the water sparkling in the sun. Sofie looked at her phone for a while, scrolling Twitter, an app Bunny did not use or understand. Bunny took out her own phone and posted a photo of the beach to Facebook after texting it to Maryellen. They had bought their smartphones together at a T-Mobile store. She felt a spray of sand on her back and turned to see her brother standing behind them.

"He lives," she said, and John unfurled his towel on the other side of Sofie and lowered himself onto it like a mantis, groaning as he lay back in the sand with his hands over his eyes. In the distance an enormous long boat made its way between Naxos and an uninhabited tiny island, no more than a rock with a small shrine to the prophet Elijah on its miniature summit. "Look," said Sofie, pointing with her beer toward the boat, its red hull low in the water. "Maybe it's from Sangachal."

"Where's that?" asked Bunny.

"Remember?" said John. "Baku."

"Oh," said Bunny. Bunny had in fact been remembering more than usual since coming face-to-face with her brother, once again overseas. She let her mind wander back to the CLO trip, the van to the desert, the tour guide's missing thumb, the petroglyphs on the rock, Charlie's hands on her shoulders.

"That was when Bunny didn't speak to me for an entire summer," said John, sitting up and idly rubbing Sofie's back. Bunny rolled her eyes.

"Are you kidding me, John? *You* didn't speak to *me*." She looked at Sofie. "John and I didn't have very much in common at that period of our lives."

"I see," said Sofie. She pinched the space above John's bony hips. "What were your respective interests?"

"John was obsessed with running. He ran around Baku that whole summer. I got catcalled anytime I went anywhere and had no friends, so I sat at home a lot. I watched soap operas with our neighbor and was in love with the boy who rented a room from her. An English guy."

John laughed. "Eddie? Upstairs Eddie? You were in love with Upstairs Eddie? He was, like . . . ten years older than you."

"He was younger than I am now," Bunny said.

"It's always the older men who are interesting to teenage girls," said Sofie. "I was in love with the guy who looked after our summer cottage. And I slept with him, *and* then in the end he turned out to be my third cousin." John looked at her in horror and she laughed, her laugh a surprising hoot. Bunny loved her. She wished she could spend time with her, that she had known her for years.

"Wow," said Bunny. "Well I never got anywhere with Upstairs Eddie, tragically for me." She paused, unsure whether to release Charlie's name into the universe.

"Do you remember that asshole journalist guy," she asked her brother. "Eddie's friend? Charlie, his name was. Charlie something."

"Oh yeah," John said, thinking. "He's, like, semifamous you know, now," he said. "He writes good stuff about the Iraq war." Bunny filed this away.

"You're fucking kidding me, Charlie Kovak?" said Sofie. "I know him! Well, I know *of* him. What? Bunny! Did you sleep with him?"

"No, Jesus!" said Bunny. "Of course not. But we had, I don't know. Tension. Something. He was a disturbing person." She thought about Gobustan, in the caves, how he had touched her. It was murky, these many years later. She almost remembered it as a kiss. She could see for a moment how memory rewrote itself.

"He is kind of handsome, in a Neanderthal way," said Sofie meditatively.

"This is gross," said John. "Bunny was, like, fifteen! He was even older than Eddie."

"He was probably thirty, I would guess," said Bunny. "Too old. I knew it, but you don't *really* know when you're fifteen, I guess. It was a long summer. I was so bored. He paid attention to me."

"All those guys are pigs," said Sofie. "Adventure guys. Trying to chat up Moldovan teenagers."

She pinched John again, now his cheek. "You're not a pig, are you, though."

"When did you even interact with Charlie Kovak?" said John to Bunny, still incredulous at the mystery of their shared childhood. Bunny briefly wondered what it was like to remember things as he did, what life looked like, what the world looked like. What had made them different, so that he ended up out in the world with a beautiful magnetic Swede and she was an oil-company administrator in Texas? "We met him, like, twice."

Bunny shook her head. "It was more than that. He came on that CLO trip too, you know?" said Bunny. "To Gobustan. And I don't know. He used to come visit Eddie in Zeynab Xanim's house."

"Zeynab Xanim," her brother said. "Oh man, yeah. You were always up there. I thought it was because she fed you sweets." Bunny pressed her sweating bottle of beer to her forehead.

"Our mom was in Texas with Small Ted that summer dealing with our grandma," Bunny explained to Sofie. "So we were mostly on our own, and John was sprinting around the city all day to beat his room-mate's 5K time. John didn't like me because I had a bad reputation at school and all his friends said nasty things about me." She enjoyed the freedom she had now, with John, to speak as she was. Seldom had they exchanged so many words on personal topics.

"Beautiful Bunny," said Sofie with warmth that made Bunny love her. "I'm sure all his friends were pigs too."

"I didn't hate you, Bunny, Jesus. I did hate that roommate. Paul de Waal! I never ended up beating his time." John patted his stomach. "And now I'm, like, five minutes away from what I could run back then."

Bunny looked at Sofie. "That was our only summer in Baku," she said. "The second summer Mom said she was sick of the former Soviet Union, and she came and rented a place in Athens with Small Ted, so we came here on break. Then Dad got the second posting here, which they had always wanted. And then he did . . . what he did." She looked over at her brother for some sign of loyalty to their mother but he assiduously avoided her gaze.

"I'm going swimming," he said, and he clambered up and ran into the water like a gazelle. The women stretched back on their elbows and watched the tanker crossing the horizon, passing a small fishing boat bobbing in the foreground.

"So what happens at that place? San-something," Bunny asked.

"The oil comes from a platform on the Caspian near Baku. Or sometimes on a boat from the other side, from Kazakhstan or Turkmenistan." Sofie drank the rest of her beer and burped. "Excuse me," she said. "Then at Sangachal they put it into a pipeline that goes through Azerbaijan and Georgia and eventually to Turkey, to Ceyhan." Bunny noted the pronunciation, *Jay-hahn*. "And then it goes on a boat again, to Piraeus, or Trieste maybe. To Europe."

"Downstream," said Bunny.

"Yes," said Sofie. "Downstream, refining. See, you do know."

Bunny drank from her beer and peeled the label from the bottle. "I sort of know," she said. She put the label into her bag, thinking of her tidy parents. "I think Charlie Kovak was investigating whether they would build that pipeline," she said. "For this creepy newspaper he had."

"Yes, BTC pipeline, it's called. It was a great geopolitical feat," Sofie said sourly. "And now of course it's a mess. There's Georgian farmers still waiting for their payments from BP even though they broke ground, like, ten years ago," she said. "And now they are working on another pipeline, the Southern Corridor, for natural gas, also for Europe. Europeans are desperate to have some source that isn't Russia, to not have to deal with Putin. They are, like, 80 percent importers, something crazy. It will start at Sangachal too." She dug a bit in the sand and looked at Bunny. "Do you like your work?"

"No. Sometimes," said Bunny. "I like to get things done. I like to get paid. I like to get my moles removed at the dermatologist. I have my own place. I was living with our mom for, like, two years." She thought of her apartment. She liked to walk through Buffalo Bayou at a leisurely pace, listening to Miike Snow. *Were they Swedish?* she wondered inanely. She liked to have a single taco and two Pacificos at a place a few blocks away from her apartment. There was always a new food to try, in some small portion, in Houston. She was trying to get to know the city, although she still did not have any friends beyond her Zumba buddy Sarah. She looked out at her brother. "Unlike him, I actually have student loans. Not a lot. But I have them. I didn't get a fucking cross-country scholarship."

Sofie laughed again. "I'm sorry, but this is such an American tragedy! You work for the oil complex so you can have health insurance and a place to live!"

Bunny felt a reflexive sting at northern-European superiority. "Well, yeah, we don't just get those things in shitty America." She drained her beer and looked for the oil tanker, which was almost out of sight. "I do kind of think there's something amazing about it," she said. "All the logistics. Like, they stick a pipe down into the ground or into the bottom of the ocean or even sideways or diagonal or whatever and somehow get the oil to flow up it?"

"It's true," said Sofie. "It's epic work."

"And then we can turn our lights on," Bunny said, feeling a bit poetic. "It has to come from somewhere, the way we all want to live."

She could hear an echo of the boy she had met at the party on Phil and Estelle's roof, confident, a little self-righteous. She ventured to wax philosophical, as her father might have done. "I mean, yes, part of it is just, like, evil Wild West shit. I can see that. But we need energy for hospitals! It's how we have modern life. Women don't all die having babies in a shed." She tried to remember his name, the boy from the party who looked like Fred Savage.

Sofie looked amused, propped up on her elbows to keep her shoulders off the sand, her midriff slightly scrunched. "I see," she said. "I agree that it's nice to have electricity and not die in a shed."

Bunny looked at her, defensive, uncertain whether she was being made fun of. "I mean, you guys flew in a plane here. This is not, like, a required trip. You flew in an airplane that burned fossil fuels to come on your vacation."

"Of course I did," said Sofie. She sat up and lit a cigarette. "You can't make everything about society dependent on fossil fuels and then require that making the good choice comes with a penalty of living like an . . . ascetic compared to the other people you know." Bunny found it touching, to see her finally searching for a word. "The only thing you can do is do a wholesale change of how these economies function. And the oil companies and their friends in politics, and as you probably know they are often the same people, they are the biggest obstacles to this." She took a drag and exhaled up into the air.

"Yeah," said Bunny. "I get how these companies are looking out for themselves," she said. "I don't know a lot about this stuff. I just think that we have this huge system that's already in place. I don't know; it's like our dad." She looked at John trawling slowly through the water. "He didn't always like whoever the president was, but he worked to do what he could at his job. And anyway, we used to live in the former Soviet Union," she said weakly, feeling that she was on difficult terrain. "Places that would, like, run out of electricity."

Sofie laughed, and then said in a voice that was serious but not accusatory, "If you had been to Iraq, I think you would feel differently that we can work with the system we have. Or if you could see this beach in fifty years."

Bunny flushed. "I believe in global warming! I'm a liberal! I hate Republicans. I was a temp when I got this job in a recession, and it was all hydroelectric and nuclear and there was no oil involved."

Sofie looked mildly disdainful. "I bet your boss is right-wing, though." Bunny stopped to think. In Texas, the need for oil was self-evident, inviolable, at least among the people Bunny had met. It transcended politics, Bunny thought. Of course Warren and Christine were Republicans; Maryellen was not one but had been one, Bunny was pretty sure, until George W. Bush, although they didn't really discuss electoral politics when she was a child. Of course Ainsley and Jeff with his dead bears were Republicans. Of this there was no doubt. Frank Turnbridge, yes, of course, he with his "Obama-nation." But Phil? It was hard for her to pin this on Phil. Unlike most of the Americans at Miles or Turnbridge, he never mentioned politics. It was one of the reasons she liked him. And in Houston it was different. People had Obama signs, even though they knew that oil kept the lights on. It had a liberal feeling to it.

"And!" Bunny said. "The engineers there come from around the world. They come from Iraq! And Nigeria. And Mexico. And Venezuela," she said helplessly, feeling stupid, as Sofie nodded knowingly at each country on the list.

John returned from the sea, drops of cold spray landing on the two women as he sat back down on the towel.

"And also," Bunny said. "It's a small company, and this is a spinoff that is going to work on renewables," she said. "It's not, like . . . Halliburton." Halliburton was a company inscribed on Bunny's heart as an avatar of American villainy, even though she wasn't sure exactly what it was or did. Like a bank that was too big to fail, it was too big to understand; she remembered only the face of Dick Cheney splashed across the Facebook pages of college acquaintances who followed the news more closely than she did.

"Well, Halliburton is an oilfield services company," said Sofie mildly. "Your company probably does work with them, in some capacity. It would be very normal. It's one of the biggest such companies."

"Well I'm not fucking . . . Karl Rove," Bunny returned, aware as she spoke that if they demanded she explain who Karl Rove was, she would be unable to answer. She laughed as she invoked him, but she was offended and she could tell that it was obvious. Among her peers in college they were used to joking about all their villainies, personal or general, their racist uncles a punchline, their own racist jokes strictly ironic, but they were not accustomed to thinking of themselves as people who had responsibilities to be bad or good. They were all probably mostly fine. For someone so kind, funny, and normal, Sofie was very serious. It unnerved Bunny.

"Hey," said Sofie, putting her hand on the top of Bunny's foot, where it sat awkwardly. "I don't mean to insult you. I'm not even sure how we got here, from Upstairs Eddie and Charlie Kovak."

John laughed at her. "Are you kidding? You always get to Halliburton somehow." He looked at Bunny. "Cheer up, Bunny," said John. "She does this to everyone." Now it was Sofie who looked annoyed.

"It's okay," said Bunny. "It's just a job. I don't care. I'm not a super political person, sorry." She walked into the water, knowing she had fallen low in Sofie's estimation and feeling offended and sad after their intimacy of the morning. She stayed in the water for a long time, thinking rebelliously about soft salt domes and ancient stones and flat-bottomed barges transported in pieces across the earth.

When John and Sofie knocked on her door after their afternoon nap, the air was conciliatory. Sofie stretched out her arms when Bunny opened the door. "Gordon's Space," she said. "Let's go out." Bunny couldn't be angry at beautiful, warm Sofie. She said, "Just a minute and I'll get ready," and she put on makeup, a dusting of golden eyeshadow and smoky eyeliner. She put on lipstick and then wiped it off. She spritzed dehumidifier on her hair and put on deodorant. She was wearing a striped wrap dress that she felt forgave her body's errors.

In the port they shared two small bottles of ouzo and a plate of tender marinated octopus parts pierced with toothpicks. They watched the sky turn pink and the lights of a few scattered fishing boats blink on in the harbor. A breeze picked up and turned to a wind and they rose to find a taverna in the village for dinner. The island was small and not crowded. Greek families were doing their volta on the pier.

They moved on to dinner in a courtyard at the back of a taverna on a back street, protected from the wind. They ate fried sardines and gave the tails to the cat who jumped in Sofie's lap. They ate tzatziki so sharp with garlic they would feel it in the pit of their stomachs late in the night. They ate giant beans and stuffed courgette blossoms. They ate airy plates of *kalamarakia* fried to perfection. Bunny and John reminisced further about the people they had known. "Remember the journalist who showed up drunk for a party the night before the party happened? He lay down on the couch and Mom made him coffee?"

"Remember the embassy guy's daughter who went to a hotel with the marine and then everyone found out?"

"Remember Murad?"

"Remember Kyria Vouvras?"

"Remember Zeynab Xanim?"

They spoke again of Upstairs Eddie. "You can find people on Facebook now," interjected Sofie. "All the villains from the past, horribly returning."

"Upstairs Eddie wasn't a villain," Bunny said. "He was trying to expose corruption in the oil industry. Like you. He was always trying to get our dad to introduce him to government ministers so he could interview them sitting on their golden toilets or whatever."

"Ah," said Sofie.

Bunny saw the soft intelligence of Eddie's face in her mind's eye. "He was like a smart, fancy do-gooder. He spoke perfect Russian."

Sofie rolled her eyes. "NGO savior guy."

"You're a hypocrite," Bunny cried. "What about John? Isn't the Peace Corps, like, the original villain of paternalistic do-goodery?"

Sofie slapped the table with satisfaction. "Bunny, I knew it! You *do* have politics. John said you have no discernible politics."

"Wow, okay," said Bunny. "And what are you, John? A communist?"

Sofie laughed. "His reeducation is long but ongoing," she said, petting the side of John's face. "Anyway, Bunny," she said. "I think maybe it's you who is the cynic. What's more cynical than believing things can't change?"

She dragged on the stub of her cigarette and smashed it triumphantly in the Tuborg ashtray. Bunny would have hated her but she was too magnetic, too open. What an odd woman for her squirrelly, taciturn brother to end up with. A table was seated next to them, four young men, white Europeans of some sort, dressed in a motif that bespoke a vague European frattiness. Sofie saw Bunny notice the men, looked at them herself, and smiled. "Swedes," she said, reaching across to give Bunny a gentle punch. "I would bet my life." Bunny ignored this.

"How did you guys meet again?" she asked Sofie, nodding toward John. She knew they had partially covered this during their first wine-soaked evening.

"At a stupid party," said Sofie, smiling tenderly at John. "I went to Kyiv to cover the gas disputes between Russia and Ukraine. And there was some kind of reception at a hotel that I went to, and the Peace Corps people were there getting drunk on their big trip into town."

"Where did you live then?" Bunny asked. Sofie laughed.

"I didn't really live anywhere. I did couch surfing while I covered stories. When I ran out of money, I would go back to Stockholm and stay with my parents and work at a café until I could go out again."

"Wow," said Bunny. "So was it long-distance, with John?"

"For a while," she said. "And then we moved in together in Kyiv when he was done with the village."

"Did you ever think about living in the States?" asked Bunny with genuine curiosity.

"As I told John," Sofie said, "I love *not* living in America more than I love him."

"But what if you have kids?" Bunny asked. "You know Maryellen needs to have some grandchildren," she said to her brother.

"Well then you're going to have to step up," said her brother. Bunny looked from one face to another.

"I'm not having children," said Sofie. "I've known this since I was eleven years old. I have a niece and nephews; I don't need my own. The world does not need another child of affluent people in the West." Bunny was shocked by this. Her brother had always seemed to her the kind of man who would have children, although every person seemed to her the kind of person who would eventually have children. Children were a thing that people had.

"How old are you?" she asked.

"Thirty-three," said Sofie. "And sterilized," she added. "So that solves that."

"Wow," said Bunny. "That's intense." She had never heard anyone say this before.

The meal was concluded, the bill paid. Sofie raised her glass of wine to the table of young men and said something in Swedish. "*Skål*," they said back. The tables naturally returned to their own atmospheres. "We can see what they are doing later," said Sofie, "if you like."

John said, "Sofie, Jesus."

"What!" she said to John. "This is Bunny's vacation! Maybe she wants to meet people!" She glanced at the men again. "To be honest, they are going to become horrible," she said in a low voice to Bunny. "Four boys on the islands for the weekend." She paused. "Although," she said, "if they were really horrible, they would probably be on Mykonos. Maybe these are more discerning."

"It's okay," said Bunny. "We can just see how the night goes." She glanced at them again.

It was dark now, past eleven o'clock, and the lights of scattered villages were visible across the sea. The wind was chilly, and the water slapped up onto the old stones of the pier. They passed the row of cafés, some of which had made the transition to sexy nighttime caves, all sparsely populated. It was late in the season. They selected one with a board advertising unlikely drink specials, Sex on the Beach and mai tais. The techno version of "The Logical Song" played softly from speakers. They seated themselves on damp sofas under the awning. A handsome waiter came, looked at them, said first, "*Deutsche?*" and then self-corrected. "English. Hello, guys, welcome."

"Do you have Gordon's Space?" asked Sofie.

"Of course," he said.

"Two, please," said Sofie.

"Heineken," said John curtly. The man left and returned with their drinks and bowls of chips and popcorn. Bunny felt a wave of jet lag and sipped the Gordon's Space with its sickly aftertaste of Lemon Pledge. "Wow," she said. "My youth." She and Sofie and John clinked their glasses.

"Give me a sip," said John to Sofie.

"It's really horrible," said Sofie. "Terrible youth."

Bunny put one of her cigarettes in her mouth and as she reached for the lighter the waiter was before her with a flame. "*Efcharisto poli*," she said to him.

"*Parakalo*," he said with a nod. He squinted at her. "*Ellinidha?*"

"*Oxi*," she said. "*Millao mono poli ligo*." She pinched her fingers for the international gesture of "I only speak a little."

"Very good," he said to her in English. "Stay in Greece and you'll learn."

"Thanks," she said, and she smiled at him. He was cute, with curly hair and a Chicago Bulls T-shirt.

At that moment the music switched to "We No Speak Americano," and then the four Swedes arrived under the awning.

"Ah," said Sofie, "*hej*, hi, hi." She gestured to the table next to them, and they gamely came over. Together they formed a shape like two amoebas trying to osmose. Bunny was awkwardly on the farthest side from the Swedes, her brother a barrier between the one she had decided was the most handsome, who was auburn-haired with a wide and slightly flattened nose like a boxer.

"Hey, guys," the waiter said to them. "Welcome, *wilkommen*, welcome." They sorted out their drinks and Sofie introduced John and Bunny to her countrymen.

"Nice to meet you," said the redhead.

"Why do Swedish people speak such good English?" Bunny asked him, feeling reckless as the Gordon's Space added its special poisons to her blood.

"Why are Americans so shit at speaking Swedish?" said the redhead with a good-natured expression.

"He speaks Russian!" said Sofie, elbowing John. Bunny sipped her Gordon's Space.

"Here, we are a strange shape now, too awkward; Bunny, come, you are very far, you switch with John and we can make a circle," said Sofie, prodding John with her hands to stand. Bunny was mortified but Sofie was so swift and sweetly tactful in her ministrations that the reshuffling was completed quickly, so that they were now an oval with John and one of the Swedes as its narrowest points, and she was seated next to the redhead. Bunny admired Sofie's management of the situation. Competence and graceful authority in group situations was rare and precious, as Bunny knew from the admin pool.

The men said their names, two of which were just sounds to Bunny. The auburn-haired one next to her was Konrad. "Is it your first time in Greece?" asked Konrad.

"No," said Bunny. "We—he's my brother," she gestured to John, "we lived here when we were kids, and then we came again when I was in university." She could hear in her voice the egregious phenomenon of changing her syntax to meet a foreigner's, taking on a ridiculous lilt, even though in the case of Konrad it was preposterous to try and match his perfect English. "Where do you all live?" asked Bunny.

"You know the city of Lund?" said the one who looked like a Hitler Youth. Bunny nodded politely.

"Are you at the university?" asked Sofie.

"We two are in a master's program," said the blond, whose name was Nils, as he pointed to himself and Konrad. "And these are our friends from university. Norwegians," he said, and he smiled pleasantly.

"What is your master's program in?" asked Bunny.

"Finance," said Konrad.

"Cool," said Bunny. She was trying to figure out how old they all were. Konrad's hair was really a beautiful shade of dark red, with a gentle wave in it, and he had a few freckles across the wide, slightly smushed bridge of his nose. He had brown eyes and eyebrows that took up a lot of space.

"Are you in school too?" he said.

"No, I work at an energy company. But I took a finance class this year," she offered. "It was called 'Managing the Firm in the Global Economy.'"

"Ah," he said. "This is basically our program." He took a handful of chips from the bowl on the table. "How did you find it?" he asked Bunny.

"To be honest, it was very confusing," said Bunny. "About supply chains and arbitrage."

"Yeah," he said. "It can be complex." John and Sofie and the Norwegians were in some version of the same conversation on their side of the oval. "So what kind of energy company?" he asked her.

"Well, it's an oil company, small, family-owned, private." She looked at Sofie, hoping she was occupied.

The guy looked interested. "Cool. It's E&P?" Bunny knew what this meant now: exploration and production.

"Yes," she said. "Well, also new technologies. I work on the renewable side." She tried to sound confident.

"Do they pay you well?" asked Sofie, who was now listening from her side of the table.

"Yeah," said Bunny. "Twenty-three bucks an hour." She had recently gotten this raise and could hardly believe how high it was. John whistled.

"That's pretty good," he said. "What's minimum wage, seven?"

"Something like that," she said, "I don't know."

Sofie shook her head. "Seven dollars per hour and no health care. This is why I won't go to America."

Bunny said primly, "Well, I have health insurance." It was not good health insurance, but she had it.

She spoke to the group, not sure at whom to look. "What kind of business are you all going to do after your master's?"

"Actually we two are interested in the energy sector as well," said one of the Norwegians. "We have domestic energy production in Norway." Sofie looked mischievous.

"Good old Statoil," she said.

"Yeah," said the other Norwegian, whose name was Per.

"Be careful," said Bunny. "Sofie is an environmental journalist. Soon she'll start yelling at you."

"Yes, it's true," said Sofie. "But I'm a socialist too, as you know. I prefer nationalized oil industries." She looked at the Swedes and Norwegians. "Although now that Statoil went consortium with BP and the other bastards and they imposed their shit management strategies on them, they turned it into a hell for workers just like everywhere else." She said this with a dangerous friendliness Bunny could now recognize.

Per laughed but looked at her with confident disdain. "Okay, but what should they do? The last ten years it's all consolidation, it's all consortiums, you know? North Sea oil is difficult to extract; they had to diversify."

"Yeah, okay," said Sofie. "But what if instead of trying to compete they take their massive subsidies and retrofit their equipment and turn to 100 percent renewables?" Per made an abrupt Norwegian sound, then returned to English with admirable swiftness.

"A net importer! So you just pay for your problems to be offshored."

Sofie smiled sweetly. "Okay," she said. "But five degrees by year 2100 is most of the human race dead."

Bunny felt a chill. Was that number true? She drank the rest of her Gordon's Space fast, and Konrad noticed and chivalrously beckoned the bartender. "You'll have another?" he said, putting his hand on the back of her arm fleetingly. The last time she had felt any part of a man touching any part of her was when Barney the engineer had placed his unwelcome hand on the middle of her back while he pointed out the text of a map that had its label misapplied.

"A Heineken, please."

Sofie spoke again. "They say already by 2030 it will be too hot for the hajj to be in Mecca. Can you imagine this?"

"Who cares?" said the Swede who wasn't Konrad with what seemed like virulence. Bunny, John, and Sofie looked at him. Sofie sat forward.

"Don't tell me you're a fucking SD Nazi man; I won't have a drink with you," she said, and Bunny admired her even as she felt upset by the directness of the confrontation. How did someone become like this, unambiguous, unassailable? Bunny held her breath to see whether the Swede would reveal himself, but he put his hands up and said, "Sorry. A joke. I don't like religion." Sofie turned away from him, still suspicious.

Bunny spoke timidly. "But what about the Resource Curse thing," she said. "Like, isn't it a thing where the countries that have a lot of oil and gas get all fucked-up because they can't manage it? People are really poor and the ruling class just mismanages all the money? Like . . . ," she reached around in her mind. "Venezuela." Sofie waved her hand, annoyed.

"Most petrostates, they do not exactly have total control over their own resources. Venezuela, Nigeria, Iran, Kazakhstan, these places, they have never had an opportunity to be true resource nationalists, to have real sovereignty, because they are left with bad infrastructure and bad economies by colonialism and they have no choice but to take the deals offered them to help upgrade. And that's just on the technical side. On the political side, they are immediately destabilized the minute they show a sign to take control of their own resources. Mossadegh in Iran got overthrown by the British and the Americans because the oil companies said so."

Konrad laughed. "Okay, Che Guevara. What about Libya? Gaddafi? These people are perfectly happy to keep the oil companies there but impose their ridiculous price sharing, 70 percent of profits, something like that. They all switched to service contracts anyway. There's no concessions; there's no colonialism. And still they can't run their own countries."

"Colonialism doesn't end in fifty years, or a hundred years," said Sofie. "Anyway, most of the supermajors like a dictatorship. Political transitions are bad for them. You have one ruler for life, you only need to deal with him and his people, launder your bribes through one government. ExxonMobil and Hess and Chevron all paid bribes to Obiang in Equatorial Guinea. He is a monster! But they loved him." Bunny remembered what Frank Turnbridge said. They think in geologic time. Not political time. Not term-limit time. The wind picked up off the dark water and she felt chilled in her dress. She moved her arm a hair's breadth closer to Konrad, who was leaning toward Sofie, challenging her.

"Fine," he said. "Let's say this is true. But globalization is here. And that raises the standard for everyone, by the way! And if every country says, 'Our economic doors are closed, we only do what we can do here and we don't connect with any other economy,' you know this won't work." Bunny was amazed at their English. How did people learn another language so well, other subjects so fluently?

"I'm not proposing this," said Sofie, her face weary but somehow still suffused with a reasonable amount of goodwill. "I am just saying that there is nothing inevitable about a country bungling its own resources that is not explained by the last four hundred years of political economy." She lit another cigarette. "And the reality is we will all die if we do not divest from the carbon economy. Well. Not you and me, probably. But people are already dying. They are drowning when their islands get wiped out from superstorms. They are dying because they can't feed themselves because the crops can't grow where they used to grow. They are dying when they cross the desert. They are dying in boats," she gestured out at the dark waters where this was happening, perhaps as they spoke. "And if they get inside Fortress Europe, if they don't get pushed back or die at sea, then they come up against fucking Golden Dawn or SD Nazis. It's sick, man." John, who had not said a word for twenty minutes, held her hand but, perhaps wisely, stayed silent. The Norwegians spoke in low voices, and Bunny wondered if they would leave. The evening had taken a dark turn so swiftly. Sofie seemed to live so comfortably with darkness, Bunny thought. Bunny could not imagine living thus. Bunny liked to be optimistic.

"Anyway, sorry," said Sofie brightly, understanding that the evening's festivities had taken a direct hit. "I'm a journalist; these are the stories I think about; it's hard to leave work at home." She picked up her drink, and each man was forced to reveal whether he would act like a dick in the face of such truth, and then such graceful accommodation, or whether he would stay and drink. Bunny considered the way Sofie was like a man in that she could speak confidently and at length, but like a woman in that she could read and direct the energy produced by the things she said. And one by one they clinked, and stayed. "Now what should we talk about," said Bunny, laughing and taking Sofie's cigarette gently to light her own.

Bunny woke up in her room alone. She remembered becoming very drunk and lurching into Sofie as they stumbled in a group down the cobblestones, their voices echoing in the narrow corridors of the village as they looked for another place to go when all the places were closed. She remembered clutching Sofie's arms and saying, "You know why I like you? Because you're serious but you're still fun." And Sofie had squeezed her arm in return and said, "And you're silly but you're not stupid." John had run an impromptu race with Per, who had also run cross-country in high school.

Somehow Bunny and Konrad had split off from the group and ended up on the small beach right by the pier where the two daily boats deposited and retrieved visitors. They kissed fervently, she remembered that, and then she remembered a mutually antagonistic fumbling. She remembered a flare of desire as she felt his surprisingly hard stomach through his shirt, the stubble on his cheeks. But she didn't feel up for unprotected sex on the beach, and Konrad had heavy hands. She didn't want to bring him back to a room that abutted her brother. Konrad meanwhile was sharing a room with Nils. She was foggy with fatigue and drink. She had wrestled with him in the sand, and then she had left him despondent and gently wrathful at his hotel—"Girls, girls, girls," he had sung, which almost made her change her mind—and walked unsteadily back to her hotel smoking her last remaining, broken cigarette with her fingers pinched over the tear. Now she lay in her sunlit bed, feeling exhilarated but also disappointed that she had squandered her chance for holiday promiscuity, which had come so easily and ended so fleetingly, but also curiously proud that she had exercised restraint, although why restraint now finally seemed like a virtue she couldn't say. Sofie couldn't infinitely orchestrate these sit-downs with her countrymen. In three days Bunny would be back on the plane to Texas.

The day before her flight Bunny decided to go to the Acropolis while Sofie and John went to the Benaki museum. She walked the narrow streets to the back of the colossal stone outcropping and wended through the warren of tiny perfect hovels clustered on one of the slopes, corrugated tin roofs, whitewashed walls, structures from another era that had somehow evaded Plaka's evolution into stately neoclassical buildings. Eventually she found the ticket booth. She stood in the line of many tongues and nations, the sun hot on her back, and bought her ticket.

Bunny felt a powerful but unfocused desire to wrest from Athens all that her memory required to feed itself. If she could just see enough balconies spilling over with plants, enough heavy doors in marble vestibules of beautiful old apartment buildings, enough multilingual graffiti, if she could hear the calls of the wood pigeons in the cool mornings, if she could imbibe enough cold weak beer and sickly frappés in the shade of tucked-away cafés, if she could lay eyes on the cast of characters who had populated her childhood—archaeologists and journalists and politicians and aid workers and wandering expats, their original reason for coming to Greece long forgotten by everyone—she could have taken it all in, could scratch the painful itch of nostalgia. But always the thing receded.

It was very hot and Bunny perspired as she walked up the path and looked down into the Herodion, where she and Ted and Maryellen and John and Small Ted had once seen a performance of *Macbeth*. She slipped on the marble of the entry portal, worn into smooth divots by millions of feet. The Parthenon itself was encased in scaffolding. She inspected the caryatids and then traversed the plateau to the lookout point, where she gazed out at Athens, stretched out in the basin that led to Hymettus. She turned to Lycabettus Hill, pinpointed their old apartment in Kolonaki. It was a day without *nefos*, no smog, the haze having blown out to the Saronic Gulf by the late summer wind. She thought of all the places of her childhood that she would never again see, barring some long odyssey or life recalibration. The towers of Meteora, the snowy streets of Kastoria in the winter. A windy night somewhere after a missed ferry, a lonely hotel smelling slightly of mildew. The rest stop at the Isthmus of Corinth where you stared down into the incredible feat of the canal, the narrow walls representing untold ingenuity and suffering, and beside which you could get succulent skewers of charred pork and toasted pieces of bread wrapped in paper. The precipitous windy roads of Pelion. When would she lay on the hot slate stones of the pool at the Petite Planète hotel at Mycenae, the wild thyme and ancient stones of the Argolid just beyond the narrow border of slate pavers? Her family had been happy here, at least in her memory. She thought about her own apartment sitting empty, the muggy streets of Houston and the frigid air of her cube at Turnbridge Energy Solutions, and felt momentarily unable to face them. A family, Turkish maybe, crowded next to her by the stone wall and she offered, in the universal language of the index finger pressing the air, to take their photograph.

There was a young woman across the aisle from Bunny on her connecting flight from JFK to Houston. She was writing cards, Bunny saw, a whole stack of them, transposing from a draft on her phone. Bunny's innate nosiness led her to read the card, a message to a potential bridesmaid in a girlish hand. The woman wrote something almost—but not quite—identical on each card. "I literally can't imagine my wedding day without you," she wrote, followed by a specific memory with the girl in question. Then: "You have watched my love for Paul grow and mature." She used the last card as a ruler so that her lines would be straight. "Will you do me the honor of being a bridesmaid?" She drew boxes for the bridesmaids to check. Bunny was mesmerized by the effort and orderliness of the operation. What was Paul doing right now? She strained to get a look at the ring when the bride set down her pen and cracked her long fingers after the exertion. A rock, in Bunny's brief glimpse; the sunlight shot through it and danced for a moment on the scratched fiberglass of the plane's hull. When the woman was done with her pile, she stood and walked, slender in yoga pants, to the rear of the plane. Bunny could almost feel it herself, the sense of accomplishment, the cramped hand, the small neat pile bespeaking a task crossed off the list.

Bunny, realizing that she, too, could be getting something done, decided to look at the pieces of memoir that Frank Turnbridge had given her. Bunny was often amazed at how difficult it was for people to put together a sentence even when it was so easy for them to do other things. "I had just about perfected my golf swing on the oil sands at

Marsa el Brega when Esso. . . ." Here Frank trailed off. What had Esso done? It would remain a mystery until she could ask him in person. The next sentence began, "In this business you have to get good on an oil sand course. And in Libya you had to get good at making toilet wine in your barracks. Masjid-i-Sulaiman in Iran had an oil sand course too. You could really get ahead if you got your swing right. But the oil makes the ball act funny."

Bunny thought of Konrad and her drunken night on the beach; he had talked about Libya. She thought of Sofie's jeremiad. She could never have shown her this document. Bunny understood, logically, that Sofie was right about everything. But it was impossible to reconcile Sofie's prognostications with the world Bunny saw before her, with all its foregone conclusions. She envied the men like Frank Turnbridge, the young man Frank Turnbridge had been, all the oil men, who had worried only about the bottom line and how they might close the deal. These men ran into each other across the world, on the course at Marsa el Brega, by the pool at Dhahran camp, on the shuttle plane at Bontang, always going somewhere new. As Bunny's plane banked over Houston she looked down over the miles of cars, the sun glinting off the windshields. She imagined herself a young man, a full moon casting its light over the shimmering oil sands.

2013

$102.96/$88.70

STORYTELLING

Bunny was late to the program at the Marriott Marquis, and she slipped into the conference room as a small brunette was speaking, gesturing at a slideshow up on the large screen. She found a seat at the back and tucked her bag under it—a LeSportsac in a fun pattern, a small rebellion against the staidness of an office where Frank still required all men to wear a coat and tie. She was disappointed in herself for being late and frazzled. She was wearing a J.Crew pencil skirt in kelly green that she also owned in purple, and a sleeveless blouse that tucked in without bunching. OPI's You Don't Know Jacques! shone dully on her recently manicured nails. Bunny was trying.

Bunny had learned about the program from the email Listserv of the Houston Community College Global Energy Center. Most of the events in the three-day conference—one of a seemingly endless series of oil-related summits and programs and exhibitions that filled up the enormous hotels and event spaces near Discovery Green every week—were opaque to Bunny as she skimmed them. This, though, was some kind of satellite event tacked onto a technical conference about the Bakken shale. It was called "Storytelling Oil and Gas" and offered a speaker followed by a networking happy hour.

The room held around fifty people, a high proportion of them young women like herself, a few men and women of middle age, mostly white. Apart from the occasional bar, her Zumba, and, lately, her spin class, this was the youngest room Bunny had been in since she moved to Texas. It was decades younger than any Turnbridge room, which was invariably 75 percent gray-haired white men.

The brunette who was speaking was small but spoke in a manner that was authoritative and sharp. She looked corporate, with neatly trimmed bangs swooped to the side. On the projection screen there was white space and the words "It's a start."

"The work we did with BP really started earlier," she was saying, "with our colleagues at Ogilvy and Mather, who, along with Landor, created an absolutely groundbreaking campaign with 'beyond petroleum.'"

She clicked into the next slide, which showed the green and yellow BP sun, instantly recognizable. She looked out at the audience.

"Our colleagues there in the early 2000s put out an incredibly engaging campaign and created an instantly iconic brand identity."

She looked at the audience, and her face assumed a somber expression.

"But because one element of our firm is reactive, helping folks out in a crisis, sometimes we have the less-fun task of thinking through and responding to problems and figuring out how to prevent those problems in the future." She clicked her remote again, now a still of a gulf scene, a stretch of white beach and blue water.

"I had the pleasure of meeting Ms. Iris Cross, BP's general manager for external relations, who comes from the Gulf region and shared the actions the company was taking after the Deepwater Horizon incident in this video, which my colleagues and I put together." She played the video, a scene of a heron in a marsh. A pleasant-looking Black woman in a blue shirt and company jacket, like Warren might wear on the Motiva floor, appeared on the screen and spoke.

"When BP made a commitment to the Gulf, we knew it would take time, but we were determined to see it through," the woman said. She explained that BP had set aside $20 billion to fund economic and environmental recovery, and the screen showed fishermen pouring bountiful buckets of healthy-looking shrimp down on a deck. "I'm pleased to report that our beaches and waters are open, for everyone to enjoy," she said, spreading her arms in a smiling gesture of welcome. When the video concluded, the BP helios beamed back on the white screen, and there was sporadic clapping in the audience. The small brunette spoke again.

"Now, that's a situation I hope none of you ever have to face. And *ideally*, the energy industry has so many wonderful opportunities for being proactive, figuring out how to meet each moment as it comes." She stopped and looked earnest before speaking again. "We know from what happened with the tragedy in the Gulf that our environment, our world, can be affected by fossil fuels."

Bunny felt soothed and comforted by this acknowledgment.

"And the reality is we know what we know about climate and the environment *because* of the scientists who work in this industry. Some of the greatest scientific minds in the world, people with the best training, the best education, the greatest commitment to human development, are workers in the oil and gas industry. These are heroes at every level—men *and* women—people I feel privileged to have gotten to know a bit as we worked with BP." She took up the remote again and looked at the screen, pausing for a beat to show a beautifully lit photo of workers standing before complicated machinery—Black, brown, and white faces together. She clicked and showed a gorgeous photo of an offshore rig in azure waters, the symmetry and intricacy of the rig its own form of art and beauty, backlit against a sunset. There was not a leak in sight; the waters were calm, the machinery gleaming. It was almost beautiful, Bunny thought. Stirring.

"The *industry* has been responsible for a major shift from heavy fuel oil to cleaner-burning natural gas, and that's something that simply can't be stressed or highlighted enough in *any* story you want to tell about your clients. Innovation has been pushed forward by the industry more than anywhere else." She paused, clicked again, and there appeared an image of a field of wind turbines.

"Now sometimes it can be tough to get our industry colleagues on board when we want to take a storytelling approach that tackles climate head-on. I don't have to tell you all that this industry is full of guys who have been doing things the same way for a long time." Everyone laughed, and the speaker paused.

"So you might have colleagues who take a view like, 'I drilled this well with my own bare hands, and I don't want to talk about fuel efficiency in my commercials.'" The laughter became uproarious, Bunny's voice joining the others as she pictured Frank, who might have said this word for word. The speaker paused again to appreciate it.

"But in this political climate, with consumers who are thinking about environmental impacts, it's really crucial that we are putting our industry's best foot forward, looking for those opportunities to tell those really important stories about how our industry has pushed human ingenuity to its limits to create more efficient technologies."

She sipped from the bottle of water. "We have *so many* opportunities now to tell those stories, a lot of venues that didn't exist even a few years ago. But sometimes companies, whether you're in standalone PR or advertising or marketing, whether you're in-house at a major or in oilfield services, are set up in a way that reflects more of the old world, so that some of these opportunities can kind of fall through the cracks. If we think in a more holistic way about content, if we're thinking about blog posts, about white papers, about earned media, if we're thinking of philanthropic programs and public-private partnerships or just straight-up traditional advertising, if we consolidate an approach so that those are all individual elements of one big portrait we are painting, we're going to have a lot more success than if we kind of just trust that each of these little fragmented departments is going to effectively tell its own story."

Bunny felt energized and motivated by the woman as she watched her walk around the front of the room, small yet supremely confident.

When she finished speaking, the room filled with applause. A thin blonde woman with waves, texturized with beach spray, Bunny thought, took to the podium. She was wearing a sleeveless beige dress with a thin patent leather belt around a very narrow waist, and she had towering black heels with the red soles Bunny could identify as Louboutins. She spoke in a broad Southern accent, not Texas as Bunny knew it, but something farther east and north, of the sort Bunny still struggled to believe was real.

"I'm Meghan Abernathy, I'm with KBR here in Houston, and I want to thank Allison for speaking with us today."

Bunny scanned her growing mental card catalog of companies, names, roles, sectors. In recent months she had decided there was no use in being cynical without actually knowing how anything worked, and also that she could never understand how anything worked if she didn't learn what all the different companies did. KBR, she knew vaguely, had something to do with Halliburton—maybe had been owned by them and then spun off. They had some problem with corruption, she knew. And some problem with Iraq, because of the Halliburton part, Bunny assumed. She wondered what this woman did at KBR. She saw the flash of a diamond on her ring finger. Bunny instinctively disliked her.

"So, I have such a super-special privilege now of introducing you to our surprise guest, who has been such a mentor to me as I've gotten started in this business. Even though I'm not on the technical side, I wanted to understand more of the science, and she just held my hand

and walked me through the entire stream." Bunny dug in her bag for gum, missing the name. "She's going to tell us about an amazing new opportunity for women in oil and gas to connect with one another. She comes with two decades of experience in the oil complex, both on the technical side and in communications and business development, and now she's starting her own thing, which she is going to tell us about. So please give her a warm welcome!" Meghan left the podium plodding with the ungainly step of someone whose shoes are too high for their feet. Bunny took a small and ugly satisfaction from this.

Another woman bounded up from her seat in the front row. She had blonde hair in what Bunny thought of as a career-woman hairdo, softly sculpted but with a little motion to it. The new woman and Meghan embraced, and then she faced the room. "I want to thank Meghan so much for letting me crash this happy hour. Allison—" here she found Allison in the room and extended a hand—"that was such a clear, concise, beautiful presentation of what we need to do in this industry, and I thank you so much too."

She looked back at the audience, and her face was serious. "I want to get started by highlighting something that she said during her presentation, which I am just so glad she brought up." She tucked a strand of hair behind her ear. There was an intensity to her movements, her shoulders moving up and down as she spoke. "This industry is filled with guys. Old. White. Guys." Everyone laughed again. "Now there's nothing wrong with old white guys, I'm married to one, there's nothing wrong with anybody." At this she wove her hands. "But this is an incredibly male-dominated field, from the drilling floor to the rig to the refinery and right on up to the boardroom." She looked around at the room. "But we know—and I look around this room and have all the proof I need—that this industry is also full of women busting their butts. And after almost two decades working in this industry and meeting so many incredible women, I realized that women in oil and gas would benefit so much from a network that's for us, for women, to network, connect with employers, something that will benefit not only *us*, but our entire oil and gas industry." She paused again.

"I won't give you my whole pitch, this is kind of a surprise, not even a soft launch, more like a preview, but pretty soon, you're going to be learning about a new network, which is going to bring together the amazing women of this industry, the women literally powering our world, and focus on bridging that major gender gap in our industry. Diversity is so important, and I'm proud to say that the industry is *listening*."

Bunny was not accustomed to thinking of herself as *diversity*. *Diversity* was, to her, a word that meant that for every group of white people there had to be some proportional number of people of other races. At Stanhope, Martin Luther King Jr. Day was celebrated by a day of service, and then the dining hall served fried chicken and invited a white preacher and a Black gospel choir to the chapel service. Bunny knew that America had a bad past and a present racial problem, as evidenced by the reaction to Barack Hussein Obama and what had happened to Trayvon Martin, and that they had to heal from this. She also knew that she had no Black people in her life, save two of the Miles engineers, who were from Nigeria and who were no longer in her life now that she worked at Turnbridge and who had not in any case been in her life at all. Bunny's mind wandered to this and wandered back to the woman in front of her, who exuded a friendly animation.

"I'm so proud to say that after a lot of hard work and hustle, we have some major backers of this new social and professional network, including Shell and Halliburton." There were scattered claps in the room. "We will be putting together professional-development programs, networking events, conferences, and job-placement services. Pink Petro. Remember that name, look for our launch, and then please join us for our conferences and events and on our socials. I can't wait to connect with you." She smiled again, thanked Meghan, and stepped away from the podium to applause from the room.

"Okay, everyone," said Meghan, "the bar is open and we have the space until seven, so please get to know one another!" Bunny wandered over to a bar table and from her place in the line watched a small crowd of young women form around the blonde woman at the front of the room, watched the first speaker as she walked briskly out of the conference hall, a Goyard bag on her shoulder—Bunny had just learned to want one of these bags herself—and her phone in her hand, vanishing down the escalator on surgically thin heels.

2014

$98.68/$54.86

THE SHOW

I f Bunny focused her ears above the freeform jazz of the opening
credits, she could hear the rain pounding with incredible force
against the roof and flimsy siding of the townhouse. Runnels
poured over the window and blurred the exterior, a neat square of sod
with a small row of juvenile azaleas, newly planted, sodden in the dark
gray, the darkness of the storm indistinguishable from the growing
darkness of the evening.

Bunny was surprised to learn that Francis owned his own house, a
trim and nondescript structure in a subdivision in The Woodlands, a
municipality he had selected for its proximity to his office and the airport and where he had found a townhouse suitable for a high-income
bachelor still paying off his business school loans. When Bunny had
expressed amazement that he was a homeowner, Francis had looked
puzzled. "Why pay rent?" he said. Bunny had never considered this.
To her paying rent was a sign of success, in that it meant she was not
living with Maryellen and that she had $975 every month earned on her

own steam to pay for her tidy one-bedroom, a space she could finally more or less keep clean.

This was her first visit to Francis's house. Until now, their third sleepover date, he had stayed at Bunny's apartment, an hour's drive through gridlock. Francis was a little embarrassed about his house, abashedly noting its emptiness. Bunny found this as endearing as she found the emptiness itself off-putting. The townhouse was two stories, two bedrooms, two bathrooms, one of which was en suite. The fridge was gleaming but empty except for five Stellas, two Vitaminwaters, and a neat stack of premade salads from Trader Joe's. Bunny herself was intimate with the salads, the three uniform slices of cucumber in the Classic Greek that was neither Greek nor classic but which she had acclimatized herself to over years of lunches at her desk, because it was a known quantity of 350 calories, fewer if you used less dressing, and required no preparation. And yet seeing them so neatly, so martially stacked in Francis's pristine fridge gave Bunny an uncanny feeling, one tinged with pinpricks of curiosity and gloom. Bunny was not quite at a place to joke with Francis, and in any case she had the perspicacity to see from his shyness about the townhouse that he would be wounded if she were to make fun, of the contents of this refrigerator, or of his sensible navy blue comforter—at home in a college dorm—or the row of identical blue shirts in his closet. Her own apartment was filled with carefully selected things she had appropriated from Maryellen or bought on Etsy after a few drinks.

Francis worked all the time and spent many days on the road, Bunny knew. This was why their courtship, such as it was, had been so halting and slow. It had taken three years from the day they first met on Phil and Estelle's rooftop for them to go on their first date. It had taken two more of Phil Miles's annual holiday fetes, two more awkward acknowl-edgments of prior meetings, canapé-greased hands wiped on cocktail napkins before shaking once again, mouths full of tartare. A week after the most recent of these parties, Francis had emailed Phil, who he knew solely in the context of being invited to his holiday party, and asked him for Bunny's number. Phil asked Bunny if she would mind his giving it out, and Bunny said that was fine. This was the most romantic thing that had ever happened to Bunny. It bespoke a boldness in Francis that immediately made him attractive to her. She remembered with an irritation tinged with eros that he had called her "baby girl" the first time they met.

Until now Bunny had been fitfully dating on Hinge and Tinder, fending off Phil's offers to set her up with this or that nice young man he had met during his hobnobbing. When Bunny and Francis met for their first date, a drink after work at a hotel bar equidistant between them, she was relieved to see that, while she didn't exactly remember him as handsome, he was handsome enough, with intent blue eyes and a good build. There was something slightly childlike about his face, but his body was hard, even intimidatingly so, sustained by early mornings in the gym. Bunny's fitness regime had been honed to twice-weekly Zumba or spin, going on a punishingly long walk on the Hershey Park trail in the evening, and not eating anything before 1:00 p.m., sometimes for several weeks at a time.

They had made a plan to be cozy in the predicted rain and watch *Homeland*, their show. Bunny was relieved that he demonstrated this ability to nest, to veg, to stay in and cuddle and watch TV instead of involving her in a marathon or seminar as she had worried he might, given his general focus and singleness of purpose. They ordered pesto pizza and now as the opening credits played they ate the pizza on his couch and drank the Stellas. There was a plaid throw arranged on the back of the couch, and Bunny wondered whether he had taken care to arrange it, whether it was a single, furtive sign of bower-building in this narrow, spartan house.

Bunny turned her head from the waterfall over the windows back to the TV, where the show's credits played. It was a new season, new credits. The old credits had always haunted Bunny with the audio headline from the Lockerbie bombing. This clip, like the show, like the craggy bonhomie of Saul Berenson, imparted to Bunny some faint familiarity, a funhouse mirror recalling those fearful moments of her youth, lying in the bed with inchoate worries of embassy bombings, plagued not only by her own memories but by whispered and inherited ones—the barracks bombing, Malcolm Kerr shot in the head at his desk, Bill Buckley tortured on video, planes falling from the sky. When the British military attaché in Athens was assassinated on the way to work, she thought of her father, who seemed so kind and defenseless. As a child Bunny had always gone to him for reassurance, for if Ted was afraid of the events of the world, he never said. She could remember being gnawed with worry listening to Bobbie Battista when Desert Storm started and American personnel overseas were instructed to be on alert. The American school in Athens closed for two days, and Bunny and her brothers stayed home watching TV with Maryellen. "The world has more good people than bad people," Ted always told her. The show brought her back to those feelings in some peculiar way, nonlinear like the jazz signifying its heroine's mental illness. But now the credits were different. Now they showed Hillary Clinton instead of Bill, a truck full of men heading toward some Asian mountain range, Osama bin Laden killed outside of Abbottabad. It was a new era.

Francis also had something comforting about him—he tended to have an answer to things, like her father, although Bunny would never have put it quite that way. Francis confided in her that he had always been drawn to intelligence, but he never got far in his CIA application. This is why, Bunny supposed, he was so interested in the show. She burrowed down and spread the blanket over them both.

On-screen, Carrie took her new position as Station Chief in Kabul. She gave the go-ahead for an air strike on a sought-after Muslim villain in Pakistan, hesitant at first, then resolute as her right hand, a Black man, walked her through it. The hit was stunningly rapid and silent, visible only on the screen in the command center, the only sound the background hum of office workers speaking into their headsets. Afterward her team brought her a birthday cake bearing the sobriquet "Drone Queen." In the rubble of the strike itself, a young Pakistani man searched the row of the dead for the bodies of his mother and sister. At the end of the episode the handsome Station Chief in Islamabad, his cover blown, was dragged from the car by a mob and beaten to death, an off-screen death whose inferred violence was sickening with its closeness.

"Oh my god," Bunny said, her hand over her mouth.

Francis walked around the small bar to the kitchen and got some Häagen-Dazs sorbet from the freezer. Bunny looked with alarm at the rain pelting the sliding door that opened onto the small strip of lawn at the back of the townhouse. "I can't believe how much it's raining," she said. "Is this normal?"

"I have no idea." Francis was from Missouri, a place Bunny could not picture. He served them scoops of sorbet so small that she protested, venturing humor, showing him her real self. "I need more sorbet than that, Jesus," she said. "Give me the scooper. You're a freak." He gave it to her with amusement and then kissed her. The ease of the moment was a relief after the tiptoeing awkwardness of some of their previous interactions. The sex itself had, fortunately, been courteous and inoffensive. A reasonable baseline, Bunny thought. Sex was always strange and sort of disgusting if you thought about it too much. Other parts had been good, too, tentatively. Evan had been a revelation with his basic decency after the string of assholes she had been drawn to in high school and college, and Francis seemed like a continuance of this upward trajectory. He was not a bro, exactly. He was incredibly focused, a little self-conscious, but able to take a joke. He was not a Republican, she had ascertained with relief, but a Decline to State, which was likewise a reasonable baseline. He read a physical newspaper. His favorite movie was *The Last of the Mohicans*. He had majored in poli-sci and played golf at a place Bunny learned was called

"Mizzou," and gone straight on to business school at Cornell. She wondered about his family. She felt he was not exactly rich, despite the golf, but she could not get a read on what exactly he was. All of her instruments were thrown off, here in the great middle and south of the country.

"You're staying over, right?" he asked, his arms on her sides. She was intoxicated by the unheimlich intimacy engendered by the sterile townhouse, as if they were two kids rattling around an abandoned hotel. The nearness of Francis, his solidity, the sound of the rain, the fizz of her second beer, the real but resistible urge for a third. She scanned his spotless counters for a bottle of wine. In its absence, she decided to lean in. "Come upstairs," she said, pulling him by the belt loop, performing. "Yes, ma'am," he said, with his own note of performance.

ALICIA

H ave you met Dad's girlfriend?" Bunny looked in the rearview mirror at her older brother, who was staring at his
phone with furrowed brow, the top of his head comically
close to the ceiling of the car, a brand-new Prius that Bunny had leased
earlier that year. The Glenn children had always been told by Maryellen
and Ted that leasing a car fed into usury, but Francis had pointed out
that if she insisted on a hybrid, the technology was changing so rapidly
that by the time the lease was over, she could painlessly hand in the car
for a more efficient version.

Bunny was at the wheel, Sofie beside her in the passenger seat,
watching with fascination as the roadside fell away from the speeding
car. When Bunny learned that John, Sofie, and Small Ted were making
Maryellen's dreams come true and coming to Texas for the holidays for
the first time in years, Bunny had worried about Sofie, whether it
would all be miserable for her. But Sofie had been a sport throughout
the days of edifying activity that Bunny and Maryellen planned. She
had brought her laser-like but appreciative eyes to every mile of the

terrain. She had admired the thousand-year-old cypress and the soupy green waters of the Adams Bayou and the magnificent orchids in the sultry greenhouse of the Shangri La Botanical Gardens. She had eaten mac 'n' cheese with burnt ends and hiked the Kirby trail at Big Thicket. She had driven around with them to admire Christmas lights in the tonier Beaumont neighborhoods. She had gone to Target and filled a cart with sunscreen and tampons. "They're cheaper here!" she said, noting Bunny's amusement.

And now they were speeding toward dinner at Uncle Warren and Aunt Christine's, which would not be edifying in the way of a thousand-year-old cypress. Maryellen had taken her own car, bringing along Small Ted, which freed Bunny to ask about their father, who would soon be arriving in Houston to visit his remaining relatives and take advantage of the novelty of all his children gathered in one place.

"I said, have you met Dad's girlfriend?" Bunny said, irritated. Bunny knew that John talked to their father more than she did. There was an unsettled, unspoken something between the older siblings, in the way they had apportioned the family relationships and responsibilities.

John looked up from his phone. "Alicia? Yeah."

"They came to see us in Kyiv," offered Sofie. "She's nice. She's young," she added wryly.

"Oh my god," said Bunny. "How young?"

"I don't know exactly, forties," said Sofie.

"Dad said she's an anthropologist?"

"Yeah," said Sofie. "She studies collective agriculture, I think."

"Does she live there full-time?" asked Bunny, who had to mine information while she could. Ted Senior had in the end gone back to Tajikistan as the public affairs counselor, his bid accepted.

"No," said John. "She's working on her dissertation or something."

"No, John," said Sofie. "She *finished* her dissertation. She's on sabbatical to finish her second book. She's a professor in England."

Bunny tried to imagine who such a person might be.

The announcement of Ted's visit had created trouble for Bunny, who had to break the news to Maryellen and then manage her mother's agitation at her father's thoughtlessness. Her agitation persisted even now that she was in hostess mode. She had not sat down once since the siblings had all arrived. She moved constantly around the house folding things and wiping down surfaces. Every once in a while she cornered Bunny and said, "Why does he have to come here? Why?" This had begun to annoy Bunny, and Bunny snapped at her that anyone could go anywhere they wanted, and she and Maryellen had been frosty to each other all week, although Bunny was nonetheless conscripted in the siege-like deployment of Maryellen's hospitality.

Maryellen and Sofie, however, were getting on like a house afire. Sofie had endeared herself by expressing great enthusiasm for the splendid garden Maryellen was making out of their grandmother's ladylike former lawn. Maryellen had in the last year taken the fifty-hour course, done the subsequent fifty hours of volunteering on the gardening phone lines, and become a Master Gardener. On visits home Bunny heard her on the phone and in the street with neighbors, advising people to plant natives and telling worried neophytes what to do with their sickly plants. Bunny was moved, in these moments, by her mother's helpful vivacity. Maryellen had met other gardeners from Jefferson County, Orange County, and even Galveston County, which had a larger membership and put together a nice newsletter for their part of the state. The garden she had made was now truly a thing of beauty and a haven for birds and other creatures. It had taken very little time, in the scheme of things, to totally remake the earth.

Maryellen had told Bunny about doing all of these things as they were happening, but somehow Bunny hadn't noticed the cumulative impact of Maryellen's transformation until she watched her interact with Sofie: showing her a new persimmon tree, or the rain barrel system she had installed around the mock-Tudor house. Bunny had lately been too focused on Maryellen's fury about Ted's visit to appreciate her accomplishments. It was nice for Sofie to interact with Maryellen instead, to bring nothing but an outsider's grace to her conversations with their mother, who was indeed a friendly and warm person. Bunny wished she had invited Francis, but Francis was working and then going to his parents' to meet his sister's new baby, people that Bunny hadn't met and still couldn't picture, although she was starting to get a faint outline—his mom was a licensed home organizer and his father was an accountant. His sister was a pediatrician. His grandparents had been a soybean farmer on one side and a Lutheran pastor on the other.

"I can't believe Warren and Christine moved out here," said John as Bunny took the exit for Lumberton.

"Yeah," said Bunny. "I haven't seen their place yet, but Mom says it's ginormous. Remember we used to think it was so fun to go to that house in Nederland? This one's apparently even bigger."

"White flight two: whiter and flightier," John said. Maryellen had begged him not to "get into it" with Warren tonight, recalling scenes of the past.

Warren and Christine's house was on a road with no sidewalks, wooded on one side and with a certain unfinished quality exacerbated by the fact that half the houses visible on the rest of the road were still under construction. It was as though some great hand had taken the former cul-de-sac of Warren and Christine's Nederland house and stretched it out into a giant loop, keeping the pitilessly shorn front lawns but expanding the space between the palatial homes. When they had parked, they all looked in silence for a moment, except Maryellen, who had seen the new house already. Small Ted looked out into the trees and expelled plumes of what looked like steam into the crisp December air, a respite after the somnolent heat of fall. "What is that?" Bunny asked, reaching for Small Ted's hand.

"It's a vape," said her little brother. "It was in the swag bag at a tournament." Maryellen slapped him on the back of his head. "It's not smoking," he protested. Their little brother still seemed small and bearlike to Bunny, dressed in a black T-shirt and jeans, unshaven, a little wrinkled, some of the beakiness of John and Ted Senior but stouter now than before. He was out of college and played poker full-time, to the great consternation of Maryellen. Bunny did not know what Ted Senior thought about it but imagined it was not good.

"Good lord," said Sofie, taking in the house.

"Jesus," said Bunny. It was gargantuan, a sort of Alamo farmhouse, and from a distance had a flattened pyramidal aspect. Bunny patted Sofie's back. "Welcome to America, baby," she said in her poor approximation of a Texas accent.

The house was lit up, and Christine opened the door and welcomed them in, ushering them into an expansive mudroom to remove their coats and then into an open-concept kitchen, where Warren greeted them while Christine poured glasses of Syrah. Christine was a plump, good-looking, relentlessly efficient woman with brown hair and indifferent highlights. She had been a nurse when she and Warren met but left the job when her kids were born. It was she who had ferried Tyler and Ashley to soccer and tap and Girl Scouts and Boy Scouts and cheerleading and football and activities at the Church of Christ seemingly every day of her life. Their cousins were not at dinner. Tyler had a successful window-blind-installation company in Dallas, where he was having Christmas with his fiancé, and Ashley, who taught second grade at a private school, was in Cancun with her in-laws. Now that they were launched, Christine was getting her realtor's license.

Warren was a tall, fairly good-looking man with a slight paunch, with youthful black hair streaked with gray. He hugged all of them, John included, and gave Sofie an approving look before hugging her too. Bunny asked with morbid fascination for a tour of the house and together they trooped through the rooms, looking at the small gym room, the enormous walk-in closet in the master bedroom, the pantry that was half the size of the kitchen and stocked with clear plastic containers and filled with snack foods and pastas.

"I've never seen so many paper towels!" said Sofie in a way that she made sound admiring. There were at least eighteen rolls, reams of paper towels, a Great Wall of paper towels. Somewhere there must be a Giza of toilet paper, a jug of detergent the size of a Bamyan Buddha. Sofie was vibrating with the friendliness that had characterized her presence throughout the trip, but Bunny felt utterly dispirited, as she sometimes did when confronted with these American scenes.

In the hallway Sofie stopped to look at a peculiar curved stick, artfully hung on the wall. Bunny vaguely remembered it from the old house.

"You've got the doodlebug!" said Maryellen with surprised recognition. They all peered at the object.

"What's a doodlebug?" asked Sofie.

"It was a contraption people used to take out to look for oil near Spindletop during the gusher days," said Warren. "Guys would set out a shingle saying they could find untapped wells and get paid to wander around with a stick."

Sofie was fascinated. "Is this an . . . ancestral doodlebug?" she asked, and Warren laughed. "It was Grandaddy's, but it was just a gag. Someone gave it to him, I think." Maryellen and Warren's far-back forebears were Sorbs, the "smallest ethnic group in Texas," who had come from Lusatia to Houston in 1854. The descendants of their particular branch made their way to Beaumont in the Spindletop boom years, a lawless sepia-toned era, during which few people actually got rich.

"You know about Spindletop?" Warren asked Bunny and John, worried that they would not. "We know," said John.

"That was the original gusher," said Warren proudly. Bunny had read about it in the Turnbridge reading room, the salt dome that made every other salt dome a sudden possibility.

Christine made creamy Cajun chicken pasta for dinner, and they ate it with yellow garlic bread and green salad at the long dining room table, a huge window looking out onto the inky dark fields behind the house, woods at the end of the acre-long tract of property. An outdoor bulb illuminated a patio and firepit surrounded by chairs. A single bug buzzed anxiously in the beam of light.

Sofie asked Warren about his job. "Have you always worked for Motiva?"

Warren nodded. "Since when it was still Texaco."

"It's a good job," Sofie said more than asked.

"Oh, yeah," he said. "Someone at Valero told me they only leave up operator postings for a day. They get, like, five thousand applications for a single job. It's one of the only jobs where you can basically guarantee six figures without a degree."

Christine looked at Warren. "It's hard work though," she said, looking at the group. "Four days on, four days off." He waved at her. "If nothing's going wrong, I can put my feet up, even watch a DVD. Don't tell anyone that part," he said.

"When did the Saudis buy their interest?" Sofie asked. Warren looked surprised. "You know your stuff," he said.

"It's my job," she said modestly.

"Sofie's a journalist," John reminded them officiously.

"Sometime in the eighties," he said. "They went in with Texaco. Then Texaco sold their share to Chevron, and then Chevron sold their piece to Shell and called it Motiva. So that's half Shell, half Aramco."

Sofie was nodding. "But I think this will expire soon, no? It will be wholly owned by Aramco."

Warren shrugged his shoulders, said, "Que será, será." Bunny raised her eyebrows.

"Really?" Maryellen interjected. "The Saudis will own the whole thing?"

Sofie nodded with amusement.

"One day we'll be a colony of Saudi Arabia," said John derisively.

Sofie looked again at Warren. Bunny looked at Small Ted, who was staring off into space, taking in the elaborate window treatments, a plaque that read "Bless this house." She wondered if it had been weed in his little electronic cigarette.

"So you like working there?" Sofie asked.

"It's a great job in a lot of ways." Warren seemed pleased to have the attention of an attractive woman, someone asking him so many questions. Warren had always brimmed with opinions, wanted only a new audience to voice them.

"Course I drive like a bat out of hell as soon as I get off the clock," he said. "Kind of a windows-up, door-locked situation down there in Port Arthur." He chuckled. Bunny tilted her head and looked at her brother, who had been waiting for a moment just as this, which Warren would never in his life fail to deliver.

Sofie looked at Warren with innocence. "Oh, why is that?"

He shrugged, reticent. "You know, just gangs and other kinds of crimes and stuff down there."

John made a sound. "You mean because Black people live there." He looked at his uncle with intensity etched across his face, which was almost gaunt now. His hair was shorter that when Bunny had last seen him and stuck up in places from where he had pulled off his hat. He wore a plaid flannel shirt under a sweater that Bunny recognized as having belonged to their grandfather and which John must have plundered from a camphor-scented closet in Beaumont. He had vertical lines on each side of his mouth. He was wearing glasses after years of contacts that now dried his eyes too much, and he looked like a handsome schoolteacher, which Bunny supposed he was.

"John," said Maryellen, warning.

Warren folded his arms. "There's a lot of poverty down there. Bad crime."

"It's got poverty because Black people couldn't buy houses any- where except there and North End," John said pedantically. John pointed at Sofie. "Ask her! She knows more than me."

Sofie smiled at Warren, a more conciliatory figure now than she had been with the Nordic boys on the island, her own people. "Black people were excluded from the best oil-industry jobs then funneled to the industrial areas to live. They call these places 'sacrifice zones,'" she said.

"Like half the kids in Port Arthur have asthma and all the adults have cancer," John said, almost pleadingly. Bunny didn't think there was any point arguing with someone like Warren and Christine.

"There's Black guys who work with me at Motiva. Great guys," Warren said authoritatively. "Not everyone down there is like that though."

Christine looked at Sofie with a saccharine, patronizing expression. "I don't know what it's like in Sweden, but here it kind of has just worked out for people to just live in their own groups."

John looked at her with disgust. "It didn't 'work out,' Aunt Christine; that's literally segregation."

Christine had a temper and now she raised one eyebrow sky-high. "Please don't put words in my mouth," she said. "What I'm *saying* is they tried it in Beaumont, get the public housing that was in the North End to get torn down and rebuilt over in the West End, and a lot of the African Americans didn't *want* to go. They *wanted* to stay where they were." She drained the rest of her wine. "You can tell us about what's going on in the Ukraine, but don't act like you know exactly how everything works down here. It is not *racist* to want to live with people who have similar values as you."

John looked at her with disdain. "Is that why you moved here?" he said mockingly. Christine smiled at him in a bless-your-heart way Bunny had always found frightening. "Why yes it is."

Incredibly, Warren seemed less combative, perhaps because of Sofie's open, pretty face and dowdy but form-fitting turtleneck. Her hair was in a low pony that fell over her shoulder and draped over one breast. "Well," he said. "I do remember Daddy"—he and Maryellen called their parents "Mother" and "Daddy," to the Glenn children's great amusement—"Daddy did say when the Blacks came into Beaumont for the wartime jobs they got run off." Then his face closed. "But it is getting crowded in Nederland. They built on that field that was behind us, and we just didn't have the room anymore. Not everything is about being *racist*," he said.

"Mr. Barack Obama sure has made things divisive," said Christine, with a sly expression, almost an expression of pleasure, as though she relished the consternation she knew such a remark would cause. Warren nodded his head in agreement. Bunny, even, was moved to comment. "Come on," she said, and John said, "Are you serious?" in something that approached a yell. Small Ted made a kind of nihilistic squawk of amusement, and Bunny looked at him. What was her little brother's *deal*, she wondered. Sofie had rolled her lips inside her mouth and was looking out of the side of her eyes at John.

Maryellen put an end to things as handily as she might have once subdued a plane full of fractious passengers. "Now y'all stop. Stop it right now." Bunny noted the *y'all* with curiosity. Maryellen patted her mouth with her napkin and put it on the table. "Somebody take me outside," she said. "I'm drooling over all the outdoor space here. Christine." She said Christine's name with firmness. "What are y'all going to plant?" A second *y'all*.

Christine poured herself some more wine. "The HOA has all these rules," she said, waving her hands.

"Well let me help you," said Maryellen. "Come on and let's look." She stood and Small Ted shoved his chair back from the table and stood too, presumably to spend time with his vape.

Warren called to the women as they retreated outside, "Save some space for the pool." He turned to Sofie and said, "This is the house where we finally build a pool, by god."

The housing arrangements for Ted Senior's visit to Houston had been a challenge. With customary thrift Ted had asked to stay in Bunny's one-bedroom apartment, but then this would leave nowhere for Sofie, John, and Small Ted, and they couldn't go back and forth between Beaumont and Houston for logistical but also emotional reasons, for Maryellen's sake, Bunny said. As the de facto host and organizer, she told her father and Alicia to get a hotel, and she put John, Sofie, and Small Ted in her apartment, Small Ted on the couch. She would stay at Francis's townhouse.

Bunny had been very anxious about having other people in her space. She had it professionally cleaned before she left, using a service she read about on Yelp. She went around beforehand appraising how her apartment looked. She had stolen various items from Maryellen and from the Beaumont storage unit. She had some beautiful painted Greek pottery and Greek embroidered pillow cases for her throw pillows. She had bought replica vintage travel posters, Côte d'Azur and Cairo and Buenos Aires, and had them framed. She had snowy dish towels and linens from a local homeware shop and a set of good wine glasses from Sur La Table. Her plates and bowls were from Ikea and perfectly fine. On her coffee table was *Greek Style*, which she had taken from Maryellen. On her small bookshelf she had *The Joy of Cooking*. She had her suite of college books: *The Scarlet Letter*, *Heart of Darkness*, *Things Fall Apart*, *The Sun Also Rises*, *Nineteen Eighty-Four*, and several anthologies of American literature, each with its yellow "Used" sticker. She had *The Omnivore's Dilemma*, *Blink*, the collected stories of F. Scott Fitzgerald, *The Stand*, *A Thousand Acres*, *Bridget Jones's Diary*, *The Poisonwood Bible*, *Lonesome Dove*, *The Joy Luck Club*, and *Anna Karenina*. She had *Ali and Nino*, the same copy she had read on the couch in Baku. She had *The Prize*, acknowledged as the bible for understanding the history of oil but which she thought was boring. She put out several *New Yorker*s, which she bought when she went to Barnes & Noble to browse every so often, to feel connected to a world of culture that her immediate existence did not quite provide. Before the visit she got several plants and put them on the windowsill. She filled the refrigerator with salami and cheese and olives and sparkling waters and Lone Star beer.

On the appointed day they left Beaumont and drove to Houston, where she installed Ted and Sofie and John and their bags in the apartment. As she anticipated, Sofie prowled around the apartment looking at everything, even Bunny's calendar, which, exactly like her mother, she had tacked up in the kitchen next to the place where she charged her cell phone.

Sofie and John elected to go with her to pick up Ted and Alicia, while Ted stayed behind, watching Bunny's TV and vaping into the herbaceous candle-scented air of her apartment. Bunny navigated the eternal hideous snarl of the George Bush Intercontinental Airport and parked the Prius. They went in and waited in the concourse until John, taller than everyone, pointed down the crowded hall. "There," he said. Bunny saw her father, completely gray now, tall, imposing, wearing desert-like pants and hiking boots. "God," Bunny said. "Here comes Lawrence of Arabia." Next to him was a very small and well-proportioned, striking woman with dark hair pulled up in a bun on the top of her head. She looked adult but clearly three-quarters of a generation younger than Ted. She wore skinny jeans and scuffed black cowboy boots and a blue button-up shirt. She had a round face but a beautifully defined jaw, Bunny reflexively cataloged with envy, and sculpted eyebrows. Ted arrived before his children and side-hugged each of them, followed by emphatic pats. He looked emotional, Bunny thought. She felt simultaneously a flood of affection and a deep unwillingness to go through with the rest of the events of the weekend.

Her father put his arm on the woman's shoulder. "John and Sofie, you know Alicia," and Sofie leaned forward to hug her. "Bunny," said her father. "This is Alicia."

"Nice to meet you," said Bunny, sticking out a hand.

"Nice to meet you," said Alicia in a surprisingly low and rich voice, a voice with gravity.

"Yes, well," said Ted. "I see our bags."

After Ted and Alicia had been given a chance to freshen up at their hotel, they all went to a nice Italian restaurant in Montrose, where they stood around a high-top by the bar while they waited for a table.

"What's it like to be in America?" Bunny said brightly, looking at her brother and Sofie and her dad and Alicia.

"Everyone's fat," said John matter-of-factly. "I forgot about that. You really notice it when you leave."

"Bunny's not fat," said Sofie, also matter-of-factly.

"Well," said John, and hit his brother in the stomach. "Teddy Bear is kind of fat." Ted punched him back.

"I'm not fat because I'm always a little bit hungry," said Bunny to Sofie, feeling that she could say these things to her. She had been with her the night of the Scandinavian bacchanal. It seemed she knew everything about Bunny. "My nature is fat, though." Out of the corner of her eye Bunny watched Alicia watch them with faint amusement on her face. Alicia was also not fat.

"Houston is cool," Sofie said, looking around. "I was not expecting this. It has so many parks and bars and things." Bunny also felt that Houston was cool, although she knew she did not have any meaningful connection to the cool part, the bars where people had gorgeous tattoos and wore crop tops and fanciful denim and were not all white and did not work in oil and gas. She appreciated being able to see, tangentially, this element of the city, to sample the foods and music of many nations, to have access to its multicultural riches at the most superficial level.

Ted Senior looked at his older son and Sofie. "What's going on in Ukraine?" he said.

"It's bad," said John. "I mean, there's a ceasefire now, but they say it gets broken every day. It doesn't seem over." Bunny knew only very vaguely that there was something going on in Ukraine, heard it in passing on NPR in the morning.

"What's happening?" she asked.

"Russia annexed Crimea," said her father, "and now Russia-backed separatists are trying to chip off parts of the east, Donbas."

Bunny looked at John and Sofie. "That's scary," she said. "Is that close to you guys?" realizing this was probably stupid, Ukraine was huge. She lamented her childhood knowledge of the world atlas.

Sofie shook her head. "No, it's the other side of the country," she said. "But it's unsettling. It's not good."

When they were seated, Sofie asked Alicia about her book project. Bunny had until now mostly pretended her father's girlfriend was not there. She simply did not know what to say. How dare this woman.

"It's about the role of women in cotton production in the post-Soviet transition," Alicia said in her gravelly voice.

"I thought Uzbekistan is where they grew all the cotton," said Sofie.

"All across central Asia," said Alicia, smiling graciously as though she was used to ignorant comments. Bunny pictured her at the front of a lecture hall. "My mother was from Iran, so I get by better in Tajik than Uzbek." Bunny slotted Alicia's face into the bracket provided by this new information.

"So is that the major export?" asked John.

"For agriculture, yes," said Alicia.

"And it's very much a group effort," their father interjected. "I went out and picked the cotton," he said proudly. Alicia smiled and put her hand on his shoulder, at which Bunny felt profound dismay.

"Yes, it's a collective obligation from Soviet times, so teachers and government officials and basically everyone in the community is supposed to come and take shifts picking the cotton for processing and export," Alicia said.

"So everyone does it?" asked Sofie with interest, ever the communist, Bunny thought. Bunny did not want to take any shifts picking cotton.

"Basically, yes," said Alicia. "It's nominally optional, but if they choose not to do it, there is a lot of community disapproval, plus you have to pay to delegate your shift to a laborer."

Sofie was looking at her with fascination.

"Unfortunately there's a trade deficit, very much so," said Alicia. "But farmers aren't allowed to plant anything else except cotton, even though they earn nothing for cotton because there is a glut."

"Unintended consequence," interjected Ted Senior. He had always spoken to his children about unintended consequences. One of his Peace Corps trainers had told his cohort a story about building enclosed ovens in huts in rural India to keep women from burning their eyes in the smoke. The smoke had kept the thatch roofs warm, and snakes had liked living in them. When the snakes left, mice and rats proliferated, and the women hated having the mice and rats more than they hated having their eyes and throats roasted by smoke. They abandoned the ovens so the snakes could return. Bunny had never exactly known what the moral of this story was.

"Where does the cotton go?" asked Bunny, now curious in spite of herself.

Alicia stuck her hand out. "Into everything you are wearing," she said. Bunny involuntarily glanced at her own outfit, skinny jeans and low boots, a perfect striped long-sleeved tee from Madewell.

"The fashion industry is very dependent on the cotton from Central Asia, for sweatshops," Alicia said. Bunny thought for a moment of her tortuous report on H&M's supply chain but couldn't remember what exactly she had written. "It's very opaque, the industry." Bunny considered with fascination the differences between this woman, not so much older than herself, and her mother. Alicia seemed content to sit and be asked questions, to receive the questions like gifts from acolytes, whereas Maryellen always had a question at the ready. What, she wondered, did this woman get from her father that she could not get from someone else? Bunny preferred not to think further on it.

"A hyperobject," said Sofie, suddenly. "I just learned this term."

Alicia smiled. "Oh, yes, me too," she said. "It's very interesting." Bunny felt left out. She could see how Sofie and Alicia were natural allies, had things in common, smart and highly informed women.

"What's a hyperobject?" she asked. Small Ted had his elbows on the table and was looking around at everyone.

"It's something so big and sticky with so many parts that it can't be seen, something that touches so many other things," said Alicia, assuming a didactic air that gave her height beyond her short stature. "I think the philosopher who invented the term had many caveats about its use, I don't remember all of them."

"Like global warming," said Sofie. "Or the oil industry." She elbowed Bunny.

Alicia tilted her head. "That's right," she said. "Your father said you worked for an oil company." She raised her eyebrows ever so slightly.

"Well," said Bunny. "I work for the non-oil part of it, the part that is moving away from oil; we are targeting batteries and energy storage, not oil." This was still the plan, at any rate. She considered the new word, played with it, rolled it around on her tongue silently. Hyperobject. It made sense to Bunny as an organizing principle.

Bunny was more educated now, but she still struggled to understand how the industry worked, what Turnbridge did, what anyone did. She had tried to break it down into the basics. There was upstream, that was exploration and production, that was Turnbridge Oil Company, for example. They needed oilfield services, Halliburton and Baker Hughes and so on. She had learned that Sofie was of course right, that everyone basically did business with Halliburton, although there were a thousand others of varying size. Then there was midstream, pipelines and storage and transportation; that was like Enbridge and Kinder Morgan. Then there was the downstream, refining, like Warren at Motiva, or Valero or Marathon, and then the petrochemical companies that made plastics and face lotion and basically everything you might ever buy in a supermarket or Target or Neiman Marcus or Walmart, everything they would stick in your arm in a hospital or use to listen to your heart.

What made it confusing—one thing that made it confusing, anyway—was that many companies were integrated, meaning they had upstream, midstream, and downstream divisions. The national oil companies—like Aramco and Statoil—and the supermajors—like ExxonMobil or Chevron or BP—of course they had a hand in every single piece of it. But then Valero, who was downstream, also had some arm that was midstream; it was just called something else. And the oil field services, Halliburton, Schlumberger, it seemed to Bunny, provided service in every single direction, to every part of the stream. Then there was the legal, Baker Botts, or the accounting, Baker Tilly. Names and names and names. There were endless permutations.

And this was before even approaching the financialization, the market side, the trading and private-equity part. Half these companies seemed to have trading wings that made financial bets on what the other divisions did, or hedged in case the main revenue stream was obstructed by something else. And then there were the companies that seemed to do a little bit of everything that violently moved the earth. KBR was like this, employer of the blonde-haired Meghan at the networking happy hour. Lockheed Martin had an energy services division, alongside its missiles, planes, and rockets. And there were the engineering companies that seemed to have taken the broadest-possible view of what engineering was. These were the mega companies— Bechtel, Fluor, AECOM—who built everything, including pipelines and oil platforms, and sometimes staffed them too, but were themselves not oil companies or staffing companies and could not slip neatly into one place in the stream. Every time Bunny learned one thing, the map she had constructed in her mind shifted.

"Hyperobject," she said. "It makes sense. It does touch everything." She touched the plastic tablecloth, feeling wise, suddenly. "Absolutely everything."

Ted Senior made a noise in his seat. "This is an ironic moment to bring up some family business," he said, and they all looked at him. "Remember the place your mom used to call the Taco Bell field?" They all nodded. "Oh god," said John.

"Your grandfather used to get some money from it every month, not a lot; it was split with all the other owners. 'Mailbox money,' they called it," he said, a little ruefully. Bunny finished her negroni and asked for another one. The evening required lubrication; she could only get through it thus. It seemed everyone was feeling this way, except Alicia, who had one glass of wine and switched to club soda. Her father was on his second or third.

"Apparently in the last couple of years the oil price has gotten high enough that they thought it was worth taking another look at the old wells. Now they're planning to do something called enhanced recovery, where they send pressurized carbon dioxide into the well and blast out the remaining oil that's stuck there." Ted Senior sipped his water. Bunny thought about this.

"Like . . . fracking?" She knew abstractly that fracking was not good. Turnbridge did it, in the New Mexico part of the Permian, knowledge she did not dwell on. John looked indignant.

Sofie answered for Ted. "No, fracking is secondary oil recovery; this is the step after that, tertiary." Ted nodded and Sofie went on. "The oil companies are saying it's the most practical way to do carbon capture because there is an incentive built into it, to get more oil," she said.

"Yes," Ted said, sipping again.

"Which is of course bullshit," she added.

Ted looked a little sheepish, but he was not easily fazed. "It's using carbon dioxide taken from somewhere else to blast the old wells. And then they store it somewhere, I suppose."

Sofie took a piece of bread from the basket and tore it in half. "Environmentalists are of course highly skeptical about this claim."

"I'm sure they are," said Ted pleasantly. "But at any rate, if this all happens, there's a good chance I'll get a pretty substantial monthly income. Which would then go to you."

John looked ill. Bunny felt mildly jubilant to see him and Sofie touched more directly by the hyperobject, whatever it was.

"I can't believe Grandma and Grandpa Glenn lived off a fucking oil well," John said.

Ted shrugged. "They didn't exactly live off it. And that nice retirement home wasn't free. In the end they didn't end up with all that much." Bunny knew that in the scheme of the Glenn finances, it was the cousins who were rich, not Ted's parents. Well, not rich-rich. Not Stanhope rich. Or Turnbridge rich. Not Miles rich.

"Can you do something to shut down production?" John asked gravely.

Bunny laughed. "He owns one-seventy-somethingth of it," she said. "Is he supposed to throw a grenade down the well?"

Ted smiled weakly at his older son, his buddy. "The next election will do more than anything I can do to determine what happens. The recovery is only valuable to them if the oil prices are high enough. But of course if oil prices are too high, then the populace riots at the gas pump." He drank more wine. "Then again, if the idea is that oil needs to be carbon neutral, then this option may be appealing to the lease-holders regardless of what the oil prices are."

Bunny remembered her father's practiced pragmatism, his measured way of speaking.

"Another thing," Ted Senior said, "if you can agree with the other descendants of the original owners, all 70-something of them, you might be able to sell the land for development someday. You'll still keep the subsurface rights."

When they finished their meal and walked toward the hotel, Sofie broke off to smoke a cigarette and Alicia followed her. Bunny watched them a for a moment, marveling at how they seemed like natural peers, Sofie less stylish but just as striking. They were beautiful, slightly weathered bookends, and one was sleeping with her brother and one with her father. Bunny sighed at the perverse thought and walked to stand with them, hoping that they would not make chummy jokes about Glenn men. Sofie handed her a cigarette. Bunny hesitated for a moment, then looked at Alicia. "I was going to say my dad would freak out if I smoked a cigarette in front of him, but clearly he has, uh, relaxed his policies." She realized as she spoke the words that they probably sounded bitchy, and Alicia responded in a tone that was cordial. "I'm sure he wouldn't be too surprised by it." For the first time it occurred to Bunny that her father had discussed her, Bunny, with this woman she didn't know.

"Do you like Dushanbe?" Bunny asked Alicia.

"It has a lot of charms," she said, smiling, and Bunny supposed that one of the charms was her own father. "You'll have to come and see us," said Alicia. "We have a nice little guest room for visitors. We can get to know each other," she smiled. Bunny found this ominous.

"Ah," she said. "That would be nice," she said, leaning her head toward the flame cupped in Alicia's manicured hand.

2015

$55.88/$32.26

ROCKY OAKS

Bunny was in her bra and underwear, laying out her makeup brushes on a towel on the vanity of their bathroom at the Westlake Village Marriott Residence Inn, when she heard the beep of Francis's key in the lock. For a moment she contemplated covering herself with a towel, as though he were a stranger. Before now, she and Francis had never traveled together, never shared a room other than their respective bedrooms, never more than a few nights at a time. Theirs was a courtship that took place in fits and starts. And now they had been together for nearly two whole weeks, a trip that culminated here in the Westlake Village Marriott Residence Inn. In some ways it had been the most romantic two weeks of Bunny's life.

Francis appeared in the doorway, his face flushed and his hair tousled and sweaty. "Wow," he said. "Hi, sexy." She had reflexively curled herself over the vanity, but when she turned toward him, the brush she would use to dust Bare Minerals in Very Light over her face gripped like a pen in one hand, she took in his red cheeks, the glint in his eye, and felt a stirring. She was thirty-two years old and had recently become fearful, as she perused articles about Korean skin care trends and slowly began spending more and more money on products every month, that certain elements of youth might soon pass her by. She was wearing pretty underwear, underwear she had bought specifically for this trip, the wedding of one of Francis's friends from business school he described as "a brother." This was the first time Bunny had met his friends and peers from B-school, as they all called it. When she pictured them she felt the old familiar concurrent sense of opprobrium and desire that they find her suitable. She had lost seven pounds rapidly by eating one large meal at dinnertime, generally composed of salad and a can of tuna fish. Last night, at the rehearsal dinner, which took place in the cavernous private room of a Michelin-starred restaurant, she had felt nervous but luminous in her Ted Baker dress.

Francis had been gone all morning playing golf with the groom and the other groomsmen. She dusted him on the nose with her powder brush, and he put his hands on her waist and leaned it, redolent of beer.

"Did you bro out?" she said, teasingly, and he kissed her neck. "Wait," she said, and she woke up her phone on the counter to see the time. "It's two o'clock. You're supposed to be on the bro bus at two thirty." His hands were in the front of her underwear and she considered that this had never happened before, a spontaneous daytime overture. "You better make it quick," she said, returning her brush and, inspired, leaning against the counter, her ass pressed out toward him.

"Oh my god," he said, falling to his knees. Bunny left her body and surveyed the scene from above, allowing the aesthetics of it to bring her into a feeling of arousal. She was in good lingerie in the bathroom of a reasonably nice hotel, and her boyfriend, who had a great body, too good, even, was on his knees behind her. Francis still sometimes felt like a stranger to her, a thought that made her hover farther above, but when she imagined that he was a different kind of stranger, someone unnamed, nearly faceless, when she thought about this she could return to her body, maintain the two states of mind, within the body and without, that would allow her to come.

Francis made it into the shower and out the door at 2:28, the bag containing his tuxedo and shoes remembered by Bunny pressed into his arms as he left. She returned to her place in front of the mirror, her brushes and products before her. She had gotten a blowout that morning in a salon she found on Yelp, and she twisted and clipped it up to prevent further damage from the shower steam. Her face was red and she re-covered it carefully with a primer she had researched on Reddit, and then her Bare Minerals, and then her blush. She filled in her eyebrows and brushed them. She lined the top of her eyes and put on eye shadow. She pressed her eyelashes into the curler. She applied mascara with her mouth open.

At three forty-five she opened a beer from the minibar and got into her dress, a black V-neck fitted sheath with symmetrical watercolor hothouse flowers she now worried was both not summery enough and not formal enough for a black-tie-optional wedding, the first she had ever attended. She sat on the edge of the bed and finished her beer before going back into the bathroom for an appraising look in its bright light. She felt pleased to find that she was actually a little bit in love with the way she looked. She spritzed Jo Malone on her wrists and neck and dusted her forehead again as a preventative measure. She coated her lips with a plumping gloss, put the gloss and her eyeshadow and compact and phone and key and ID and credit card into her clutch, also purchased specially for the wedding, and slipped into black patent leather pumps with a slight platform. She put a stick of gum into her mouth, turned out the lights, and stepped into the frigid hallway of the hotel.

She joined the scrum of wedding guests at the appointed entrance to wait for the shuttle. She scanned the crowd of guests, mostly young people, white and Asian, and saw with relief that she was neither overdressed nor underdressed. She was first into the back of the second shuttle, and a raucous cluster followed her on. "Can we sit with you?" asked a friendly-looking white girl in a short, strapless hot-pink dress with a peplum waist, clearly already a few drinks in. She slid in and directed her friends, three good-looking men and another woman, into the adjacent rows.

"I love your dress," said Bunny. "I love *your* dress," the pink dress said, and Bunny was warmed by the swift and immediate kinship of drunk women, although this drunk woman immediately became wrapped up in a game of catch-up with a couple sitting across the aisle. She worked for Apple, did something with commercial real estate, and flew to places in East Asia every month. Bunny looked out the window and eavesdropped, envying the woman both her innate air of youthful vivacity and her professional importance. She seemed *fun*. That she made an incredible amount of money went without saying. The group she was with seemed to have all gone to Tufts. In Bunny's taxonomy of colleges, this was for people who were possibly less preppy than the people at Connecticut College but smarter. Definitely with better grades.

Bunny wanted to ask how this woman had gotten her job. She had been strategizing with Francis about this during their long vacation, which had started with a flight to Seattle and a rental car and moved into a slow trip through the rainforests of the Washington coast, down through Oregon and into the redwoods, meandering between the One, I-5, and US 101. They listened to audiobooks as they drove. Francis was lightly obsessed with September 11 histories, because in his mind September 11 was a glaring example of unforgivable process error. Bunny had protested the selection of books in his Audible library, books whose titles made ominous reference to looming towers and black banners, but as they listened and drove, she was caught up. For one, the books affirmed the Glenn family's longstanding disdain for the CIA, which Maryellen felt endangered regular diplomats by posing at embassies as something they were not. They also informed Bunny that the group in the joint FBI-CIA office that was supposed to prevent things like September 11 was largely composed of young women, and that they had derisively been called "The Manson Family" by their colleagues. There were a lot of women involved in the whole thing, actually, Bunny was surprised to learn. She was likewise surprised to learn that perhaps the first men to be extraordinarily rendered, by some iteration of this cadre, were snatched up in Baku just after the embassy bombings. Bunny felt a shiver at this. She had been there! It had not seemed like a threatening place, she told Francis. Francis told her that whenever he was tempted to obfuscate a mistake at work, or hoard information, or big-time someone, he remembered September 11. Bunny had laughed but stopped when she saw how hurt Francis looked. His current consulting project was streamlining returns processing to mitigate loss and maximize profit for a major athleisure retailer.

Somewhere during the trip, as they traveled these long stretches of road, as they walked around in beautiful old damp trees holding hands, as they drove through sprawl and bonded over their shared hatred of the ugliness of most American commercial zones—something that surprised and pleased Bunny about the typically pragmatic Francis— as they listened to the story of the nameless woman who senselessly detained the wrong man at a black site for months and months and months, Francis told her that statistically speaking the only way for someone to earn a lot more money was to leave a job and find another one with a higher salary.

The thought of doing this made Bunny feel uneasy and vaguely treacherous. Bunny had become—in addition to being the de facto cohead of marketing with a woman she cordially loathed named Margaret who was an idiot and Frank Turnbridge's niece—Phil's right hand, and Frank's right index finger. Phil could not send so much as a two-sentence email without Bunny looking it over first, while Frank trusted her to the extent that he looped her in on things that were decidedly outside the Turnbridge Energy Solutions purview. And yet every four months, Phil would say, "You have to aim higher," almost willing her to get a new job, and she would come up with some scheme to learn more. Right now she was learning how to make websites, overseeing the development of a separate, standalone Turnbridge Energy Solutions website while also fixing the Turnbridge Oil Company website. She had traded in Microsoft Word and its secrets for tutorials about WordPress templates. She maintained a spreadsheet of every energy event and conference taking place around the country and world.

She had more work than she could do, but it felt good to do it. And in many ways Phil had been making good on his promises. After months of strategic chatting on Bunny's part he had asked her to propose a budget for what she was calling Outreach and Communications, which would allow her to travel to conferences and network. Francis chided her, but he also said that loyalty was undervalued in the modern era.

Bunny occasionally looked at job descriptions. She had seen communications positions that made her feel a tug of ambition and want. When she read requirements like "enthusiastic communications specialist who knows how to craft compelling content about people, projects, skills, and culture," she recognized something she could do. But it was also upsetting, even as she was wrapped increasingly in the social world of Houston young professionals, to read the names attached to these job descriptions: ExxonMobil, Bechtel Energy, Baker Hughes. She felt it would be crossing some gulf. Something balked. And she also felt certain she was not truly qualified for these positions. The big companies seemed frighteningly standardized and corporate. There was something loose, wild, flexible, about her arrangement with Phil and Frank Turnbridge. A family dynamic.

The wedding was at a vineyard in Malibu. Bunny had never been to California and was mesmerized by the terrain as the shuttle took the curved rocky roads in the sun-baked canyon. It looked like Greece to Bunny, and she felt such a powerful feeling of homesickness she wanted to pull out her phone and get on Kayak to find a flight. She and Francis had talked about going to Greece, but she had put it off for reasons she couldn't quite articulate. What if he didn't like it, the Paris of the Balkans? If he said something against it, she would have to leave him. He was slightly fastidious, in his way. She couldn't tell how he would travel. She put her face close to the window, gasping as the villa came into view at the top of the mountain. The shuttle let them out at the top of the winding road, and they spilled out in front of the formidable stone house. Handlers ushered them through a garden path and down a precipitous road to the helicopter pad, which had been set up with a flowered altar.

As Bunny took her seat and accepted a fan and a parasol from an attendant, she saw Francis standing in the row of groomsmen and made eye contact. The groom was his B-school roommate, who now worked at Bain, and he was marrying a colleague. They were both vice presidents, which Francis had explained was like the bare minimum you had to be as a consultant by this point. Francis saw her, held her gaze and mouthed "wow" like a boy in a movie. A hot breeze blew obligingly over the rocky promontory where the guests waited.

A violin and a cello on the grass by the helicopter pad began to play "At Last," and everyone stood. Bunny looked behind her and saw the bride, a gorgeous Asian American woman in a bright white strapless dress, a tight bodice with a skirt that exploded out into exuberant yet controlled tulle panels. It was a world apart from the boring dresses currently being touted as classic, dresses Bunny had seen in a million wedding photos on Facebook: dresses with sweetheart necklines and lace overlay that were formfitting through the hips and then trumpeted out as they approached the knee, flowing into a train. The bride had the kind of collarbones that were so symmetrical and gently prominent Bunny absentmindedly put her fingers to her own and traced them under her flesh. A necklace would have been superfluous, and instead the bride wore a jeweled hairpiece in her simple updo. Her gown, the venue, everything called out couture, bold but incredibly tasteful. Wildly expensive, wildly fun for the guests, not a detail left to chance, pleasure and hospitality at the fore.

When the vows concluded, irreligious personalized statements of commitment, the guests cheered and stood and the hot air of the mountain became suffused with license and release, guests migrating to the delicacies transported by caterers, to the stations for signature cocktails (a "Meet Me in St. Louis," a nod to the couple's first meeting at a work offsite) or whatever they liked from the top-shelf open bar. Bunny got herself canapés and a paloma, and she stood at the edge of the infinity pool and looked at the vineyards spread out down the mountain. On the helicopter pad the bridesmaids and groomsmen hammed it up for the photographer. A drone camera buzzed over them all.

One of the boys from the bus sidled up and held up his glass to be clinked. He was a built white ginger with narrow brown eyes.

"From the shuttle," he said. "Sorry if we were being dicks; we were at the bar before we got on the bus." Bunny clinked and sucked in her stomach just because. "How do you know Matt and Kelly?" he asked her. She felt the slightest twinge of regret that things would be wrapped up so quickly, his question having only one egress.

"I don't," she said, her regret transmuting to her delivery of the phrase. "My boyfriend is a groomsman." She nodded toward the helipad, where Francis and his cohort were lifting up the groom and holding him horizontally across their bodies.

"Cool," said the guy, and his recalibration of the moment was so perceptible she decided to take it as a compliment.

"What about you?" she said, to be polite.

"I work with Matt," he said.

"I was going to go and get my table assignment," Bunny offered, a kindness so he could mingle elsewhere. "Do you know where you're sitting for dinner?"

"Not yet," he said, and they went to the board inside the soaring foyer of the villa and learned they were at Machu Picchu (him) and Cinque Terre (Bunny)—the tables named for places the couple had traveled.

Bunny felt hands on her shoulders and turned to see Francis, a little sweaty but trim and dapper in his tuxedo. The ginger drifted away, the pretense abandoned.

"You look beautiful," said Francis, and held her hand and she felt something similar to love. "You ready to rage?" Francis said. "How crazy is this place?"

She kissed him. "It's ridiculous," she said. "Let's go get fifty drinks."

At Cinque Terre Bunny ate chateaubriand and drank the best white wine she had ever tasted, slightly effervescent yet somehow also golden and syrupy. She set about learning all there was to know about Jenny, the woman seated on her right, and her new husband, Paul. Jenny worked for an arts nonprofit. "Tell me everything," said Bunny. "He"—she pointed at Francis—"thinks I need to get a new job, and I don't know any jobs but I feel like maybe that could be interesting." As she said it she felt embarrassed, being thirty-two and not knowing, but she also knew that ignorance was disarming and people liked to talk about their work in detail if you allowed it.

"Well," said Jenny, "I'm in nonprofit fundraising, so right now I'm helping put on a music festival to raise money for our low-income-youth program." Bunny leaned her face on her hand and looked very intently at Jenny, who was white with flat-ironed dark brown hair that was probably supposed to be curly. "That is so interesting," she said. "So how exactly do you do that?"

"A lot of it is like working with the PR firm, liaising with the press and making sure that there's coverage of the event, reaching out to all the prospective donors and getting them plugged in, coordinating invites, that kind of thing." Jenny had a very long narrow face and a very long narrow torso. Bunny hypothesized that she had not been considered pretty in high school but was pretty now, because everything kind of went together, a unity to her unusual proportions. She enunciated her words very clearly and maintained eye contact. Bunny decided she appreciated her.

"That sounds so cool," said Bunny. She looked at Paul, who was wearing a Vineyard Vines bowtie and cummerbund and pouring sweat. "And what about you?" she asked him.

"I'm in sales," he said.

"Ooh," said Bunny. "What do you sell?"

He swigged his beer. "I sell a component used in cobalt extraction," he said. Bunny was intrigued by the world of possibilities that this suggested, but he spoke again. "Who knew when you turned thirty you would just talk about work all the fucking time," he laughed, and Bunny felt stung.

His wife hit him. "Rude," she said. It occurred to Bunny that if she and Francis got married, these might be the people at their wedding. She decided to be fun.

"Hey, bro," she said. "I'm just trying to learn about the group." Another woman at the table, a blonde wearing a truly killer sequined dress, leaned forward.

"Hey, girl, hey," she said. "I'm all for it. I'm Mallory, I am a certified Scrum Master, and I'm training for a half marathon."

"Love it," said Bunny, loving the woman. "Quick question, *what* is a Scrum Master?" she said exuberantly, but the woman looked momentarily at the caterer asking whether she wanted wine.

"We must be the business table, ha ha," Mallory said when she looked back at the group. "That table over there is the doctor table. What about you, Bunny? What do you do?"

"I'm in the energy industry," she said. The man who sold the extraction component flicked his head idly in her direction. "In Houston," Bunny added.

"Oh, word," said the man. "Where at?"

"It's small, privately owned—Turnbridge Oil Company?"

"Ouch," said a man across the table who had not previously spoken to her. "Thirty-nine a barrel," he said. Almost with surprise she realized she knew what he meant.

"Yep," she said, sipping her drink. "It's in the shitter. What do you do?" she asked the man across the table.

"I'm a trader," he said, rueful. "Glencore. I might not even have a job when I get back from this wedding." He lifted his glass.

The cobalt extractor said, "You in Geneva?" and the other man nodded.

Glencore looked back at Bunny. "So are you, like, E&P?"

"Yeah," said Bunny. "Although I'm in a kind of . . . ," she reached for another word. "Futurecasting division. We look to invest in new technology and renewables."

The man nodded. "Nice."

She forged ahead. "We're a little insulated from the price shock though. We had already started pulling out of Bakken; it was burning so much cash." She had heard Frank and Estelle talking about this. The men at the table looked at her with shrewd interest. She felt exhilarated. "We have a reversionary interest though, so it's in play if the technology or the market improves, either one, ha ha." This was the first time she had ever spoken of "we" in just such a way. She tried to pull the other man out. "I don't know much about the financial side, the arbitrage or whatever. It seems very confusing. What's the deal with being a trader?" She tried to look winning. The guy looked weary.

"I'm on the physical trade, not paper. It's all fucked-up now because the prices are so divorced from the demand. The end of QE fucked everything." Bunny noticed that some of the people at the table looked bored, like it was peculiar to talk about work. Before she could decide to ask what QE was, a glass clinked over a mike and they all turned to the pool patio, where the bride and groom stood, the bride in her second dress of the evening, this one a slinky and satin slip with an ephemeral second layer over it. The sun fell behind the mountains and the sky was bloodred as the speeches sounded out over the hillside.

When the dancing began, inside the great room and spilling out onto the patio, the bride was in a third dress, short and poufy. They all danced to a remix of Edward Sharpe and the Magnetic Zeros. Bunny was transfixed by the DJ, a real DJ who appeared to be spinning records and who was scruffy and incredibly hot. As she swayed by the pool, smoking a cigarette she had bummed from another guest, she watched the DJ and wished she knew him, wished she knew someone like him, wished she could both bottle the feeling of being three sheets to the wind in a beautiful villa with unlimited food and drink and assuage it. Francis came up, handed over her millionth paloma, gently took the cigarette, dropped it in a glass at an abandoned table, and led her toward the dance floor.

2016

$47.12/$25.52

THE LUNCHEON

It was always freezing in these conference halls, almost windy with air conditioning. Bunny had brought a thin cashmere sweater to put over her blouse. She had now been to enough women's industry events to know that there would be a baffling array of attire—Texas in spring, impossible to dress for. There would be stylish suits, incredibly sleek; there would be elaborate bouclé blazers of another era and sundresses that Bunny could only think of as slutty and far too young for work. There would be one or two women in khakis and company vests, needing only hard hats to signify they had line jobs and felt no need to prettify the hard, serious, difficult, technical work that made all the other jobs possible. There would be chunky statement necklaces and wrists and ankles adorned with tiny heart and butterfly tattoos. There would be blowouts and updos. Most, not all, of the women would be white, although Houston was not a white city and Texas not a white state. Bunny saw Black and brown people everywhere in the city, and yet they were mostly not here. But it was also not an East Coast room, not a Stanhope room or a Conn College room, although there was always a chance of there being someone from Stanhope or Conn College in any such room. Bunny was years from understanding Texas, but she did appreciate the slightly different composition of its circles. The eastern name game was mostly a thing of the past, at least for Bunny.

No one from Turnbridge Oil Company or Turnbridge Energy Solutions was being honored at this celebration of women in energy, but Bunny had bought the ticket with Turnbridge money for the networking opportunities. The "women in energy" stuff was slowly ramping up, industry-wide. Bunny herself had only ever worked with women in the non-oil admin pool of Miles Engineering Consultants, where they were the small, disgruntled army that supported everyone else, confined to the Repro Room and shouting over the roar of the printer. But now there was a growing, generalized chatter about how women could be elevated, or included at all, in places like Turnbridge Oil Company, where there were currently no women engineers or geologists.

Before the awards there was an opportunity for chitchat at the assigned tables. Bunny's table included a tax lawyer at one of the many firms whose name was simply a pairing of men's surnames, a VP at a company that made pipes for routing compressed steam, a geologist who was not attached to any company, and an LNG market analyst for Statoil who had previously held some kind of line job.

They introduced themselves around the table. When Bunny named her workplace, the unattached geologist smiled. "I graduated from Turnbridge School of Earth Sciences," she said, one of Frank Turnbridge's lavish gifts to his alma mater, which now produced a cadre of excellent engineers and geologists every year. "Oh, that's great," said Bunny. "I'll have to tell Frank." The women were presented with their lunch, a green salad upon which sat a chicken breast and dried cranberries. Mimosas from the prelunch mingling hour and glasses of iced tea sweat beads of water onto the polyester table linens. Bunny took the smallest sliver off the side of a soft, sculpted butter ball and spread it carefully across half a roll. "Where did you go after you graduated?" she asked the geologist, an open-faced woman with a pretty smattering of freckles. "Exxon," she said. "I did an internship with them in school, and they were hiring a ton when I got out." She looked around the table a little sheepishly. "Unfortunately I just got hit by the big crew change," she said, and the women nodded sympathetically.

Bunny knew that a huge number of people had gotten laid off in the last year after oil prices cratered. Frank talked about this a lot, because his reductions had stayed at only around 10 percent, while some companies were doing 40, 50 percent. It did not occur to Bunny that she was in many ways the lowest hanging of low-hanging fruit until Phil had urged her, "Keep making yourself indispensable." Her website development and outreach intensified, as did her performance of small personal tasks for Phil and Frank.

"I'm so sorry," said the woman who made steam pipes. The geologist shrugged. "It is what it is. In 2012 I was getting a recruiting call every day, now . . . nada." She sipped her iced tea. "It's actually been kind of nice, though. I have twins. I have a lot more time with them now." The other women murmured supportively.

"They always lay the moms off first," she said, and looked over at the woman from Statoil, who was visibly pregnant. "Just kidding," she said. "When are you due?" she asked, the first public acknowledgment of the woman's bump.

The Statoil woman laughed. "Two months to go," she said.

"You all get pretty good maternity leave, right?" asked the laid-off geologist.

"Not as good as they get at HQ," she said. "Like three months. Better than most."

Bunny, the only woman of childbearing age in the current Turnbridge family, had no idea what their policy was.

The tax lawyer joined the conversation. "Did you find daycare yet?"

"God, no," the Statoil woman said. "It's rough out there, my Lord!"

The other women nodded and she went on, her face open and vulnerable. "All the places have the wrong hours. My husband has a line job, so we're kind of scrambling. My mom is going to watch the baby for a while, but then I'm not sure." She looked at the geologist who had formerly worked at Exxon. "What did you do with two?"

The geologist laughed. "Panicked," she said. She became serious. "The most affordable thing you can do is get an au pair, if you have space," she said. "But we didn't have the room. We got a nanny, and I had a manager who worked with me on the hours a little bit. We had a schedule where the nanny would come at five thirty, we would get in to work by six fifteen, and then she would bring them to preschool and school, and then I would try to go home so I could get them by three thirty." Bunny's jaw dropped.

"Five thirty in the a.m.?" she said aloud. She had had two of the mimosas somewhat in spite of herself. The geologist laughed. "I know. But honestly it was working." She seemed conscious that she was at a networking event and that positivity was queen in this room. Bunny noticed that everyone kept themselves bobbing well above the line at which they would sink into overt bitching.

"That schedule actually worked out great. I could be with them in the afternoon, and I would try not to bring work home too much," the geologist said. The tax lawyer nodded sagely. "That's so important. I always say from 6:00 to 8:00 p.m. is my absolutely no-work zone so I can do the dinner and bedtime, and if I have to work I always do it after that." She looked at the woman from Statoil sympathetically.

"Are we scaring you, hon? We haven't even got to talking about labor." All the women laughed. Bunny felt faintly repulsed. She had been suspicious of mothers ever since her time working at the baby-and-child consignment shop in Pittsburgh. The harried customers who came into the shop stressed her out with their nervous energy, and the serene customers struck her as smug. They talked down to her, she always thought. She could count on one hand the number of men who had ever come inside the store. Bunny thus associated motherhood with stress and bad smells and the absence of men. And yet Facebook told her that many of the women she had gone to school with had embarked on the journey of procreation. A fever had come over them.

One of the few men in this room wove through the tables, stopping every so often to greet people. He came by their table and put his hand on the shoulder of the woman from Statoil. "What are we talking about here?" he said. "Shoes?"

Bunny laughed out loud. The tax lawyer, who appeared to know the man, rolled her eyes. "Shoes go on our feet, Larry," she said. He wandered away uncowed.

"Unbelievable," said the woman from Statoil. "They sponsor this lunch, and they still think we only want to talk about shoes."

The women listened to a series of speakers before the keynote. The first spoke of the rocky times for the industry. "These are painful, volatile, hurtful times," she said, and Bunny glanced at the laid-off Exxon geologist and felt again how lucky she was that Phil seemed committed to keeping her on, that she was important to him and even a little to Frank.

Bunny and Phil were trying to show Frank how the disaster of the oil market was an opportunity for the Turnbridge Energy Solutions side of things, which was still struggling to fully define itself. She knew that their competitor among the scant number of private companies was going in on battery storage and utility ventures, buying tracts of land and grid infrastructure, buying water rights, had even hired a venture capitalist from California to come and acquire smaller technology companies for the patents. At Phil's request Bunny scoured trade publications and patent data to keep him abreast of what they were doing. Phil was sensitive about comparisons with this company, she knew, in a field where they had so few peers. He had gone from the awkward small middle of dam building to the awkward small middle of oil and gas.

He had Bunny plan a trip for him to California, asking her to "set up some meetings" at a list of start-ups. Knowing what she knew of Phil, and his ultimately not-very-technical grasp of the industry, she wondered what benefit there was for anyone in California to meet with him. She had the impression that Silicon Valley was where people had left the traditional corridors of power and were soaring away in some other direction, pulling humankind with them. The benefits for workers at these jobs were legendary, and the path to getting one of those jobs, the noncomputer kind, was opaque. They were empyrean. And yet when she called or emailed the admins at these companies—engineering technology and AI and battery companies mostly—and said she was calling from Turnbridge Energy Solutions out of Houston, Texas, someone always took the call. Frank joshed Phil about his schemes—"Disneyland is the only reason to go to California"—but he didn't tell him not to go.

Bunny was distracted by her phone for the beginning of the keynote, which was a woman who had been one of the first Black women special agents in the FBI. Her presentation began with a picture of red high-heeled shoes and an anecdote about how she had worn them to work knowing that it was a male-dominated space and there was no use trying to blend in. "Be your own person," she said, and there were loud hoots of assent from a white woman in one of the bouclé jackets, who kicked one of her feet up high to show that she herself was wearing red stilettos, maybe Jimmy Choos.

The speaker talked about being so tied up in her work on 9/11 that she forgot to pick her son up at school. She teared up when she recalled this moment. "Look to your family," she said. "Don't forget who and what really matters." The anecdote hung strangely in the air, although the room clapped to it with what seemed like real feeling. Bunny ate the other half of her roll and thought about Francis's audiobooks. Surely 9/11 was the one day to put aside family feeling, she thought. Surely on that day of all days she could be forgiven her devotion to her work. Bunny wondered how many of the women in the room had gotten up at five in the morning, how many were paying someone else to live in their home and deal with their children. She took one foot out of her shoes, Tory Burch square-heeled croc pumps that didn't have quite enough room in the toe box, and flexed her toes, one foot then the other, before turning her attention back to the podium.

2019

$63.00/$48.00

THE RETURN

E lizabeth, for she had finally decided to make the change from Bunny when she assumed her new title of Director of Outreach and Communications at Turnbridge Energy Solutions, was sitting at a glossy conference table looking out through the windows at downtown Baku, a skyline she could no longer recognize. The Caspian, blue as ever, stretched out into the horizon, dotted here and there with miniature tangles of infrastructure. She marveled at the view and then turned her head toward her colleagues at the table, ten women: one from the local office of BP; one from Baker Hughes; one from a university in Russia; one from the Interior Ministry of Azerbaijan; one from the Turkish Ministry of Culture; consular officers from the embassies of America, Canada, and Pakistan; and two from local NGOs devoted to women's affairs. A lone man was present, also from the Azeri ministry, and the women made much of him with gentle mirth.

They were in one of the buildings that anchored the new and unrecognizable skyline—now its most distinctive architectural features, defining the city's silhouette as much as the Maiden Tower itself. The Flame Towers were seven years old, built on the outcropping in the highest point of the city, across from parliament and Martyrs' Lane, and immediately replicated on refrigerator magnets, on postcards, on tour brochures. They soared over Baku from every vantage, three curving towers of glass—gray or black or blue in the daylight, reflecting the sky and the buildings around. They changed their shape and aspect depending on where you were: sometimes there appeared to be two; sometimes only one peeked out from between two old buildings; sometimes all three were visible, illuminated at night with the flag of Azerbaijan or with images of flames. *Azerbaijan: Land of Fire*. Elizabeth remembered the book on the embassy-assigned coffee table in their apartment; it was probably sitting in a box in a storage unit somewhere today. A publication of British Petroleum, now BP, one of their hosts this week as the women planned their conference.

BP's sizable new office building sat at the other end of the Bulvar, near the new looming tower with an open oval maw gaping at its top and a half-finished crescent skyscraper, a massive and architecturally remarkable offshore semicircle currently being built by AECOM and delayed, they were told, for years now. Baku seemed to be a playground for skyscraper architects; Elizabeth had seen shapes utterly foreign to the Houston skyline. The city was full of fanciful new buildings, rolled like carpets, twisted like DNA, perched like spaceships that had landed, it seemed to Elizabeth, overnight. Cranes made striking cuts across the sky. She often found herself turning to the Caspian to orient herself, the only thing that seemed to remain constant.

The conference planners had just come from a beautiful catered lunch, and Gulbahar, the representative from BP, had cups of tea brought in for the day's final session. They were gathered this week to plan the Celebrate Global Women in Energy conference that would take place the following spring on International Women's Day. They had spent the morning and the previous day assigning participants to the rubric of panels decided on over months of emails and Skypes. Now they would make tentative plans for what they were calling "the extras," the things that would make the participants feel appreciated and showcase the beauties of Azerbaijan. The woman from the Turkish Ministry of Culture, a stunning and syrupy person also in her thirties, was bringing in a Turkish children's chorus to sing, coordinating a musical program with a group of Azeri musicians on the theme of "Turkic Worlds, Global Connections" to highlight the traditional linguistic and cultural ties between Turkey and Azerbaijan. It was evident to Elizabeth that this Turkish woman, Ebru, had a mission. She also had a tremendous budget for these kinds of activities, although she was cagey about the numbers themselves. Bunny noticed Turkish flags all over the place in the city. Then again, the entire purpose of the conference was the promulgation of various agendas, from all sides.

The NGO representatives had each been given lunchtime keynote spots, with a request from the ministry that their presentations be sent over for approval before the conference. From one of them Elizabeth had learned that in the last decade there had been a decline in Azeri women entering college of more than 25 percent. She would not be including this information in her keynote, not exactly, she indicated discreetly.

Azerbaijan, it seemed to Elizabeth, had quietly entered a media blitz. Gulbahar showed them a beautifully produced video for the tourism board, *Take Another Look*, put together by Landor & Fitch, Ogilvy's partner for the old BP rebrand. Elizabeth had recently flirted with the idea of a job in marketing or PR or advertising, which she thought she might be good at, and she had done a little clicking around on LinkedIn and AdAge, mostly learning that all these agencies were owned by WPP, an umbrella that put Halliburton to shame with its reach. It seemed like a staggeringly large and slippery enterprise with its own conventions and language; Elizabeth wasn't sure she had it in her to network her way into another opaque world. The Azerbaijan ad was gorgeous, though; they had done a nice job. Gulbahar told them BP, too, was launching a major campaign this year, the first since those soothing videos about tourism and restoration after the disaster in the Gulf.

Gulbahar had an enviable balayage and a British accent and was chairwoman of the committee. "Okay," she said now as they stirred their tea in its tulip cups. "I know we've had a long two days, so let's make sure everyone is clear on their action items before we have our next Skype meeting, which is going to be in six weeks." She tapped briskly at her iPad with a stylus. She was incredibly efficient and kind.

Soon they were dispersed, free until that night's dinner, and Elizabeth stood on the road beside the Flame Towers cluster and tried to photograph the way the spindly towers of the Turkish Martyrs' Mosque were almost perfectly reflected on the curved mirrorlike glass of Tower 3. She had an expansive feeling, released after listening to Gulbahar's tense parrying with Rupa from the American embassy about the bus schedule for the Ateshgah excursion or the afternoon at the National Carpet Museum, the beautiful swiss cake roll of a building curled up on the Bulvar. But she also felt at sea, fifteen years old again and let loose in the known and unknown city. She began the walk down the curved road that led from the Flame Towers to the center of town, grateful for her new Birdies loafers as she navigated the incline. She paused to turn back up toward the towers and take another photo when a black Mercedes pulled over and Gulbahar craned her neck to speak out of the open passenger window.

"Can I give you a lift?" she asked.

"I'm just wandering," Elizabeth said. "I don't really have a destination."

"Please get in," she said. "I can drop you somewhere." Gulbahar had been beautifully hostessing all day, and Elizabeth hated to keep her longer. She knew little of Gulbahar's life outside of her work. She assumed she was unmarried—no ring—but she didn't know for sure.

Elizabeth had been amazed to learn that the receptionist in the BP office, a very young woman, had two small kids. Their photos were on her desk; she had first assumed they were her younger siblings. Elizabeth was constantly being surprised by the revealed information of people's lives.

Elizabeth got into the car and after effusive thanks began to watch the city go by. "It's changed a lot, right?" Gulbahar said, looking with amusement as Elizabeth craned her neck out the window. She knew that Elizabeth had been in Baku before. "It's unbelievable," said Elizabeth. She had thus far seen only the briefest glimpses of the place she had known. On a walk down the Bulvar the first night, expanded for kilometers and beautifully paved, she felt the new pavers rattle gently beneath her feet, little rivulets welling up here and there from the changeable Caspian, the faintest hint of instability beneath their smooth perfection. When she strayed a bit from Sahil and Fountains Square—a McDonald's in the square! A Cinnabon on Zarifa Aliyeva!—she looked into old buildings and saw the beautiful old cracked mismatched tiles, the miscellaneous planters set on landings to catch the sun through grimed casement windows that opened into interior courtyards, a glimpse of the past.

"They say between 2005 and 2007 it's two different cities," said Gulbahar. "Before and after BTC."

"Unreal," said Elizabeth. She noted the cement blockades hugging the curve of the main road as Gulbahar turned onto it. "Is that a security thing?" They reminded her of the barricades that blocked the road to the American embassy in Athens.

"God, no, it's bloody Formula One," said Gulbahar. "Azerbaijan paid to host it, and now they've put up these awful cement blocks all over the nicest part of the city." She deftly steered the car past a man who had braved the overland street crossing and slammed on her breaks to avoid colliding with a car that had recklessly changed lanes. "And now everyone thinks they're a bloody Formula One racer too."

Elizabeth marveled at how much smoother the roads were now—no cracks, no cavernous potholes. The city seemed immaculate. Every so often she saw elderly people in orange vests with brooms made of twigs, sweeping sidewalks and picking up trash and watering newly planted landscaping.

Gulbahar glanced at Elizabeth as she dodged cars. "Have you gotten to do any sightseeing? Did you see the Hadid building yet?"

"Not yet," said Elizabeth.

"Ah," said Gulbahar, "that you have got to see. Let me take you by there now."

Elizabeth remembered this element of being in the world, in another country, that suddenly your day was out of your hands, you were beholden to other people, an obligation, both you to them and them to you, the push and pull of knowing what was offered genuinely and what was out of a sense of duty. Suddenly Elizabeth yearned for the quiet of her hotel room, worried the day would somehow get away from her.

"You're so kind," she said. "But I'm sure you want to get home."

"Please," said Gulbahar, making a swatting gesture as if to bat aside Elizabeth's fussy little courtesies, and Elizabeth let herself be taken.

Gulbahar navigated the car up onto the road that Elizabeth had taken into town from the new airport, a vast gleaming conservatory of a building that shone like a beacon during Elizabeth's incredibly bumpy descent into Baku.

"There's your president's hotel, Trump hotel," Gulbahar said, laughing, pointing at a huge—she heard the man's awful voice in her head—building standing alone in the middle of a roundabout. It was a strange, heavy structure—a giant wedge of fruit or a sail from one side, something vaginal but somehow unwelcoming from the other.

"Oh god. I have to pretend he doesn't exist," said Elizabeth, which was true. When she heard his voice she turned off the TV, left the room. She still couldn't believe it; she had been so sure it was impossible. It was Sofie who had issued the warning she did not heed. "I will bet you a million dollars," she typed over WhatsApp when he began winning primaries. "Ask your bosses. They'll vote for him." She should have heeded Sofie, who was so informed about everything. Sofie's career had been going gangbusters. She had been one of the main European journalists covering Standing Rock. ("Where's John Wayne when you need him," Frank Turnbridge had said, about that situation.)

Just past the tangle of roads and raw landscaping that surrounded the Trump building, Elizabeth gazed upon another building, an otherworldly white edifice. "That's it," said Gulbahar, pointing out the window. It was a surreal building, surrounded by emerald-green grass: a white cloud, a desert dune, an ocean whitecap, a hambone, incongruous and beautiful, monumental in a way unlike anything Elizabeth had ever seen. This was Zaha Hadid's Heydar Aliyev Cultural Center.

Gulbahar found parking and they crossed a broad street and walked up the escalators, which weren't working, past the giant freestanding #Baku sign—"for Instagram," Gulbahar said—up the slightly stained white steps and across the expanse of polished white pavers that led into the flowing white concrete and polymer of the building itself. In the shadow of its undulating waves of white a bride in a glorious dress with a full poof of skirt was being photographed, the white that flowed off of the building and beneath her feet like the train of another gown. An elderly woman carrying groceries trudged across an expanse like desert sand, her head down against the wind. Clouds traveled low and fast above them in the darkening blue afternoon sky. It was an utterly exhilarating building, against which every scene took on glamor and significance.

The Aliyev Cultural Center—a monument to its namesake, the handsome matinee idol now dead and replaced by his weak-chinned son—was surrounded by a park and, behind that, an apartment building, also monumental, the breadth of a city block, lined with small businesses on the first floor, teeming with uniform balconies above. Elizabeth puzzled over her mental map, now so askew. "I'm trying to think of what was here before," she said. Gulbahar raised an eyebrow. "Apartments, houses, some shops," she said. She looked slightly regretful. "There was some protest about the process," she said. "But that's how we do it in Azerbaijan," she said, waving her hand with a look of amused weariness. "Tear the old thing down, build something new." Elizabeth admired her garnet nails.

They circled the building, Elizabeth taking photos from different exposures, trying to capture all the building's sinuous lines. Young people played an impromptu game of volleyball on the grass of the park and were spread out under trees. It was a lovely scene.

"Shall we go somewhere for a tea?" said Gulbahar.

"You know, if it would be okay, I really think I'd like to walk around a bit more," said Elizabeth. "And rest for a bit before dinner." Elizabeth hoped that she had not offended her. But she knew Gulbahar and her colleagues had been trained in the foibles of Americans, their deep rudenesses marked down as quirks of their generally inhospitable culture. Gulbahar had been to America, anyway. When Elizabeth was a teenager in Baku, Gulbahar had been at a high school in Oklahoma, one of the Freedom Act exchanges that Elizabeth's father himself had probably helped to arrange. They had laughed about the coincidence when they met in the lobby of the Houston Marriott Marquis in 2017.

"Absolutely," said Gulbahar, understanding everything and waving her garnet nails again. "Go, go. I'll see you at dinner."

Elizabeth walked the busy street around the Hadid building, looking for one of the underground passages that had proliferated in the last two decades and which were the only way to cross some of the streets for what seemed like miles at a time. She made her way in the direction of the waterfront, propelled by a new burst of energy after the administrative minutiae of the day. As she drew close on Rustamov Street, she realized she was in the site where the Black City had once begun, that warren of storage tanks and pipes and infrastructure that had been a no-go zone for her on the map. And she saw now that everything there was gone. The streets were lined with enormous blocks of apartments, in a grand old style with mansard roofs. But as she looked closely at the apartments she realized they were brand-new, mostly empty, light from the sinking sun illuminating motes that floated in empty rooms through glassless windows.

She walked east on 8 November Street for a while, farther and farther away from where she eventually needed to go, noting block after block of new construction, cranes and bulldozers, the rest of the city visible through steel and concrete skeletons. It became overcast as she walked, the breeze cool. In the distance she saw a hillside with crowded houses, finally something that seemed the same as it had been before. She could see the green leaves of the mulberry trees that poked over the walls and gates, their berries gone for the season, and yearned to teleport across the massive blocks of empty apartments and vacant hotels to get to the warren of streets she remembered. It had rained right after lunch, and petrichor was in the air, both the smell released from the patches of unlandscaped dirt, and the pavement itself, the faint and pleasant acridity of bitumen within the asphalt, oil everywhere, oil in the ground, oil making the ground.

She opened Google Maps and saw herself as a blue dot on the screen. She thought of the internet café filled with smoke and boys playing video games, cash carried in suitcases, precious, once-a-week phone calls, letters with stamps that might take weeks to arrive. Things changed so fast. She opened Uber and called a car to her location. It used a third-party app in Azerbaijan but provided the same service. "Baku White City," the map on the screen read, a place all new.

The lobby of the Flame Tower that housed the Fairmont Hotel was splendidly appointed. A leviathan asymmetrical glass chandelier cascaded from the vaulted entry to the hotel, the front desk dwarfed beneath it and beneath the two-story-high turquoise bas-relief mural that formed its backdrop. Feet sank into the acres of dusty rose carpet that stretched across the floor. The effect of the lobby was glittering but serene and tasteful, luxury creating a quiet that was textured, almost audible in its comfort. Elizabeth loved the giant egg-like chairs in the café that snaked off the lobby, soft nooks made for discreet conversations while you drank a Turkish coffee and munched a small cookie. She loved her room, with its floor-to-ceiling windows and its perfect view of the city, and she marveled that it had been relatively cheap, like a midrange Holiday Inn back home.

Elizabeth took off her loafers, stripped off her slacks and sweaty blouse, and gave herself what she reflexively thought of as a whore's bath at the sink. She put on a soft T-shirt and pulled the comforter off the bed. She poured a small plastic cup full of vodka from the minibar, wedged under her heels the little specialty foot ice packs that she had made cool in the ineffectual freezer, and lay back on the bed against the mountain of pillows. That she was here in her underwear in the preposterously nice hotel room with her aching feet on tiny bags of blue coolant represented the pinnacle of Elizabeth's professional life. She felt, in this moment, deliriously happy.

When Turnbridge Oil Company had decided, at Phil's urging, to expand and proliferate like so many cells; when Elizabeth had made herself the director and sole member of the newly christened Outreach and Communications team based on a principal of consolidated storytelling; when she was commissioning, editing, and posting YouTube videos of oilfield workers and support staff lip-syncing to Pharrell's "Happy" and dancing at a project site; when she was writing grants and contacting the State Department's Bureau of Educational and Cultural Affairs to look into recruiting female engineers from Algeria, Kazakhstan, Turkmenistan, Jordan, any countries not affected by Donald Trump's Muslim Ban; when she was writing text to be read over footage of smiling Azeri women in hard hats; when she was finding footage of women holding their healthy babies in brightly lit hospital rooms, machines fueled by boundless energy cleanly sourced from around the world; when she was navigating the minefield of Turnbridge leadership's politics in the Trump era; when she was earning $83,000 per year and gunning for $95,000; when she and Francis were in Ireland on a hiking vacation she had planned down to the minute and Harvey landed sixty inches of water on Nederland and Houston sank an inch into the earth under the weight of water; when the floods took thousands of homes but not Francis's home, not Elizabeth's home, not Phil and Estelle's home or Frank's home or Ainsley's home or Warren and Christine's new home, although Lumberton had gotten deluged, by god, and it had been so close; when she had organized and participated in two 5K runs to fundraise for Harvey repair, one of which was cosponsored by Pink Petro—that's when Elizabeth met Gulbahar, who was in Houston for a conference to fuel her own prodigious ambitions, and sounded her out and hitched her wagon to BP's communications budget and Gulbahar's star.

In the end, of course, Sofie had been right. Donald Trump had won the election. Warren and Christine had of course voted for him, Elizabeth knew—Christine thought he had "good kids," as if that were a reflection of him or a requirement for office. Warren, from his office at Saudi Aramco's wholly-owned Motiva, appreciated that he was going to put America first. Even Phil Miles sheepishly admitted to Elizabeth over friendly drinks that he was thinking about pulling the lever for him, though he was, of course, a buffoon, until he saw the look of horror on Elizabeth's face and backpedaled, in word if not deed.

Elizabeth was profoundly shaken, to the point that she had taken a day off work after the election, but then she had moved on. She chose to focus on the things she could control. While she sometimes found herself rigid with rage, sitting through a long dinner in the Conrad & Marcel Schlumberger Room of the Petroleum Club listening to Frank's folksy droning, she refused to become obsessed with "The Orange Man," as people called him on Facebook, "Cheeto brain." After all, as Frank Turnbridge never tired of reminding people, during what she now realized was a set speech he could give every day of the week, in oil and gas—in *energy*—as she made a point to always say in every company communication she put her hands on—they thought in geologic time, not presidential administrations.

Elizabeth worked fiendishly hard at Turnbridge, trying to push the *energy* side, the futurecasting side. And she had finally gotten her wish expressed to Phil Miles eight years ago at his holiday party—to go somewhere. Back home people were rebuilding their houses in exactly the same places; people who could afford it were putting their houses up on steel beams. But Elizabeth got on a plane, economy plus, and flew to Baku for conference planning. Truly she was reaping the benefits of the private, family-owned company.

Elizabeth had a better education now. She could contextualize the majestic buildings on the streets she had roamed as a teenager looking for tampons and perfume and listening to Dave Matthews. Baku had been the boomtown of the world. Stalin himself had been an oil worker in Baku, a Georgian roughneck. Baku had indeed defeated Hitler, Soviet tanks filled with Caspian oil. In her small way Elizabeth had become knowledgeable, although the scale of the oil complex still escaped her. But now, rather than trying to understand the hyperobject, she let it wash over her, focused on her own projects. She planned her wedding. She organized donation drives for Big Brothers

Big Sisters and jogged next to Estelle Turnbridge Miles to raise awareness for breast cancer. She helped Maryellen harvest her first yields of fruit in the garden and then sat with her eating custardy figs and drinking white wine.

And now she was lying on the bed sipping her vodka and idly flipping through the Fairmont TV's offerings. The hotel had a stunning array of channels. She thought of her teen self, lying inert in the hot silence of their apartment, watching dubbed soaps from America and Mexico, and marveled again at the pace of change.

She picked up her phone to FaceTime Francis, who was on a team-building retreat, fishing on the Colorado River, but he didn't answer. She wanted to hear his comforting, steady voice. They had been apart for some time; he was midway through a six-week project somewhere in the Midwest, and when she remembered him she missed him. He had told her he would wait until they were together to watch the *Homeland* finale, but she told him to go ahead. She felt fatigued by their show now, the way it had converged so strongly with the present reality before she could process the preceding one, or the storyline of Carrie, annoyingly, finding new work to atone for her past sins.

She paused on Fox News, where a plasticine doe-eyed blonde sat at a glass table and looked concernedly into the camera, and then at her guest, who Elizabeth immediately registered as both attractive and oddly familiar. The man was speaking in a peculiar accent, one that took her a moment to realize was American but of such a high Waspiness it sounded foreign.

"No, we don't owe anything to the Kurds." He said to his host as though it was comic. "Let's be serious here: the YPG is a group of Maoist- *and* Marxist-Leninists—"

"Not people we would typically make friends with," said the woman. A name flashed on the bottom of the screen, and Elizabeth sat up.

"Holy shit," she said into the silence of her hotel room.

It was one of the Ivy Leaguers, serene and confident, no longer a young man but a tanned silver fox speaking derisively of the Kurds. Before the impulse could wane she picked up her phone and called her father on WhatsApp. It was late afternoon in Dushanbe, and he answered with surprise in his voice. He had left the Foreign Service, finally. People left in droves under Trump. He was a visiting professor now at a Central Asian university where he gave a course on America's role in the world. He played his surnay in a mixed Tajik-expat band. He was still with Alicia, who maintained a baffling dual life flying back and forth between England and Tajikistan. Elizabeth wasn't sure what he lived on, money-wise.

"Bunny," he said. "What a nice surprise."

"Guess where I am?" she said.

"I wouldn't have the faintest idea," he said.

"I'm in Baku," she said, and she was ambushed suddenly by grief.

"Baku!" he said. "How neat. What are you doing there?"

"It's for work," she said, half listening to the man on the television. "But listen," she said. "Remember that guy here? The guy who rode the horse to Almaty or wherever it was? The preppy guy? You told him he could show his slides at USIS."

"That's right," her father said after a pause. "He never did."

"I'm flipping channels at the hotel and he's on Fox News!" she said. "He's shitting on the Kurds. Saying Trump was right to pull out American troops."

"Oh dear," her father said, and she could picture the deep furrows forming above his nose, lines that now plagued her in their nascent form.

"He's wrong, right?" she asked her dad, remembering her childhood, when he had answered every question she ever had.

"Of course he's wrong," cried her father. "They're getting slaughtered."

She could hear her father's clicking internet connection in what she knew was the small apartment he shared with Alicia. Elizabeth had the impression, when she spoke to him, that the world had also taken him by surprise—not only the events of his own life, brought about through his own efforts though they might have been, but the world as a whole. And yet his job had been to understand and shape it, or that's what they'd all believed.

"Small world," she murmured. The sight of the young man, no longer young, on the television had thrown her off-balance. There was a feeling of coming full-circle.

"This is the second person from the Baku era I've randomly seen on television," she said.

"Oh?" he said.

She and Maryellen had been watching CNN at Maryellen's house when Maryellen had cried out and gestured at a mousy brunette on-screen.

"The CIA director, that woman. Gina something."

Her father laughed bitterly. "Oh, Haspel." She had been in Francis's audiobooks, unnamed until her confirmation hearings, the Station Chief who snatched the embassy bombers, then went on to do god knows what in Afghanistan and Thailand—she had all the tapes destroyed. Elizabeth remembered Charlie, extending his hand to blow her cover at the Fourth of July picnic.

"There was quite a Baku moment," he said, now in a voice of reminiscence. "You remember Dick Cheney was there too," he said. "He was in the Chamber of Commerce. Before his vice presidential days. Before his Iraq adventure." She had not heard her father sound so disgusted before.

"The world really went to shit, huh?" she said, feeling for a moment the years, seeing them as one horrible montage of buildings on fire, mangled bodies, beheading videos, drowned babies, blonde faces on Fox News. "What happened?" It had been a long time since she had asked her father to explain anything to her. He was silent for a moment on the other end.

"There were about five minutes after World War II when there was a chance at agreement on how to proceed as a world order," he said. "And it was bungled by a combination of greed, cruelty, and incompetence at every possible turn."

"Wow," said Elizabeth. He sighed. "It used to feel easier to focus on the positive," he said.

She felt the voice of childhood wanting to ask "What happens next," but she didn't.

"As nice as it is to hear your voice, I have to go," her dad said. "Alicia and I are going to the Residence to have drinks. The new ambassador is a nice guy, it turns out. Career guy."

Elizabeth laughed. "What appointee would they possibly put in Dushanbe?" she said.

"I don't know," said her father. "Trump couldn't find it on the map. Anyway, call me again soon and tell me what you're doing in Baku," he said. "I love you."

"I love you too," she said.

Elizabeth thought about how different Maryellen had been when she told her that she was going to Baku. She had rushed to her desk and removed from it one of thirty years of address books with a Liberty London print. She transferred something from the notebook to an index card and pressed it into Elizabeth's hand with a beseeching look on her face. "You have to look up Zeynab Xanim. You absolutely have got to call her and go and see her. Can you imagine if she knew that you were in Baku and you didn't go and see her?"

Then she fretted about how Bunny could find and contact Lale and Murad. At the thought Elizabeth felt a deep and painful guilt. And yet she hadn't been able, even once she had oriented herself to the city, even during a lull between her meetings, to take herself to the old building and ring the buzzer for the Qadirovs' door. They would be in their eighties or nineties, she told herself. She wouldn't want to startle them. But really she dreaded the interaction, the accounting for herself, the catching up, the sharing of news, the hospitality her presence would obligate and the difficulty of extraction. She knew how deeply this would disappoint her mother and felt ashamed. So she decided not to think about it just as she avoided thinking about so many upsetting things.

Elizabeth clicked off Fox News and got her laptop and checked her work email and the social media feeds for the Celebrate Global Women in Energy conference. She looked at Pinterest. She hated how wedding dresses lately had thigh-high slits. She wanted something classic but not something too old-fashioned. Kate Middleton's look was too fussy, but Meghan Markle's was too plain. It was a problem. She and Francis were planning their wedding for the following year.

She retweeted a cute video of female office staff from Tengiz field in Kazakhstan, from where she had recruited an engineer from Tengizchevroil to present at the conference, along with a KazMunayGas worker from the Kashagan megaproject. She quote-tweeted a photo of the Russian Women's Oil and Gas working group, tough women in hard hats giving a thumbs-up to the camera at Sakhalin. "Love it!" she wrote in the tweet above the photo. And she did love it, more or less. These were good and important jobs, Elizabeth knew. They empowered women and gave them options. And still there were men who hated it. Elizabeth had to block an account called "Shale Dale" who kept replying to the Celebrating Women conference account with a photograph of shit on a pig's balls, after Pink Petro retweeted it.

Whenever Elizabeth felt cynical and bad she soothed herself by thinking of the female engineers and the scientists and the technicians. She and the other women who made the conferences and the promotional videos and steered the retrograde men to be more open-minded, sure they had navigated in male-dominated spaces—they had always started out working for some man, some series of men—but they eventually rose up, and now they had each other. The women on the rigs and out in the field were truly alone, and everyone could see if they made a mistake, because their potential mistakes were mechanical and momentous rather than putting the wrong formatting on a spreadsheet or making a typo in a tweet. All Elizabeth did was relay information, tell stories, shape narratives, soft things, things that didn't really matter. Even now Elizabeth knew there was nothing that she personally could not wiggle out of, should something go wrong. These women went somewhere every day where they had to know and use the same exact information as the men, had to know it even better. She celebrated them.

While her computer was open she searched for names. The former explorer on Fox News had already tweeted his video appearance. She scrolled through his feed, op-eds he had written about how to invest in unstable locations. With some trepidation she searched Charlie Kovak. It seemed he was still a writer and still had the radio show John told her about in Greece. "A Night at the (Looted) Museum," he had written for *Rolling Stone*. Then there were the articles *about* him. "Charlie Kovak Has Nothing to Apologize For." ("Narrator: In fact he had many things to apologize for," a female journalist had tweeted in reply.) She found a video clip of him talking about extraordinary rendition. He was on a major network, rumpled and slightly grizzled with stubble. He looked so much older than he was in her memory.

She searched for Upstairs Eddie, which she had done before, now and again. Here he was presenting his old Baku documentary at a film festival. Here he was presenting his new documentary on dissidents in Putin's Russia. He was married to a beautiful woman and was the head of some foundation with vague and noble-sounding goals.

Elizabeth looked at herself in the mirror across from the bed. She was thin thanks to a rigid schedule of exercise. She had gray hair now, early grays like Ted Senior, and she spent several hours in a salon chair every six weeks to make sure they were covered. She was thirty-six, in shape after finally submitting herself to Barry's Boot Camp and suffering on some form of machine every other day. She had very good skin thanks to a standing rotation of Biologique Recherche products, one that was made of placental cells and one that was meant to mimic the white substance that coated babies when they were inside the womb. She was thinking about cosmetic dermatology but she saw too many unfortunate fillers on Instagram. She would consider microneedling, maybe some sort of peel. She had a few beautiful items of clothing. For a while she had bought herself an endless supply of perfect white T-shirts, but lately she realized she didn't need them. She got a manicure once a month, but had not yet tried acrylics, even though they were ubiquitous now and came in all sorts of shapes and designs. She had come up in a time when acrylic nails were not the province of Wasps.

Elizabeth was not sure why she had spent so much time unmarried when so many of her peers were on their first, second, third children. Evan and his wife had twins and lived in Phoenix, an inconceivable state of affairs. The time had passed very quickly, all things considered. She was bewildered to find herself at an age where the absence of children, absence she had assumed would be temporary, was now a possibly permanent state. Francis was laser-focused on his work and had taken a long time to ask her to marry him. Then again it had taken Elizabeth a long time to envision spending her life with him and comingling their Trader Joe's salads. She took her feet off the cooling pads and started preparing for dinner.

The farewell meal for the planning session of the Celebrate Global Women in Energy conference took place at one of the cavelike tourist traps off Fountains Square. Elizabeth's innate meter for authenticity, the snobbishness she and her siblings and parents had honed over years of eating in foreign countries, was instantly activated by the modern stone walls made to look medieval and the servers in traditional garb. It was beautiful, though—the women all oohed and aahed at the decor. They were seated at a long table in one of the gemlike caves, hung with rugs and instruments and folkloric weapons. A woman from the Deloitte office in Baku met them there, along with a woman who ran a turnkey workforce-solutions provider, a giant specialized temp agency providing workers for the oilfields.

They ordered wine and salads and toasted Gulbahar, and each other. Gulbahar made a short speech. "As we have been hearing during our planning sessions, women are only around 20 percent of the global energy workforce, downstream to upstream, and only around 10 percent of boardroom positions in oil and gas. Here in Azerbaijan, we are the cradle of the oil industry, where some of the first women oilworkers ever existed, and still we are in total a fraction of the industry. I am so honored to work with my colleagues around the world—" here she looked at the other women, each in turn, "—to highlight the achievements of this minority workforce and the opportunities that we must create for ourselves in the industry that powers our world." Elizabeth cheered her colleagues with genuine warmth. The shah pilaf arrived, a stunning cake of crisp browned rice. One of the servers cracked it and deftly pulled back its pieces to show the mounds of fluffed and steaming rice within, dotted with jewels of dried apricot and lamb.

At that moment a baffling scene appeared in the main room of the restaurant, visible from where the women sat. A crowd of mostly young people of various descriptions, all holding up their cell phones a full arm's length from their bodies, all trying to separate from one another to the extent possible in a relatively small space, some fanning out and walking the periphery of the restaurant while holding their phones and speaking to themselves with animation. Elizabeth watched as a harried but obsequious manager tried to corral them to the three large tables with reserved signs in the central room of the restaurant.

He spoke rapid Azerbaijani to a man and woman who had the clear look of handlers in that they were nicely but unassumingly dressed and stood at a politely watchful remove from the guests, who wandered like children, gesticulating and holding up their phones.

The women from the conference looked at each other bemusedly. "What is this?" asked Elizabeth to Gulbahar. One man drew near to them, a slight sandy-haired white boy in a dorky outfit who was speaking inaudible but clearly English words with incredible plasticity and animation on his face. "It can be vloggers," said Ebru. "They have travel channels on YouTube. They are all around Turkey now."

A very young woman came near their table, speaking an East Asian language. They heard the slight American man say, "This is *awesome*, you guys," as he fingered an ancient musket hanging on the wall. The maître d' corralled the remaining vloggers and sat them at the tables, where several set their phones down and the remainder kept speaking for a few more beats. There was something uncanny and unsettling about the sight of so many people broadcasting all at once, or not even broadcasting, recording for a future broadcast but maintaining a facade of immediacy. Nonetheless, Elizabeth wondered if she could get her KazMunayGas conference recruit to do something like this, and show everyone her day at the Kashagan Workers Accommodation Camp.

When the meal was over, Elizabeth begged off going out for drinks and walked up to the gate of the old city wall, now restored into an almost Disneyfied state of newness, all the old worn stones replaced with new, old-looking stones, just as the Palace of the Shirvanshahs had been restored, just as everything old had been seemingly made new, newer than new. In front of the digital sign at the gate she flagged a cab and, after ascertaining with her memorized phrase, "*Siz ingiliscə danışırsız,*" instead of giving the Fairmont address she gave the address of the Glenns' old apartment near the Landmark building. She would drive by first, she told herself, and if the light was on she would knock. It wasn't too late, although of course, it was late; it would be so rude to show up now. She mostly just wanted to look.

Her cab driver spoke some English. He was young, handsome, a little effeminate. "I love America," he said, and the sentiment shocked Elizabeth. It felt so anachronistic, the kind of thing someone would have said in their childhood, not *now*. Not after, well, everything. "Really?" she said. "It has some nice places."

"I have a visa appointment in two months," he said, looking in the rearview.

"Oh," said Elizabeth, worried for him. "Where do you want to go?" she asked.

"Anywhere!" he said. "Miami. Phoenix. Los Angeles. I want to drive Uber." This sounded to Elizabeth like a terrible plan. She wouldn't encourage anyone, really, to show up in America without money.

"Ah," she said. "I live in Houston," she offered. "In Texas." She wished she had something to offer other than a warning, but he pre-empted her.

"People in Azerbaijan say if you are going to America, you have to fix your teeth first," he said. "Because there it's very expensive."

Elizabeth laughed with embarrassment. "That's true," she said. "You do want to do your teeth before you go to America." He fell into silence as he navigated around a jam on one of the narrow streets.

When the cab pulled down the old street, Elizabeth strained to orient herself. It took her a moment to understand that the building was gone, in its place an entirely different building, a dress shop on the gleaming ground floor. She asked the friendly driver to continue on, feeling simultaneously pierced to the heart and relieved.

Elizabeth was on the Lufthansa flight to Frankfurt, then JFK, and then on to Houston. She had set her alarm for 2:30 a.m. All the international flights arrived and left at ungodly hours; that hadn't changed. Rain spattered the windshield of her cab as it raced down the main thoroughfare in the dark, and the skyscrapers that lined the road were illuminated with LED flags even at this late hour, casting an eerie glow on the streets. It was a cab that someone had smoked in, and the old tobacco smell was comforting. Elizabeth was bereft, coming to the end of her brief foray into the uncanny streets; she could only bear to leave with the knowledge that she would be back for the conference next year. If she stood in the right moment at the right spot, she had felt, she might see a knobby-kneed ghost with her foam headphones, her Discman in her bag, walking fast, praying for invisibility yet desperate to be seen.

Elizabeth got through the passport line and into the upper deck of the airport, which she had not seen during her arrival. "Cocoons area," read one sign, and indeed the hall was dotted with house-sized architectural basket structures magnificent and vaguely comic, and recognizably cocoons once you had read the sign. Some had a place to order food and a seated area. Some were two-story. One had a library. One was for prayer. She loved them, these giant nests.

The flight was delayed and she had hours to kill so she found a cocoon with an open restaurant and ordered a coffee and a pastry. She finished these and read her emails, which contained no action items. And even though it was only now, somehow, 6:00 a.m., she ordered a beer. Time had no meaning. Normally Elizabeth didn't drink beer anymore; she had found that any extraneous carbs collected around her middle and in the place under her chin, which was getting soft and which she knew ultimately only cosmetic intervention would truly fix. But she would make her time in the Baku airport a holiday. She had a

Vogue and a *Vanity Fair*. She returned to her banquette with her beer, a beer at which the bartender had looked slightly askance while handing it over, and folded her legs in their yoga pants underneath her. She had a big soft comfortable sweater for flying, and she had patted extra cream onto her face for the desiccating air of the plane, a special blue cream she bought for $180.

She munched her sandwich and looked around at the faces in her cocoon, which had filled up as the hours passed and the delays piled up. At one table by the cocoon opening sat a blurrily good-looking man, a white man with brown hair and a faintly olive complexion. It was a sight that mirrored some other sight, one that floated just out of reach. Elizabeth let her gaze linger on him in puzzlement and then registered with deep and profound surprise that it was Charlie Kovak. "No fucking way," she said aloud.

She looked down and then looked again to make sure it was him. He was hunched into the corner of the couch, which looked uncomfortable for his size, an echo of his posture at Zeynab Xanim's table, his saucer on his knees. He had a cup of coffee, a laptop, a phone, and a bunch of papers spread before him on the too-small table. She was amazed at the conjoined sensation of fear and affection she felt, the sense of kismet born of sheer improbability. He looked around and saw her staring at him and started. She was caught. He looked bemused and issued a look of faux suspicion that made her laugh. He was far-enough away that, awkwardly, she had to scoot herself over to the table between them to be heard. "Are you . . . Charlie Kovak?" she asked. He looked angry but then in a split second appeared to soften, taking in Elizabeth's incredulous face, her frail wrists in her big sweater, her hands held together in an almost prayerful gesture.

"That depends who's asking," he said. "Are you a hired goon?" His voice was exactly the same. She tripped over her words. "I'm . . . we met a few times . . . here, actually. I was a kid. Bunny Glenn. Well, now I'm Elizabeth. Then I was Bunny. My dad was embassy." She was surprised by the time it took him to reach back and place her. He was so crystalline in her own memory. His eyes widened, although she wondered, after the time it had taken him to remember, if it was merely a courtesy on his part. She helped him.

"Eddie Mantell lived upstairs from me, with Zeynab Xanim. You came and watched *Santa Barbara* with us one day." She thought of his hands on her shoulders at Gobustan.

"Yes, of course, I remember, wow, hi." He looked befuddled and shook himself as he began to stretch out his arms, an endearing, slightly canine gesture, somewhere between a handshake and a hug. "How the hell are you?" She scooted toward him on her banquette, and he mirrored her so it was as if they were seated at arm's length apart at the empty table between them. "This is so weird," he said. "I'm amazed you remember me."

Elizabeth laughed again. "How could I forget? You were larger than life."

He clicked something on his computer and closed it, giving her attention, a gesture of courtesy she noticed.

"What are you doing here?" he asked.

"I'm here for work," she said, as if it were commonplace.

"Did you join the Foreign Service like your dad?" he asked.

"No," she said. "I work for an energy company, actually."

He humphed, almost a laugh, but mirthless. "Wow," he said. "BP?"

"No, but I'm doing a conference with them," she said archly.

"Christ," said Charlie.

"What's your beat now?" asked Elizabeth. "Where are you going?"

"I'm going to Frankfurt, then Kabul," he said. "My beat got worse. I write about drones," he said.

"Ah," said Elizabeth. "I'm on that flight too. The first one anyway." She took a sip of her beer.

"Is your dad an ambassador somewhere cushy?" He cracked his back, a noisy somehow-familiar motion.

"No," said Elizabeth. "He left the Foreign Service. He lives in Dushanbe and teaches. He's anti-drone war."

"Well that's something," said Charlie. He looked at Elizabeth. "What year was it again? When you were in Baku."

"'98," said Elizabeth.

"Okay, yeah," he said. "The last *Intercock* I ever did was about how Unocal invited the Taliban to a pool party in Houston. Then I got my ass beat for something unrelated and it kind of soured me on running an independent newspaper. Then the events of September 11 happened, and both Unocal and I could move on to new topics."

Elizabeth laughed, loudly, energized by her beer and the proximity of Charlie, whose voice made the hair stand up on the back of her arms. She had heard someone tell that story about Unocal before, maybe Frank Turnbridge himself, in one of his frequent diatribes against the majors. Unocal didn't exist anymore, of course.

She registered that he wore a wedding ring. Almost as if he saw her notice he gave her an appraising look, took in her body and the plain solitaire on her left hand, a ring that was a source of tiny, secret disappointment to Elizabeth. She had allowed herself to covet something different, an emerald-cut diamond buttressed by baguettes, but she also believed it was cheating to pick the ring with the man. Francis was into things that he deemed classic, and what was more classic than a solitaire, unadorned? The diamond, at any rate, was fairly large and, Elizabeth was told, of perfect quality.

"Bunny from Baku," said Charlie. "It all vaguely comes back to me." He looked over at her table.

"You're having a beer, huh?" he noted. "Maybe I'll have one too. We have hours, apparently."

"Don't let me keep you if you have to work," said Elizabeth, hoping he would stay.

"Nah, it'll be good. Catch up with my old friend Bunny." He stood, wearing functional but not particularly stylish black jeans, and stretched the length of his body. Elizabeth noticed with a start that he was well into middle age. He must be fifty, maybe more. How had that happened? He was probably better-looking now than he had been then, his vague bulk seeming like the accumulation of experience. He had a solemn face, for all the rancorous joviality he had once projected. He looked serious and tired.

Charlie went to the counter and came back with a tall glass of beer to match Elizabeth's, which she had gotten from her table and moved over to his. He sat down, and she reflected on what a rarity it was to be near someone she had known in youth. She didn't go to her high school reunions, had only the most glancing of connections with any of her old friends. There was no one from anywhere she had lived that she still knew. No children she had grown up with, barring her brothers. Small Ted had moved in with another poker player in Toronto. He still came to Beaumont at Christmas.

"You know," she said as Charlie clinked his glass solemnly to hers and then drank, "you were the first person who ever explained the oil industry to me. I remember how exciting you made it sound. To me it was just boring old men throwing watermelons at that Fourth of July picnic, but you explained it all to me, remember, at that party at that old mansion?"

He looked pained. "I remember very little of that era, to be honest," he said. "What party?"

She felt alone in the memory, alone as she had felt in the embassy apartment, the loneliest days of her life and more vivid to her, some-how, than most of the years that intervened. "It was in some reno-vated old mansion, that guy, Mr. Two Percent or whoever. He had a big party there, and my dad brought my brother and me. I was wear-ing a pink dress with beads," she said flirtatiously. "It was a very big deal for me."

"I'm sure you were very fetching," he said, almost nastily, and she recoiled slightly.

"Sorry," he said, sensing the affront. "This whole experience is catching me by surprise, to put it mildly."

"You were explaining to me about the Contract of the Century," she coaxed him. "I came and sat with you, and you were threatening some guy about having gone to a weekend away with a prostitute. Sex worker." He threw his head back and laughed.

"And I was doing this in front of you? Jesus."

"You made it seem interesting, I guess."

"And now you work for an oil company. Christ. Well that's not what I meant to do," he said. "That's not the outcome I would have hoped for." He looked at her intently, but with a curiosity stripped of vehemence.

"I didn't seek it out," Elizabeth said simply. "It just worked out that way. And I'm on the non-oil side anyway. I'm on the renewable side, the energy transition. I've been there long enough that I get to make my own work, sort of. It's interesting."

"Who's the lucky guy?" Charlie asked, nodding toward her ring. Elizabeth noticed that he had noticed, noticed that he had said "lucky."

"His name is Francis," said Elizabeth.

"What does he do?"

"He's a consultant," said Elizabeth, and she forged ahead. She didn't want to discuss Francis. "Why are you in Baku?" she asked, finishing her beer. Charlie looked at her.

"It's mostly a detour," he said. "But Turkey is selling Azerbaijan drones at a discount. War-winning drones. Israel is selling them stuff too, for surveillance. Little secret unholy alliances. It doesn't bode well for the Armenians in Artsakh. Karabakh. Whatever you want to call it. Aliyev has a hard-on for it. I was in Istanbul, and then I came here to see if anyone would talk to me about it."

Elizabeth thought for a moment how interesting Francis would find this, his private love of geopolitical intrigue.

"Azerbaijan and Armenia are still fighting?" Elizabeth asked. She had not kept up.

"Yeah," said Charlie. "With some different allies. Iran's low-key supporting Armenia; Russia is dancing around it, selling weapons to everyone. America will privately support Aliyev slaughtering the Armenians while crying sad little crocodile tears."

Elizabeth's phone buzzed at the same time that Charlie's did and simultaneously they reached for them. "Fucking flight is canceled," said Charlie, while Elizabeth apprehended the same information.

"Shit," said Elizabeth, thinking of her calendar and then deciding it didn't matter. Charlie opened his laptop and began typing. He paused and looked up at Elizabeth.

"I guess we should go find out how they can reroute us," he said, draining his beer and standing.

"Maybe I'll go to Kabul with you," she said, unexpectedly saucy. It had been too early, her stomach too empty, to drink that beer.

"There's no way I'm going to Kabul today," he said. "Unless I fly to Frankfurt. They fly like twice a week direct." Elizabeth stretched. She collected her magazines and put them into her tote. Together they walked toward the escalators, down toward the ticket agents.

Later they stood in the taxi line outside the splendiferous airport, the sun illuminating the great gauzy tufts of cloud that the winds pushed across the sky. Elizabeth had gotten herself onto the same flight to Frankfurt, leaving the next morning at the same ungodly time. From there she would go back to Houston. Charlie had put himself on a direct flight to Kabul leaving the next evening. She wanted to stay within the tenuous but cozy web that surrounded them, one charged with nervy possibility but also a kind of comfort.

"Are you going to go back to your same hotel?" she asked Charlie, helpless to find a way to put it that carried no hope or insinuation.

"I stay at a guesthouse downtown. Where were you?"

"The Fairmont," she said. "I guess I could go back there. I'd rather stay down the hill though, somewhere near Fountains Square."

Charlie looked at her. "What are you doing the rest of the day?" he asked her, his face open and guileless but intent.

"I don't know," she said. "Sightseeing. Going shopping." There was a beat during which her stomach roiled.

"You ever been to Shamakhi?" he asked.

"Who knows," said Elizabeth. "Maybe. But yes, let's go. I'll go anywhere. You decide." She pointed to her bag. "I just have this carry-on." Elizabeth had always been an excellent packer. Charlie had a backpack.

"Nah," he said, reconsidering. "Too far." She felt disappointed, anxious to find a replacement.

"What about the beach?" she asked. It was the absolute tail-end of the season, and unseasonably warm.

Charlie considered. "There's an insane hotel east of town. I met a source there once. Like flaming chandeliers, mirrored walls, the works. It has a beach club. It might still be open."

"Perfect," said Elizabeth.

They got into a taxi and Charlie said something in Russian, a question. The old man at the wheel spoke back, and then they had an exchange at the end of which he began speeding down the road that led away from the airport. Elizabeth heard bilingual people all the time in Texas—people moved between Spanish and English with incredible ease—although these were people she simply overheard, not people she actually knew. Most of the women in the Celebrate Women in Global Energy conference were speaking their second or third language. And yet the incongruity of an American man speaking a language that wasn't his own would never fail to be alluring, provided, or course, that it was not her father or brother. Charlie leaned back in the seat.

"Where are we going?" said Elizabeth.

"To the beach," he said. "I'll pay this way if you pay the way back." Elizabeth had a thrilling feeling that the veil that shrouded the world was being lifted and that something would finally be made plain, some subtext made text, a secret spoken aloud.

They rode for a while mostly in silence, looking alternately at their phones and out the window at the wide, improved streets and the new apartment blocks and sprawling new single-family housing developments, done in an American shape, a Texas shape of infinite sprawl, but with an architectural style that was not quite American. There were roadside signs advertising new homes with photos of houses that were nowhere to be seen but had exactly the look of Warren and Christine's place in Lumberton.

"It's so different," Elizabeth said, to make conversation. She told him about the White City and the broad road surrounded by the huge empty blocks, the vast spaces for the apartments and parks and promenades yet to come.

"They tore everything down in that zone," said Charlie. "People were living there, and they just cut off the pipes one day and said get out. There were videos of old women crying in the street." She told him about the new building on the site of their old apartment, although that neighborhood had not been the site of wholesale destruction like the Black City had been. It seemed like a week had passed since she had asked the cab driver to make the stop in the night.

"How do you make money?" Elizabeth asked him now, watching as he tapped on his phone.

He looked up from the phone. "I have a podcast," he said. "People subscribe to it. If I do that and sell an article occasionally, I get by."

"Why did you switch from harassing oil guys to covering drone strikes?" she asked. He shrugged. "There's more people with a deep state paranoia who will subscribe to your podcast than there are people who want to hear about oil companies. Or were, at least. I don't know about now." He put his phone in his pocket.

"It wasn't really ever just oil that was my thing," he said. "It was about . . . rapacity. And it was so obvious the way the oil stuff dovetailed with the Iraq War. I mean fucking Blackwater had a little private navy to patrol Caspian oil fields for a while there and the US government paid for it." He looked out the window at the rows of doors for sale propped against fences lining the road.

"Then I got interested in how little oversight there was over these drone strikes."

Elizabeth named an audiobook she and Francis had listened to by a former CIA officer who allegedly consulted on *Homeland* and who had grown disillusioned with the scattershot methods of assassination favored by the recent administrations. "A name on every bullet" was his philosophy, the correct way to approach espionage. Elizabeth could never figure out if he was real.

"Is it true they let an AI pick their targets?"

"It's a million times worse than you can imagine," said Charlie. "Hundreds and hundreds of dead kids. Thousands of adults. Pine nut farmers, pomegranate farmers, poppy farmers." He wiped his hands on his stubble and looked out in front of him. She had nothing to say to this, so she just said, "Awful," her response to most awful things she heard about.

The hotel was a behemoth, a stepped-down cascade of concrete and glass with two mismatched observation decks like saucers perched on the roof. It was surrounded by a waterpark that was obviously closed for the season. But the beach they found when they navigated around the hotel was wide and sandy, dotted still with holiday structures, and the water was blue. There was no trace of the activity that took place on the surface miles across the sea or down in its depths.

"It looks like they still have cabanas and shit you can rent," Charlie said. She was struck by the youthful quality of his speech, for a man she would have until recently considered old. "Or we can do this free beach."

"I don't have a towel," Elizabeth said. She looked up at the hotel, a gaudy spaceship set down incongruously by the seashore. "Let's do the cabana. We can stay for a while and then go back to the city," she said, artfully shaping the day into a foregone conclusion. Her mouth went dry.

"Okay," he said simply. "Let's get a cabana." They walked to a part of the beach roped off and masked by flopping and ill-cared-for banana plants, only a few straggling tourists unwilling to let go of the summer. Charlie paid the lone attendant, then motioned courteously for Elizabeth to go first inside to change. She felt his presence outside while she wriggled into her one-piece, scooping her boobs up so that they would sit better.

They pulled their chaise longues out of the cabana and contemplated the water. It was nearly noon, and the sun was warm on the sand and the water. She looked at Charlie and saw he had a tattoo on his chest, below his collarbone, navy blue, blurred and partially obscured by the fur of his chest. Looking close she saw the letters, faded unadorned capitals reading "NOBODY GETS HURT."

"What does it mean?" she asked.

"I got it when I was high," he said. "ExxonMobil's workplace-safety slogan. They put it on billboards in their compounds overseas."

"It's poetic," said Elizabeth. "Why did you get it?"

"It turns out its ironies extend to every facet of life," he said grimly.

"Over your heart," said Elizabeth. "That's a nice touch."

He got up and jogged toward the water.

They spent several hours on the beach, mostly quiet. Charlie worked on his computer and his phone and Elizabeth read a novel set in Soviet Baku by someone who had defected to the United States after a chance encounter with Armand Hammer in Moscow. She wondered if this was real too. After some back-and-forth and laughing with the cabana attendant Charlie caused mimosas to materialize. They finished one bottle of champagne and then, after very little discussion, another. After a while Elizabeth stood up on unsteady legs.

"I want to see the hotel," she said.

"It's something," he said. "Come."

He stood and stretched and put on his shirt and she put on a dress over her suit and they walked loosely and unsteadily toward the absurd hotel. Inside the freezing lobby the splendor was breathtaking, although, Elizabeth told Charlie, a far cry from the Fairmont. A shimmering geometric chandelier the size of a small house hung from the ceiling. Elizabeth left Charlie and found the bathroom, covered on every side by silver and mirrors. A woman with lip fillers, who looked nearly indistinguishable from Kim Kardashian, was taking photos of herself and Elizabeth apologized gesturally for getting into her shot. She peed with lightly drunken relief, and by the time she had come out the starlet was gone. She inspected herself in the slightly too-bright light. She looked lively, she thought, very plain next to the stunning influencer but possibly as good as she would ever look again. She had a vision of bringing Charlie upstairs to some trianon-like suite and tearing off his clothes.

But in the end what happened, happened ignominiously in the cabana, wooden walls and a curtain separating them from the rest of the beach. It had to be silent, or as close to silent as possible, and accomplished on the hard, narrow daybed built against the back wall. "Ouch," he said when she sat on him, the frail mattress pressing down to the wood below. It was very hot in the tent, and halfway through her drunkenness wore off and she could see, as though from a bird's-eye view, what they were doing. It was the kind of moment where she could have recoiled in horror but there was enough desire and pleasure to see her through, perhaps the only time those elements had aligned with reality in quite that way. She was overwhelmed by the experience. She came, and he came shortly after, pulling her off him at the last minute. She had an IUD but had neglected to tell him, had neglected even to think of it. They sat shoulder to shoulder on the bench, Charlie nearly wheezing with effort.

"That was fucked-up," he said. "That was amazing."

Elizabeth regretted immediately that they had done it before nightfall. It should have been a culmination, taking place at the last possible minute of their time together. How would they now spend the remaining hours? She prayed he wouldn't get up and leave. She could almost hear the plea on her lips, for him to stay, to be kind to her, but she held it in. She ran her hand across his chest, the faded ink of his tattoo. She couldn't remember the last time she felt her whole life hung on what the next utterance of a man might be. She had been with Francis for five years, had never been unfaithful, never considered being unfaithful, never had a real opportunity to be unfaithful. She could see how this event now put her beyond the pale, but it also seemed to put her into the stream of life itself, instead of beside it.

"Will you spend the rest of the day with me?" he said to her, his chest moving under her hand, and she nearly wept with relief.

Later, in a boutique hotel near Fountains Square that Elizabeth had picked from Trip Advisor on her phone in the cab on the way back, they had sex again, instigated by Elizabeth. Afterward they lay side by side in a wide bed, and as if by unspoken agreement each got their phones, Charlie pulling his from his pants pocket along with a pouch holding a pair of reading glasses and Elizabeth, first drawing her sweater back over her head, pulling hers from her bag on the table. Charlie fit the glasses onto his face and squinted at the screen, a gesture that made Elizabeth laugh out loud.

"What?" he said, looking at her. "I'm old, I need my specs."

Elizabeth felt young. Wildly, absurdly young. She looked around the hotel room, this one a neo-Orientalist style, patterned tiles, very unlike the Fairmont, and said, "I can't believe this."

Catching sight of the TV she remembered the previous shocks of the trip. "Oh my god," she said. "This really is crazy. Remember those guys, the Ivy League guys, who were in Baku? You called them prep-school jerkoffs."

"Oh, yeah," said Charlie.

"I saw one of them on Fox News!" she said. "Saying Trump was doing a good job overseas."

Charlie grunted. "That guy's inches away from full MAGA."

"Really?" Elizabeth asked.

"Oh yeah," he said, tapping on his phone. "The hilarious thing is he's such an obvious patrician prep-school douche," said Charlie. "He's just a Cold Warrior born at the wrong time, Gen X like me. And he doesn't want to pay taxes."

"How does a guy like that like Donald Trump?" she wondered aloud. Charlie looked at her with disdain.

"Did you miss the night when a bunch of little fuckers in khakis and polos marched arm and arm with militia chuds carrying tiki torches and swastikas? Preppy people are fascists too, Bunny."

That was one day Elizabeth had let herself feel that things had gotten really, really bad. She looked at Charlie needfully. His face became suspicious, suddenly, in the glow of the sculptural lamp beside him on the nightstand, and then mean.

"You're not going to Me-Too me, are you?" he asked her, peering over his glasses. "We're both consenting adults here, I feel compelled to state for the benefit of any recording device." Elizabeth stared at him. "Unbelievable," she said.

"Listen, it's tough out here for a white man," said Charlie. "Like our preppy friend knows."

Elizabeth shook her head. She opened the news packet from a subscriber service they used at Turnbridge. She clicked a link and skimmed a report about the summer's Tengiz melee, when a foreign oil worker posted a suggestive photo of himself with a female Kazakh colleague and started a riot. "Jesus," Elizabeth said, and Charlie peered over her shoulder.

"Oh, yeah. I saw that," he said. "The oil companies hire a bunch of foreign workers to come, and they pay them a shitload more than the Kazakh guys, so they already hate them. This guy was an Arab I think. So when he posts a picture with one of their women, it pops off." *Their women*; Elizabeth noted this silently. The conclusions of the report did not include any details about the woman involved. Elizabeth pictured the frozen northeast Caspian, which she had read about during her autodidact period in the Turnbridge reading room. She had always wanted to go there. Tengiz. Korolyov. Kashagan. "Cash-all-gone," it was called, a flabbergasting scale of engineering required, dodging ice blocks and frigid winds, a boondoggle, a clusterfuck, plagued by sour gas that ate through the pipes. But they were forging ahead anyway. She thought of Dilnaz the engineer, her conference panelist from KazMunayGas.

"BP does the same thing here," Charlie said. "The guys who come from South Asia or the Philippines to work offshore get twice what the Azeri guys get."

"Hmm," said Elizabeth, her mind still on Kashagan.

"So what is it you do exactly?" asked Charlie.

She considered what to say. Her new title let her inflate herself a bit. "Well part of it is I tell stories about women in STEM." She issued this challengingly.

He threw his head back and laughed. "Oh my god," he said. "Let me guess: oil propaganda videos with lady roughnecks."

"Laugh it up," she said. "I know you used to make your sexist fucking newspaper and it's all a joke to you, but it's actually hard for women in this industry." She felt unprepared to defend herself, weak and worn-out, but offended. "Why should women from oil-rich countries not have a role in supplying cheap and plentiful energy for their own benefit?" This could have been marketing copy she had written for the conference.

"Jesus Christ, Bunny," said Charlie. "You believe that?"

"I believe that women should have educations and jobs and refrigerators to put their fucking food in and that they should be able to give birth in hospitals with incubators in the NICU," she said, genuinely pissed. "That's not a controversial statement."

This was what Francis had said to her on Phil Miles's roof the first time they met, and it was such a just and tidy logic she had never really moved away from it.

"Oil companies don't care about incubators," said Charlie. "They don't give a fuck about you, or any woman in Kazakhstan, or any woman anywhere."

"Neither do you," said Elizabeth. "You're wearing a fucking wedding ring."

He stood up, picked up his clothes from the floor, and walked toward the bathroom. "There it fucking is," he said. "Yes, I'm a bad person. Chevron or Tengizchevroil or whatever the fuck it is will boil you alive, and you'll still be screaming that I'm a misogynist pig so you don't have to care."

Elizabeth suddenly worried that he would leave and that this interlude would end before what she felt was its known expiration date of tomorrow, when she got into the taxi that would take her back to the airport. She felt suddenly that she would miss him. She was too proud to beg, felt so ugly and undignified, so exposed with the cellulite of her thighs pressed against the bed, but knew there must be some word she could say that would make him stay.

"I'm just as bad of a person," she made herself say. "I just *fucked* you," she said, the words feeling lewd and ungainly in her mouth.

He stopped in the doorway of the bath and looked at her for a while. "I guess it's hard to be a feminist oil and gas shill too." It was such a pungent way of putting it that she couldn't help but laugh, and she felt her strength return.

"Don't leave," she said to him, and she tried to look beautiful. Francis said when she looked at him a certain way he was powerless to say no to her. She looked that way at Charlie and prayed that it would be enough to buy her just the scant hours until morning.

"Want to go get something to eat?" he asked her in a gruff but conciliatory voice, and she was consoled.

After several false starts where Charlie either failed to remember where something was or learned that it had closed, they found a restaurant he liked, downstairs in the basement level as so many restaurants were, on a side street near the square. It was an unassuming place with a cold case in the back where the proprietor sat and smoked a cigarette, the kitchen invisible behind him. There were small rugs and a few paintings and posters on the wall, and a Pixar movie played on a flat-screen TV. There were only men in the restaurant, groups of two or three, most with a bottle of vodka at the end of the table. Their table was covered with a worn carpetlike cloth. Elizabeth looked at the menu, which had pictures. "Dolma in quince leaves," she said, "and whatever else you want." In Russian Charlie ordered and soon the dolma came, and pickled things, tomatoes and peppers. They had a salad of beautiful cucumbers and decent tomatoes and a pile of very green, very fresh, very flavorful herbs. Elizabeth approved of the restaurant, which felt unassuming and authentic. The toilet was a very clean porcelain squat. Eventually another woman came in with a group and was seated, so Elizabeth wasn't alone.

While she drank her beer and ate her dolma, tiny bundles like gifts, she told Charlie about the vloggers.

"That's a thing," he said. "The government pays for the whole trip. There's influencers going to Saudi and Syria now on state-sponsored junkets." Charlie used his warm puffed bread to sop up the oil on his plate.

"Azerbaijan is spending a shitload of money on its reputation," Charlie said. "Positioning themselves to fuck the Armenians. I bet the vloggers will all have a little interlude about Azerbaijan's long history in Karabakh."

"That's creepy," said Elizabeth.

"It's fucked," he said. But then he smirked. "Aren't you doing the same thing?" Elizabeth looked at him evenly.

"You make me out to be this villain, but I started out as a temp at an engineering company and I read boring reports all day and I turned it into a real job with real money and a real purpose of celebrating women workers of the world, and that's exciting to me." She drank her beer, wrinkled her nose, and suddenly felt her age. She would get a headache if she didn't drink a lot of water very soon. She could feel Charlie looking at her less with malice than with curiosity.

"You want to stay where you are?" asked Charlie.

"I don't know," said Elizabeth, truthfully. "I want to keep making money and doing something that's interesting. I have a lot of freedom where I work, compared to when I started." The *piti* arrived, lamb and chickpeas steaming in clay pots.

"And it's changing," she added. "Everyone's on board with decarbonization now. My company invests in batteries and new tech. The transition is happening." She heard this more and more—the energy transition, a foregone conclusion.

"It won't be fast enough," he said, looking sort of bemusedly at her. Elizabeth ate the bread, warm and dotted with seeds.

"The scientists who worked for Exxon predicted with insane fucking precision the extent of global warming ten years before you were born. And when you were a teenager, Lee Raymond stood in front of a room with the world's eyes on him and said humans don't cause climate change and if they do it doesn't matter because we need energy." He looked at her intently.

"I don't work for Exxon," she said.

"It doesn't make a difference," he said. "Actually, since your company is private, it'll be even less accountable. Public companies will get activist shareholders and divesters who will get inside and change the DNA. But private companies can keep on pumping in the dark. And they're all the same, no matter how they're structured, what they're called. Their only goal is to keep profitably existing. They want to live like any organism wants to live."

They sat in silence for a minute.

"I believe that soon it will become more profitable for them to change," said Elizabeth, the closest she had come to making a statement of belief on the issue. This is what would happen, she thought.

"A lot of people will die before that happens," said Charlie. "And the people who did it will die peacefully in their beds."

Later they were in their bed, the window open to the breeze, an hour before Elizabeth had to leave for the airport. Their day together had reached a peak and started to curdle, just past its prime. Elizabeth imagined the relief of being back in the café at the Aliyev airport in the big sweater and yoga pants, drinking a coffee and reading her magazine. She had seen on her phone that emails from Phil and Frank were filling up her inbox. The terms of her expanded role still had her doing things for them that they needed. They were still a family company, and she was part of the family. She knew from her crowded Gantt chart that they had a number of projects coming online, and Phil was always adding new things at the last minute because he knew he could count on her to get them done. She was going to ask for a raise in six months.

"When's the wedding?" Charlie asked, gently running his finger over the diamond on her finger, with something she took as perverse tenderness. She felt for the first time the weight of her betrayal of Francis, but shook it off to preserve the last shreds of intimacy in their dark room, the noise from the lively restaurants on Rasul-Zadeh Street coming in from the window, the streetlights illuminating Charlie's silhouette against the crisp sheets.

"In the spring," she said. "At his grandparents' farmhouse in Missouri," she laughed as she said it in spite of herself. She had met his parents now. His mother was a friendly but rigid person who planned out their weekend visits to the minute. His father was a history buff and had lively conversations with Francis about World War II. The farmhouse, his maternal grandparents', sat on the edge of what had become a soybean farm, the acreage of which no longer belonged to them.

"Jesus," he said, and she felt disloyal.

"It's a beautiful historic building," she said. She began now to think about how she could explain what she had done to herself or anyone else, as if it were only a problem of storytelling. He traced a finger again over the ring and on her palm and wrist and arm.

"You gonna have kids?" he asked. She knew the thing he would say before he said it. Everyone was saying it, in some version or another. "What are you, thirty-six?"

"I know, I'm geriatric, thanks," she said. The number 35 had been inscribed in her consciousness the way the number 28 had once been.

Until this point she had said nothing about Charlie's wife. She had decided too early in their reunion that she wanted to sleep with him, and asking with this knowledge already in mind felt immoral. She would not ask now.

Charlie murmured and then looked vacant. He rustled in the bed, suddenly no longer there. She could feel the pull of his phone, his clothes, his laptop, his life in the small bag on the table by the TV. She felt a mixed revulsion and sadness, seeing for a moment what this might have been to him, how that might differ so much from what it was to her. That would make it indescribably sordid. She tentatively stroked his hair, realizing that she wouldn't see him again, in fact could never see him again, because seeing him again would make what happened real, something that counted, and would make the gulf in their realities matter too. She would put the experience in a black box. She traced a finger over his tattoo. "Nobody gets hurt," she said again.

THE RING

Maryellen and Elizabeth met at a Houston boutique that Elizabeth had found online. When Elizabeth put on the first dress, a Monique Lhuillier because she had read over the years that Monique Lhuillier was one of the finest purveyors of wedding dresses, she had not wanted to come out of the dressing room. She and Maryellen had agreed that she should not do a strapless dress, and yet so many of the dresses, including this one, were strapless. Elizabeth didn't like her back, didn't trust it, because it was a part of her body she couldn't quite see, and she imagined it freckled, pimpled, hairy. She envied the brides at the weddings she had attended, their knifelike and unblemished spines rising from precipitously low backs or peeking out from architectural keyholes.

This dress nipped in at the waist, or was supposed to, and then ballooned dramatically out in a sculptural ivory bell, and it cost $7,000. She looked at herself in the mirror and felt appalled. She was so thin now, she felt, and yet in the dress she looked wide and squat, not aquiline and hungry the way she felt when she stepped off the Peloton. Her shoulders were rounded, as her mother had always prophesied they would be if she didn't stand up straight. Her face looked drawn and tired, washed-out in the custardy but nonetheless surgically bright light of the dressing room area. There was a smell of perfume with something antiseptic beneath, and the faintest smell of feet. The sales associate, who was named Michelle, sent her voice over the top of the weighted curtain.

"How are we feeling?" she said brightly, empathetically. Elizabeth waited a beat too long before she mustered, "Great!" and Michelle, who had seen it all, immediately apprehended the vibrations of the small, brightly lit space.

"The first one is always a doozie," she said. "Why don't you just come out and you can tell me what's feeling good and what's feeling like maybe we want to see something different."

Elizabeth yanked the bodice up over the little wings of flesh that it made under her arms and pulled the curtain aside, meeting Maryellen's eye on the settee where she sat holding a sparkling water that had been pressed upon her. Maryellen smiled and said, "Ah, look at that," which Elizabeth knew was not good.

"Talk to me," said Michelle the sales associate.

Elizabeth let her face fall. "I don't really like it," she said, deflated, to the vibrating presence of Michelle at her elbow in the mirror. "It's a gorgeous dress," she said, to be nice, although the word ceased to have meaning inside the heavy weight of so much fabric. "I guess I just feel like I look a little blah in it."

"It hits in the wrong place," Maryellen said firmly. "Her waist is high, and this is treating her hips like her waist, so she looks dumpy."

Elizabeth looked at her. "Mom," said Elizabeth, instantly twelve years old. Michelle looked wisely and patiently back and forth at the women.

"This is very different than the others you picked to start with—the ones that are more sort of vintage feeling, kind of flowing, you know. This one is very structural and *very* dramatic." She put her hand on Elizabeth's back, and Elizabeth hoped that there were no pimples or hairs under her hand. "I promise you this will get easier and we will find your dress," she said, and Elizabeth could have wept.

"One second," said Michelle, and she went behind another curtain, returning a moment later with two flutes of champagne. Elizabeth admired the burgundy brown shade of Michelle's lipstick, shiny like a polished loafer, against her pale skin. She drank half the champagne in one gulp while Michelle removed the clips and unzipped the dress, and then she went back behind the curtain. She got a whiff of herself as she shimmied out of the dress and lay it gently on the ottoman in the dressing room. A faintly sour smell came through her natural deodorant. Elizabeth believed that real deodorant would give her cancer.

She drank the rest of her champagne and pulled the curtain tighter against the boundary of the dressing room. The enclosure and the smell of herself brought her to the cabana of the Caspian beach hotel with a swiftness that made her put her hand against the wall, off-balance with her feet in the stiff peaks of the dress on the floor. She remembered the solidity of Charlie's body, the warmth and the doughy human but not unpleasant smell in the cabana, which had gotten so hot, where they had sweat so pitilessly from the effort of what they did that for a moment she had seen stars swimming in her field of vision.

It took a moment for guilt to rush in, followed rapidly by paranoia. She had gamed out scenarios. She couldn't be pregnant, and she had gotten an STD test at a Planned Parenthood on the other side of town the day after she got home. But she imagined Charlie's avatar popping up in the replies of a tweet about the conference. "Remember our conference in the cabana on Bilgah beach?" But then she thought, he wouldn't. He was married too. And he liked her. She had felt it, unequivocally. It couldn't be taken away, that he had liked her, and had wanted her, that they had spent the day together. His tweets, in any case, were increasingly baffling when she peeked at them; he was always embroiled in gladiatorial exchanges with other male journalists about topics on which she was not informed.

The next dress she tried on was slinky, with elbow-length sleeves split at the seam and a deep V, too deep. The dress was satin and showed every fold of skin. She couldn't even bring herself to come out of the dressing room and hear Maryellen say she could see her belly-button through the fabric.

When they left the store Elizabeth had the name of a dress written down on Michelle's card that she wanted to come back and try again after she had gone to some other stores. It was the least of a bad lot, she thought, but it was plain, made of a fabric that was secure without being heavy or structural, and had an empire waist that she worried was too Jane Austen-y but flattered her body. She and Maryellen sat at an outdoor café and shared mussels with white wine.

Maryellen asked her about her trip to Baku. She told her what it looked like now, what it was like to be there. Maryellen, misty with wine, began to reminisce. "All of those bigwigs were always coming in on CODELs and VIP visits because Clinton wanted to get that pipeline done," she said. "Holbrooke. Strobe Talbott." Maryellen had an encyclopedic memory for past events, probably because she had once had to memorize the names of reception guests, and she would sometimes recount these memories to Elizabeth over dinner. Elizabeth wondered if Alicia had taken up the task for Ted of remembering everyone's name, their wife's name, where they came from, where their kids were at school, who had gotten too drunk at the Fourth of July.

"Your father must have started taking retirement," Maryellen told her, and Elizabeth flinched. She did not want to have a sad and serious conversation with Maryellen. But she had also had enough wine that she couldn't trust herself not to get into it.

"Ah," said Elizabeth.

"Do you know anything about that?"

"I don't," said Elizabeth, truthfully.

"I assume he's still living with that woman," said Maryellen.

"His life is a mystery to me," said Elizabeth.

"Well I get half of it, his retirement," she said.

"Ah," said Elizabeth. "That's good."

"It helps," said Maryellen.

Maryellen paused and then spoke again. "I was actually thinking of going to school," she said, and Elizabeth looked at her in disbelief for a moment. "For horticulture," she said. "A master's degree."

"Seriously?" she had no idea what that would look like.

"I found a program where they have nontraditional students," said Maryellen. "Sixty-two years old. That's about as nontraditional as it gets."

Elizabeth thought for a moment.

"Sometimes I think about nursing too," Maryellen went on. "Did you know that?" Elizabeth did not. "Did you know nurses were the first flight attendants?" said Maryellen. She sipped her wine. She had drunk more wine than was customary. "The first planes flew so low that the turbulence was awful and everyone was sick all over the place. They wanted people with medical experience." Elizabeth couldn't tell where her mother was going with this.

"So is it horticulture or nursing, Mom?"

Maryellen laughed. "Why not both?" she said. She looked adrift for a moment. "But no, horticulture. You see what I've done with the garden. My peachcot is coming in now." Maryellen had taken a class on grafting and begun doing her own fruit experiments.

Elizabeth decided quickly that this news was good, the best she'd ever heard. She reached out a hand for her mother's hand. Life did not make sense if it did not have a forward direction, an upward direction, an uplift. She was always encouraging her mother to date, and Maryellen had sporadically gone to the movies with a widower named Frank from Orange, in a relationship that didn't quite get off the ground. Why had it been so easy for Elizabeth's father, Elizabeth wondered. Why was it so easy for men? A master's degree in horticulture was even better than the movies with Frank. She felt relieved even while she felt puzzled.

"That's so great, Mom."

Maryellen suddenly changed tacks. "Francis is such a nice man," she said.

"I think so," said Elizabeth, but Maryellen was not finished, and she gripped her wrist. "I pray that what happened to me will never happen to you," she said. Elizabeth hated and feared these moments, when she could offer nothing useful and was simply reminded of the pain that still bubbled up from the ground, like gas bubbles in a marsh.

"Everything worked out," she tried to assuage her. "You're doing *great*." Maryellen was not assuaged.

"I'm serious," she said. "Make sure it doesn't happen." Elizabeth was puzzled. How was she supposed to do that?

"But if it does . . . I don't know . . . you didn't work, which made it a lot harder for you when Dad did that." Elizabeth had gamed out what she would do if Francis left her. She would apply for a job overseas, she thought. Somewhere big. Maryellen withdrew her hand and put it into her lap, and Elizabeth realized she had made an error.

"You think it wasn't *work* to follow him around the world and raise three children?" she said, looking at Elizabeth with something so close to scorn Elizabeth couldn't hold her gaze.

"That's not what I meant," she said, now exasperated that her mother was willfully misunderstanding her. "I know that was fucking work. I *meant* that I have a job and I always will, so I won't be, I don't know, financially dependent." She tried to make her feel seen and heard, as the Instagram therapists might say. "I can't imagine what it was like, Mom, truly." Maryellen raised an eyebrow.

"No, you cannot," said Maryellen. "If you have kids—and you don't have an endless amount of time to do that, I hope you know," she said, looking narrowly at Elizabeth, "you'll see." Elizabeth felt stunned.

"Believe it or not, mom, it's actually kind of difficult to have kids for people in my generation." Maryellen waved this away. "Hard!" she laughed. "You were born with a silver spoon in your mouth, like your father." Maryellen continued, now just angry at Elizabeth, for no reason Elizabeth could identify. Her accusation struck Elizabeth as so untrue that she laughed out loud, which made Maryellen look even more scornful. "Those fancy schools, all those opportunities." This stung Elizabeth, with the unspoken implication that she had not done anything by herself, or done anything worth doing. She wouldn't have come to Texas at all if not for Maryellen.

"That's not fair," she said. Despite the last decade of analysis of privilege, having it and checking it, it was insulting to hear that you got something you didn't deserve, especially from your own mother. No one had applied to the ManPower temp agency but her. That had been nothing but Elizabeth's own steam.

Maryellen dabbed her mouth with a napkin, put it by her plate, stood, and turned with such poise that Elizabeth was transfixed as she watched her walking away, one foot in front of the other as she must have once walked down aisles, unfazed by the turbulence that shook the great machines around her.

Elizabeth sat for a while, angry and chastened. Why was her mother so angry at her? She remembered the announcement that precipitated their argument. More school, at Maryellen's age? She drank the rest of her wine, thought about the dress, and looked at some photos she had taken of it on her phone. She stewed and decided to put it out of her mind. She and Maryellen fought. That's what mothers and daughters did. She not want to "process," as they said. She paid their bill and slowly stood and walked toward where she had parked her car. She dawdled, looking in the shop windows she hadn't perused in years, stores she had ogled when she was living with Maryellen in Beaumont and came into Houston to escape.

In one window there was a small, beautiful array of antique jewelry that was obviously very expensive. There was a ring of some kind of jet-black stone, a night sky against which were set tiny stars made of diamonds. There were pearl rings and cameos, the face of a fox with two sapphires for eyes. Elizabeth found herself opening the door and going inside the shop, which was empty, cool and quiet.

"Welcome," said the stylish blonde woman at a desk in the back, getting to her feet in towering black Swedish Hasbeens that Elizabeth had been eyeing for herself for a while.

"Everything here is so stunning," said Elizabeth, looking over the cases. She had never been compelled by jewelry, apart from engagement rings, but now she let her eyes wander and appreciate as though she were in a museum. Her eye caught on a gently ornate signet ring, words and a harp etched into some ethereal pale blue stone, set into an embellished warm gold. Elizabeth read the words aloud to herself while the woman walked over to stand beside her.

"*Je réponds à qui me touche.*" She leaned into the pronunciation, tipsy and feeling herself. "I respond to whoever touches me?" Elizabeth asked the woman searchingly, laughing as the words left her mouth.

"You got it," said the woman approvingly. "We've been translating it as 'I respond to every touch.'" Elizabeth laughed. "That sounds nicer," she said.

Elizabeth asked to try it on, and when the woman brought out the ring she slipped it on her finger, looking at it from every angle. She would never take it off, she decided. She would keep this forever. "I'll take it," she said, not asking the price.

"Yes, girl," said the woman. "When you know you know." Adrenaline coursed through Elizabeth's body when she handed over her credit card and signed the iPad showing the charge of $2,500 plus tax. She walked out of the store wearing it on the ring finger of her right hand, floating on air.

THE FLOOD

All the car alarms in the neighborhood were going off at odd intervals, muffled by six feet of water. Lights flashed rhythmically in the drizzle that still fell in gentle bursts from the low gray sky, a remnant from the storm. Everything else was silent, the surface of the floodwaters still and belying the currents below. The deluge had receded from the main roads, but Elizabeth, dazed in the front seat, could look out of the passenger side into subdivisions and see the lights flashing through the rippling green brown depths, semicircles of mid-century homes resting serenely under the waters. Windows peered from the water like eyes over a fence.

Elizabeth had huddled with Francis in his townhouse in The Woodlands, which was dry, and they were dry. The idea of being high up, in her old apartment, where she still had a few months on the lease, scared her—the idea of it swaying back and forth in the wind—although she learned in the subsequent days that high was preferable to low when the waters came. They knew they were going to buy a bigger place, but Francis said it wasn't logical to get a big mortgage when they didn't know what they were looking for in a neighborhood, hadn't done the research about the schools for their hypothetical kids.

The Woodlands was mostly spared, although not everywhere. They had stayed in the bedroom on the second floor watching the news and the Bourne movies all in a row, braving the downstairs only to cook frozen pizzas and look out the window at the road.

Maryellen couldn't relive the anxiety of waiting through Harvey to see if her street would flood, even though it hadn't then, thank god. So when this storm approached, she drove up to Warren and Christine's in Lumberton. Lumberton had flooded again, but not all of it, and their street remained above the waters. On the second day Elizabeth had called Warren's house to check in and Maryellen told her in a leaden voice that the Beaumont house was most likely gone. What hadn't flooded during Harvey had flooded now. A neighbor with a jet ski sent her a photo of the strange Tudor folly with brown water past the windows of the first floor. "Mom," said Elizabeth on the phone. "It will be okay. We'll come." They waited until the same neighbor told them that the waters had flowed back out, and they got into Francis's car.

Now Elizabeth and Francis drove the glistening streets, and Elizabeth couldn't understand what made the difference between the places that flooded and the ones that didn't. Port Arthur, which was usually walloped, flooded less than usual, while Winnie was completely inundated. Vidor was inundated. Port Neches was mostly spared. Harvey had been a thousand-year flood, they said. And here they were, two years later.

They stopped first at Warren and Christine's house and picked up Maryellen, who was as wan as the days after Ted had left her. Although Elizabeth had grown a subterranean hatred for Warren and Christine, she felt grateful to them when she saw them standing with their arms around her mother, when Warren got the big fans and the Shop-Vac out of his garage and put them into the back of the Silverado and followed them to Beaumont.

The waters had receded, but there was a skim of black mud over the walkway. The native perennials in the front yard had been snapped off, and the prairie grasses were flattened. The front door buckled in its frame.

Francis and Warren got out of their cars and instantly began to handle things with a male fluency that Elizabeth found profoundly comforting. Somehow Francis had known to adopt the perfect attitude with Warren, a sort of assistant manager, deferring to Warren but seamlessly tucking in the loose threads of his planning, adding darts here and there to pull it together, pointing out what should go in the back of Warren's truck to dry out somewhere, what should be put in a pile as garbage, who they needed to call to haul it all away. Francis was wearing the fishing waders he had bought for the team-building retreat on the Colorado River. He radiated calm, consolatory efficiency.

When they pried open the swollen door, Elizabeth was stunned by the violence, the incredible movement, that the waters had visited on the house. It was a mausoleum for destroyed things. Driving by the flooded subdivisions in their placid brown lagoons, Elizabeth hadn't understood the force of the water in motion or the speed with which it must have moved through homes and neighborhoods. She had missed Harvey, after all. She and Francis had been hiking across a moor. They had watched the disaster on their phones with thoughts and prayers.

End tables from a nested chinoiserie set had traveled across two rooms into the foyer and splintered against the wall. Cabinets had opened and sent forth their contents, china and glassware buried, in pieces and whole, in the scrim of mud and weeds and tumbled ceiling insulation matted against the floor. Elizabeth thought of her quiet evenings in this house with Maryellen, drinking G&Ts and cataloging items for eBay, writhing with quiet dissatisfaction. All that was left was now lying in meaningless, miscegenated rubble—her grandmother's leftover things, porcelain things, English things, alongside the miscellany of the Glenn family travels. A painted wood panel from Moldova lay atop a family of bonnetless Madame Alexander dolls as though to cover their shame. Maryellen slumped against the doorframe while Francis, Warren, and Elizabeth moved awestruck through the rooms and regarded the damage.

In the guest room stacks of archival boxes had been ripped from the closet, their contents disgorged across the floor. Elizabeth picked up a sheaf of photographs now befouled and gummed together, and picked them apart. Ted and Maryellen and John and Bunny in Buenos Aires in their small embassy apartment. Ted and Maryellen and John and Bunny and Teddy Bear in Athens in that rare snow. Bunny goofing on the stage at Epidaurus. Small Ted on his first day of school in Yerevan. Bunny and John in Baku, Bunny in her dress and John still sweaty from his run, in his shorts and his T-shirt, standing with visible reluctance by Bunny, both of them ghostly pale in the light of Ted's flash. Elizabeth sat down in the mud and wept.

She watched Francis in his waders pull up a waterlogged Anatolian rug that must have weighed a hundred pounds and carry it laboriously to the front yard, to the pile of things they would try to salvage. She felt a bayonet of guilt, the memory of what she had done with Charlie on the beach. She let it pass violently through her, a river through a house, and addressed herself to the task at hand. She knew she would have to harden her heart against this memory, to let it become like a scene from a movie that had nothing to do with her. She would never tell Francis.

Maryellen was in the back garden, where she had brought all of her Master Gardener knowledge to bear on fruit trees and native plants, now a snarl of branches and dead baby trees. Maryellen was reciting a litany: her persimmon, her figs, her pecans, her apples, her pomegranates, her peachcot. Elizabeth was transported to the days when she had come to Beaumont and Maryellen could do nothing but ask

Elizabeth perplexedly what had gone wrong, when they both cried all the time. She couldn't go back to that time. There was no room for grief, her own, her mother's, anyone's. Her mother had hated this house anyway. Elizabeth's brain worked to assemble a new story from the wreckage before her. They would have to see this as a blessing. Maryellen would simply have to find a way to begin again, again. That's all there was to it. Elizabeth hugged her mother. "It's okay, Mommy," she said. "It's okay."

2022

$113.73/$80.33

THE PANEL

The conference room at the Marriott was frigid and cavernous, and the women on the stage looked incongruously small before the projection screen upon which their faces were superimposed, every pore and flyaway magnified by the HDR camera that was recording the event. The panel was called "Communicating the Energy Transition: Opportunities and Change." There were four women on the stage, all white, all smartly yet somberly dressed. They were from Baker Hughes, TC Energy, Bain, and Turnbridge Energy Solutions, the latter represented by Elizabeth, who watched attentively, her face set in its smiling, listening angle as a pale, serious brunette with perfectly straight hair was speaking.

"We are at an inflection point, but I think energy companies have a tremendous opportunity, in many respects a missed opportunity, to emphasize to the public, to regulators, to our investors, and even within our own corporate structures, that the energy transition has always been part of our story—that we are in fact the drivers of that transition. At Baker Hughes, for example, we have been leading in carbon reductions, safety improvements, technological innovations, since long before ESG became such a clear benchmarking tool and an instrument of financialization."

It was a coup that Elizabeth had managed to be here, one brought about purely as a consequence of her networking and hustle on the Baku conference—which she was there to talk about and which had gone off without a hitch on International Women's Day, right before everything locked down for COVID, right before she and Francis had scheduled and rescheduled and rescheduled their wedding again. Now, two years later, she was representing a small, private family business alongside the bigwigs at a conference in Houston. After finagling her way onto the panel through dedicated LinkedIn interactions with one of the organizers, she had convinced Phil to let Turnbridge Energy Solutions buy a table at the ceremonial luncheon hosted by Ally, proceeds to support the prevention of sex trafficking. Ally had once been Pink Petro. The name had changed, although not its commitment to serving as a professional network for attracting and retaining women in the energy sector.

It seemed in the last few years that everyone had changed their name. Pink Petro had become Ally. Statoil became Equinor. *Oil Magazine* became *World Energy*. Turnbridge Energy Solutions itself now stressed the non-fossil part of its solutions, a slap in the face to Frank Turnbridge, who had enriched himself and his children, and promoted America's energy independence with Turnbridge oil, Permian oil, Anadarko oil, Bakken oil. Frank was not there to see the change, having died of an aneurysm while taxiing in a Piper Malibu on the way to the Colorado Oil and Gas Association's annual golf tournament, which he had attended faithfully for twenty years. Elizabeth smiled when she heard the Baker Hughes woman say "ESG." It had been Frank's bête noire. "What does it even *mean*, for god's sake," he would say. "It's just three words jammed together."

Elizabeth was dizzied by the swiftness with which they had all adapted their language. It had been twelve years since ManPower sent her to the doors of Miles Engineering Consultants. In the last few years they had learned, it seemed to Elizabeth through an almost-silent accord, to speak a completely new vernacular. Elizabeth was always looking at other companies in the "energy space," as they now called it, instead of "oil and gas," to see how they were positioning their businesses. Baker Hughes, she knew, now called itself an "energy technology" company. "We take energy forward—making it safer, cleaner, and more efficient for people and the planet," their homepage promised. You would hardly know, from its sun-kissed landing page, that ExxonMobil had ever drilled for oil. BP had gone from an international oil company to an integrated energy company. Halliburton's landing page read "The Energy Evolution." Even Miles Engineering, a certified woman-owned business with a frightening photograph of Ainsley at the top of its home page, now offered "Sustainable Engineering Solutions for a Net-Zero Tomorrow."

They all spoke of environmental, social, and governance as they steered the public through the energy transition. Elizabeth did not understand how someone had come up with that phrasing, two adjectives and a noun, but she understood that it was one of the things that had ultimately driven everyone to change their names: the idea that investors were making their choices based on this brief acronymic nod to a company's virtue. Charlie had been right: the Turnbridge umbrella, a private company, was less in thrall to ESG than were Elizabeth's peers on the conference stage. There were no shareholders to apply this rating to their firm. ExxonMobil had recently had their ass handed to them by the activist shareholders at a hedge fund, of all places. So Elizabeth had been right too: it was getting too expensive to do nothing, and the money guys knew it. But changing a website was the easiest, cheapest thing in the world.

Turnbridge began as a family, and they were a family still. Phil continued to crave style, respect, refinement; Elizabeth craved power, every year adding to her small allotment, no bigger than a plot in a community garden. She wanted to recommend things and have people do them, within the comfortable familiarity that Turnbridge supplied. But she thought maybe, just maybe, she might soon be ready for something more.

Phil, as though sensing Elizabeth's restlessness, as though hearing Francis's whispers in her ear that it was time for her to move on after more than a decade in the Turnbridge orbit, had recently signed off on a bonus of $15,000. This was paltry in the scheme of corporate bonuses but such a far cry from Elizabeth's original fifteen dollars per hour that she immediately wove it into the story of her career and herself, as though she had started out working the commissary on an oil rig instead of formatting reports in an air-conditioned office. She was proud that she had shown herself to be of value, that she was no longer consigned to the long nights of Repro in the admin pool but invited to sit with the women with business degrees and speak of ESG on a projection screen. She used the bonus to take Maryellen—now living in a small condo in Houston, her garden limited to a line of terra-cotta pots, her horticulture plans temporarily abandoned with the onset of COVID—to Paris after they got vaccinated. They flew economy plus. Maryellen couldn't believe how awful airplanes had gotten, how bad the service, how nasty the passengers. Elizabeth and Maryellen had fought the whole trip, but they also bought new handbags in the Bon Marché and would always remember their walks along the Seine, the best trip they'd ever taken.

Elizabeth had finally, in her own way, achieved fluency. Not a fluency in the language of her fellow panelists, necessarily—she still felt a vague resentment at their ability to throw around business terms. But she had learned a language that was proving valuable. It did not matter that she did not understand the stock market and still asked Francis to explain things to her—she knew that messaging mattered more than ever. She took the down-home style of Frank Turnbridge and mixed it with feminism. This was her niche, among these women. The "social" part of ESG. She spoke of lifting women up, supporting women in their intersecting struggles. In recent years it had been pointed out that the celebrations of diversity, group photos of empowerment sessions or new home pages, typically revealed an array of *white* women. It was unacceptable, female leaders earnestly said at keynotes and roundtables, and they promised to do better, although Frank Turnbridge insisted to the end it was merely an issue of *qualifications*.

In Elizabeth's Women's Energy Professionals book club, they said that they would do better too, so now they were reading *Roberts Vs. Texaco*, about the disgusting treatment of a Black Texaco employee by Texaco executives. Before this they had read the first autobiography of Condoleezza Rice, who was a figure of admiration among many of the Women's Energy Professionals. Elizabeth had difficulty with this because of the Iraq War. Then again, as some of the women reminded their peers during their meetings, "diversity, equity, and inclusion" didn't just mean of skin tones and genders—it meant of ideas! All ideas should be welcome. Ideas, it seemed, were the true diversity, and sometimes seemed to matter more than the other kinds. It was important that no one feel left out, especially the men.

Sometimes Elizabeth marveled at how simultaneously irrelevant and critical the shaping of narrative was to reality. Decarbonization was more important than ever. The majors were pulling out of the Permian and Bakken right and left. Shell was sending out packets offering to recalibrate refineries to make plastic instead of fuel. "Opportunity out of Uncertainty," their collateral materials read. And yet Europe was preparing to freeze without Russian gas. The EU had signed a deal to double its supply of LNG from Azerbaijan, great news for Azerbaijan and BP. Azerbaijan had retaken Karabakh in 2020 with the help of Turkish and Israeli drones Charlie had been so interested in, and some of Elizabeth's colleagues from the Celebrate Global Women in Energy conference had posted disconcerting nationalist memes on social media. Sofie and John had meanwhile evacuated Kyiv just before the Russian invasion. They were in an Airbnb in Athens, volunteering at the squats for the people they called the real refugees, the people who had been coming to Greece for ten years from across the sea.

When it was her turn with the mic, Elizabeth looked out at the audience of professionals who were there to collectively perform their sense of urgency. No one was wearing masks—masks in Texas were as rare as prairie chickens—and she hoped that nobody had COVID. It had ripped through Turnbridge, putting Frank in the hospital for four weeks before he recovered just in time to die of something else. Elizabeth had mostly stopped worrying about it herself but occasionally paused to feel sad at how stupid and mean the conversation around the pandemic had gotten. She had noticed that if she stayed off social media, she felt better about everything. She knew things were a mess, and yet on blue-sky spring days, when she was in her brand-new all-electric Kia Niro, when she drove through the glinting green soft places of Texas, past the rioting wildflowers, she couldn't help but think that her life was going very well.

She looked at the women arrayed before her. "Like so many of us, I have a personal stake in the energy transition," she said simply. She had practiced her talk a dozen times. She described the devastation of the house in Beaumont: generations of heirlooms and documents and photos gone, all the things that make up a life. While she spoke she placed her hands on her stomach, beautifully round in a navy-blue stretch maternity sheath, rubbed them in circles, and felt the oceanic movements of the stranger within. In the end, her speech was powerfully received.

Downstream

2051

$312.53/$178.12

THE FUTURE

Elizabeth was standing in the delivery room by the hospital bed where her daughter lay groaning and heaving. To her continual amazement, Elizabeth was about to become a grandmother. Pamela had refused an epidural for reasons that Elizabeth could not comprehend. "I want to feel everything," Pamela had said, and now she was feeling it, caterwauling with pain every two minutes in a way that Elizabeth was helpless to soothe. Elizabeth periodically smoothed her hair and called for ice, fingering her ring for reassurance. *I respond to every touch.* She had worn it every day since she bought it. One day she would give it to Pamela.

Pamela had chosen not to learn the baby's biological sex, in keeping with her generation of Portland youth. Either way she was going to name the baby after the baby's father, who had been hit by a car when Pamela was only a few weeks pregnant. This was a pain of an immensity that simultaneously dwarfed and magnified the pain of labor. Elizabeth felt profoundly sorry for her only child, a beautiful twenty-nine-year-old widow stuck with her mother.

When Pamela was ten years old, Elizabeth and Francis had finally heeded the writing on the wall and left Houston. They had spent a lot of time thinking about where to go. It was generally agreed that west of Pennsylvania and north of Kansas was the place to be. Francis had approached the problem with the meticulous attention to detail that he brought to his career and that had put him at the partner level of his firm by the time he hit forty-five. They had picked Portland because, while the 2028 earthquake had shredded infrastructure for several years, the destruction hadn't risen to the level of the direst predictions; it had led to a lot of new building and cleared out old housing stock, leaving only strong survivors from among the beautiful historic homes. Elizabeth and Francis and Pamela had taken another road trip to look it over and had found it lush and pleasing, the climate dreamy after the Gulf, the months of rain and spikes of vicious summer heat notwithstanding. If you had money, the charming old houses could be retrofitted tastefully to filter out the torpid smoky days that began in March and stretched into October, to pump out the torrential rains and occasional deluges of wet snow of the winter, and to cool down the heat of the summer. And they had money, so they had bought a 150-year-old charmer on a triple lot whose previous owners had been unable to afford the upgrades to make it livable in the new era. Eventually they persuaded Maryellen to come and live in the lovely ADU they built behind the house. Maryellen surprised everyone with her unwillingness to leave Texas. The weather had driven her from one home, and she did not want to leave another. They built her a workshop off the ADU and left the rest of the lot to her. They said they were counting on her to make the garden beautiful. In the end she did do her master's; she taught informal classes as she set up a small orchard on the lot.

Francis and Elizabeth had only become stronger as a couple as all the things happened, all the cascading events. They were their own corporation, themselves and Pamela its individual shareholders. They had not only money but combined decades of experience with spreadsheets, projections, logistics. Francis's job was to analyze possibilities, and he had a way of looking into the future that Elizabeth found reassuring throughout their life together. Francis was never out of work. He still worked on supply chains, although now they focused on equipment, the necessities of life. Companies and governments were always cycling in and out of disaster and scrambling to catch up; they never found a model to right themselves that didn't involve paying someone else for advice. Francis and Elizabeth were never closer than when they sat at their kitchen table with a laptop, making their plans.

Every few years Elizabeth looked at the blue ring on her finger and thought of Charlie, imagined a life full of days on the shores of the Caspian—although Azerbaijan was in the midst of a grinding, killing drought, like half the world, a third of the US. Now and then she saw herself young on that beach—how young she still was then she couldn't have comprehended. Charlie would be old now, a truly old man. She had long ago stopped searching his name online; she thought of him when she heard on NPR that they had transferred the remaining detainees from flooded Guantanamo Bay to undisclosed locations, probably in Saudi Arabia.

Mostly Elizabeth felt grateful for their life. Jobless, she had managed the retrofitting and renovation of their Portland house, bringing all her idle scrolling on TikTok and in Meta rooms to bear on the selection of tiles and wallpapers along aesthetic lines, but applying her fluency to securing the house, thinking about their individual energy future and availing herself of some of the innovations that had come about in the last decades. They were fully solar, built on a relative of the same perovskite technology Phil Miles had doggedly pursued in the early years. Often in the reno she found herself in a room full of men, dealing with engineers, contractors, plumbers, electricians, and she smiled to herself at the way the conversations re-created themselves throughout time. She deferred, she wheedled, she flattered, she played dumb, all to bring them around to her view, and if she couldn't, she fired them. Francis ceded the project to her and was grateful that she did such a good job.

She and Maryellen spent time together in the garden. Elizabeth knew nothing about plants but loved going to the nursery with Maryellen, drifting down the green rows, picking based on the shape or color of leaf. They planted six figs, which loved it in Oregon, she was surprised to learn. Three olives. Plums and cherries. Two kinds of mulberry. One day, a beautiful spring day after the rains had stopped, she was hanging laundry on the heavy-duty retractable clothesline she had installed between her house and Maryellen's ADU, and she felt the sun on her shoulders and smelled the heavy scent of fig leaves and it was almost as if she were somewhere she had been before, somewhere good, just out of reach. On the first 120-degree-Fahrenheit day she ever felt, nearly everything shriveled and died and the crows fell out of the trees. On that day Maryellen comforted Elizabeth the way Elizabeth had comforted her after the flood: tersely. The way they supported each other was to simply move forward. "Look," Maryellen said gently, bending a piece of wood from a fig to show the green within. "Wick. It might come back." They tried not to think too long of the hundreds of people who died that week.

Sofie and John stayed in Greece for years, on one of the islands that still had a supply line for water, living what appeared to be a spartan, monastic existence in an old island house whitewashed futilely against the 122-degree heat that struck every year and killed the very young and the very old. Ted Senior had come to live with them when Alicia died of viral pneumonia, and before long they had all gone back to Sweden, where they now lived in what had once been Sofie's family's summer cottage. So it had gone how it always had gone: Maryellen to Elizabeth, Ted to John. Small Ted was still in Toronto, still playing poker, still a bachelor, as far as Elizabeth could tell. She thought sometimes of getting in the van and going to visit him. She and Francis had long ago bought a Mercedes E-Sprinter that they had kitted out with a kitchen and four beds, which they jokingly called their apocalypse van.

Elizabeth wondered whether she would see her father and brother and sister-in-law again. Flying was out of the question for Elizabeth; the turbulence had gotten too bad, and even though the airlines still stood by the old line that turbulence never shook a plane out of the air, she had seen too many videos online, was spooked by the waivers they made you sign now just to buy a ticket. They could always drive the van somewhere to get out of the smoke for a while. But they felt safest at home. They had a generator that cost the earth. They had a cistern that could hold a six-month supply of water. The winter rains could fill it within a few weeks, the atmosphere was so heavy. She doubted she would ever again see the Aegean lapping at the warm sands of the Peloponnese.

Port Arthur and Nederland and Beaumont were unrecognizable, many parts functionally gone. So many people had left. On Google Drone you could see whole neighborhoods abandoned, structures denuded of every valuable material without or within. After transitioning nearly 100 percent to plastics and byproducts before pivoting to focus on its Corpus Christi plant, Aramco abandoned Motiva, leaving parts of it to rust and melt into the Gulf. Warren had died of cancer and Christine had gone to live with Tyler and his wife in Dallas, where they trucked in water.

The Maldives were functionally gone too, but Elizabeth couldn't grieve places she had never seen, although she had seen, every year, the footage of people washed to sea, towns simply removed from the face of the earth during storms, or disappearing into sinkholes in spongy, baking permafrost. There was no language to communicate these things, no feeling that could encompass it.

The feuding heirs of the Taco Bell field south of Houston sold their remaining surface rights just in the nick of time—developers knew it was a floodplain but still felt sure they could do something with it. It was right next to Friendswood, which had been underwater in Harvey but which its residents mostly rebuilt, jacked up their houses, dug in, some never believing it would happen again. Roughly half of the field's joint owners argued vociferously against the offer they had eventually accepted—it was low, they said, pitched toward the wettest, most dubious parts of the tract and not toward the smaller, higher-up, freeway-facing pieces that were still legitimately valuable. Eventually the ones who believed in climate change had produced enough actuarial data to convince the group to get out while the getting was good. The proof was everywhere; by 2030 the US military had left its every coastal base. Ted Senior's share of the field was something like a million dollars, and that was before even the brief florescence of production that came with tertiary recovery, that process of producing more oil that somehow still counted as carbon capture. Thus Elizabeth and Francis and Pamela had for several years been getting $14,000 times three every year, the federal gift limit, from Ted Senior from across the sea.

Long ago their financial planner had taken oil stocks off even his darkest portfolio of wealth-management options—anything that didn't change its name, that is, and in the end that was almost everything. When Elizabeth gave birth to Pamela and cut back her hours, Turnbridge Energy Solutions was acquired by Mobil Green Futures, probably for its patents, after Exxon and Mobil broke apart. Phil had cashed out in a serious way, mostly because he had eventually gone in with his rival on supplying a big portion of new utility infrastructure to Texas through a scheme Elizabeth never quite understood. He and Estelle had retired to British Columbia, a place called New New Zealand; the joke went it was for the folks who couldn't afford the real thing. Phil had given Elizabeth a gift of Mobil Green Futures shares and she kept them, still barely grasping the mechanisms that made them wax and wane.

In her last years at Turnbridge Energy Solutions, Elizabeth had created the materials that showed not just prospective clients but prospective buyers how Turnbridge Energy stood apart. She explained that their company was not like the supermajors, who had turned oil and gas from the thing that powered the world and empowered women, into the thing that brought down pension funds and destabilized nations. But after the acquisition, Elizabeth was let go.

The oil companies changed their names, they pivoted, they called what they did something different, they became part of the solution, they called themselves indispensable. There were some fines, some show trials, some FCPA convictions, but the system had worked so seamlessly that many of the people who got rich from oil put themselves directly atop the next generation of energy just in the nick of time.

Elizabeth eventually came to accept getting laid off. She was finally part of the crew change. In any case, caring for Pamela had exhausted her from the very first moment Pamela was born. Even with one child there was plenty to occupy her; there was so much need for an involved parent. She always believed you had to take care of your own kids, was too embarrassed to hire a nanny and have a stranger see her life, apart from the cleaners before whom she assiduously precleaned. She got by with babysitters and carefully vetted preschools and Maryellen, who vacillated between wildly helpful and detached, her childrearing days in the rearview. Elizabeth was amazed, sometimes, at how little she thought about work or even remembered what the work had been as the time passed. She loved Pamela with painful intensity, and there was so much to do, and time had a way of carrying everything away and out of sight. But sometimes she looked at the clock at two fifteen, school-pickup time, and thought she would suffocate. In the end she pivoted too.

In the warm hospital room, Pamela cried out again. The machines wheezed, the air pumps working at capacity to filter the wildfire smoke out of the room. Elizabeth prayed there would be no brownouts. The hospital was less well-equipped than their house, all things considered. A nurse checked Pamela's dilation. "You're ready to push, Mama," she told her gently. "Do you hear that, sweetheart?" Elizabeth said to her daughter. "You're going to meet your baby." Pamela batted her hand away and then reached for it again. The OB on duty came in and was officious, telling Pamela to push in this or that way. Finally, she summoned the last reserves of her strength, gripped a bar they wheeled over her bed, and pushed with everything she had.

The baby came out small and purple. Pamela cried out with exhaustion and relief. She reached down as the OB, looking at the baby, said, "Baby girl," and Elizabeth searched the doctor's face for other information. When the lights blinked off, the auxiliary systems whirring and beeping, Elizabeth held her breath and waited, her ears straining in the dark, listening for a cry.

ACKNOWLEDGMENTS

There are many climate activists fighting against the currents described in this novel, all of them with far fewer resources than oil and gas companies. Nothing is inevitable. Please support the work of organizations like Taproot Earth, Climate Justice Alliance, Indigenous Environmental Network, the Sunrise Movement, or your local mutual aid organizations, which are crucial to surviving the catastrophes caused by climate change.

Thank you to Claudia Ballard, who saw several incoherent early pieces of this book and stuck with it and with me, and to Emily Bell and the remarkable team at Zando and Crooked Media Reads.

I am extremely grateful to Jale Sultanli and Shane Austin, who read portions of the text and contributed valuable insights into life in Baku in the 1990s. Any misrepresentations of that time period, or of Baku, are mine alone. Many thanks to Professor Katy Pierce for making the introduction. Thank you to Molly Gartrell Earle for her introduction to Bev and Tom McAloon, and to Bev and Tom for sharing recollections and photos from Azerbaijan. Dr. Gregory Brew provided his expertise in the fields of oil history and energy policy and the book is stronger as a result; any factual errors about oil and gas are mine. Thank you to the brilliant Emma Harper for being the best possible travel companion in Baku, and to Ibrahim and Samir for their insights during that trip. Many thanks to Chris Matthews, whose expertise and efficient summarization of the oil and gas industry helped me to solve a plot problem, and to Stephanie Matthews for a kind welcome in Houston. Thanks also to Serena Roberts Houlihan and her family for their hospitality, and to Clark, Allison, and William Kellogg for break-fast, infrastructure stories, and a tour of Muffintown. Thank you to my mother, Phyllis Graham, for her recollections of overseas posts, her careful reading, and for introducing me to the work of Professor William Caraher; his blog *Mediterranean Archaeology* contains many valuable scholarly resources about the global petroleumscape. Thank you to my father, Brady Kiesling, for his reflections on the Foreign Service, Texas lore, and for helpful tweaks. Thank you to both of my parents for wonderful times in Greece and elsewhere. Thank you to Michael Youhana for recommending useful sources. Thank you to Christine Berkes and Megan Faris for our shared time at PCR. Gratitude and love to the memories of Catherine Mohr, Lalu Kiesling, and Dr. Athanasios and Georgia Prosalentis.

The bulk of this book was written during the COVID-19 pandemic, an experience that would have been far worse without the support of Rahawa Haile, Meaghan O'Connell, Jen Gann, Angela Garbes, and many other friends who provided solidarity, humor, and love. Thank you to the Hedgebook Foundation for the incredible opportunity to do a short COVID residency at the same time as my friend Manjula Martin. Thank you to my immediate community in Portland: Serena, Aurelien, Margaret, Alex, Diane, Rupa, Kartik, Tiffany, Tim L., and the many wonderful teachers and caregivers who helped us through chaotic times, among them Ren Dominguez, Rose Benge, Megan Chavez, Tyler Hutson-Lytle, Rachel Vidalez, Hollie Kissler, Dr. Tina

Lageson, and Michelle Naglis. Thank you to Emily von W. Gilbert and the Universal Preschool Now! team, who continue to show me that a better world is possible, and to mutual aid groups like Defense Fund PDX for saving lives during the Pacific Northwest Heat Dome of 2021.

Finally, thank you to my adored children, and to my husband, Tim, without whom this book would not exist.

CONSULTED WORKS

Many works of journalism, scholarship, memoir, and fiction informed the world of this novel, among them: *The Oil and the Glory: The Pursuit of Empire and Fortune on the Caspian Sea* by Steve LeVine; *Gaslighted: How the Oil and Gas Industry Shortchanges Women Scientists* by Christine L. Williams; *The Oil Road: Journeys from the Caspian Sea to the City of London* by James Marriott and Mika Minio-Paluello; *Fly Girl: A Memoir* by Ann Hood; *Private Empire: ExxonMobil and American Power* by Steve Coll; *Azeri Women in Transition: Women in Soviet and Post-Soviet Azerbaijan* by Farideh Heyat; *This Changes Everything: Capitalism vs. The Climate* by Naomi Klein; *Revolutionary Power: An Activist's Guide to the Energy Transition* by Shalanda Baker; *The Secret World of Oil* by Ken Silverstein; *Under Sand, Ice and Sea* by A. Bryce Cameron; *A Geophysicist's Memoir: Searching for Oil on Six Continents* by Albert Hrubetz III and Nina P. Flournoy; *The Great Derangement: Climate Change and the Unthinkable* by Amitav Ghosh; *Working for Oil: Comparative Social Histories of Labor in the*

Global Oil Industry edited by Touraj Atabaki, Elisabetta Bini, and Kaveh Ehsani; *More City than Water: A Houston Flood Atlas* edited by Lacy M. Johnson and Cheryl Beckett; *Hyperobjects: Philosophy and Ecology after the End of the World* by Timothy Morton; *Oil!* by Upton Sinclair; *Tales from the Derrick Floor: A People's History of the Oil Industry* by Mody C. Boatright and William A. Owens; *The Orphan Sky* by Ella Leya; *Fossil Capital: The Rise of Steam Power and the Roots of Global Warming* by Andreas Malm; *Mineral Rites: An Archaeology of the Fossil Economy* by Bob Johnson; *Losing Earth: A Recent History* by Nathaniel Rich; *The Looming Tower: Al-Qaeda and the Road to 9/11* by Lawrence Wright; *The Dark Side: The Inside Story of How the War on Tower Turned into a War on American Ideals* by Jane Mayer; *The Watchdogs Didn't Bark: The CIA, NSA, and the Crimes of the War on Terror* by John Duffy and Ray Nowosielski; *The Perfect Kill: 21 Laws for Assassins* and *See No Evil* by Robert B. Baer; *Roberts vs. Texaco: A True Story of Race and Corporate America* by Bari-Ellen Roberts and Jack E. White; *Around the Sacred Sea: Mongolia and Lake Baikal on Horseback* by Bartle B. Bull; *The eXile: Sex, Drugs, and Libel in the New Russia* by Matt Taibbi and Mark Ames; *Nine Lives: A Foreign Service Odyssey* by Allen B. Hansen; *Propaganda, Inc.: Selling America's Culture to the World* by Nancy Snow; and *Subterranean Estates: Life Worlds of Oil and Gas* edited by Hannah Appel, Arthur Mason, and Michael Watts. I am grateful for the oral histories of William David McKinney and others made available through the Foreign Affairs Oral History Program of the Association for Diplomatic Studies and Training.

The Bertolt Brecht epigraph was borrowed from Imre Szeman's essay "How to Know About Oil: Energy Epistemologies and Political Futures" in *The Journal of Canadian Studies*.

I am additionally grateful for the documentary reporting of the late Stanley Greene, Marcel Theroux, Alana Semuels in *The Atlantic*, Amy Westervelt in *Drilled* and *Hot Take*, Mary Annaïse Heglar in *Hot Take*, Kendra Pierre-Louis in *DeSmog*, David Wallace-Wells in *New York*

Magazine, Adam Davidson in the *New Yorker*, Thomas Goltz in *Soldier of Fortune*, Jonah Goldberg in the *New York Times Magazine*, and countless journalists at *Azerbaijan International*, *Texas Monthly*, the *Houston Chronicle*, *Dallas Monthly*, *Vice*, *Eurasianet*, the *New York Times*, the *Wall Street Journal*, the *Guardian*, and elsewhere. Finally, my research was helped enormously by the public library systems of San Francisco and Multnomah County and their excellent librarians, free audiobooks, and periodical access. Public resources are precious.

ABOUT THE AUTHOR

Lydia Kiesling is the author of *The Golden State*, a 2018 National Book Foundation "5 under 35" honoree, and was a finalist for the VCU Cabell First Novelist Award. Her essays and nonfiction have been published in the *New York Times Magazine*, *The Cut*, the *New Yorker* online, and elsewhere. She lives in Portland, Oregon.